.SEN

THE HIVE

"Mesmerizing! Gregg Olsen tautly reveals layer after layer of lies, secrets, and betrayals in an increasingly horrifying exposé of one cult leader and her terrible sway over others. Forget the evil men do. These women will have you fearing for your life."

—Lisa Gardner, #1 *New York Times* bestselling author

"*The Hive* is a riveting thriller, a tsunami of a story that starts out strong and absolutely knocks you over at the end. The characters are fascinating, their world so real and absorbing—I was transfixed from the very start. Gregg Olsen is such a compelling writer."

—Luanne Rice, *New York Times* bestselling author

"In this gripping thriller, everything is not as it seems, and beauty is only skin deep. *The Hive* is a brilliantly engrossing read—exactly what we have come to expect from Gregg Olsen."

—Karin Slaughter, *New York Times* and internationally

bestselling author

"A charismatic wellness guru, a dead young journalist, and a slew of secrets are the ingredients that make up this fiendishly fun thriller. *The Hive* will have readers buzzing."

—Greer Hendricks, #1 *New York Times* bestselling coauthor of

The Wife Between Us

"Gregg Olsen's *The Hive* is a fast-paced, intriguing, intense, and suspenseful read that is as creepy as it is fantastic. Brilliant, thought-provoking, heartbreaking, and original, *The Hive* will keep you up at night and leave you reeling long after you've finished it. Every page carries weight in this novel. There are plenty of twists and turns to satisfy even the most seasoned crime fiction reader, and the characters feel authentic and alive in ways that only Olsen can achieve."

—Lisa Regan, #1 *Wall Street Journal* bestselling author of the Detective Josie Quinn series

"Die-hard Gregg Olsen fans will love *The Hive*; new readers will become fans. Olsen deftly guides the reader through the pages, cranking up the suspense as long-held secrets rise to the surface. The result is compulsively page turning as Olsen keeps the reader's mind buzzing in suspense. He hooks the reader as a dark crime from the past collides with a crime from the present."

—Kendra Elliot, *Wall Street Journal* bestselling author

"Gregg Olsen's *The Hive* begins with a fascinating premise and a spellbinding opening scene that held me in its grip as I flew through the pages. Olsen expertly weaves together a multilayered tale told by a complex array of unforgettable characters in his latest jaw-dropping thriller. In this dark and dangerously addictive read buzzing with secrets, betrayal, and murder, queen bees and wannabes take on a whole new meaning. Not to be missed."

—Heather Gudenkauf, *New York Times* bestselling author of *This Is How I Lied*

IF YOU TELL

"This riveting account will leave readers questioning every odd relative they've known."

—*Publishers Weekly* (starred review)

"Olsen presents the story chronologically and in a simple, straightforward style, which works well: it is chilling enough as is."

—*Booklist*

"An unsettling stunner about sibling love, courage, and resilience."

—*People* (book of the week)

"*If You Tell* accomplishes what it sets out to do. The result is a compelling portrait of terror and a powerfully honest, yet still sensitive, look at survival."

—Bookreporter

"A true-crime tour de force."

—Steve Jackson, *New York Times* bestselling author of *No Stone Unturned*

"Even the most devoted true-crime reader will be shocked by the maddening and mind-boggling acts of horror that Gregg Olsen chronicles in this book. Olsen has done it again, giving readers a glimpse into a murderous duo that's so chilling, it will have your head spinning. I could not put this book down!"

—Aphrodite Jones, *New York Times* bestselling author

"There's only one writer who can tell such an intensely horrifying, psychotic tale of unspeakable abuse, grotesque torture, and horrendous serial murder with grace, sensitivity and class . . . a riveting, taut, real-life psychological suspense thrill ride . . . all at once compelling and original, Gregg Olsen's *If You Tell* is an instant true-crime classic."

—M. William Phelps, *New York Times* bestselling author

"We all start life with immense promise, but in our first minute, we cannot know who'll ultimately have the greatest impact on our lives, for better or worse. Here, Gregg Olsen—the heir apparent to legendary crime writers Jack Olsen and Ann Rule—explores the dark side of that question in his usual chilling, heartbreaking prose. Superb and creepy storytelling from a true-crime master."

—Ron Franscell, author of *Alice & Gerald: A Homicidal Love Story*

"Bristling with tension, gripping from the first pages, Gregg Olsen's masterful portrait of children caught in the web of a coldly calculating killer fascinates. A read so compelling it kept me up late into the night, *If You Tell* exposes incredible evil that lived quietly in small-town America. That the book is fact, not fiction, terrifies."

—Kathryn Casey, bestselling author of *In Plain Sight*

"A suspenseful, horrific, and yet fascinating character study of an incredibly dysfunctional and dangerous family by Gregg Olsen, one of today's true-crime masters."

—Caitlin Rother, *New York Times* bestselling author

LYING NEXT TO ME

"*Lying Next to Me* is a clever, chilling puzzle of a tale. A riveting, sharp-edged page-turner, it's Gregg Olsen's best book yet."

—A. J. Banner, *USA Today* bestselling author

"A dark, claustrophobic thriller filled with twists and turns. A brilliant book."

—Caroline Mitchell, #1 international bestselling author

"In *Lying Next to Me*, [Olsen] has given us a first-rate work of psychological complexity as well as a mystery that is full of twists and is quite a grabber."

—Popular Culture Association

THE LAST THING SHE EVER DID

"Gregg Olsen pens brilliant, creepy, page-turning, heart-pounding novels of suspense that always keep me up at night. In *The Last Thing She Ever Did*, he topped himself."

—Allison Brennan, *New York Times* bestselling author

"Beguiling, wicked, and taut with suspense and paranoia, *The Last Thing She Ever Did* delivers scenes as devastating as any I've ever read with a startling, pitch-perfect finale. A reminder that evil may reside in one's actions, but tragedy often spawns from one's inaction."

—Eric Rickstad, *New York Times* bestselling author of *The Silent Girls*

"Olsen's latest examines how a terrible, split-second decision has lingering effects, and the past echoes the present. Full of unexpected twists, *The Last Thing She Ever Did* will keep you guessing to the last line."

—J. T. Ellison, *New York Times* bestselling author of *Lie to Me*

"Master storyteller Gregg Olsen continues to take readers hostage with another spellbinding tale of relentless, pulse-pounding suspense."

—Rick Mofina, international bestselling author of *Last Seen*

"Tense. Well-crafted. Gripping."

—Mary Burton, *New York Times* bestselling author

"With *The Last Thing She Ever Did*, Gregg Olsen delivers an edgy, tension-filled, roller-coaster ride of a novel that will thrill and devastate in equal measure."

—Linda Castillo, *New York Times* bestselling author

THE
HIVE

ALSO BY GREGG OLSEN

Fiction

Silent Ridge

Water's Edge

Snow Creek

Lying Next to Me

The Weight of Silence

The Last Thing She Ever Did

The Sound of Rain

Just Try to Stop Me

Now That She's Gone

The Girl in the Woods

The Girl on the Run

Shocking True Story

Fear Collector

Beneath Her Skin

The Bone Box (novella)

Dying to Be Her

Closer Than Blood

Victim Six

Heart of Ice

A Wicked Snow

A Cold Dark Place

NONFICTION

If You Tell: A True Story of Murder, Family Secrets,
and the Unbreakable Bond of Sisterhood
A Killing in Amish Country: Sex, Betrayal,
and a Cold-Blooded Murder
A Twisted Faith: A Minister's Obsession and the Murder
That Destroyed a Church
The Deep Dark: Disaster and Redemption in
America's Richest Silver Mine
Starvation Heights: A True Story of Murder and Malice in the
Woods of the Pacific Northwest
Cruel Deception: The True Story of Multiple Murder and Two
Devastated Families
If Loving You Is Wrong: The Teacher and Student Sex Case That
Shocked the World
Abandoned Prayers: An Incredible True Story of Murder, Obsession,
and Amish Secrets
Bitter Almonds: The True Story of Mothers, Daughters,
and the Seattle Cyanide Murders
Bitch on Wheels: The True Story of Black Widow Killer Sharon
Nelson
If I Can't Have You: Susan Powell, Her Mysterious Disappearance,
and the Murder of Her Children
The Confessions of an American Black Widow

THE
HIVE

GREGG
OLSEN

THOMAS & MERCER

Published by Thomas & Mercer, Seattle

www.apub.com

Amazon, the Amazon logo, and Thomas & Mercer are trademarks of Amazon.com, Inc., or its affiliates.

ISBN-13: 9781542016469
ISBN-10: 1542016460

Cover design by Rex Bonomelli

Printed in the United States of America

For Chris Renfro,
simply the best. Really. Truly.

Beauty is more than a skin-deep issue. Our outer covering is our calling card. In order to feel great, to do great things, we need to understand that undeniable truth. Everything I've ever done has been to help others in a world that judges them every second of the day.

—Marnie Spellman, *Dateline NBC*

PROLOGUE

Late summer 2019
Whatcom County, Washington

Only days apart and a few miles from each other, two women read the same pages from their copies of a dog-eared memoir. One found it among her mother's things. The other borrowed a reading copy from an archive. They'd highlighted passages with yellow or pink markers. Scribbled notations and a blizzard of question marks splattered foxed pages as they ruminated over the veracity of Marnie Spellman's story. At each turn of a page, they questioned the reliability of every word in *The Insatiable Heart*. One of the readers sought answers for things that happened when she was only a girl. The other studied the book for insight into the mind of the writer.

Over and over, even when the unthinkable transpired, the book served as a guide, then an arrow sharply pointed at their hearts, vexing and urging at the same time.

My parents were running errands for the afternoon on the mainland, and my brother and I were left to work on the farm. Dad had insisted that we muck out all the stalls and, for added measure, change out the straw in the chicken coop. I detested those tasks and was sure that my parents left it for me to do while they were away just so they'd be out of earshot when I complained. Casey was six at that time and, quite frankly, of very little help. That's not to say that he didn't try, but as usual, the lion's share of what needed to be done fell on me. It always did. Added to that, of course, was my mother's edict that I needed to weed the garden and clean the kitchen floor.

"Until it sparkles and shines, Marnie."

I respected her. I guess it had more to do with her role than how she treated me. The singsong quality of her commands always put me on edge.

Casey told me he was tired of helping—which, of course, he wasn't really at all—and we decided to take a break by the overlook, the highest point on our property, crowned by a trio of old-growth cedars I named the Supremes after my mom's favorite musical group. I brought sandwiches and apples.

Later, I'd be blamed for the choices I made that afternoon—that maybe things would have been different if I'd brought bologna instead of peanut-butter-and-jelly sandwiches. That maybe the soap that Mom had made started it all. It was lavender from our own herb garden, triple milled by the both of us. And later there would be those who said it was all a lie.

Casey saw the swarm first.

We were lying on our backs, looking at the sky and feeling the breeze as it filtered through the green fringe of the canopy.

"Look up there!" Casey called out. There was both excitement and fear in his voice.

I followed my brother's frozen gaze. It appeared above us, first as a dark cloud, then as a heaving and undulant mass of something that I couldn't identify at first. It was the noise that told me. Bees. It was morphing into shapes that at once stirred and then mocked me.

A running horse like the weather vane on our barn.

A sea star from the beach.

An archway like the one at the church we attended on Christmas Eve and Easter, the sum of my religious upbringing.

As I peered at it, I felt as if I were falling. Maybe rising. Something. It was as if gravity had ceased to exist. As if Newton's apple had floated instead of fallen. I could hear my brother calling my name, but even that receded to silence. I was flying. I was drifting. It was the strangest sensation. One that could never be duplicated. It was like I was inside a kazoo. Tissue paper over my face, a slight dampness blowing over my skin. A soft humming lifting me skyward, then swirling me toward the sun.

Up.

Then down.

I remember thinking that I had died. Not sure how. Whatever was happening, I knew the experience was transformative, unearthly. I was only a vessel of thought and memory being carried away.

Can you understand?

Do you even dare?

The Insatiable Heart
Marnie Spellman

Chapter 1

Monday, September 9, 2019
Whatcom County, Washington

Renae Jones pushed the denim-blue stroller along the damp trail. One of the front wheels, clogged with mud from a late-summer rain, was stuck in a position that made the effort more difficult than it needed to be. Add it to the list. *Everything* about being a mother was harder than she thought it needed to be. Sleepless nights. Baby bawling, caterwauling. A yearning for time to speed toward the moment when reason or bribery would elicit the kind of response she longed for in the child. Quiet. That was all. Peace. Stillness.

Renae sucked in forest air, strained with more effort, and kept moving the stroller onward. She wore earbuds, but there was no music filling her ears. No podcast. Nothing. Indeed, the earbuds weren't even connected to her phone; their cord ran to the zippered pocket of her jacket. She wore them purely as a defense mechanism. The last thing she needed was company, an audience for her agony.

She prayed that the pills her doctor had given her would break her out of the endless sulk that had consumed her since Carson was born. The last six months had shown her the worst of the demands on a young mother.

She shook her head at the thought of how her mother and her friends had told her that being a mom was the greatest joy she would ever know. That was a lie, a trick. The kind of thing that someone says because you're suddenly in a club in which there is no real understanding of what is involved after the parties, after the well-wishes, after the pretty blue and white ribbons are undone and the gift wrapping removed and the boxes opened. The initiation into the club had been a blur of fragrant peonies and golden sponge cake with Mount Baker–sized peaks of white icing.

The best kind of cake.

The kind that keeps people foolishly going back for more.

Even when they ought to know better.

Carson was a beautiful little girl. Renae knew that was true because she'd been told so repeatedly by her mother, her sister, and all her friends. Even strangers at the Haggen market at the base of Sehome Hill. Yes, Carson had big brown eyes and lashes that almost tickled onlookers from across the room. But beautiful? Renae couldn't quite see her that way. She looked at the baby as she cried all night and screamed all day, and wondered how this child had ever been a part of her.

And him.

Him. The baby's father. Kirk Lane's devotion had proven elusive to Renae even months before she gave birth.

"I'll be there for you, babe," he'd said.

Liar!

As her belly grew to a Jiffy Pop roundness, so did her disdain for Kirk. His teeth were oddly small. His eyes seemed dull, almost cloudy, like those of an old dog on his last ride to the veterinarian's windowless side room, where pet owners huddle, lean over their animal, and cry goodbye. Kirk even had a peculiar odor about him that started to turn her stomach in her second trimester.

Renae named her daughter Carson, a family name. The funny thing, some noticed, was that she almost never used it. It was always *she* or *the baby*, and once or twice, she found herself referring to Carson as *it*.

One time her mom noticed her doing so.

"Renae!"

"What?" she said, though she knew she'd been caught again doing that weird thing she'd done since she brought Carson home from the birthing center. It had just slipped out as she'd been numbly multitasking her way through another interminable conversation with her mother.

Now she'd have to pay for it.

When at last Renae lifted her eyes from her phone, where she'd been scrolling through job postings, holding on to the hope that a change of employment would snap her out of the funk that had overtaken her life, she found her mother looking at her with those same eyes that had tricked her into the motherhood club.

"Renae, is everything okay, honey? You seem . . . I don't know . . . a little distant."

"I don't know, Mom," she said. "I don't know why I feel the way I do about it."

"But . . . *it*, honey? Her name is Carson. Your baby has a name."

"Right," Renae said. "That's her name. I know she's my baby, but, Mom . . ." Her words trailed off into tears.

Renae's mother got up and placed her hand on her daughter's shoulder. "Honey, you need to get yourself together. Carson is yours. Just like you are mine."

Wrong thing to say.

The exchange didn't help one little bit. Stating the obvious didn't move her. Simple made sense, but not now, in the complexity of what she knew to be postpartum depression, a black hole that drew her downward from the moment her eyelids rose to wakefulness.

As she shoved the stroller through the trail's gummy mud, Renae chewed her lower lip and held back the words that circulated through her brain. *Something is terribly wrong with me. A baby is forever. Until eighteen, at least.* Or, please, until the medication her psychiatrist had prescribed kicked in. But when would that be? She ate the pills the way she ate bunches of the stuck-together jelly beans her mom kept in an uncovered dish on her glass-topped coffee table.

I should have gotten a dog. I shouldn't be a mom. I don't even feel like Carson's mine, or that I even like her. I'm the worst mother the world has ever known.

She stopped the stroller at the edge of the ravine and looked downward as the falls sent spring runoff into the deep channel of the Nooksack River. Pondering how she was going to survive, what she was going to do.

What she *should* do.

With effort, she allowed herself just then to believe that the medication had, after all, begun to make her feel better. Far from 100 percent, but the new dosage, she hoped, was moving in the right direction. Carson stirred, and she looked down at the brown-eyed baby. The roar of the water seemed to calm her, much like the sound of the Dyson when Renae ran it next to the crib in the nursery she had yet to completely decorate, vinyl appliqués of rabbits and badgers still to be affixed to freshly painted walls. Then Carson's brow puckered, precursor to yet another meltdown, and Renae tore the pacifier from her fanny pack, bent down, and thrust it between the startled baby's lips. After a moment of silence, Carson started making that irritating sucking sound.

Anything was better than another round of caterwauling, though.

The young mother stared at the waterfall, wondering now if she was getting better or if that flash of hope was another false promise. The answer gained weight in the back of her skull. Storm warning.

She recalled the words of her friends and relatives: "You don't know love until you are a mother, and that's a fact."

Renae's hands gripped the stroller. She started to ease it forward, timidly, toward the edge of the ravine, which opened wide like a granite and earthen jaw. Her hands felt moist, her brow soaked. Her heart raced.

She pushed the stroller a few inches farther. She would keep pushing. She would follow the stroller down.

It would be over.

As she gathered her nerve, her eyes latched on to a chalky figure below.

Is it real? Or some kind of prank?

Whatever it was, it snapped her out of what she was going to do.

Down by the falls, slumped on the mossy bank, was what appeared to be a human body. A woman. Naked. Legs akimbo. Pale. Wet. Dead.

Renae let out a gasp and pulled back. She released her fingers from the stroller. Her racing heart was now hammering. She found it hard to breathe. She moved closer to get a better view and looked around to see if anyone was nearby.

She was within a cave of evergreens. Stony quiet, save for the sound of the water as it cascaded down into the bottom of the ravine.

Except for the naked, ghostly pale woman below her, she was alone. She felt it in her bones. This was the kind of place where one could surely count on solitude.

It had been the reason she'd come here.

She jammed the cord of her earbuds into her phone and pressed three digits.

"I think I found a body," she told the 911 dispatcher.

Carson started to cry.

"I need to hold my baby," Renae said. "Just a minute."

She didn't need to stop talking to the operator. Her hands were free. But she needed the time. And as she'd said, she needed to hold her baby. She reached down, fiddled with the pesky safety straps, and gently lifted Carson from the stroller. She was warm, and only a little fussy. Renae rocked her a bit, that jiggly way that her mother had shown her. Carson stopped her halfhearted fussing at once, and mother's and daughter's eyes met in that unmistakable way that communicates more than just want.

"You still there?"

"Yeah," Renae said. She told the operator where she was, what she could see, then promised to wait for the police to arrive. "I'll wait. I'll be here."

Her baby held against her with both arms, Renae kept her gaze locked on the lifeless figure more than a hundred feet down. Suddenly, life seemed so fragile, so precious. Certainly, death would end the pain that had consumed her since her baby was born. But death was final. It was absolute. There was no turning back. No second-guessing.

Had that girl down on the rocks come there with the same idea?

Had she still been convinced during her fall?

Or had she, as Renae had at that very moment, changed her mind?

And fallen, anyway.

CHAPTER 2

Lindsay Jackman managed to breathe. Somehow. Her hands gripped the wheel and her heart raced as her mind fought to stay on task. The call that morning and the warning from her lieutenant left her angry, heartbroken, and confused.

"You're too close to him," Martin Madison said, his voice low but emphatic. "I'm working the scene."

"I'm coming."

"You can't."

"He's my partner."

"We have a body at Maple Falls. Dispatch will update."

As she pulled out of the lot at the Ferndale Police Department, the dispatcher repeated the location. Lindsay felt the presence of the empty passenger seat beside her.

Phantom limb.

She'd been trying to compartmentalize the numbness that comes with sudden and nonsensical loss. Earlier that morning, the wife of her partner of nearly a decade had found his body behind a curtain of car exhaust, at the wheel of his SUV, in their garage.

Once she'd absorbed the blunt facts, her mind set to cycling point-lessly through the same thoughts.

Goddamn you, Alan!

How could you do this to me?

To Patty? To Paul?

Lindsay shifted her thoughts back to the dispatcher as she drove out toward Maple Falls, on the North Fork of the Nooksack, a river running along the Mount Baker Highway, south of the Canadian border.

"Woman says she found what she thinks is a body at the base of the falls. Scared. Not sure. Probably nothing. You know the falls, Detective?"

"Kids are always messing around out there," Lindsay said, ending the call with a request for some backup.

The Nooksack's waters emanated from a melting glacier in the Cascades, and it flowed rapidly, almost milky white, then softer and clearer as it lazily eased into Bellingham Bay. One of its showiest spots was Maple Falls, a hundred-foot drop that saw a good number of visitors in the summer and on weekends. Weekdays, especially after the Labor Day rush, not so much. It wasn't Niagara, that's for sure. More of a destination for locals than for the tourist looking to be dazzled, although drunk selfie takers had found purpose and met their ends at the location. Three had fallen to their deaths over the past five years. One kid from Canada managed to survive only to spend the rest of his days taking selfies in a wheelchair.

That the spot was dangerous, of course, was its lure. When the bro-chure *Discover Whatcom!* was released by Bellingham Whatcom County Tourism that year, the falls weren't even mentioned—for safety's sake.

By that time, the omission didn't matter. No one read *Discover Whatcom!*, anyway. Social media owned the promotion of anything worth doing.

Or, apparently, worth dying for.

Lindsay was driving from the police department in Ferndale, thinking about the latest stupid tragedy and how such incidents only brought more people to test their daredevil picture-posing prowess. The landscape was a green blur as she zipped along the river. No lights. No sirens. No need.

A body. A woman's.

She looked once more at the empty passenger seat.

"Probably a local showing off for some friends," Alan would have said.

"You always think that," she'd have offered after a prolonged beat.

"Well, I've been right all of my life. You know that, Lindsay. You've seen me in action."

He'd have grinned those bright-white choppers and waited for her purposely feeble retort.

It had been a game of theirs, a teasing give-and-take between two people who work closely on a job that requires such a personal bond.

Alan Sharpe had occupied a space somewhere between father figure and best friend. His suicide, she knew, would haunt her forever, in part because she didn't see it coming.

She hadn't known how fragile he was, how a deep-seated hurt lurked behind his ready smile. He was devoted to his family and his work. Sometimes when Lindsay arrived at the office they'd shared, she wondered if Alan had even gone home the night before. She had stopped asking about it because he always denied it—even after she'd found a pillow and a blanket in the lateral file cabinet next to his desk.

And yet he had always smiled. He'd never acted sad. Not even a little.

The detective's tires crunched the jagged-edged gravel as she drove up in her county-issued SUV and parked alongside a Toyota sedan, the only other vehicle in the small lot. A young woman with a baby in her arms was waiting next to it.

"Ms. Jones?" Lindsay said, getting out.

"That's me," the woman answered. "Renae."

"Are you two all right? I know discoveries like this can be very traumatic. And I see you have your hands full." Lindsay smiled at the baby.

"I'm going to be fine," Renae said. "But I need to take Carson home. She's going to need to nap."

"Understood. Let's take a walk down the trail, and you can tell me about what you saw. It won't take long, but I need to make note of what you found, how you found it. Coroner and techs are on the way."

"It's down there," Renae said, indicating with her eyes. "*She's* down there. Under the falls."

"Right, but I need you to show me," Lindsay said. "Can we put your stroller in your car? No sense horsing it down that trail." Though Lindsay could see its wheels were already caked with mud. What had this woman been thinking?

She helped Renae put the stroller into the trunk of the Toyota, then watched as she pulled a baby carrier from the back seat and strapped the child into it.

"It won't take long," Lindsay said again as Renae hoisted the carrier onto her back. "Just tell me everything you heard and saw. Tell me when you got here, why you came, just the basics for my report."

Renae snapped the buckles of the carrier into place and led the detective down the muddy trail.

"I came out here maybe an hour ago. I like it here. Quiet. Kind of lonely. I don't know, I thought it was peaceful. Just needed a break."

"How old is she?"

"Carson is six months," she said. "Almost seven."

"She's beautiful."

Lindsay saw Renae's slight, sad smile dissolve as they drew closer to the falls. She could hear the water as it started its dive one hundred feet to the rounded rocks below. Light seeped in through the maple trees that arched over the trail before giving way to the dark cavern of the Douglas firs and the weeping forms of the western hemlocks. The sunny circles of light that illuminated the path faded as they approached the precipice that was the primary overlook.

"You were out here all by yourself?" Lindsay asked.

"Yeah."

"Did you see anyone?"

"No."

Renae adjusted a strap from the baby carrier, wincing as it dug into her thin frame. "I've never seen anything like this," she said. "Really. You know, just something I wished I'd never seen."

Lindsay nodded, gave the young woman's elbow a gentle squeeze. There was nothing else to say.

As they walked closer to the roar of the falls, Lindsay noted how the ruts of the stroller and prints from Renae's muddy shoes had marked the sodden trail. No other footprints. She knew her partner would have lamented the rainfall the night before, erasing tracks, washing away evidence. She found herself thinking those very thoughts in Alan Sharpe's voice.

Her phone pinged and she looked down, a quick, bruising glance.

Patty wants small memorial on the 17th. Damn suicide. She's a mess.

Lindsay swallowed and went back to the business at hand.

Renae stayed a few steps from the edge of the ravine. She didn't need another look.

"Down there." She pointed. "To the right."

Lindsay held her breath and took in the scene below. It was as if the falls were a long, misty ribbon, pointing to the place where the dead woman's body lay.

The dead woman was nude.

There were no signs of any clothing.

This wasn't likely a suicide, but there was no way of really knowing that right then, and guessing was never a good idea at the start of an investigation. Collecting the evidence, finding out who the woman was, how she died, and tracing her steps—all of that had to be done before any games of supposition. Games that Alan had been adept at, frequently uncannily so.

Which means exactly nothing now.

CHAPTER 3

A couple of Ferndale officers arrived to secure the scene, and a few minutes later, two of the county's crime techs, Tim and Tam, trudged forward to help with the most crucial part of the investigation: gathering evidence.

Lindsay and the techs started the climb down a switchback to the body.

"My mom walks the beach on Lummi," Tamara Oliver said as they made their way down. "I always kind of cringe inside that she'll be the one to find a foot or a body washed up from the straits. Despite what I do for a living, my mom can't take the sight of a speck of blood."

"You sure she's your mom?" Tim Arthur said.

"That's what the evidence suggests," she said. "Maybe you don't understand because you grew up in a family of doctors and paramedics, Tim. Blood and guts was dinner-table talk for your people."

"The family business," Tim said, with a toothy grin.

Lindsay felt a pang, listening to the two of them. They had the same kind of teasing relationship that she and Alan had had.

As if she'd read her thoughts, Tam said, "Really sorry about Alan, Lindsay."

News of tragedies among their ranks traveled at lightning speed.

"Yeah," she answered. "He was one of the good ones, for sure."

A light mist hung over the chasm by the time the trio reached the bottom and made their way to the figure that Renae Jones had seen that morning.

The acrid smell of a decomposing body met them when they were twenty feet away.

The body was facedown. Ashy white. Smudges of dried, coagulated blood that were more bronze than red streaked her back like tiger stripes. The body was in bad shape, though possibly preserved some with the cold water that encircled it. Lindsay took photos with her phone for reference, and the techs moved methodically over the body, capturing images and diagramming the scene. Lindsay noted red marks along the upper back to her neck, exposed by the part in the victim's black hair.

"Get a close-up here," she said, pointing.

Tim's digital camera clicked with the sounds of old SLR—for effect, of course. Lindsay thought it was silly for new technology to mimic the analog world. She had told Alan more than once that his old-school ringtone—an actual ring—gave away his age as plainly as his pleated slacks.

He had poked her back about her penchant for energy drinks and mindless scrolling on her phone.

The woman appeared to be in her twenties, maybe younger. She'd been dead a day or two; rigor had come and gone. Her skin was pale. Her body was thin but not malnourished. No tattoos. No defining marks other than the abrasions that had caused the striping on her back. Lindsay wondered if those injuries had been a result of the fall. Or maybe from before. All questions of what had happened when would be determined by the coroner in her office, forty minutes away, in Bellingham.

"No tracks," Tim said after examining the victim's arms.

"Yeah," Lindsay said. "Looks pretty healthy. Fit. Hair's been trimmed recently. Not a single split end."

One of the officers called down from above and said he'd recovered some cigarette butts and some trash.

"No clothing," he said.

"No shit," Tam said.

The officer's face went red.

"I meant up here," he said.

Mist dampened the victim's shoulder-length hair, and Lindsay moved it away from her neck, exposing bruising that indicated strangulation as a possible cause of death—providing the victim was dead before she hit the rocks at the bottom of the chasm.

She called up, "Pull your search back from the immediate trail and see what you can find."

Tam pulled Lindsay aside.

"We still can't believe it about Alan. We all know you were close. We're here if you need us, Linds."

She nodded but said nothing.

What could she say?

After almost ten years, this would be Lindsay's first solo case. Alan Sharpe had always been there, initially as a mentor, then a partner, then a close friend. And then, finally, a pseudo father figure. They had been yin and yang, yet never really to the point of any measurable friction. She knew as she looked down at the body that Alan would have been suggesting a zillion theories about what might have happened to Jane Doe. They'd have been the same scenarios that she'd already run through her head, but she would have let him list them because it was something he had liked to do. He hadn't been a show-off. Not really. It had been his MO. His way of processing a scene.

She supervised as the techs finished, and the coroner's unmarked white van carried Jane Doe's body to the county morgue.

Lindsay was the last to leave. She surveyed the parking lot and glanced over at the trail to the falls. It had been years since she'd been there. Serenity punctuated by the sound of rushing water from a distance, a natural white noise. Lindsay could think of no scenario that would have a woman wind her way naked along the trail to jump. No clothes had been found anywhere nearby. No car had been left behind.

Someone had carried her there, unconscious or dead.

And tossed her like garbage onto the mossy rocks below.

Chapter 4

Tuesday, September 17, 2019
Deming, Washington

The stone chapel in Deming, built in 1933, had been restored recently by a group of citizens convinced that if the old building wasn't repaired, it would become a hangout for drug addicts and teens with nothing better to do than spray-paint some colorful nonsense on its walls. Even a whiff of degradation would be picked up by those who sought the pleasure of destruction, and before one knew it, it would be gone.

That afternoon, the parking spaces and the shoulder alongside the road were filled with law enforcement cars from all over Washington. Alan hadn't died in the line of duty, but he'd taught a yearly class at the academy south of Seattle on working with all resources to stem the meth epidemic that was ruining so many little towns and rural outposts. His sudden death brought out a good number of the millennials he'd taught over the years.

Lindsay and her ex-husband, Jack, sat in the second row, just behind Alan's wife, Patty, and their son, Paul. Lieutenant Madison and his long-suffering wife, Peg, sat at the end of the same row, close enough that the smell of smoke wafted from him every time he exhaled.

A portrait that had been taken for the newspaper when Alan was honored for his work with young people was on an easel in front. Enlarged, rendered in black and white, the image that presided over the mourners captured his spirit completely. His silver hair. The flinty sparks from his eyes. And the smile. It was the kind of grin that dared a person not to smile back. His arms were folded across his chest, the obligatory hero pose that looked silly on local real estate signs, but on Alan, it worked.

Paul Sharpe put his arm across his mother's shoulders as she melted into the pew.

Lindsay reached for a tissue as the pastor, a tall man with oval-shaped wire-framed glasses, talked about the mysteries of depression and hidden pain and how the love that had surrounded Alan was never going to be enough to save him.

"Some tragedies are readily apparent as to cause and effect," the pastor said. "A terrible car crash, for example. It happened, we say. It was an accident. It is heartbreaking, but there is seldom the word *why* attached to such things."

Paul bolstered his mother as each word came at her.

Alan Sharpe wasn't a religious man, although his wife certainly skewed that direction. Patty had been brought up in the Lutheran faith but switched to an evangelical congregation years ago in hopes her husband would attend. Which he did, but only very occasionally. Patty had selected a middle-ground church for her husband's service, partly because she didn't want to face the questions that came with it in front of people she knew, but also because she knew that the old stone church held some appeal to him.

They'd been there for a wedding the year before.

"This is nice," he'd said. "A church with a little age and historical significance seems a lot more authentic than the modern, guitar-playing kind we attend."

Patty only smiled.

As she sat there with her grown son and they listened to the pastor talk about a man he didn't know as if they had been close friends, she did the same thing she imagined Lindsay Jackman did. She streamed the morning of his death in her mind.

It was a movie she couldn't stop watching.

Monday, September 9, 2019
Ferndale, Washington

Patty reached over and felt the emptiness in the bed. *Strange.* She'd been the first one up with very few exceptions from the day she and Alan had gotten married. She put her feet on the floor, slipped on the ridiculously pink robe Paul had given her for Christmas the previous year, and padded her way to the kitchen, thinking Alan would be there, poring over the paper with a K-Cup of coffee.

It was just after 5:00 a.m.

"Alan?" she called out.

No answer.

She placed a coffee pod in the machine and snapped down the lid. As the rumbling water forced its way through the coffee grounds, she tried to remember if he'd had an early appointment that day. Yes, coffee with Lindsay. But it was very early. No one had an appointment at that hour. He'd come late to bed last night. She asked if he was okay, and he nuzzled up against her, saying everything was fine.

"Just couldn't sleep."

"You're freezing," she said.

"Sorry. Sorry about that, too."

Only now did it occur to her to think about those words. Really, only one of the words.

Too.

What exactly did that mean? *Too?*

The coffee steamed in the cup, and Patty sipped. *Too hot.* Looking around, she noticed the sink was empty. Alan hadn't made a morning cup and left it there, rinsed and ready for the dishwasher. That had been almost a game with them. She couldn't understand why her husband didn't go the extra step and put it in the dishwasher. *Maybe he did.* She opened it, and no, it was completely empty.

Alan couldn't make a move in the morning without a decent dose of caffeine.

Their house wasn't large, and she'd passed his empty office on the way to the kitchen. She paused in the living room a beat. A sound was coming from the garage.

A running engine.

Oh, she thought, *he's leaving just now.*

When she flung open the door to the garage, a stinking fog poured inside. Her coffee fell to the floor, burning her leg, and she screamed. *Oh no!* Alan must have had a heart attack or something. She turned her head away from the car exhaust and felt for the opener. Got it. As the door began to rise and the exhaust leaked from the space, Patty knew that it had been no accident.

A dark-green garden hose led from the tailpipe to a passenger's-side window, crimped tightly to hold it in place.

She screamed a second time and ran for the driver's-side door, where she could make out the shape of Alan's head leaning against the steering wheel.

"Oh God no," she said. "Alan, what did you do?"

Frantically, she tried to open the door, but it was locked. She circled the car, trying all doors. She felt woozy, and she coughed out fits of carbon monoxide. She ran back into the house and grabbed her phone and the extra key fob from the rack by the refrigerator.

As she gave her name, coughing into the phone, 911 recorded her call.

> Patty: This is Patty Sharpe. Help me. I think my husband is badly injured or maybe dead. God, please hurry. I'm at 589 Semiahmoo Way. He's Ferndale Police Detective Alan Sharpe. Hurry!
>
> 911: Stay calm, Patty. An ambulance is on the way. Four minutes out. Tell me what happened.
>
> Patty: I found him in the garage with the car running. A hose . . . [Coughs and cries, the beep of a key fob.] Alan, God, no . . .
>
> 911: Patty? Patty?
>
> [A muffled noise.]
>
> Patty: [Coughs.] I'm here.
>
> 911: I need you to get out of the garage, Patty. Right away. Carbon monoxide can make you very sick. Do you understand?
>
> Patty: Yes. I do. I don't understand anything else. Oh God, Alan. Why has this happened? Why?

[The sound of an ambulance siren.]

911: Patty, help is there now. Stay on the phone until you see them. I hope your husband will be okay. Take care, Patty.

Patty: Thank you.

Tuesday, September 17, 2019

As she sat in the church pew, remembering, Patty Sharpe wondered how much she should say about that morning. How it would hurt. How it might invite questions she didn't want to answer.

It was a movie.

CHAPTER 5

Tuesday, September 17, 2019
Ferndale, Washington

The Sharpe family's backyard was set up with picnic tables covered in pale-pink tablecloths—not because the hue was Alan's favorite, but because the linens were leftovers from a baby shower Patty had hosted for a church member a week ago.

After arriving from the memorial service, mourners filed past Patty and Paul as they thanked everyone for coming.

Paul did the talking. His mother stood next to him, her arms folded around her trembling body.

"My mom and I really appreciate it," he said, his voice breaking. "Never forget to tell people you love them. You don't know when there will never be another chance to say those words."

The house became a moving mass of memories and condolences that expanded and contracted each time the doors opened. There were two distinct groups of mourners. The first was those who waited in the receiving line to say something kind to the widow and her son.

They stood, silent and immobile, racking their brains for something to say that might ease the pain. The other group hovered around the dining table, a classic Danish modern piece blanketed with room-temperature cold cuts and solidifying casseroles sharing the same sad DNA—post-memorial-service fare.

Later, Lindsay found Patty in the kitchen. She'd spilled something on her pale-blue dress and was trying to remove the spot. She was a compact woman, under five feet, with a decidedly old-school approach to life. She wore an apron when cooking and clipped coupons—not to save money, but because it was like muscle memory from a meager childhood. Alan brought extra coupons to the office every week.

"Can I help you?" Lindsay asked.

Patty finally looked up. Her eyes were puffy, and the makeup she had applied so carefully that morning had rubbed off onto a tissue.

"No one can help me, Lindsay."

"I'm here."

"Right. You're here." Her tone was flat, maybe a little dismissive. "I know you mean well, Lindsay."

Patty's words stung. It was confusing. Lindsay wondered if she'd meant to hurt her.

"What's going on?" she asked, moving closer.

Patty took a step away. "Look," she said, setting down the sponge she'd used to remove the stain. "I'm not angry at you."

By saying that, you are, Lindsay thought.

"What is it? Let me help."

"Alan is gone. He killed himself. I don't even have any idea why he would do that. I'm angry. And frankly, Lindsay, I'm jealous that you probably knew him better than I did."

"I don't know why he did what he did," Lindsay said. "I never saw anything that would point to this. Alan was happy. He loved you and Paul. This doesn't make any sense to me, either."

"You spent more time with him than I did."

"He loved you, Patty. Is something going on?"

Patty looked down at the stain. "I just can't get this damn spot out. Alan loved this dress. I wore it today for him, and now look at it."

Patty was deflecting.

"Any club soda?" Lindsay asked.

"No. Just 7Up."

Both women smiled and shook their heads.

Lindsay put her arms around Patty. Alan's wife, now his widow, smelled of a light woodsy perfume. Her neck was wrapped in a double strand of coral beads from their anniversary trip to Hawaii; its silver lobster claw clasp had inched its way to the front. On any other day, Lindsay would have mentioned it to her.

Not today.

Instead, she said, "I honestly don't know what I'll do without him."

"He thought of you like a daughter," Patty said.

"Thank you. And I'm so sorry."

After Patty pulled herself together, she sat outside picking at a plate of food, occasionally thanking people for coming when they presented themselves to her. She didn't cry anymore. She knew that she'd have to find a way to accept the nightmare handed to her when Alan died.

There had been moments of worry and depression, of course, but she had to dig a little to recall them. Alan had presented a happy-go-lucky persona to everyone, despite the dark nature of his work as a detective. He obsessed over it. Sometimes she'd see him in his office, looking at files with a clinking tumbler of Scotch that he'd filled more than once. He'd be poring over something and muttering. Slurring, sometimes. She knew better than to move close enough to see; she'd made that mistake one time. She could never erase that image of a little brown-haired Ferndale boy disfigured by his mother's cigarettes in the pattern of the Little Dipper. She had let out a gasp, and Alan had swiveled his chair.

"Honey," he'd said, "don't come closer. You don't want to see any more of this."

"Alan," she'd replied, moving back toward the door. "You're right. I don't. Tell me: Is he okay?" Her eyes had been fixed on the photograph and the boy's upper thigh. He'd been burned in a place that no one could see.

It was a hidden torture.

"He's in foster care," Alan had said, shifting the folder from her view. "He's going to be all right."

From her vantage point, she'd seen the notation, a date and a single word written on the top of the photo.

Homicide.

Lindsay had experienced her own share of grief. Her mother had died of breast cancer shortly after Lindsay joined the Ferndale Police Department. It turned her world upside down, but it had been known to her that the day would come. She and her mom had had those moments in which they could muse about the future and laugh about the past. Patty and her son hadn't had that kind of opportunity.

Alan was here. Then he was gone.

Lindsay found Paul standing in a corner, a small plate—like hers, barely touched—in his hands.

"Dad never knew so many people loved him," he said.

Lindsay picked at a piece of salami and provolone rolled up tight like a cigarette. She wished she had a smoke. Drawing on a cigarette was a go-to move for thinking about what to say when you haven't got a clue.

"He was good," she said. The blandest, most obvious thing to say. But it was all she had.

Paul was twenty, with broad shoulders and a chiseled jawline. His eyes were dark like his father's, and he was handsome like him, but in a different way. Lindsay thought about how men had become preening affectations of manhood in the past decade or so. Shaved. Muscled. Cocky.

He was sweet.

Sensitive.

"I know I'll never work with someone like your father again. I'll miss him forever."

Paul nodded. "Yeah. He was a great man. Good heart."

Lindsay swallowed the last of her salami-and-cheese cigarette. "I just don't get it," she said, looking toward a table with his father's photo, badge, and awards.

"Yeah. Me neither."

When a woman approached Paul to offer condolences, Lindsay slipped away.

I would have helped you, Alan.

Chapter 6

That night, Lindsay shut the front door of her house on Alder Way and took in the empty feeling that greeted her. Silence filled the small bungalow, her share of the proceeds from her divorce. She was in her midthirties, single, and without children. She wouldn't have said she was one of those people married to a job, but in reality, she lived and breathed everything crime related—TV, books, podcasts—and would be hard-pressed to name anything else approaching a hobby, much less a passion.

She placed the memorial program on the counter, swung open the fridge door, and popped open a very cold beer. Lindsay came from a big family, one that considered alcohol a necessity at any gathering to remember the dead. She could have used a drink while at Alan's.

She sat at the classic fifties kitchen table she'd stabilized with a folded napkin under one leg and scrolled through her phone.

Jack hadn't come with her from the memorial service to the reception, but he'd sent a small flurry of messages.

Alan was a great guy.

I always liked him.

I'm sorry you are going through all of this.

And finally, I miss you, babe.

She sipped her beer. Jack had been gone for more than a year. He was a manager at the paper mill in Bellingham and had done the predictable. It had been so obvious it was embarrassing. It was like all of a sudden, the guy she was in love with—married to for six years—had hit forty and become the poster boy for a midlife crisis. First, he hit the gym. Then the new clothes started arriving from some Internet stylist. Then out of nowhere he started wearing cologne.

Who is this man?

She wondered that for longer than she should have, before finally switching gears.

Who is the other woman?

That turned out to be classic, too. She was twenty-five, slender, beautiful, and adoring. She was also his secretary. Lindsay tried not to hate her. After all, *she* wasn't the cheater. Her husband was. God knew what he had said about their marriage when he and his new lover spent afternoons at the Shangri-La Motel on Samish Way.

That, too, was embarrassing.

"Really, Jack? The Shangri-La? What are you, some college kid without a credit card?"

"You don't have to be so hostile, Lindsay."

"You don't have to be so stupid, Jack."

"I'm sorry, Lindsay," Jack had said when she confronted him. "Really. I didn't want this to happen. It just did."

Lindsay didn't even cry. She was too angry for tears. Too embarrassed to be the last to know. She didn't even raise her voice.

"Things don't just happen, Jack," she finally told him. "*People* make things happen. *You* made it happen. And I don't even care why. The why will never make a difference to me. This is all on you."

"You weren't around much," he said. "I was lonely."

"Seriously, Jack? I knew you'd say something like that. Me? I'm not running around to conferences—and now I know why you were. I'm working hard. I'm doing something that matters, though I don't work half the hours that you do. Let's amend that: when I thought you were working."

Jack pushed back. "A lot of those times I was," he said.

"I don't want to argue. You think you're in love. Fine. Our marriage is done. I'm not even going to fight to save it. I can't. Betrayal is black and white."

"You're taking this better than I thought you would," he said.

Lindsay thought of telling him that she still loved him, that inside she was a mess and that she'd give anything to make this moment vanish. She didn't. She had a kind of outer shell that she used to protect herself. She'd let him inside. That was what hurt. He knew her. And still he had done this.

"This girl you are fooling around with doesn't even care about you," she said.

Jack stood to leave. "Her name is Willow," he said. *Willow*, for God's sake. "And I'm sorry. I never meant to hurt you, Lindsay. Willow and I *are* in love. We want to make a life together, maybe in Bali or somewhere."

Bali? Who is this stranger?

Lindsay bolted for the front door, twisted the knob, and jerked it open.

"Go," she said without looking at him.

And that was that. At least, that was that until two weeks ago, when Willow decided she was no longer in love with Jack or the idea of living in Bali. She'd left him a goodbye text and vanished. Jack, according to mutual friends, was stunned. He hadn't seen it coming. Willow was his fantasy girl, his dream come true. She was the quintessential arm candy who hung on every word. She'd waxed herself into alabaster smoothness and told Jack that he was the best lover she'd ever had.

She'd never want another.

Until she did.

As predictable as the trajectory of his midlife crisis, so was its inevitable and sputtering end. Jack told Lindsay that he felt like a fool, and she wondered if he knew that everyone else thought he was a fool, too. He had rented a condo downtown over an Italian restaurant and smelled of olive oil and garlic when he arrived in the office each morning. For her part, Willow wasn't a conniver. She didn't whistle-blow about their relationship and how it had violated company rules.

She could have.

She simply didn't even think enough of Jack to bother. She did, however, take a new job as the administrative assistant to the president of the mill. It was, as everyone in the office thought, a big step up. Not only that, the president was single.

The night of her partner's memorial, as she sat in the darkening kitchen, another beer in her hand, Lindsay didn't even allow a sliver of regret to envelop her. Alan had been her shoulder to cry on. He'd been the one to tell her that if she wanted to forgive her husband, that was fine.

"Whatever you decide," he had said, "please understand that it is never going to be the same. You will spend the rest of your life wondering if you did the right thing. You can't hide your feelings, either. They will tear you apart. Trust me."

At the time he said that, she had known he was right. Now something ate at her as she thought about his advice. *Trust me.* What was he talking about? Had he and Patty had problems? Or had it been something else?

Lindsay slept on the same side of the bed as always, although she'd chided Jack for claiming the one next to the window. Breeze in the summer. Moonlight in the winter. She climbed in bed, feeling as alone as she'd ever felt. Lonelier than when her mother had died. She closed her eyes and replayed the day in her mind. She thought back even further to when Patty had found Alan dead in their garage. Then further. She thought about how Alan had been distracted by something the week before at Der Dutchman. At the time, he had told her it was nothing.

"Just stuff."

She refrained from asking for details while they waited for coffee. She wanted him to break the silence between them by explaining. Instead, Alan switched gears.

"Lindsay, do you mind getting my coffee?" He handed her ten dollars.

She pushed the money away. "No," she said. "I mean, yes. I'll pay. My turn."

"Thanks," he said, turning toward the door.

As the line moved, Lindsay caught a glimpse of him. Alan was outside on the sidewalk next to his car, on the phone. She held the image for a second, then turned away. It seemed as if she was intruding on something personal just then. The look on his face was peculiar.

Was he agitated or excited?

She couldn't be sure.

As Lindsay lay there with her eyes shut, she pondered that incident—whether it was a sign she'd missed. She wished she'd asked Alan about the phone call. He'd been so private about "stuff" and she hadn't wanted to push him away. She had respected him. *Admired* him. Being helpful, she had come to know, can feel intrusive and prying. She turned on her side and faced the pillow—the same one on which her ex-husband had laid his head. She shifted and pulled up the covers.

When she had asked if he was all right, he'd apologized for being uncharacteristically distant.

"Just stuff on my mind," he'd said.

His words now carried a sense of finality, like the remembered last lines of a closed book.

She wondered, if she'd pushed harder, might she have found a way to save him?

It was a futile mind game she was playing with herself, and she knew it. Answers about Alan might never come.

The dead girl at Maple Falls was a completely different matter.

CHAPTER 7

Wednesday, September 11, 2019
Ferndale, Washington

The desk across the hall from Lindsay was nothing if not a reminder.

The mentor she had leaned on was gone.

Maple Falls was hers alone.

She looked at the time and got to work. The victim would be autopsied that afternoon in a fluorescent-lit, tile-walled examination room in the Whatcom County coroner's office in Bellingham. A records search turned up a list of missing women between the ages of fifteen and forty, some matching the description only a little. A few, though, were ringers. Lindsay studied the proximity of where the body was found and the location of those reporting a missing person. There were at least six that seemed more likely than others, but the reality of such things is much more random. Some killers are methodical and smart, having read up on police procedure on the Internet and from the endless parade of TV crime shows that serve as how-to guides to avoid detection.

As Lindsay saw it, there were three principal rules embraced by the informed killer: Keep your mouth tightly clamped. Make sure the body is clean of all forensics—fluids, fibers, latent prints. And finally, never dump a body in your own backyard.

Each of the principles was important; together, they formed a trifecta to ensure being free to kill again.

Lieutenant Madison poked his head into her office.

"Any update on Maple Falls?"

She told the lieutenant Jane Doe's autopsy was after lunch and that she'd report back on any preliminary results.

"A few potentials here," she said, indicating the list of missing women and girls on her computer screen. "We'll know more in a few hours. Also ran a check on sex offenders in the area, new releases and whatnot. Nothing there. We'll know more where to look once we find out where she's from."

"And where she was killed," Lieutenant Madison said.

"That, too."

The lieutenant glanced in the direction of Alan's office. "We probably need to pack up his personal stuff. Patty will probably want it." His eyes scraped over Alan's collection of Mariners baseball bobbleheads and black-framed citations for his stellar police work—including the photo for his work with school kids. A family photo of Alan, Patty, and Paul was placed next to the phone.

"I'll take care of it," Lindsay said.

"You sure?"

"I can do it. I *want* to."

After Lieutenant Madison left, Lindsay printed out the list of names and set it aside. She looked for a box to put Alan's things in but couldn't find one. She started to fill his gunmetal-gray trash can with his things. It was undignified, but Alan probably would have laughed about it. She laid the bobbleheads flat and then added a second layer, keeping Ichiro Suzuki for last. He had been Alan's favorite player.

"I love the guy," Alan had said one time, "but for crying out loud, he's lived here for decades; you'd think he could say a few words in English. He's got enough money to hire a dozen language teachers."

"Maybe he doesn't *want* to learn English," Lindsay had countered.

Alan had shrugged it off. "Don't get all PC on me. He should. That's all there is to it."

She opened the top drawer of his desk and went through its contents: receipts, a collection of paper beer coasters, and other odds and ends. In a small manila envelope were two flash drives. She knew how Patty deplored the ugliness behind the work they did, so she set those aside for the Records Department to review and either destroy or catalog. Alan had been sweet, smart, and very sloppy.

On top of the pile, Lindsay stacked the citations and the picture of the Sharpe family. It was taken on the beach in Hawaii when Paul was a gangly teenager. The light was low, setting in the west, and everyone was bathed in a peachy, golden light. She remembered how he had talked about that trip and how he and Patty always planned to go back.

"Maybe for our next wedding anniversary."

More rain fell, and the wipers on Lindsay's SUV did their best to sweep the water from the windshield as she drove down the interstate from Ferndale to Bellingham. Autopsies never bothered her. She wasn't sure if that meant she was a pro or that she'd been born without the capacity to be grossed out by things that sent others running to the toilet.

She turned on the radio and listened to the news. There was no mention of Maple Falls. Not really surprising: the news staff at both the radio and the newspapers had been cut to the nth degree. That meant that social media picked up stories first, reported half-truths, and swiftly moved on to whatever would get a host of likes and follows. *Viral*, that insidious word, was everything.

She drove past her estranged husband's downtown condo and into the parking lot next to the coroner's office. A homeless man approached her as she climbed out of her rig, and she waved him away.

"I give directly to the food bank and the shelters," she said. "Do yourself a favor and go there. You don't have to live out here."

He flipped her off and disappeared down an alleyway.

With that, Lindsay went inside, pushed the buzzer, and announced her arrival. "Darlene is expecting me," she said.

"All right, come in," said the woman controlling the entrance to the coroner's office.

The door was unlocked, and waiting in her office, scrubs on and hair pinned back, was probably the most beautiful woman in Whatcom County. And the smartest, too.

Darlene Watanabe looked up from her coffee, then at her Cartier watch. She was rich, too, the money having come from a family that had made a fortune in a multitude of businesses that ranged from agriculture to tech.

"Right on time, Detective. Let's see what Jane Doe has to say. She's on the table, ready to tell us about how she ended up at the bottom of the ravine. And who she is. At least, I hope so. But before we start, I want to tell you how sorry I was about Alan."

Clad in pale-blue scrubs, Lindsay stood adjacent to the autopsy table and watched the pathologist as she examined the body. She'd made it a practice to attend autopsies, though not because she enjoyed them. Far from it. She came to watch because she felt the victim deserved the respect of being seen as more than mere evidence, although ultimately anyone who landed on a table in Dr. Watanabe's suite was firmly placed in that category. Before that, however, the body on the stainless-steel table had been someone's child, husband, wife, sibling . . . any number of roles ascribed to the living.

Dr. Watanabe went about her protocol, methodically documenting what she was seeing, now and then adding the occasional non sequitur.

"Decomp extreme. Dead a few days."

"Late teens, early twenties."

"Good health."

"Tried the new Thai place on Railroad yet?"

"Perfect teeth. Orthodontics for sure. Not a street girl."

"Some bruising on the wrists. Hard to tell how recent."

"No sign of rape. But with this kind of decomp, I'll swab, of course."

"You ought to try it. Best satay in the state."

While the pathologist went on with her exam, a picture emerged of the dead girl on the table. She wasn't likely a member of any of the risk groups that sometimes get caught up in something nefarious. In the past few years, there had been an influx of homeless people in Bellingham. Substance abuse and mental illness were often what linked those newcomers.

"No obvious signs of drug use?" Lindsay asked.

"None that I can see. Tox will have to tell us that story." Dr. Watanabe paused a moment and ran a light on the girl's neck. Bruising in the shape of fingertips wrapped around it.

The killer's hands.

Lindsay waited for Dr. Watanabe.

"Manual strangulation is definitely a part of the equation here."

"I noticed the bruising at the scene," Lindsay said.

"Very good, Detective," Dr. Watanabe said in a way that didn't seem derisive. She was direct and compassionate. The previous pathologist was the flip side of that. Always puffed up about what he knew and how inconvenient a traffic fatality was. "What's the point? Crushed and dead? End of story."

"Doctor," Lindsay said, "any thoughts on whether she was alive when she was dumped?"

Dr. Watanabe looked at her through her plastic face shield. "My guess now is that all of these scrapes and abrasions were postmortem. Not a lot of blood loss here. That indicates, as I imagine you know, that she was in fact dead before she hit the bottom of Maple Falls."

Lindsay turned away as the pathologist ran her scalpel in the Y configuration to unzip the body and reveal the organs. It was the only part of the procedure—along with the sound of the Stryker saw as it cut into the skull—that made Lindsay uncomfortable. Looking at the contents of the body as they were weighed and measured wasn't nearly so bad. Just the unzip. And the sound of the saw.

Blood oozed, and the cheerful pathologist applied suction, letting the blood and other body fluids swirl into the drain that ran around the table like a little moat.

"This one's messy, Detective. Sorry. The fall. Ribs shattered. Organs look like they were run through a Vitamix as she fell into the ravine."

Lindsay nodded.

"Any travel plans?" the doctor asked.

"Not really."

"Heard that Jack already got himself dumped."

"Yeah."

"Such a moron."

Lindsay couldn't argue with that.

"Hyoid's broken," she went on. "Strangled before she was dumped."

"Someone dragged her," Lindsay said. "Dirt on her heels."

The pathologist nodded. "Good eye."

Near the end of the autopsy—Dr. Watanabe photographing everything as she went, weighing each organ, and noting details into the mic that hung from the ceiling over the table—Lindsay thought of the missing girls that she'd pulled from the records. At five feet five inches and 108 pounds—the same height and weight as the victim—one had emerged as a frontrunner.

Later that day, Dr. Watanabe confirmed through dental records from a family practice in Everett that the victim was indeed Sarah Baker, a student at Western Washington University, reported missing by her roommate.

CHAPTER 8

Just after ten in the morning, a young woman opened the door to the basement apartment in an old house on Bellingham's North Forest Street and, without even letting Lindsay Jackman say a word, blurted out, "I knew it was Sarah."

"Are you her roommate, Zoey?"

"Yes. Zoey Carmine."

Lindsay identified herself.

"I reported her missing," Zoey said. "I told campus police and Bellingham police that I was pretty sure something bad had happened to her. She wasn't the kind of girl to just run off. She wasn't at all."

"Can I come in?"

Zoey, a lithe brunette with green eyes and a long, narrow nose, motioned Lindsay inside. The young woman wore faded jeans and a white top that gave off the intended bohemian vibe. Her jewelry amplified the look. Silver earrings nearly the size of wind chimes almost reached her shoulders. Lindsay could barely tolerate a small stud earring. Those would drive her crazy.

Once the door was closed, Zoey let out a cry. "I saw it on Facebook! The girl from Maple Falls. It's Sarah! She's really dead, isn't she?"

"I'm so sorry, Zoey," Lindsay said, trying to calm her. "You have suffered a terrible shock. I'm here to find out what happened. For you. For Sarah. Catch your breath. Tell me about her and when you last saw her?"

They sat next to each other on a hand-me-down sofa that had been covered with a red-and-green quilt. It wouldn't be Christmas for months, but when it was, the couch would be ready.

Zoey put her face in her hands and let out a cry that reverberated around the room. It was the ugly, messy kind of sobbing that leaks from a broken heart and a jolt of utter shock.

"I'm so sorry," Lindsay repeated, leaning in, her face full of concern. "I know this is agonizing for you."

Zoey dropped her hands and looked up at Lindsay. Her eyes blurred by tears, her mouth agape.

"Oh God," she said, tears running into her mouth. "Detective, what happened?"

"We don't know exactly."

Which is the truth.

"Was she in an accident?"

This round of twenty questions was leading to where it always led.

"No," she said.

Zoey let out a scream. "Someone killed her! She was murdered! Oh God. This is so wrong!"

"I'm sorry," Lindsay said.

And there's nothing we can do about it now.

"I've known Sarah since we were kids. She was my best friend. I *knew* something bad happened. I *knew* it. But murder? Who would want to kill a girl like Sarah? She was nice to everyone."

Lindsay gave Zoey a moment and then, as gently as possible, redirected her to tell what she could about Sarah.

Both of the girls had grown up in Everett. Sarah was an only child, raised by her aunt. When the girls were fourteen, Zoey's family moved next door.

"Her parents were dead," Zoey said, fumbling around for a tissue before settling on a paper towel. "We really were like sisters. I *needed* a sister. I was the oldest. Me and four brothers. We slept in the same room, and well, it was a mess."

"Her folks dying must have been terrible for her," Lindsay said.

"Right. Really hard. She never got over it. Especially her mom. She talked about that a lot."

Lindsay let the girl blow her nose before prodding her to continue.

"Tell me about her disappearance."

"We were at the farmers' market late in the day Sunday. The last time I saw her, she was looking at some earrings from one of the vendors. I was chatting up a guy, and then . . ."

Zoey fell silent.

"Then what?"

"She was gone. Just gone."

"Did you see anything?"

"No. I just figured she went back home. Got mad at me for talking to that guy. Or something. She could be like that. Impatient. Not really mad."

"Did you call or text?"

"Right away. No answer. That's what kind of made me worried. It wasn't like her. She kept her phone with her at all times. In her *hand*. Not even in a pocket. She lived on that phone."

Lindsay noticed Zoey had her iPhone in her hand, too.

Zoey started to scroll.

"I hate seeing how her texts have dropped lower and lower. You know, on the list of texters? Every day after she went missing, all of our last words have fallen further and further down."

Lindsay hadn't thought of that, and she understood what Zoey was getting at. Alan's text messages and voice mails had already tumbled deep into the quicksand of newer messages since his suicide. It was like

46

his voice was being shoved downward to silence. Every message since had pushed him lower, to that place on a phone no one ever scrolls to.

Zoey showed Lindsay the messages she'd sent Sarah.

Girl, where are you?

Hey, want to meet up before dinner?

Sarah! Where did you run off to?

I'm getting kind of worried.

Okay, now I'm worried.

Text me.

This isn't funny.

I don't know what to do.

If you don't answer, I'm calling the police. I really am. And if you're pissed off for some reason, this will all be on you!

Really, I will.

"And then I did. Late Sunday night, when I saw that she hadn't come home, I knew that something serious had happened. I didn't know whether, you know, she was hurt or abducted or what. Just that it was serious. I called her aunt. She wasn't home. Then I called the police."

"What did you tell them?"

"Pretty much what I told you. Probably the exact same thing, because, well, that's what happened. She disappeared from the market."

Zoey got up, dropped her crumpled paper towel onto the table in front of the Christmas couch, and went to the kitchen. "You want water?" she asked. "Anything? I have coffee from this morning. I could microwave it."

"I'm fine," Lindsay said. She looked at a photo of the two best friends on the wall, taken in front of Old Main on the Western Washington University campus.

Zoey reentered the room. "That was taken last year, when we were freshmen. We were so excited to be getting out of Everett and moving up here."

"What was she studying?"

"Environmental science and journalism. In the summer, she worked on a farm on Lummi Island."

Lindsay nodded. "I'd like to look in her room if that's okay with you."

"Sure." As Zoey led her there, she said over her shoulder, "But brace yourself. You'll see. I always told her that her room looked like a nature show barfed on the walls. So much stuff."

Zoey hadn't understood the room's contents and Sarah's design aesthetic. The walls were a nearly floor-to-ceiling array of images and scientific renderings of Pacific Northwest plants, insects, and wildlife. Her desk was tidy. A laptop, open but asleep, sat with its big blank eye facing the bed. Behind the laptop sat an assortment of specimens from the natural world: a bird's nest, a moon snail shell, and a gargantuan pine cone that Lindsay recognized as one from a sugar pine. A dried-up wasp nest that perfectly imitated a Chinese lantern. An array of textbooks was neatly stacked on a nightstand next to the bed.

Zoey watched from the bedroom door.

"Everything is tidy," Lindsay said. "Is this how she left it?"

"Pretty much. I made the bed because that editor from the *Front* came to do a story about her being missing."

"The *Western Front*? Campus paper?"

"Right. Carl or Carlton something."

"Did the story run?"

"Yeah. Online."

Lindsay scanned the inside of the closet. Nothing remarkable. She opened the drawers of the dresser. Again nothing.

"Did Sarah have a boyfriend?"

"No, not really."

"Anyone even a little special?"

"She didn't really have much time for boys or anything else. Sarah was too busy finding ways to save the planet from destruction. I told her that the planet could wait—that we were in college and the earth would want us to have a good time."

Lindsay slid the top drawer of the dresser closed.

"Did she say anything—anything at all—that indicated she was in any kind of trouble? Or that someone was bothering her? Anything like that?"

"Not really. I mean, I can't think of anything. She was quiet. Kept to herself. Just wanted to do good and never be the center of attention."

As Lindsay started to leave, Zoey called out.

"Just a minute. There was something kind of weird. I mean, not crazy strange. Just a little off."

"What is it?"

"Her car was parked out front—where it is now—the morning after she vanished from the farmers' market."

"Okay," Lindsay said. "Why is that significant to you?"

"It means she came back here, but never made it inside. Something must have happened in the parking lot."

The detective gone, Zoey perched on the edge of Sarah's bed. She and Sarah had met in junior high and had been on-and-off best friends. Mostly off at the moment owing to different interests. No drama between them. Just college. Work. Life.

The same forest-green comforter Zoey was stroking now had been in Sarah's room back then. Zoey thought it looked like the felt on a pool table, but Sarah insisted it was the color of everything important.

"Green isn't just my favorite color," she'd said. "Green is the color of life."

Zoey lay her head on the pillow and looked through her phone messages, wondering if what she'd said to her best friend that afternoon at the market had been the reason she fell into the wrong hands.

She found the text that appeared before the others she'd shown to the detective. She'd been careful to start with the messages that followed this one.

> I can't babysit you, Sarah. I want to hang out with Brendan. Can't you just get lost for a couple hours?

Guilt seized her, and she closed her eyes, squeezing tears into the pillow.

I didn't mean it, Sarah. Really. Promise. This is all my fault.

Chapter 9

After grabbing a sandwich to eat on the way, Lindsay listened to the overly cheerful guidance from her GPS as she drove from Bellingham to Everett, a somewhat sad mill city north of Seattle that seemed always on a futile hunt for a lasting jolt of optimism. To expedite the process of contacting Sarah's family, local police were asked to make the notification. Too much risk with social media channels always open, twenty-four seven. Mary Jo Baker's address was an apartment on Rucker Avenue. Not the best part of the city. A bunch of kids were playing in the parking lot and parted like the Red Sea before Moses when Lindsay edged her car into an empty space.

A woman in her seventies with red-framed cat-eye glasses and thickly penciled-on eyebrows answered her knock.

"I'm here about Sarah," Lindsay said, identifying herself. "Are you Mrs. Baker?"

The woman lowered her glasses. She'd been crying. "Everett police just left. Did you already catch the SOB that killed her?"

How she wished.

"No. I'm here, though, to find who did it. May I come in?"

Lindsay stepped inside, and Sarah's aunt started talking.

And talking.

"Sarah was a very bright, wonderful girl. And beautiful. Really. Kind. She'd never hurt anyone. She was so sweet," she said, her voice cracking a little. "First her mother. Now my beautiful Sarah. God must hate the shit out of me."

"I'm sure it isn't that," Lindsay said.

"It feels that way the longer I live. Have a seat, Detective."

The sofa was covered with small blankets arranged in neat stacks. Lindsay carefully nudged her way in.

Sarah's aunt perched on a straight-backed chair and nodded at the blankets. "I sew those for the families with little ones around here. Just something to pass the time. Some people don't have a lot."

"They're beautiful," Lindsay said.

She shrugged her thanks. "Now, what more can I tell you? Honestly, I don't mind helping. I've told the officers who came what I knew."

Lindsay found her notepad in her purse. "Right. I'm here to follow up. Tell me more about her. What was she like?"

"Stuck to herself. Didn't really socialize with many people. She was a girl with the weight of the world on her shoulders. Never had it easy. Mom left her to follow some misguided dream, then committed suicide. And dad was killed by a drunk driver, a kid who ruined his life along with Sarah's."

"That's awful. She listed you as her mother on the university data card."

"I was as close to one as she had. Took her in when she was little. Been here ever since."

"Not an easy thing to do."

"You're right. It wasn't, yet it was the right thing to do. My sister was gone. Drove down to California and got little Sarah. Took her to Disneyland. Poor kid. I brought her back up here, got her started in school. She wasn't my biological daughter, but I was one hundred percent determined to be her mother. You know, for my sister. Anyway, I never once regretted it. And really, my heart aches so much right now that I don't even think I could feel any more pain if I had given birth to her."

"I'm so sorry," Lindsay said.

"None of this is your fault, Detective," Mary Jo said. "You can be sorry if you don't find Sarah's killer."

Point made.

Lindsay nodded. "Do you mind if I take a look at her room?"

"Down the hall. Have at it. It's pretty much the way she left it when she went off to school in Bellingham. I haven't been in there to dust or vacuum or anything. Now I just can't imagine going in there. Not for some time, anyway."

Sarah's bedroom was all white wicker and pale-yellow walls. It was cheerful in a way that was utterly at odds with everything that had happened to her—in her life as a child in California and in her death at Maple Falls. By the looks of her desk, nightstand, and bookshelf, Sarah was as organized at home as she'd been in college. Almost obsessively so. All the books were pulled forward to the edge of the shelf. Her nightstand had a spare phone charger and a box of tissues. Lindsay went through the desk and it, too, was tidy. It appeared that Sarah was a girl without the need for a junk drawer. The only semblance of clutter was a light-blue file folder that peeked out from under the desk blotter.

Inside the folder was a black-and-white photograph of a group of women. She took it with her when she returned to the front room.

"Found that in my sister's stuff after she passed," Mary Jo said when Lindsay showed it to her. "Sarah wanted it. Don't know why. Her mother's not even in the picture."

Lindsay asked if she could borrow the image.

"Suit yourself. Just find out what happened to her. All right? Do that for me. And for Sarah."

Lindsay tucked the photo into her bag.

"I will do my best, Mary Jo. That's all I can promise you."

On her first big case with Alan, Lindsay had promised a woman that they'd find her son's killer. "We can't make promises like that, Lindsay," he'd told her on the way back from the notification. "We can only promise we will do our best."

Lindsay had felt embarrassed then but had never forgotten it. Ever since, she'd paid strict attention to the promises she made. That was the kind of mark the man's words had made on her.

She'd give anything to turn the clock back to the day before his suicide. She'd send some more of his words back his way. She'd tell him what he'd told her when her mother passed. "She's gone, yes. She'll live on in the people who loved her."

It took less than an hour for word about Sarah's murder to get out after Lindsay met with Sarah's roommate, Zoey, and students at Western went into social media overdrive. Texts and posts ricocheted from every platform to every student on campus. Girls who had barely noticed Sarah proclaimed broken hearts and missed opportunities to hang out and spend more time with her. Boys said they thought she was cool and "super smart" and the like. Someone started a GoFundMe page because they heard Sarah had a cat and it would need to find a new home. "Sarah's Cat" clicked up to $144 before someone posted that Sarah hadn't had a cat at all.

It was still light out when a mound of flowers and teddy bears started to form by the fountain in Red Square, the university's central plaza. Some students made hand-lettered signs proclaiming their loss—for a girl none really knew. They were propped up against the concrete edge of the fountain.

YOU ARE IN A BETTER PLACE
WE DEMAND JUSTICE
CATCH SARAH'S KILLER

In the basement of Haggard Hall, Carl Flanders logged on to the *Western Front* website to respond to comments on the article he had written about Sarah's death.

WWU Student Murdered at Maple Falls

Carl was twenty-five, a sixth-year senior with more than enough credits to graduate. That is, if he could simply determine what he wanted to be when he grew up. Carl sat alone at a table and tapped on the keyboard, updating the story of the dead student and the vigil students planned. It bothered him a little that students used the "like" button on the paper's Facebook page on the story. There was nothing to "like" about murder.

"Update: Friday night's vigil will be led by her roommate. Be there at 7:30."

He wasn't sure how he felt about Sarah Baker's death. He had nothing against her, personally. It was all professional jealousy. She had had everyone's ear. And eyes, too. At the top of it, she was a rival. She went around the journalism department talking about "something big" that she was doing, but it was secret.

"If I tell you," she'd said, "I'll have to kill you."

Candlelight vigils and makeshift memorials go hand in hand.

Both are a show.

And both bring out the best and worst in people.

Lindsay found a parking spot on Billy Frank Jr. Street and hiked up the hill to campus with Lieutenant Madison huffing and puffing behind her. The air had cooled by at least ten degrees, and rain threatened to fall during the vigil. Lindsay wondered if she should stop and let the lieutenant rest, though thought better of it. He needed the exercise. His wife would almost certainly agree.

They would stand out in the crowd, owing more to Martin's age than how they were dressed. Lindsay wore dark slacks and a blazer. The lieutenant wore his usual uniform: blue Dockers and a camel-colored windbreaker. His gray mustache screamed cop or out-of-shape, over-the-hill ex-porn-star.

More than two hundred students congregated by the fountain, milling around and hugging each other. Some were crying. A few acted as if they were at a party, laughing and swaying to music coming from their earbuds. The thick and unmistakable scent of marijuana filled the air.

"It's legal," Lindsay said, eyeing the lieutenant.

"Shouldn't be," he said. "And it's not legal in public."

"We're not here for that."

He gave her a nod.

She regretted asking him to come. He wasn't Alan. His extra set of eyes would likely be of little value. And that had very little to do with the fact that his vision, even behind his thick glasses, was poor.

A girl with spiral curls handed them each a candle inserted into a paper cup.

"Light-up is in five minutes," she said. "You need a light?"

"Nope," Martin said, pulling out his lighter. "This isn't our first vigil."

Although, of course it was.

The girl with the curls walked away, passing out her supply of the candles to the gathering. It occurred to Lindsay that there was nothing makeshift about this memorial. Someone must have had a stash of these candles ready to go.

Promptly at seven thirty, with candles struggling to stay lit, a mid-dle-aged man with the collar of his overcoat turned up against the chill stood on the edge of the fountain and called out to the crowd.

"I want to thank you all for coming tonight," he said. "I'm John Evans, dean of students at the university. Times like this are very hard, and I know all of you are hurting over the unfathomable loss of your friend and fellow student. Tonight, all of us have joined here to remember Sarah Baker and share our grief."

A girl standing next to Lindsay cried out, "It's so wrong!"

"Yes," the dean called back. "All of it. I think we can say we all share a sense of anger, as well. We want the police to catch the killer."

Students cheered, giving the moment the feeling of a very strange pep rally.

The dean introduced a young man named Calvin Harper. The crowd parted and let him come up to sing. His voice started out soft and was absorbed by the bodies that enveloped that side of the fountain. He sang a more-than-passable "Amazing Grace."

Lindsay continued to scan the crowd to see if there was anyone or anything out of place. She told the lieutenant to take as many photos of the gathering as he could.

"Get video, too," she said.

She caught a glimpse of Lieutenant Madison doing just that.

Good.

Alan would have stood there in shock to see the lieutenant following anyone else's orders.

If only he had still been alive.

After the song, the man said a few more words, and a very shaky Zoey Carmine stood up to speak.

"Hi, everyone. My name is Zoey. Sarah was my best friend. We grew up together. We were roommates here at Western. I just want to tell you a little bit more about her. She was the nicest girl ever. She loved all animals and plants. I used to tease her about that, you know, asking her if she ever got any answers back when she talked to a tree or a goat or whatever. She laughed and said it wasn't about getting answers as much as it was about letting other beings know that she loved them."

Zoey stopped for a second, and a boy yelled out, "We're here for you, Zoey! We're here for you and for Sarah!"

Zoey looked in his direction. He was tall and had a full beard and wore a navy stocking cap. She gave him a little nod and continued.

"It would have brought tears to Sarah's eyes if she were here and could see how much she was loved. She was kind of a loner, actually. Everyone wanted to be her friend, but she didn't always want to let them in. Anyway, I'm super heartened by everyone here."

A kid in a blue WWU hoodie leaned into the girl next to him. "I heard she was raped and beaten to death."

Lindsay glared in his direction. "She wasn't raped," she said. "Where did you hear that?"

"Online," he said with a look that was an attempt at a smirk. "What's it to you?"

Lindsay flashed her badge.

It had been a smirk, after all. It melted away. "Sorry," he said, stepping back. "Just a rumor, I guess. Never trust the Internet."

"That's right."

Zoey wrapped up her eulogy.

"She was like a sister to me. I will never get over what happened to her." She started to cry and then touched her lips before muttering, "I'm really sorry."

The crowd dispersed after that, and Lindsay found Martin, still recording video like he'd been told.

"See anything?" he asked. "I haven't been out in the field like this for years. Kind of fun if it weren't so fucking cold."

Lindsay watched the students leave.

"Not really. There was one thing."

"What?"

"Never mind. Probably nothing."

Martin looked her in the eye. "I want to hear your thinking, Detective. No bad ideas, remember?"

Lindsay didn't trust him the way she trusted her former partner. They could muse about any stupid, ridiculous idea and not judge.

Lieutenant Madison . . . well, he was the boss. He wasn't a trusted colleague.

Lindsay gave in.

"I thought it was kind of odd when Zoey said she was sorry."

His brow narrowed.

"At the end," she said.

"Sorry for what? Breaking down? Or what?"

"Like I said, I don't know. Just kind of felt odd to me."

The lieutenant let out a sigh. "I guess I've been in the office too long," he said. "I didn't see it that way at all. When you're out in the field, everyone is a goddamn suspect. I know that's right. But really, I think the girl was just upset because her friend was dead, and she was sorry about it."

Lindsay shrugged it off. "Let's get out of here. I have a dinner to microwave."

Martin grinned at her. "I thought you cooked."

"Not anymore. Cooking for one is a pointless endeavor."

They were walking across Red Square when they heard a voice call out.

"Hey, are you the detectives working Sarah's case?"

Lindsay spun around and found a young man hurrying up to them.

"We are," she said. "How can we help you?"

"I'm an editor for the *Western Front*. Carl Flanders." Lindsay recalled his name. He was the student journalist who'd interviewed Zoey.

"I promoted the vigil," he said. "Got a great turnout. Would like to interview you about the case."

"We don't have anything to tell you right now," the lieutenant said.

"Come on," Carl said, turning to Lindsay. "She was one of our own, in the journalism department."

"You knew her?" Lindsay asked.

"Yeah. She was kind of every guy's crush."

"What else can you tell me about her, Carl?"

A little disoriented to find himself the interviewee, he settled quickly enough into the role. "She was smart and pretty. She wasn't interested in hanging out with the group. She just kept her nose down most of the time. Working on a book or something. It wasn't for the paper. She was kind of standoffish. Private."

Lindsay gave him her card.

"Call me later," she said. "I'll see about talking to you then."

Carl walked away satisfied, a little worried, too. He'd admired Sarah but knew his admiration had turned to jealousy. Not about her occasional articles. Not about the project that she'd been quietly working on for months. He hadn't a clue what that was about, anyway. No, he was jealous of how everyone else thought about her.

"She's the only one that's pretty enough for broadcast TV. She'll go places," the paper's sports editor had said when a bunch of the staff went out for beers.

"I'd do her in a heartbeat," said the ad manager, straining as always to fit in.

It didn't work that night, either. Rolled eyes all around.

Except for Carl's. His were closed nearly to slits, as though he were fighting a headache, and failing at it.

Carl was tired of hearing Sarah's fan club prattle on about her.

Just sick of it.

Chapter 10

Paul Sharpe planted himself at the far end of the sticky bar at the Rusty Nail off of North State Street. It was the end of a long Saturday night—Sunday morning, really, a half hour to closing time—at this Bellingham pub, and the smells of beer and whiskey and sweat were heavy both in the room and rising from the pores of his skin.

He knew he smelled, too, still he didn't care.

Normally, Paul had a very alert and engaging appearance. Now, he was sullen, his eyes heavily lidded and his hair made do without gobs of product. His world had been upended in a split second, and booze and late hours were only making things worse. He'd made a point to be careful to rotate the bars he'd frequented, because he didn't want to besmirch his father's name.

The word about his suicide had already done a good job of that.

Paul had been proud of his dad. He kept a photograph of the two of them from when he was a little kid in his wallet. He was wearing his father's cap, and it swallowed most of his head. That was the idea, though: showing that he was small and that he admired his daddy. Which he did, more than anything. The thoughts of those days played fleetingly in his mind. His dad had been nothing if not supportive, kind, and loving to him his entire life. His father was his hero. He set the benchmark for what a good dad and husband should be.

Big hat to fill.

Big shoes, too.

And now, he was gone.

"Sorry about your old man," the bartender said.

"Thanks. Yeah. Me, too."

Her name was Josie.

"This one is on the house, Paul. You're going through a lot of shit, and I'm going to serve you two drinks; then you're going to go get some sleep."

"Yeah, Josie. Thanks."

She was a little older than he was. Good-looking, too, no matter what time of day it was in the bar: often a drunken fantasyland, soaked in desperation, where most people started to look better only around 2:00 a.m.

She got his first glass of Jack, no ice.

He put it to his lips as she stood there.

"I know it doesn't really help," she said, "but I've been there. My first serious boyfriend jumped onto the tracks at Tukwila Station. I stood there like a statue as the train went over him. Just, like, froze."

"That's horrible," Paul said.

"It was eight years ago, but it crosses my mind every day. How was it that I didn't know?"

"I feel you," he said. "I never saw even a hint that Dad would do what he did. Just didn't see it coming."

Josie offered a world-weary smile as she watched him drink.

"People keep secrets, Paul."

He nodded at his empty glass, indicating he was ready for one more.

"Yeah," he said. "I guess they do."

Woozy, not falling down drunk, Paul left the bar for an Uber ride, his mind consumed with thoughts about one of his last encounters with his father. It had been about a week before his suicide. Paul had been home getting a free meal and his laundry done, courtesy of his ever-giving mother. He was watching TV when his father arrived. Paul immediately knew something was off. Alan Sharpe had been known to dive deep down into depression and worry, but only for a short time. This felt different. Deeper. Underwater with no lifeline, it seemed.

"Dad," Paul had said, "what's happening?"

"Just a case. Same old. Reporter hounding me. Just getting me down when I know it shouldn't."

"Tell me about it. Maybe I can help."

Alan's eyes suddenly went damp. "Don't know much, Paul. Dead baby found in a rest stop off the interstate."

"Wow, that's terrible."

Alan sat down on the sofa next to Paul. "Right. Really beyond terrible. Baby girl was wrapped in a black plastic garbage bag like she was nothing. Not my case, thank God. Even so, it really got to me."

"Dad, I'm sorry. Whoever did that must have been sick."

Alan brushed it off. "Sick or just couldn't be bothered. Had a baby, didn't think to find a home for their daughter, and treated her like garbage. Literally. Left her to die in a bathroom stall."

"Baby was alive?"

"Yeah. That's what the doc says."

Patty came inside just then. She'd been running errands in town. She set down her purse and keys and noticed straightaway that something was amiss. Father and son were slumped on the sofa, looking as if they'd melted into the cushions.

"You two all right? What's going on here?"

"Just a case, babe," Alan said, getting up to embrace her.

"Baby dumped at a rest stop," Paul added. "Dead."

"Oh no," Patty said.

Alan whispered in his wife's ear.

"Right, honey," she said softly when he'd finished, stepping away and looking at Paul. "I made green enchiladas. Staying, Paul?"

Paul had climbed under the covers of his old bed that night after the enchiladas, in a room that remained pretty much untouched since he went away to college. Trophies from Little League marched across one of the shelves. His mostly worthless collection of various trading cards—football, baseball, and whatever else he'd liked as a teenager—was in pristine condition in binders piled up next to the bed. It was always good to be home. His mother doted on him in the way that moms do, sometimes a little too much. His dad was the same, never distant, always there to take him places, work on his homework.

He fell asleep right away, only to be awakened by a noise he'd never heard before.

His father was crying.

Paul pushed his legs into a pair of pants and followed the sound coming from his dad's office down the hall.

The door was slightly ajar, so Paul nudged it open. Without making a sound. His dad was sitting on his chair, looking at some paperwork.

"Dad?"

Alan tried to shake off his grief. He wiped his eyes on his arm before turning around.

"Want to talk?" Paul asked.

"I don't want you to see me like this, Paul. We can talk tomorrow."

"Sure?"

"Yeah," he said. "Now let's get back to bed."

Alan turned off the desk light.

Paul watched his father gather up the papers, slide them into a manila envelope, and place them into his bottom right-hand drawer— the only desk drawer with a lock. He turned the key and put it into his bathrobe pocket.

"Things are always better in the morning," Alan said. "Now go to bed."

Paul went back to his room, unlocked his phone, and searched for information on the dead baby. He scrolled through the news sites, the *Bellingham Herald* and even the *Seattle Times*. He was sure that something as sensational and tragic as that would have made the news.

There wasn't anything.

The next morning, Paul got up early and went into his father's office. Something was tearing his dad apart in a way that seemed far beyond any kind of depression. Blue days, his dad called them.

Paul jiggled the bottom desk drawer. Locked. As quietly as he could, he pulled out the middle drawer, releasing it from the desk and leaving the contents of the bottom one exposed.

He stooped down on his knees and felt around.

Nothing. The drawer was empty. There was no file.

Whatever it had been that had made his father so upset, baby or something else, was gone.

CHAPTER 11

Monday, September 16, 2019
Ferndale, Washington

The caller didn't want to identify himself at first.

Lindsay Jackman had no use for anonymous tips. Alan had insisted otherwise—saying they could be a better-than-nothing first step to solving a crime. Lindsay frequently pushed back on such occasions, insisting to her partner there were too many crazies looking for attention, and sifting out the bad from the good was too much work.

"Just tell me who you are," she said to this man, "then let's go from there."

The man exhaled, and for a second, Lindsay thought he'd hung up. "Sir?"

"I'm here," he answered.

"Tell me your name and what it is that you think I need to know."

"I suppose you need my name for your records or something."

"Yes," she said. "Something."

"My name is Reed Sullivan."

He let his name float in the air. It brought no immediate response from Lindsay.

"Mr. Sullivan, how can I help you?"

"I read about the vigil on campus for the girl murdered at Maple Falls."

"Yes, Sarah Baker. Did you know her?"

"No," he said. "I can't say that. But I think you should come talk to me. The paper said she worked at Spellman Farms in the summer. My wife did, too. My wife was murdered. That makes two girls with ties to Marnie Spellman."

"When did your wife die?"

"Twenty years ago," he said.

"All right," Lindsay said. "I'll come and see you."

She wrote down Reed Sullivan's address and told an officer she was heading to an interview on her way out the door.

"Reed Sullivan?" the officer said. "Wow. Poor SOB. His wife was found murdered on the beach out at Lummi Island. That was a big case. And yeah, no one trusts Marnie Spellman. Good luck."

Lindsay was too young to remember the Sullivan case, but not so young that the name Marnie Spellman was unfamiliar. These days, Marnie had faded into self-imposed exile on her Lummi Island estate, but Lindsay knew she'd once been a cosmetics queen. A savvy marketer who had somehow turned herself into a wellness and lifestyle guru before the likes of Martha Stewart or Gwyneth Paltrow.

There was a weirder—and perhaps darker—side, too, Lindsay would come to learn when she plunged into her self-directed course in Marnie Spellman studies after hearing what Reed Sullivan would have to tell her.

Marnie purportedly communed directly with Mother Nature, indeed, claimed all recipes of her various potions came from that kind of spiritual connection. That brought devotees and detractors. A million or so in the former. Devotees would do anything she asked. Detractors would chant that Marnie Spellman was evil.

The Truth of Beeing was Marnie's slogan.

It was not a typo. In time, even outsiders came to recognize the spelling as the invention of Marnie Spellman, glamorous entrepreneur, glamorous charlatan. Which label they applied depended upon which TV shows they watched or magazines they read.

The tagline appeared on every product, in every book, and with the advent of the Internet, eventually it took its place there, too. Marnie's famed childhood incident with a swarm of bees had framed all that she would do, all she had been about.

It had not been a mistake that it had been honeybees that selected her, showed her, and changed her. While not entirely unique in the animal world, a beehive was a monarchy. The leader of any hive, the one around which everything revolved, was the queen. She was superior to the drones and scouts, which lived only a short time to serve her. There could be no hive without her. There was no future for the planet without her. Honeybees were the primary pollinator of most of the world's plant life. Vegetation was the building block of all foods.

Without queen bees, not only would the hive wither and die, the consequences for the entire world would be catastrophic. Without queens, a famine unlike any previous one would ravage Earth's human and animal population.

Marnie cast herself as the queen. And really, why wouldn't she? She was stunningly beautiful. She was razor sharp. Most importantly, she had an undeniable charisma—a kind of bright light—that pulled others into her orbit.

Even seasoned, cool-headed Detective Lindsay Jackman would come to feel that pull as she lowered herself down into the Marnie

Spellman rabbit hole. Ridiculous as they often were, there was no denying that Marnie's words would find purchase in Lindsay. This would
trouble her, but very much interest her, too. As she tracked the growth
of this unwanted feeling, probed her psyche for how and why it had
been granted entry, she would come to recognize it as a potentially valuable aid in her investigation.

No argument, it was creepy as hell—it could also prove a gift.

In the meantime, she would gather others' stories, wherever she
could find them. Like a post and accompanying video on the Internet
from a North Dakota woman whose husband had hired a cult depro-
grammer to kidnap and "knock some sense into her"—his words—
and who later went on national TV to talk about her experiences with
Marnie and working on Spellman Farms.

Lindsay started scribbling notes.

"Marnie is magnetic," the woman said. "That's the word that keeps
coming back to me. She's the kind of person that makes you feel as if
you are special, important. There were times I was with her when I just
started to cry. It wasn't because I was sad or anything like that. I cried
because I was in the presence of someone so gifted, so smart, and so
loving that I couldn't even comprehend why she had any interest in
me, just some regular mother of two from Bismarck. Again, as I tell
everyone who gives me the same look you are right now, you had to be
there. It cannot fully be explained in words."

The interviewer asked if she regretted leaving her family for Marnie's
compound on Lummi Island.

"I know what you did just then, by using the word *compound*.
You're making it out to be a cult, aren't you? You can't accept that a
woman could assemble devotees without manipulation and trickery.
Marnie was no Jim Jones."

She stopped and looked off camera.

"People want me to regret it," she went on. "People—including
members of my family—tell me that the prudent thing to do would

be to disavow Marnie and all she stands for." She turned back to the interviewer. "I won't. I can't. I do, however, regret missing my sons' birthdays, and I regret hurting my husband. Those things were necessary, though, for me to achieve my becomingness."

The interviewer shifted his weight and smirked, but it made no difference to his subject.

"As long as I live," she went on, "I will never deny the importance of what I learned from Marnie Spellman. Never will you find me saying to anyone what the mainstream media longs to hear. I know how this game is played. So does Marnie Spellman. The undisputed reality here is that she is the best of what we all can be."

The video over, Lindsay read a note purportedly posted by the husband. He mentioned how after the program aired, his wife, Marnie's defender, received two dozen yellow roses and a handwritten letter, delivered by special messenger to her job at a telemarketing center outside of Bismarck.

She told him how she went into a stall in the center's bathroom to read Marnie's note.

> *You will never know how much this means.*
> *You are everything I knew you could bee.*
> *Come home to me when the time is right.*
> *Love, M*

"She said she held that little paper close to her breast, savoring the message and passing love to its sender. Then she shredded it into confetti, dropped it in the toilet, and watched it swirl downward. She knew the deprogramming had been a colossal failure, but going on TV had lent a measure of credibility to her claim that it had succeeded. It provided her cover until she could sneak off to the Pacific Northwest again, and for good."

Lindsay stopped taking notes. Takings notes felt like the composition of a fairy tale. A ridiculous dream. Marnie Spellman's pull on others was absolute.

"My wife said she still loved me and our kids," the man wrote, "and maybe she did. Only enough to call me and tell me what had really gone on before she disappeared to Lummi Island. Of course," he'd concluded, "maybe that was only so I wouldn't try to follow her."

CHAPTER 12

Y2K brought out a sense of urgency in some people. Not just preppers. Normal people, too. After all, when the new millennium came, there was no telling what would happen. People were still adjusting to having seemingly everything about their lives spring from or revolve around the computers that had been hogging every available inch of desktop space for the past ten, fifteen years. Computers whose creators hadn't, evidently, programmed them to account for a world that extended beyond the year 1999.

Would that world stop spinning?

Would planes drop from the skies?

Who knew?

Nobody, it seemed.

When calendars finally turned to 2000, nothing happened. Y2K was the dud of all duds.

But not for the Jenners—Dan and Linda. The approach of Y2K was the impetus to accelerating a lifelong goal of taking a grand tour of every national park in the US. "No monuments, just the parks," Linda had informed each of their skeptical grown children before they packed up in the fall of 1999 and headed out on the adventure of a millennium.

"Just the parks," Dan had chimed in, each and every time, from the green leather recliner across the room. "You have to draw the line somewhere."

"But the line might get a little wiggly," Linda had said, bringing down the curtain on their little skit. "We'll be living in the moment, too."

Olympic National Park had been the last on the list for Washington State, and it easily ranked in their constantly recalculating top ten. Maybe top five. Dan, a retired school administrator, and Linda, a former software manager, had pulled every penny out of one of their savings accounts for the trip. Linda was in remission from a battle with breast cancer, but as positive as she wanted to be about her prognosis, she knew that the odds were not in her favor. Both of her sisters, her aunt, and her grandmother had died of the disease. At sixty-nine, she'd lived longer than any of them and wanted to enjoy the beauty of nature before the world was stolen from her.

Not by Y2K.

By cancer.

They'd already hit Mount Rainier ("The meadows were starting to bloom!") and the North Cascades ("Talk about an elk herd . . . There must have been a hundred!"), and they'd finally made it to the Olympic Peninsula and a historic lodge not far from magnificently craggy Ruby Beach. The weather on the Washington coast is predictably unpredictable. One minute, rain. The next, a sunbreak that stretches out for a couple of days or lasts only as long as the flutter of a gull's wing. Ensconced in the cozy lobby at the lodge, they sat by the fire and sipped coffee laced with Kahlúa.

"Just a splash of cream," Linda had said to the waiter.

Dan rolled his eyes upward. "Give her a good dollop," he said. "She's not watching her weight."

Linda didn't argue. Letting her husband do something kind on her behalf gave him great pleasure—something that had been lacking in what she called the "cancer years," that took up so much of their time before the big national park trip was conceived.

It rained buckets that night, rain pelting the roof of their room like a continuous spray of pellets from a BB gun.

Linda sent an email to her kids on the blasted Blackberry their oldest had given her when they set off on their adventure.

> *We're in a rainforest, so I guess the torrent that hit us last night at the lodge was nothing out of the ordinary. I'm telling you I was almost scared. The rain turned the parking lot into a river. On to Alaska tomorrow. Maybe it will blizzard there ☺. Life is precious. Life is good.*

The next morning, the Jenners, fueled with coffee and almond croissants, drove to Seattle, then Bellingham, where they'd catch a ferry to Alaska. With a couple of days to kill, they explored the city and drove farther north to Lummi Island.

The couple layered their bodies with fleece and rain jackets and walked down to the beach. Even that was an adventure. The trail was washed out from the storm the night before. A tree had fallen. Its roots were an umbrella turned on its side. And yet it was warm, calm.

Dan took off his raincoat. Not needed. Linda kept hers on; the breeze was gentle, but it tugged at her, and she needed to stay warm. As they wound their way to the beach inside the sodden tunnel of the understory, they came to the open space of the Salish Sea. The clouds had parted to reveal a flawless blue sky. The waves were meringue. Rocks jutted in the surf like the remnants of a lost city revealed.

"If I live to be a hundred," Linda said, "I'll never see anything that matches that."

Dan put his arm around her. Even through the layers of her jacket, he could feel the smallness of her frame. Linda had never been a large woman. Now she was a stick figure.

"Denali's supposed to be pretty amazing," he said, referring to their next stop.

She leaned into him and gave him a kiss. "I can't wait."

And really, they had no time to lose.

They walked along the shoreline, miles of stunning emptiness all around them. It was as if they were the last people on the earth, and they felt nothing but the love of each other and the kind of peace that comes when one knows the end of a love story.

"One of those Japanese glass floats," Dan said, pointing down the beach to a white orb on the waterline.

"Our lucky day!" From the minute she'd arrived on the Washington coast, she'd had two desires. She wanted a really good fried razor clam. That had been struck from her short list at dinner the night before. The clams were meaty and tender. She loved them.

"They taste like the ocean," she'd said.

Dan smiled at her.

"The ocean tastes like tartar sauce, then," he'd said.

And now this. The dream discovery of any beachcomber.

A glass Japanese fishing float.

They moved closer, leaving a trail of their tangled footsteps on the wet sand.

"Still has its netting," Linda said, moving in front of him. She wanted that float more than anything.

"No," Dan said, reaching out, trying to stop her from getting any closer. "Not netting." His blue eyes crinkled at what he saw. "It's hair, Linda."

Linda turned to meet her husband's gaze with a kind of look he'd never seen. Not even when she'd been diagnosed with cancer. Not when she'd felt the first twinge of the agony that came with a miscarriage early in their marriage.

She was terrified.

Linda pressed her face into Dan's shoulder. "Oh God," she said. "That's a body."

Dan held her so tightly he feared her brittle bones would snap. "I think so, honey. Some lady's body."

"We need to get the authorities here," she said.

Dan looked down the stretch of beach. Suddenly, they were no longer alone. A young couple with two little kids was heading toward them. He let go of Linda and cupped his hands by his mouth and called through the suddenly choppy breeze. "Back! Keep your kids away from here!"

"Everything all right?" a young man with a goatee and a Mariners baseball cap called back.

"Police," Dan said. "We need the police!"

Linda remembered her Blackberry.

It wasn't so stupid anymore.

She dialed 911.

CHAPTER 13

Monday, September 16, 2019
Bellingham, Washington

Reed Sullivan's house was at the end of a quiet street in the Happy Valley neighborhood south of Bellingham. An overgrown purple-and-white wisteria coiled its way over a sagging trellis and up onto the ebony sheet metal roof and started snaking downward to the other side. It was as if the vine intended to make a meal of the place.

Lindsay bent low to dodge the tentacles of foliage as she made her way to the front door and knocked.

A man with round glasses and a mass of black hair streaked with gray answered. He wore an oatmeal-colored cardigan and black slacks. His button-down shirt matched his pastel-blue eyes.

"Mr. Sullivan?"

He studied her. "That's me."

"I'm here about your phone call about the girl found at Maple Falls."

He looked into her eyes; his own were magnified by the lenses, blinking hard.

"I shouldn't have called, Detective."

"Maybe," she answered. "I still need to talk to you."

With that, he shut the door.

"Mr. Sullivan," she said, hoping he was still on the other side of the door and listening. "I need to know what happened back then. I need to know why you think your wife's murder is connected to our Maple Falls victim."

It was the last bit of chum she could toss into the water. Reed Sullivan's chance to say what he might not have been able to say twenty years before. Lindsay held her breath and watched as the doorknob turned.

Reed Sullivan's living room featured high ceilings and a pair of fans that whirled overhead as he and Lindsay took seats across from each other. He sat on a leather armchair, she on a high-backed sofa so deep and devoid of pillows that she felt herself shrink a little. A white Persian-mix cat curled under the coffee table.

"She's my final feline," he said, smiling slightly at the cat, or maybe the alliteration. "Kind of a habit having one. Calista liked the furriest ones, and well, I just continued on with the tradition."

"Lots of maintenance," Lindsay said, noticing the snowy fur already clinging to her slacks.

"Tell me about it," he said. "I brush her twice a day, and still I have all of this to contend with." He indicated an accumulation of drifting white cat fur on the armchair.

"Mr. Sullivan, an officer told me about your case. It was before my time. I'm sorry about your wife and everything that happened to you. You called because you see a connection between your wife's death and the case I'm working now. Sarah Baker."

"Right," he said. "I know there is a connection because Sarah called me."

Lindsay gave him a hard, deliberate stare, trying to size him up on the spot. He looked normal. But they often did. Was he a crazy? An attention seeker?

"You spoke with her?" she asked.

He didn't fidget. He didn't shift his gaze.

"Only for a minute," he said.

"Go on," she said.

"Right. She said she was working on a story, an exposé maybe. I told her I would talk to her. The next thing I knew, I saw the article in the *Herald*. The one about the candlelight vigil the end of last week."

The cat jumped up and landed softly on his lap. A cloud of fur floated in the current created by the ceiling fan.

Lindsay probed for more on Sarah's call.

"I agreed to do the interview," he said. "She felt that my wife's death had been covered up and that there was more to the story. That Marnie Spellman was at the center of it all. And she said there might have been others."

"What others?"

"She didn't say. I didn't ask. I figured she'd tell me when we met. Obviously, that's never going to happen now."

"What about Marnie? What did she say about her?"

"Not more than that. She didn't have to. I know what kind of dangerous fraud Marnie was, and almost certainly still is."

"All right, Mr. Sullivan, let's talk about you and Calista. How was it that the two of you ended up here in Washington?"

"You mean, how was it that Marnie Spellman took control of my wife," he said, "and then control of my life?"

Lindsay had sliced open a wound. His face had gone flush.

"I guess that's what I mean," she said.

He stroked the cat. Fur snowed again upward into the ceiling fan.

"It started with that stupid home shopping channel. My wife was mesmerized by her. She started buying all of her products. The soaps, the scrubs, the bee pollen elixirs. Every day, it seemed, there was something from UPS on our doorstep."

He stopped, and Lindsay filled the gap.

"A lot of people bought her products—"

He cut her off. "But they didn't leave everything behind to be with her. Look," Reed went on, "I thought it was a problem, a compulsion, a shopping addiction, or something like that. I even suggested to Calista that she go to a counselor for help, but she shut me down—and honestly, I thought about it and pulled back."

"That helped?"

He petted the cat. "No. Not at all. I didn't know it. Something else was going on. She'd started to get the recordings by then."

Winter 1998/1999
Los Angeles, California

The way her husband and friends had viewed it when it had begun manifesting itself that Los Angeles winter of 1998–1999, Calista Sullivan had simply retreated from their daily lives in favor of some kind of personal quest. She was still there, though not all *there*. Friends who lunched with her on weekends found it impossible to arrange a suitable date. She was too busy, too distracted. She was finishing up a nursing degree at night. Calista missed so many shifts at her day job at the restaurant where she worked as assistant manager that she was fired.

She didn't even bat an eye over that. Instead, she focused more of her attention on the CDs she'd ordered from Marnie Spellman's growing holistic enterprise.

"Something's calling me," she told Reed one afternoon in February.

Her words didn't track. "Calling you?"

"Telling me that I need to leave here—that I have something more waiting for me."

"More than *your boys*? More than *me*?"

"I don't expect you to understand. It's something that I have only been able to grasp recently. It's about having a greater purpose."

Reed's eyes filled with tears.

She stood there, a concerned look on her face. She reached out to him, and they embraced.

"I don't understand you," he said.

"I know. You can't. You are part of the world designed the way man means for it to be, with you and the boys at the center and me on the periphery, Reed. Try to see it, though. Try to understand that being someone's wife or someone's mother isn't the be all, end all. I feel empty. There's a void in me. Can you see it?"

Who is *this woman?*

"No," he said. "I can't. I think that being a mother to our boys is a great honor, a gift that only you can give. There's no greater calling."

He was trying, struggling to speak in a language mirroring the one that she'd been using.

A gift. A calling.

She pulled away.

"Reed," she said, "I love you. I do. I love our boys, too. This is hard to say to you. It is time for me to love myself more. It's supposed to be that way."

Reed's attempt at understanding ceased. His face flushed hot. "Be *what* way? Calista, our marriage, it's always been a partnership. Neither of us is more important than the other."

Calista took a step away. "Of course. And that's the problem. Why should I be a partner to you when I could lead? Why couldn't I, as a female being, be the one who decides the way we live, how we grow?"

"You picked this house, Calista. We have two boys because you wanted two kids. You chose their names."

Calista stayed calm, serene. "You led me to those decisions, Reed. This house was the one *you* wanted; I only acted as though it had been my favorite. I much preferred the place with the cutting garden on Fillmore Street."

Reed's frustration escalated. "That was practically a teardown!"

She gave a little shrug. "So you said. I saw potential. And as far as our sons' names go, Brady was your best man's name, and Christian was your grandmother's maiden name."

Reed knew she was right, but he had to say something.

"You were the one that suggested those names."

"Because I knew you would love them."

She looked down at the CDs she'd been listening to.

His eyes followed hers, and he lurched toward the table and swept the plastic cases to the floor.

Instead of getting angry, she looked wistful. She even smiled a little. It was a sad smile, he thought later. It hadn't been directed toward her husband with any measure of unkindness. It came from what she called "a knowing" deep inside that reminded her that her turn was now and there was nothing he could do about it.

"You can't have the boys," he said.

"I know," she said. "They belong to you."

He was beside himself. "Seriously, Calista? What are you thinking? You're their mother. They need you."

She shook her head.

"Reed, *I* need me."

Monday, September 16, 2019

Lindsay had grown up on *He Bear, She Bear* and other books that gently prodded girls into understanding they could be whatever they wanted to be. She hadn't even thought twice about her gender when she wanted to be a cop. Her mother, who'd gone into teaching instead of architecture because she was the only girl in high school mechanical drawing, considered Lindsay's choice an affirmation that the old rules that had held her back were no longer in play.

If Reed Sullivan's take on it was accurate—and there was nothing to suggest it wasn't—Marnie Spellman's philosophy echoed that, but shot past it into territory icy enough to excuse abandoning your spouse and children. To require it, even.

"That must have been very hard for you," Lindsay said, "having her leave like that."

"Understatement, Detective. Yes. Very."

"Did she go right away?"

"That night. She took only what she could put into an old pair of Samsonite suitcases and called a cab for LAX."

"What about your sons? What did she say to them?"

"I wasn't there," he said. "She sequestered them in our bedroom and shut the door. Brady told me later that she promised she'd only be gone a short time. Visiting a new friend. Something vague like that. Nothing to indicate she was never coming back."

He stopped to pet the cat.

"For all of her talk about evolving and being something greater than merely a mom and a wife, Calista was a chickenshit liar. She didn't have the courage to tell the boys the truth."

"What truth was that?"

"The truth that none of us mattered to her. Not anymore. That there wasn't room for anyone but herself. And her."

"Marnie Spellman?"

"Yeah, her."

CHAPTER 14

Reed Sullivan played with a loose string on his cardigan. He looked a little lost, like he'd been transported back to a time that now felt foreign. Lindsay noticed a bead of sweat roll from his brow.

Remembering those days was hard work. Painful. He talked about putting the house on the market and how he'd hoped that their marriage was worth a second chance to her.

"She had been sending letters and leaving phone messages that said she missed everyone and wanted us to sell the house and move up to Washington. The boys were six and nine. I guess I was weak. I figured that the only way to move forward with our broken lives was to acquiesce to her new life and the demands that came with it."

Reed was the flip side of the generation of men who'd insisted that their wives' professions be secondary. That she should always follow him. To a new job. A new city. Didn't matter what she had going. He was primary.

"What was she doing?"

"She was living in Bellingham at the time, commuting to Lummi Island to work at Spellman Farms. She bragged in one letter that she'd never known true happiness until she started working for Marnie."

"What was she doing?"

"Marnie was on the bubble back then. She was working on one concoction after another, each not only promising eternal youth, but a kind of euphoric happiness that comes from . . ."

He stopped.

"From what?"

"I don't really know. Her mystical connection to nature. Like she was some kind of chosen conduit, some goddess of nature. Something like that."

Reed got up from the armchair and went to an antique mahogany secretary. Without saying a word, he fished in the back of the lowest drawer. His eyes met Lindsay's as he held out a bundle of a dozen or so letters tied with a faded yellow ribbon imprinted with what proved to be the Spellman Farms logo, a hexagon surrounding a honeybee.

"They're in order. Not long. Read them while I make some coffee."

Lindsay untied the bundle while Reed disappeared into the kitchen.

He didn't oversell their brevity. Calista barely put words to paper.

I am becoming. It is what I need.

Miss you and the boys.

Marnie is the most amazing being I've ever had the privilege to know.

I have never been happier. This is what heaven must be like. Long days in the sun, hard work. Bliss.

I'm moving closer every day.

She read that one aloud to him when he reappeared with two steaming mugs of coffee. "What is she talking about? Moving closer to what?"

He set one of the mugs on the table in front of her.

"I really don't know. Wish I did. Read the last one."

Lindsay opened the final letter. It was the longest of the bunch, though still only a single page.

> *Reed, I need you and the boys to come up here. We can't be complete if we aren't together. I need you to understand that all that I have done—even if it hurts you—has been done for a greater purpose. That purpose is the being I am today. Sell the house. Take the boys out of school.*

Lindsay looked up.

"So you came."

He'd sat back down. "Seems stupid, I know. There was a time when I could have killed her . . ." He stopped for a moment; his word choice had been an awkward mistake. "I was angry. But yes, I did what she asked. I had two children to think about, and I weighed all of that. Having them live a life without their mother was somewhat acceptable when it was her doing. Her leaving us. Yet when it became my turn to do something, I couldn't keep them away from her. They loved their mom. It just, you know . . ."

When he reached for his coffee, Lindsay noticed a slight tremor in his hand. Parkinson's? Nervousness?

Reed saw her looking and redirected his hand, clamped it on the armrest. The movement was sudden, jerky.

"What happened when you got up here?"

He paused for a moment. "You know, I imagine. You know some of it, the worst of it, Detective."

"Just the barest outlines," Lindsay said. "I'd like to hear it from you. Tell me about Calista and Spellman Farms."

"Tell you about Marnie Spellman."

"Yes. Her, too."

"All right. It all starts and ends with her. She was the queen bee, excuse the pun. She led the group of women, an inner circle, who ran the farm on Lummi. They were thick as thieves. Calista was one of them—until someone killed her."

CHAPTER 15

June 1999
Bellingham, Washington

Reed Sullivan and his sons, Brady and Christian, would have to wait three days for Calista to show up to see them in Washington. She was on her own time, not anyone else's. Every movement, she later told Reed, was dictated by the powers of nature. The wind. Sun. Life.

Reed rented a house on Alabama Hill. It came with a BigToys play structure in the backyard, and they quickly turned it into a hideout, a fort.

They needed one.

Their mother had upended their lives.

Reed watched the movers off-load the family's belongings from California. He instructed them to put all of Calista's things in the master bedroom—next to his own, of course.

It was a natural assumption that would turn into a bone of contention.

Reed was startled by Calista's appearance when she finally showed up. He even held his breath, thinking that any reaction would be the wrong reaction. Her hair was cut short—not a crew cut, but nearly so. Dark semicircles underscored her eyes. She was about the same weight, maybe a little more muscular. In any case, she didn't look like the woman who'd left California. Her demeanor was different, too.

He'd expected that. She'd left him, after all.

He didn't think her perceptible indifference would extend to the boys.

But it did.

When they got to her, Reed thought he saw her recoil, a split second of distaste in her reaction.

Calista said all the right words.

"My babies! I have missed you so much!"

The boys climbed all over her. Especially Christian. He had cried about her absence more than his brother. He'd been the one to sit by the wall phone in the kitchen, waiting for her to call and tell him that she'd be coming back.

When she did call and Reed tried to talk to her, the conversation ended in an ear-to-ear boxing match.

"Let me talk to Brady and Christian. We can't talk like this, Reed. It's not good for me."

For her.

It was always for her.

It was a bitter reality, one that he had no way of influencing. He wanted to hate her. That would have made it so much easier. He couldn't stop loving her. He couldn't stop wondering if she'd lost the core of who she was by immersing herself in what he derided as the Cult of Marnie.

That afternoon, when this woman who sounded and vaguely looked like his wife appeared, he told himself that he'd back off. He didn't even allow himself to think the words *give her time* because that would have implied that he had control over her. He didn't. He didn't want to manage her every move.

He just wanted her to come home.

He and Christian went to a Chinese takeout place and brought back food for the family. Calista refused to eat.

"You love fried rice," Reed said.

"I used to love it," she said, offering a slight smile to lessen the impact of her words. "I just don't put anything into my body if I don't know where it came from."

"It came from Ming Garden," he said. "It's good. Right, boys?"

"Yeah, Mom," Christian said. "Really good."

"It's fine. I brought some Marnie Bars." She took a foil-wrapped bar from her purse.

"That's silly, Calista. You need to eat real food."

Wrong thing to say.

"In case you don't know, this is made of the sun and sea," she said. "Nothing silly about what she can do for us."

"Marnie isn't in charge of what you eat, is she?"

"You misunderstood, Reed. It's like you to do that. I'm reminded now of so many things that I left behind when I moved up here."

"Can we not go there?" he asked, looking at the boys, who were no longer eating and who had braced for another family quarrel.

Just like old times.

"Fine. Just so you know, when I say there's nothing silly about what she can do for us, I'm not talking about Marnie, but God. That's the she. That's the creator of all that I am and all that is around me."

She looked at her sons.

"You are proof of her divinity, boys."

"What?" Christian asked.

Reed put his hand on his son's shoulder. "Never mind."

Calista ate the rest of her Marnie Bar and retreated to the bedroom the boys shared. Mattresses on the floor. Boxes everywhere. Reed watched as she shut the door. When the boys were done eating, they turned to him with questioning looks. He nodded toward the door, as though to tell them that yes, of course they should follow her. Pretending confidence he didn't feel. Who knew what this version of their mother might do?

She let them enter, and the door settled shut again.

About a half hour later, Calista emerged.

"I miss them."

"They miss you."

"I miss you, too," she said, leaning in and giving him a kiss. It was tender and passionate at the same time. Reed kissed her back. A minute later, they were behind another door, on the mattress in the master bedroom. Reed had tears in his eyes as they made love. He doubted there could ever be a woman like Calista. She could let him twist in the wind like he was nothing, then crook her finger and he'd be devoted to her once more.

It went on like that for about a month. She came to visit, would play with the boys, have sex with Reed, and leave.

The last time she came to the rental house, she was different. Cooler, especially toward Reed. He expected sex after the boys were asleep; instead, she picked up her purse and jacket.

"I'm glad you came to Washington. How long are you staying?"

Reed wasn't sure how to respond. It must have showed on his face.

"Oh no," she said. "There's been a misunderstanding."

"What do you mean 'a misunderstanding'?"

"I'm sorry, Reed. I thought . . ."

"You thought what?"

"I thought you knew that this was only a visit. A few weeks. I didn't expect you to actually move here with everything we owned."

Actually, he'd tossed most of her clothing and burned her photos when she left California for the Pacific Northwest. But yes, he'd brought all the rest.

"You told me to sell the house. To come here."

"Right. I need the money. My share of the house. I thought that you would know that. California is a community property state. We are done. I've already met with a lawyer."

His glasses started to fog, though he hadn't moved a muscle.

"Lawyer?" he asked, staring at her. "Money? That's what this is all about?"

"Look," she said, stepping toward the door. "What else could it be?"

"Your boys?"

Calista shifted her eyes downward. "They are happy. The boys look well taken care of, Reed. I knew you would be able to manage."

Her tone was condescending, and Reed removed his glasses, wiping the condensation on his shirt. He wondered if she was hoping he'd call her out, tell her off, remind her that she had given birth to them and they belonged to her. Yet he didn't. He didn't know her. This wasn't Calista.

"I'll need your account number," he told her.

"I don't have one."

"You need one. I'll wire the money."

Her eyes were cold. "I want cash. Bills."

She opened the front door. A dog barked in the neighbor's yard. The boys were asleep in their bedroom. Everything about that moment was normal—or at least had the semblance of normality. Not everything, of course. Not his wife. Not his life.

"I'm glad you came," she said. "I really am."

And with that, the door closed, and she vanished again.

Monday, September 16, 2019

Lindsay set down her coffee and let the air out of her lungs in a protracted sigh before speaking.

"What did you make of all of that?" she asked.

"She was gone. I knew that she was gone, and I knew that Marnie Spellman had taken her away. My wife was a searcher; I see that now. I didn't know what she was looking for until that night."

"What was it? What did she want?"

"Her own life. A life unencumbered by me, by the boys. She'd found herself on Lummi Island. She'd found the home she'd wanted, and it just didn't include any of us. If I hadn't been so prideful, I'd have known that earlier, when Karen Ripken came to see me."

"Who is that?" Lindsay asked, making a note of the name.

Abruptly, before answering, Reed got up and went into the kitchen. Lindsay heard a cupboard door open, a pill-bottle top being popped, and then the sound of running water.

"Time for my meds," he said, returning, nudging the cat aside and sitting back down.

His eyes were riveted on the letters. "I felt so stupid," he said.

"It had to have been a lot to take in."

"Yeah. That's right. I'd have been better off if I'd listened to Karen. She knew. She'd been through it all."

"Tell me about her. Who is she?"

"I met her through a flyer she posted at Ralphs, a grocery store in California. 'Have you lost someone to Marnie Spellman?' it said. 'Join my support group.' The bottom was cut into a fringe with her telephone number on each strip, and I tore one off and stuck it in my wallet. When I got home, I stuck it on the refrigerator and stared at it for a few days. Getting up the nerve to call."

Chapter 16

Karen Ripken's mother, Annette, left her family in California for Marnie Spellman's farm in 1998, the year before Calista Sullivan went north. Annette left her second husband; Karen, then a teenager; and a two-year-old, Sarah.

Karen was in her senior year in high school and was a frontline witness to her mother's burgeoning fanaticism over all things Marnie. First, like Calista Sullivan, she'd ordered every product the woman hawked on the home shopping channel; then she jumped into what she told Karen was "the movement." This was thirty years after the bloody chain of revolutions and unrest of the 1960s, yet that's how her mother talked about Marnie. For her and the other women who'd turned their lives over to the woman, the times were still very much a-changing.

The Pacific Northwest was a perfect home for them. For whatever reason, the region had clung more insistently to the sixties' aesthetic than most places. People there were still climbing rocks at sunrise or burrowing into the confines of sweat lodges in order to become more in touch with their inner beings. Crystals, pyramids, and sage bundles were staples of every hippie-dippie street fair, of which there were many. It made for fertile ground for all manner of spiritual-skewing groups that, especially if they revolved around a leader with any degree of charisma (or at least prophet-worthy facial hair), outsiders tarred with unkind labels like *sects* and *cults*.

Not that Marnie Spellman fit that mold. Even young Karen could see that. There was something decidedly square about her. To Karen, she looked more like a glossy blond suburban housewife—or an actress playing one on TV—than some kind of messiah figure. She just confused Karen, really.

"What's so special about Marnie?" Karen asked her mother.

"Look at her," Annette said, holding up one of Marnie's CDs. "Don't you *see* it?"

Karen took the CD. Marnie's portrait nearly glowed from beneath the shimmer of the plastic. Her eyes were sapphires. Her skin, flawless. Her blond hair was a halo, an effect created by backlighting and a savvy photographer.

"I guess she's beautiful, Mom." At least, her mom's idea of beautiful.

"Beautiful? Is that all you see?"

"What else is there?"

Annette tapped her finger on the CD's plastic case. "Look at the wisdom in her eyes. Look at the aura that springs from her portrait. Tell me, Karen, do you see all of that?"

She didn't. Not at all.

"I guess so," Karen said, trying to be kind. Her mother had gone through a very lonely and difficult time when her husband, Karen's father, left them. She'd managed to marry again, to a nice enough guy, and to have Karen's little sister . . . but she was damaged in some permanent way that stuck to Karen's heart.

"She is *beautiful*. Now look at me," Annette said. "What do you see?"

Karen ran her eyes over her mother's face, her green eyes, her silky brown hair. "I see my mom. Just as beautiful. Just as amazing."

Annette gave her daughter a knowing and slightly sad smile.

"Be truthful. You see your mom," she said, putting the CD on top of the stack of Marnie Spellman recordings. "That's not me. That's a role that I played, one that, frankly, is played out."

Karen bristled a little. "What does that mean?"

"You're an adult," her mother said. "You'll be studying at the university next year. I'm not going to live my life just being a mother. That's just not who I am. I'm going to move up north."

"To what? Be with that bunch of weirdos?"

"You only say that because you're young. And you see a future of easy choices to happiness. Get a college degree. Get married. Have babies. Be a grandmother. A life like that is charted by society. I fell for it. This is my turn. My chance. I hope by my example of taking that leap of faith that you and your sister will see—"

"What are you *talking* about? Focus on what's real, right here in front of you. You have a two-year-old! What about her, Mom?"

"I've made arrangements."

"What? What are you going to do with Sarah?"

"She'll be with family. She's not going to an orphanage. Good God, Karen, you can be so dramatic."

When Karen began to cry, Annette only stood stone faced, looking at her with eyes that merely scraped over her own. She wasn't engaged. She was calm. It was Karen who suddenly found herself spiraling downward.

"Mom, you are twisting my words," she said after a long moment of silence passed between them. "That's not what I meant. You're not just a mother. Of course, you are more than that."

"Honey," Annette said, softening a little, "you can't possibly understand my truth when you don't even understand your own."

"I do understand, Mom. You're not being reasonable."

She didn't know it at the time, there was no "reasonable" for those drawn inside the growing sphere of Marnie Spellman's influence.

Karen felt hot tears against her cheek.

"I don't understand, Mom."

"You will when you are my age. Trust me. And if you don't find yourself before that time, you will be as lost as I've been my entire life."

Monday, September 16, 2019

Lindsay noticed Reed glancing at the wall clock, his eyes lingering on the hour.

"Are you expecting someone?" she asked.

"Not at all. Just aware of time. How little we have. How little Karen had with her mom. How we all got sucked into something that was beyond our comprehension. I didn't understand what kind of hold Marnie had on her followers. Neither did Karen. We thought that reasoning would save us. That finding some little fissure into my wife's and her mother's psyches would somehow bring them back. Marnie's hold on them was unbreakable."

"You said you should have listened to Karen. What do you mean by that?"

"She told me not to move up here. She told me that she'd been up to see her mom three times, and she said each time she came away convinced that all efforts were futile. She couldn't stop the hope from growing back, couldn't stop herself from trying. She learned from hard experience that it was useless. And it was hammered home by the people in her support group. None of them were a match for Marnie."

"What did she say when you told her you were moving, anyway?"

Reed stayed quiet.

The room suddenly felt very uncomfortable. Lindsay gave him space. She didn't interrupt whatever he was processing in order to fill the awkward air between them.

"She told me coming up here would be the biggest mistake of my life. That I'd live to regret it. And you know what?"

"What?"

Reed put his hands together as if preparing to pray. "She was right. I wish I never came, and at the same time, I didn't know what else to do. I came up, and I stayed because I thought . . . I thought . . . that she'd come back to us. I thought she'd snap out of whatever it was that had gotten ahold of her."

"But she didn't," Lindsay said.

"No. I saw her only one final time after I gave her the money."

July 1999

Shortly after Calista's demand for the proceeds from the sale of their house in California, Reed put the money—$128,000—in the freezer. The boys were exploring the neighborhood when she arrived a week later. Calista looked better this time. The dark semicircles were gone. She was buoyant as she took a seat in the dining room. She even kicked off her sandals. She was tan. Fit. And it seemed, more open. Less standoffish.

It was a completely different Calista than the one who had demanded cash a few days before.

"Can I get you a glass of wine?" Reed asked, hoping for a reversal of what she'd asked for, that perhaps she had come home to stay.

She flipped up a palm to indicate no. "Water. Room temp. Bottled, if you have it."

Reed resisted the urge to roll his eyes or make a comment. He was looking at her with new eyes. She was not his wife anymore. She was a stranger. Yet he still loved her. That didn't make sense.

He should hate her.

"Coming right up," he said.

"I don't expect you to understand, Reed," Calista said as he returned with the water.

He refused to play that game again. "I don't need to understand."

She finished her water and regarded him with those pretty eyes of hers. "Do you have the money?"

Whoosh went any hope, no matter how unlikely.

"Really, Calista? Is that all you want?"

"Actually, no. I am all I want. The money . . . well, that's something that is owed to me."

Inside, Reed was saying goodbye. Outwardly, he said nothing. He went to the freezer and pulled the huge pouch of bills from behind a box of frozen lasagna. When he turned around, she was right there, sandals back on her feet.

"Here," he said, holding out the cash.

She leaned still closer to take the money. Closer than she really needed. He could feel her breath against his face.

Was she offering a kiss?

Not again.

He pulled away, his back brushing against the refrigerator door. The bill from the moving company and a shopping list for grocery items were dislodged from a Seattle Seahawks magnet and fell to the floor.

"Goodbye," he said.

She disappeared out the door to a waiting car.

And then she was gone.

Monday, September 16, 2019

Lindsay could hear the clock ticking behind her. Reed's cat scurried off to the kitchen. She could see the pain on the man's face, even after so many years had elapsed since his wife's final goodbye.

"You never saw her again after that?"

"Just once."

July 1999

It had been a few weeks since he'd forked over the proceeds from the house. Not so much as a phone call or card for the boys, both of whom had birthdays during that time. It was like she'd never been a part of their lives at all. Reed noticed how they'd stopped asking about their mother, and he thought better of his attempts to inject memories of her into their daily lives. So he stopped talking about her. It ran through his mind that she might even be in danger; it didn't provoke him into any action. Karen Ripken had gone that futile route. She'd hired private detectives, made calls to the tribal police on Lummi Island. She'd even appeared on one of the daytime TV shows about the grip cults have on their followers.

"It's a conspiracy," she said one time when they talked on the phone. "I'll bet our phones are tapped."

"No, Karen. That's going too far."

Reed's voice, his thoughtful countenance, soothed her.

Only for a short time, though. Then she'd circle back to conspiracy theories and the belief something nefarious was going on. That Marnie Spellman's hold on her mother had been unnatural.

"Demonic," she insisted.

"Oh, Karen. That's not so."

"Well, Reed, you can believe whatever you want. So can I."

He wondered if she'd been drinking. Or high. Or if she'd been pushed so hard in her quest to bring her mother back home that she'd been broken in the process.

In Reed's mind, Karen's approach was a template of what not to do. He'd let go of Calista. He'd try to start over. He wouldn't let his rage and helplessness over what had happened rule the rest of his days.

That was the plan.

Until he saw her one last time a month after he'd given her the money. Six weeks after they'd made love for what he now accepted had been the last time.

CHAPTER 17

August 1999
Bellingham, Washington

It was August, the time of year when Bellingham was about to be over-run with university students in search of cheap beer and sunshine. Reed was dodging the mass of returning students and their parents on South State Street when he heard a familiar voice.

"Reed?"

He spun around. It was *her*. Calista was wearing black jeans and a yellow top; yellow and black were the colors of Spellman Farms.

"I wondered when our paths would cross," Reed said. "Not that big of a town."

"You're still here," she said. "I thought you and the boys would have gone back to California."

He wanted to tell her the truth: that they'd waited for her to come back to them. Instead, he offered a plausible lie. "Couldn't afford California anymore. And besides, we like it here. Except for the rain."

"The rain makes things green," she said.

He stood there looking, almost staring. She looked good. She even smelled good. Sweet. A beguiling fragrance that likely was a part of Spellman Farms' burgeoning product line.

She stood close to him, and he breathed her in some more.

Lavender.

"Cup of tea?" she asked. "Coffee?"

Her suggestion snapped him away from his thoughts. "Yeah. Sure. There's a place right around the corner."

She asked about Brady and Christian.

"Doing well," he said. "Adjusting to things."

It was a subversive little dig about their missing mother, but it went right past Calista.

They went inside Coffee Haus and ordered: tea for her, coffee for him. An awkwardness filled the space between them. Reed wished for a split second that he'd pretended not to hear his name on the street. It wasn't that he didn't miss her. It was that he now truly no longer knew who she was. Her transition to this new Calista, the woman who had apparently found her place in the world, was now complete.

"Are you all right?" she asked.

"Just strange sitting here with you."

The server brought their beverages. Calista took a packet of honey from her purse and stirred some into her tea.

"Want some?" she asked.

Reed shook his head. "No. I'm good."

"Life is strange, Reed. It's a big mystery. Being here with you feels right."

Her choice of words once more confused him. What was she really saying? Was there something between the lines?

"You really hurt me," he blurted out.

"I know," she said. "I don't want to hurt anyone. Life is not a winner-take-all affair."

He recognized her words from a Marnie Spellman card he had found when she left California. The stinging irony was off the charts. Hadn't Marnie won it all, at least as far as they were concerned?

"I know we're done," he finally said. "I know that you have no use for me. Or the boys. I know all of that. I just struggle with it. It's really like we lost you. Like you disappeared before our eyes."

Calista reached out to stroke his hand. He let her. Her palm was smooth; her fingertips brushed against the hair on the back of his hand. Her touch. He missed her touch so much.

Fool. Idiot.

"You might have lost me—and I know this is very hard for you to understand—I found myself, Reed. My purpose. I thank God for her blessings every day."

Reed caught a glimpse of a young couple engrossed in the exchange. The server was taking it all in, too.

"I need something," she said. "Will you give me what I need?"

He didn't understand.

"What do you want now? You've taken just about everything someone could take without carrying it off. Our boys don't have a mother. Our house is a rental. My job at the paper mill is second rate. Now you want more?"

"Keep your voice down," she said. "Everyone is listening."

He turned to the couple, who quickly averted their gaze and pretended to be immersed in whatever was in their coffee.

"I need money," she said. "My lawyer did some calculations based on the sale of the house. You shortchanged me, Reed. Maybe you didn't mean to. Maybe you did. You owe me eighteen thousand dollars more."

Reed shot to his feet, knocking over his cup. Coffee streamed from the table to the floor. In another time and place he would have been mortified.

"You *bitch*," he said, unable to contain his rage. "I had to pay your share of the taxes."

"That wasn't your decision, Reed."

"You left me. We still had to file jointly."

"Reed, you lied to me."

"I never lied to you once. *You* were the liar. *You* were the one sneaking around, chatting with your fellow believers of that fraud Marnie Spellman. I never said a goddamn word about any of that. I should have."

Calista didn't take the bait. She was solely focused on one thing.

"The money, Reed. We have lawyers."

"'We'?"

"That's not the point."

He ricocheted for the door. Should've left without another word, but stopped, turned.

"Calista, honestly, I wish you were dead. I wish that you'd died in some freak accident on the Long Beach Freeway. That would have been really hard, but this? Seeing you with your hands stretched out for money? I could never have called that in a hundred years. So cold, so the opposite of what you were—and what you profess to be."

Monday, September 16, 2019

Now the cat was on Lindsay's lap. Purring, no less. There was nothing she could do about it, either. It wasn't that she didn't like cats. Cats were fine. What she didn't like was that she was wearing dark slacks. Undoubtedly, when she got up, she'd look as though she'd rolled around in a bin of cotton balls.

"And that was the last time you saw her?"

He snapped, "You know it was."

"Sorry," Lindsay said. "Not my intention. I can't imagine how it would feel to be accused of a crime I didn't commit. I didn't mean to strike a nerve."

With some effort, he calmed himself, sank back into his seat. "It stays raw, Detective," he said in a ragged voice. "I know I invited it this time—I called *you*—but every time I talk about Calista's murder, it's another poke in the gut. And it's usually delivered by someone just looking to raise their own profile. Reporters, TV people—and yes, every so often even cops. All of them set on digging in and laying bare the sum total of a man's life for their own gain. It's the way the world works." He shook his head. "Can't make myself like it."

The detective left. Reed's thoughts and misgivings about Marnie Spellman had been scratched at, wounds reopened. He thought of the last time he and Karen Ripken had talked. It was brief, a late-night call shortly after Calista's body had been found.

"I saw what happened to your wife, Reed," she'd said. Again, she sounded as if she'd been drinking. "I'm really sorry. Any news on what's going on with the murder investigation?"

He thanked her for her condolences and said he'd talked to investigators.

"I figured as much. You being the husband."

"Ex-husband, yeah. That's always the first target, I guess."

"I suppose," she said. "I just wanted to check in, tell you how sorry I was. And wanted you to know that my mom died."

"Jesus, Karen," he said. "What happened?"

Silence over the line.

"Karen?"

"Suicide," she said. "I guess she couldn't 'find herself' after all. Or if she did, she didn't like what she found. I bet a lot of Marnie's followers end up with the same conclusion and follow her to the grave."

"I'm not sure what you're getting at," Reed said. "What conclusion?"

Karen's voice seemed like she was a million miles from the phone. "That her goddamn 'outside-in' philosophy is just a marketing ploy to move product." He could barely hear her sigh. "Can't heal a troubled mind with bee pollen face cream."

Reed heard ice tinkling against a glass as Karen took another drink. "Get some rest, Karen. Really sorry about your mom."

CHAPTER 18

Lindsay continued to tick off a list of potential leads into Sarah's murder.

She talked with the campus police about the surveillance camera where Sarah's car had been parked.

The camera was out of commission, its power cord cut. "It happens around here," she was told. "Kids think we're watching them all the time, and they don't like it. Last year, ten cameras were knocked out by a single drunk freshman with, of all things, a slingshot."

She consulted with Lieutenant Madison and got help from a junior officer to comb through Sarah's background, looking for boyfriends or any other girlfriends besides Zoey.

It was quickly confirmed that Sarah was a loner. And if she had a boyfriend, no one had seen him, let alone met him.

Carl Flanders from the *Western Front* was ruled out when it was established that he'd been at a party with two dozen other kids the night she died.

The folder on the Sullivan case that she'd requested from Records was waiting on her desk. Before she dug into the file, she went through her messages on the police department server. Sarah's dental records, autopsy report, a video file from the vigil. She logged the Sullivan interview and pondered the curious yet unclear connection between Reed and Sarah. She'd called him for an interview. She was working on something, a story. He'd used the word *exposé*. Whatever it was, it was something that Sarah didn't want to talk about over the phone.

Was she going to challenge him on his wife's death? Or did she know something about the case that he didn't know?

Lindsay couldn't make Reed Sullivan for Sarah's killer. Just did not compute. He was a cat guy, for one. More to the point, he was also too old and too shaky to have carried her body down the trail to the falls.

All right. He wasn't the killer. Was he a liar?

She ran through her list of things that would make up the body of her investigation. She'd track Sarah's past, dig into any relationships she might have had, figure out how it was that she ended up at Maple Falls. Moreover, she'd root out every nugget of information she could find on Marnie Spellman. Whatever really happened on Lummi Island and had never been resolved.

A woman was murdered. A man acquitted. And then poof. Nothing. No one was ever made to pay.

Maybe that's just what Sarah Baker had in mind. She was going to make someone pay . . . and they stopped her.

She found an interview with a Lummi Island ferry captain among the papers in the folder. It was brief, and it hinted at something that the investigative detective thought was interesting.

Vinnie Barenfanger had worked on the route for sixteen years and prided himself on winning on-time departure awards four years in a row before the ferry system decided to allow only major routes to compete for the honor.

An officer wrote:

> Barenfanger said he knew all of Marnie's staff and that Calista had been a regular. She told him that her hus-band was angry at her for leaving him with the kids in

California. She was a nice woman. Chattier than most of them that came over. Said he remembered Calista coming to the island early in the week. Said he never saw her leave the island, which he thought was odd. Unless people have a boat of their own, they can only get there on his vessel.

Later, when Reed Sullivan's photo was on the news, Barenfanger called the Ferndale Police Department's tip line.

The message was transcribed:

I've seen that guy. Real standoffish, and kind of angry, too. Not that I ever talked to him. Just the way he carried himself. I'm pretty sure I saw him leave the day after the girl went missing. Had a pickup with some junk in the back. Maybe in a hurry. That's kind of fuzzy, but I do know that the line was pretty long and he kept revving his motor and touching his horn to get the group in front to get on the boat. I can see why Calista ran away from him. As far as Spellman's people go, Calista was probably the nicest of the bunch. You better catch the guy.

An addendum was added by the detective: "No reports of any mechanical failures the week before Calista Sullivan went missing."

Lindsay couldn't reconcile the interview with the ferry captain. Reed Sullivan hadn't seemed the kind of guy that would honk his horn to get a spot in line. In fact, he was passive. He'd let someone frame him for a murder he didn't commit.

Lindsay selected her late lunch/early dinner from the break room vending machines—a cup of noodles and Diet Dr Pepper. She took her sad meal at her desk as she continued poring over the Reed Sullivan file, filling herself in on more of the backstory.

The content was interesting, if more than a little confusing. It seemed that nothing was as cut-and-dried as the officer had let on when she'd left to interview Reed.

Reed wasn't immediately charged with Calista's death. He had an ironclad alibi, having been camping on the coast with a group of singles and their kids. More than a dozen witnesses verified that he'd been there for five days, and there was zero possibility that he'd been able to make the trek back to Lummi to get his wife, kill her, and dump her body.

The *Seattle Times*, chasing a regional readership, wasn't so sure about that.

In a fortuitous stroke of luck, just two weeks before Calista's body was found by the out-of-town beachcombers, Washington State's largest newspaper opened an office in Bellingham's downtown on Railroad Avenue. The sole reporter manning the phones was a young recruit from the *Bellingham Herald*, twenty-eight-year-old Tedd McGraw.

For two months, McGraw managed to turn a murder case in which no charges were filed into front-page fodder. Some of his reporting focused on the Sullivan marital split and the perceived threats Reed directed at Calista at the coffee shop. The rest weaved in the mysterious empire at Spellman Farms, which had attracted surprisingly little notice in the press to that point.

Headlines, on paper yellowed with age, told the story:

Beachcombers Find Woman's Body on Lummi Island

Lieutenant Asks for Help: Who is Lummi Beach Victim?

Body Identified as Bellingham Woman, Spellman Follower

Husband Questioned, Released in Key Spellman Follower's Death

Holistic Guru Marnie Spellman on Victim: "She Was a Bright Light"

Café Owner Says Sullivan Threatened to Kill Wife

And finally,

Two Hairs on Victim's Body Match, Sullivan Charged with Murder

Murder Trial Promises Glimpse into Spellman's "Hive"

The last article was twice the length of the others. Lindsay could picture McGraw drooling onto his keyboard. After holding the world in the palm of her hand for nearly a decade—Lindsay had no idea she'd been such a big thing; Marnie had only been a name to her—Marnie Spellman had all but vanished a few years before the Sullivan case. Spellman Farms rolled on, growing in leaps and bounds, but Marnie kept herself wrapped up tight. Now, thanks to this unexplained death of what turned out to be one of her key people, McGraw clearly thought he'd worked a fingernail under the wrapping.

What was actually there didn't amount to much, though. Calista had been established as one of the group's central figures, a member of what they called "the Hive," a core circle of five women devoted to helping Marnie Spellman . . . well, take over the world, near as Lindsay could gather from Tedd McGraw's histrionic prose. Not in any nefarious way, he took pains to make clear. (Obviously, he didn't want to jeopardize the small measure of Marnie access he'd won.) No, she and her followers supported a revolution that showed women they could be more than what society had prescribed for them.

Her interview with Reed Sullivan fresh on her mind, Lindsay felt sure that he and some other members of Karen Ripken's support group might take issue with the notion that such a revolution would be a bloodless one.

The rest of McGraw's article mostly repeated itself in various ways, except for a quote from Dina Marlow, a film actress who followed Marnie. "Calista's death was a tragedy. We don't know what the outcome of the trial will be, but we all know without a shred of doubt that our sister is free, unencumbered by the physical. Free to bee [sic]." (McGraw explained that *sic* with a parenthetical comment relating Ms. Marlow's insistence on the misspelling of the word.)

"'Free to bee'? What in the *hell*?" Lindsay muttered to herself. These Marnie Spellman acolytes did present a united front, though. Dina Marlow dishing PR to McGraw could've been Calista Sullivan spreading the Marnie gospel to her ruined husband. The same high-flown spiritual rhetoric delivered in the same robotic manner.

Lindsay gave her head a shake and wrote, "Hive?" in her notebook. Two dead young women, twenty years apart, connected by this honeybee-charming face-cream guru. Lindsay would clearly need to talk to Marnie Spellman, and sooner rather than later. First she needed to finish boning up on her, which meant talking to the surviving members of her "hive," starting with Dina Marlow, if she was still above ground.

This was getting curiouser and curiouser, with no end to the amplifying curiousness in sight.

For the moment, though, she'd stick to terra firma. She phoned the crime techs who had worked the scene at Maple Falls. It went to voice mail. She looked at the time. It was after six. Crime scene techs must work bankers' hours when there wasn't a corpse to get in the way.

"Lindsay here. Following up. Let me know if the dogs found anything. I know they didn't, because if they did, you would have called me, right?"

She hung up and looked at the note to call Carl Flanders, but again nixed the idea. It could wait until tomorrow.

What couldn't wait surprised her.

She found she needed to know more about Calista and Sarah's connection.

Chapter 19

Lindsay's cup of noodles had congealed into a starchy cylinder.

A very salty one.

She went back to the break room, passing by Alan's office. She resisted the urge to poke her head inside. Like she always had.

When he was alive.

She watched as a second soda can kerplunked into the tray across the bottom of the machine.

The office was dead quiet. The HVAC system shut down promptly at seven. Officers were on patrol, and the lieutenant and the support staff had left for the day. Lindsay cracked open her pop and went back to her desk to read more about the Sullivan case.

As she read on, it seemed the primary stumbling block for the Sullivan defense was the DNA profile Forensics had collected from Calista Sullivan's body during the autopsy exam. After the OJ trial five years before, DNA was mainstream, powerful evidence. Yet during the time of the Sullivan trial, the defense had staked their client's future on the fact that he wasn't anywhere near Lummi Island. They told the court that they could put up more than a dozen witnesses who saw Reed, spoke to him, and interacted with him on a camping trip with his boys.

How could he have been in two places at the same time?

The prosecution countered by insisting that Reed had been seen by two people on Lummi the day of his ex-wife's murder.

"Mr. Sullivan, so enraged by his wife's betrayal, got up in the middle of the night, drove to Lummi Island, stalked and killed her, and had time to return to the camping site undetected."

As Lindsay saw it, the prosecution and defense played volleyball with the timeline and the evidence.

The defense: No trace of him going anywhere near Lummi. He was camping with a dozen others.

The prosecution: He could have slipped away in the middle of the night.

The prosecution: The hairs with his DNA were transferred when Calista was fighting for her life.

The defense: The hairs—if there were any—must have been on clothing she wore. Besides, she was in the water! They had to have been introduced after the body was found.

And then there was the testimony of Calista's closest friends from the farm. ("Hivemates?" Lindsay wrote in her notebook. Seemed likely.) Heather Hanley and Trish Appleton both said Calista had expressed some concern about her ex-husband.

Heather: "She said that he had become unhinged after she told him that she wanted a divorce and the money from the sale of their home in California. In fact, he never paid her, and she was thinking of taking legal action."

Trish: "She never said she thought he would physically harm her. She insisted he wasn't the violent type; otherwise she never would have left her little boys with him as primary parent."

For a woman who loomed over nearly every aspect of the trial, it surprised Lindsay that Marnie never took the stand. In one of Tedd McGraw's articles, the prosecutors said they felt Marnie Spellman's notoriety would work against their case. The same with Dina Marlow, the actress. Once it was made public that neither woman would appear in court, the case whimpered to its conclusion. Only a handful of spectators showed up for the verdict.

The headline on the front page of the *Seattle Times* was only two words:

Sullivan Acquitted!

Chapter 20

Lynden, Washington

Dina Marlow was in her late sixties. Maybe. Probably. Hard to really know. Lindsay encountered differing opinions of her exact age; some reference books had her four years older than what she professed. It didn't matter much. She looked to be in her fifties and was as lovely as always. She wore her beautiful auburn hair in a chignon, a look that she'd held on to. Her eyes were a brown that many called copper. And in certain lighting conditions, the irises did indeed reflect a coppery hue—the color of a slightly burnished penny.

She'd been a devotee and close friend of Marnie Spellman for more than twenty years. After she filmed her last movie, a comedy in which she played a hapless mother, she left Hollywood for the Pacific Northwest. For a time, she lived on Lummi Island, on Spellman Farms, before moving out to an estate just south of Abbotsford, British Columbia. She was known in Canada, of course, but Canadians are the politest of people, and they gave her no reason to feel that she was anything other than just a well-heeled woman living on her own.

A rich woman.

A movie star.

A follower.

On only one occasion during these years did she make the news, and it was vintage Dina. She was an advocate for homeless pets and was photographed at a shelter where she volunteered once a week. A tabloid headline made some remark that she'd "gone to the dogs," and there was such an immediate backlash from her most ardent fans that the magazine retracted the story.

Her estate was built on ten fenced acres at the end of a quiet road. A sign that looked to be hand painted with blue flowers indicated that there was no throughway and asked wayward motorists to **PLEASE TURN AROUND HERE**.

Lindsay identified herself through an intercom at the gate and was buzzed in. A large house and several outbuildings, including a barn, came into view. Lindsay hadn't seen pictures of the estate, but she'd imagined that a Hollywood star would build something grander, maybe something completely modern. Or maybe a hacienda or a Mediterranean-style mansion that would be wholly out of place.

Not Dina. She'd apparently shed the trappings of her old life, and while large, the home was designed to fit into the landscape, not dominate it. It was painted dark brown with green shutters and black trim. A massive river-rock chimney was the only nod to the potential grandness of what was inside the double doors at the entrance.

When Dina opened the door, a stream of sunshine washed over her face that would've done any cinematographer proud.

She looked exactly like she did on film. Older, yes, but not tired. Not haggard. Her eyes sparkled. Her features were softer, the kind of suppleness that comes from wear, not the ravages of age.

Lindsay wasn't starstruck. She'd been too young to have watched any of Dina's old movies or the TV show that had made her something of a household name for a time. Lindsay knew who she was only by reputation—and one earned primarily from the YouTube video of Dina's DUI arrest that had circulated among law enforcement in Whatcom County.

And of course, the rest of the world.

Lindsay felt a tiny pang of shame. She'd laughed right along with everyone at the downfall of someone who'd once had it all.

And still did, by the looks of the place.

After introductions, Dina released a small sigh. "As I said on the phone, Detective Jackman, I doubt I can help you any more than I already have. I only talked to the girl once, and it was a brief conversation."

The girl was Sarah Baker.

"Nonetheless," Lindsay said. "I'd appreciate a word."

Dina's smile still generated serious wattage. "Certainly. Come on in. It's a little breezy today. I put the coffeepot on when you called on the intercom at the end of the road."

Lindsay followed her to the kitchen. The space was as she imagined from the home's outside appearance, both impressive and comfortable. Some of the tables and chairs were rustic, large, and solid. Formidable. There were a mass of pillows, Navajo blankets, and metal pieces.

"This is beautiful," Lindsay said, taking it all in. "I see the influence of your love of Westerns, that part of your career. Beautiful, as I said, but it projects strength, too."

Dina smiled as she poured two cups of coffee.

"It has that look, certainly, but if you saw my bedroom, you'd think a pink bomb had gone off in there. And I don't know about strength. Like everyone, I'm a work in progress. Trying to be helpful to the planet, its people, and, of course, its animals."

She put the coffee on the farmhouse-style table and motioned for Lindsay to sit.

"I understand you and Marnie aren't close anymore?"

"No. Not at all. There was a time when we were joined at the hip. That was a long time ago. We're still friendly. In fact, I saw her the other day. She texted me that she was coming out this way to check out some property and wondered if I was busy."

"Was that unusual?"

"Not particularly. Marnie was always like that. She liked to keep things spur-of-the-moment whenever possible. She said she'd had enough of the rules that enslaved her. Her words. Anyway, she brought a nice bottle of wine."

"What rules enslaved her?"

"Like I said, her words, not mine. I'm a rule follower to a fault. I did what was expected of me to get the part, and I'm not ashamed of it. She felt like men had ruled the planet long enough, and she didn't like the way they—the government, the FDA—controlled her products."

"You mean as far as approvals?"

"Correct. That kind of thing. I understood. Not Marnie. She just wouldn't take no for an answer. That's what made her. You're not here, Detective, to talk about Marnie, are you?"

Lindsay set down her cup. "Not exclusively, but yes. I need to know more about the movement, and that means more about Marnie. You were there nearly from the beginning and were said to have been a foundational figure."

Dina studied Lindsay's blue eyes.

"That's kind of you to say, but I really can't imagine I'll be of much use to you. Marnie was a very public figure. Easily researched."

"Right. Even so, you have an insider's knowledge of the movement, the farm. The woman behind all of it."

Dina shook her head. "It was a different time, Lindsay. You probably weren't even born when Marnie started her farm."

"No, I wasn't."

"It's so hard for girls your age to really understand what it was like for women your mother's and grandmother's age and before."

"I have an idea. I know that in my grandmother's time, there was scarcely a job in law enforcement for women other than dispatcher or meter maid."

"That's a good example. Now imagine a world in which you are mostly invisible to everyone unless you possess good looks—conventional good looks at that—and money. Men didn't need either to be seen or heard. Women, well, that will always be another story."

"I really do understand. What I don't understand is how Marnie Spellman fits into that story. Her fame, after all, was founded on cosmetics. Aren't those used to attract male attention?"

Dina brushed that aside.

"Those that don't understand her story or her unbridled commitment certainly think so. They miss the point. Hers is the story of a powerful woman who built something from nothing. Her products were created from Mother Earth to empower women, make them stronger. Looking better is only skin deep. Feeling stronger is something held within every fiber of your being."

"Exactly how does a face cream empower?"

"Great question, and likely the main reason people can't quite get Marnie and what she did, and the impact she has on so many of us right now."

Lindsay passed on a refill, and Dina poured herself another cup.

"Here's the answer, and you either believe it or you don't. There is a life force; call it God if you like. Many do. God is the sum of all the love, all the possibilities, each of us possesses. God is part of who you are. And most importantly, God is female. We are built in her image, to nurture, love, have children. Create life. That's the basic principle of what Marnie taught us. Nature is our mother."

"It sounds a little pagan to me," Lindsay said.

"Some have said that. In many ways it echoes those beliefs—beliefs that were snuffed out by men. Churches led by men. Cities built by men. A culture was created that pushed women further and further away from true power. Marnie saw a world with women at the center."

They sat in silence as the wind outside whistled through the stand of alders next to the house. Dina appeared moved by her own soliloquy, and she produced a tissue tucked inside her bra to dry her eyes.

"I'm sorry," Lindsay said. "I didn't mean to upset you. Just trying to inform myself, find out what happened to those women."

"Tears are good," Dina said. "They remind you of feelings that you don't have every day. I can't help you with Marnie. I love her. I see no connection between the deaths of two women twenty years apart."

"There are similarities," Lindsay said. "I can't disclose them. Trust me."

"Trust is earned."

"Of course. Did you hear of anything about Calista Sullivan when you grew close to Marnie?"

"I came after," she said.

"But I was reading in the papers online that you and Marnie actually became friends a couple years before Calista went missing. There was a photograph of the two of you at a Hollywood fundraiser. For the Humane Society, I believe."

Dina gamely tried to furrow her brow. "You have your dates wrong."

"No," Lindsay said, "I don't think so." Lindsay retrieved a photocopy of the article from her bag. She'd already circled the date in red.

"I don't know," Dina said, taking the paper in her slender fingers, one of which was adorned with a ring featuring a canary diamond the size of a sparrow's egg. "Now I recall. Sorry. So many of these events that one seemed like the other. Yes, the paper doesn't lie—at least it didn't back in those days. That's me right there. And that's Marnie there. We were so young."

"You look like sisters," Lindsay said. "Twins, even."

Dina Marlow brightened a little. "You really think so?"

"I do."

Dina's eyes returned to the clipping.

"You haven't been completely honest with me," Lindsay said.

"I've done my best."

"The article says that you had been up to Washington and were considering making it your permanent home."

"It does?"

Lindsay pointed to the passage.

Dina started to read, then looked up.

"Yes, it does."

"You did know Calista, didn't you?"

Dina looked away toward the windows, watching the alder saplings as the wind bent them northward.

"I did. I'm sorry I wasn't fully truthful. If you keep a lie inside you, you begin to believe it. Marnie says lies often manifest into cancer. No one knows it, but I've had a double mastectomy. I think Marnie could be right."

"I'm sorry you were sick," Lindsay said.

"I'm sorry that I brought it on myself. My agent wanted me to go on *Today* to talk about my recovery. I didn't think it was a good idea. I couldn't. She kept telling me over and over that it would help other women, but I just couldn't bring myself to sit there with a smile when I knew that I'd caused this."

"You didn't cause your cancer."

"Do you believe in God?"

"Yes."

"Can you prove God's existence?"

"No, I guess I can't."

"Then, Detective, please don't challenge me on what I know to be true."

Lindsay nodded. "Sorry."

Dina ended the awkward moment. "I'll tell you what I know. It won't be useful, but I will tell you, anyway."

Drawn by a distant movement, Lindsay's gaze drifted out the floor-to-ceiling window behind Dina, which let the spectacular landscape outside into the room in a way that Lindsay had never experienced. It was as if they were watching a nature show on an IMAX screen. A pair of elk—the motion she'd seen—rooted through the edge of the field.

"A couple of laggards, part of a herd that came through before you arrived. Magnificent animals, don't you think?"

Lindsay nodded. "Yes, they certainly are," she said finally, then forced herself to focus on Dina.

"So. Calista. What I knew of her. That's what you're after?"

"Your name was on the witness list from the prosecutor's office, but there's nothing in the file about what it was that you'd told them. Why did they think you could be helpful in the case against Reed Sullivan?"

"It's a fair question," she said. "Just not one I have an answer for. I'll tell you what I told them: Calista was a lovely person. Hard worker. Dedicated to the cause. Like all of the girls around the farm. She was there because she needed to be."

Dina offered something to eat, and Lindsay declined. "This kitchen is terrific," she said. "You must be a gourmet chef, Ms. Marlow."

"Dina, please. And no. In fact, I don't cook much at all."

"Really? I read that you wrote a cookbook."

Dina gave a sheepish shrug. "The subtitle tells the story: *A Collection of My Favorite Recipes*. I didn't make them; I collected them. Macmillan thought we'd do great business, but the book was a flop. I guess I'm not that good of an actress after all. I couldn't play the part of a cook on a *Good Morning America* segment."

They both laughed.

"I know you didn't come here for a chitchat about my hits and misses," Dina said. "You came about the girl, and Calista. And Marnie, of course."

"Right," Lindsay said. "Sarah Baker. Let's start there. Tell me about her."

"Well, she came to my door seeking an interview. She said she was a freelancer for the *Hollywood Reporter*, and they were doing a 'Where are they now?' story or something awful like that. I told her I wasn't interested, and she could have saved herself the trouble of the drive out here."

"You invited her in, though."

"I did. She was polite, and she said she needed to use the bathroom. So yes, I invited her in. I also told her that I didn't want to do the interview. I didn't say why. Even saying *why* you don't want to do something gets misconstrued these days. The press used to be my friend. Not anymore. Probably not anyone's friend, when you get right down to it."

"Did she ask you about Marnie Spellman?"

Dina shrugged. "She might've. Sure, yes, she did. Marnie's a big part of my story."

"I'm curious about that. What did she want to know?"

"Same thing everyone does. Was Marnie magical or something like that."

Lindsay leaned a little closer. "Was she?"

"Look, I don't know anymore. There was a time when I would have bet my life on it, and I guess, in a very real way, I did."

"How do you mean?"

"I'm here. I came here to be a part of something. Something that was going to shed light into all the dark places that we don't dare to even peer into." She laughed. "Now, when I say it aloud to you, I feel like a certified moron."

Dina fiddled with an earring, another large diamond. Like the kitchen, the stone was the largest of its type Lindsay had ever seen.

Lindsay pressed her. "You know Sarah was a college student, not a stringer for the *Hollywood Reporter*."

Dina kept her eyes on Lindsay. Sparkling, like topaz, or embers in a dying fire. Like cracked marbles. "I know that now, from reading the paper, but really I think I just hoped she was an actual reporter, even though I intended to decline the interview. It would have at least indicated some whisper of interest in me, that maybe she'd see something in me that was still relevant, write a story even without interviewing me, and maybe, just maybe, I'd find my way back."

"I'm very sorry about that, Dina. Really, I am. You have a beautiful home here."

"Yes," she said. "That's all I have. No husband. No children. Just a big, beautiful, empty house."

They fell silent for a moment.

"So it sounds like Sarah had the chance to ask a few questions. What was she trying to get you to talk about? Marnie, you said. How about Calista?"

Dina thought for a moment that went on too long. "Yes," she said at last. "About Calista and Reed Sullivan."

"What about them, specifically?"

Dina wore a harried expression, as though Lindsay were giving her the third degree. Lindsay waited her out. She knew the look of someone bursting to have a story "forced" from them. Alan had taught her that lying back was often the way to pop it free. "Shutting up and just blinking at them is like giving them an information Heimlich," he'd said. "Be patient, and they'll cough it up all over you."

Sure enough, Dina hacked it up. "She said she'd found some things—*discrepancies*, she called them."

"Did she say what?"

"No. No."

Maybe regretting what she'd said, Dina went back to playing hostess. "I see you've finished your coffee. Would you like some tea?"

Lindsay's impulse was to decline—she needed to move this interview along—but, well. This kitchen. This view. Those elk. "Sure, I'll take some tea."

"Lovely," Dina said. After several minutes of fuss, she brought it to the table in nearly transparent porcelain cups. "The cups were Mary Pickford's. It's black tea. You take anything in it?"

"Some honey, if you have some."

Dina teasingly rolled her eyes upward. "Of course I do," she said, retracing her steps and returning with a small glass jar. "Don't be disappointed. It's from down the road here. Not Spellman's."

"I'm sure it'll be great," Lindsay said. "You mentioned Sarah speaking about some 'discrepancies' she'd discovered, relating to Calista and her ex-husband."

"Just secondhand rumor, supposition."

"At this point I can deal with secondhand, Dina."

"I don't know," she said.

"Look, Dina, a girl is dead. You talked to her. You might know something. Please."

Dina set her cup on the table. *Here it comes,* Lindsay thought. "Something happened on the farm a week before Calista's body was found," Dina said. "Something that scared some of the girls. I don't know what it was, not really."

"Think, Dina. This is important."

"Look, I was a bit of an outsider. At first, I thought the other women—you know, the inner circle—"

"The Hive?" Lindsay asked.

"Right. The Hive. They were standoffish at first or maybe—and this might be my vanity getting in the way—a little shy around me because I was so well known. I'd say *famous*, but to say that word when referring to oneself is completely hideous. Same with the word *celebrity*."

Lindsay didn't know if Dina was dealing in humility or hubris. "It wasn't standoffishness or shyness that kept them from you, was it?"

She looked into her empty teacup. "No. They had some kind of secret that no one wanted me to know about."

"Who, exactly, are 'they'?"

Dina looked down, as if trying to remember.

"It has been a long time, Detective. Let's see . . . well, Marnie, Greta Swensen, Trish Appleton, and Heather Hanley, now Jarred."

The last name brought a flash of recognition to Lindsay, but she set it aside.

She asked if Dina knew of any of their whereabouts, and the actress proceeded to tell what she could.

Lindsay wrote the information in her notebook.

Greta Swensen. Local. Gorgeous house off Chuckanut Drive. "Long career at Whatcom Memorial. Beautiful hair."

It came to her. Heather's married name. She was Heather Jarred. US congressperson. US Senate candidate. Married. Two kids.

Trish Appleton. A nurse like Greta. Married unlike Greta. Left the area years ago.

"Did you ever find out what the secret was? That the women in the inner circle had kept?"

"Not really," Dina replied. "I mean, it was related somehow to the Sullivan matter. I know that much. I was there at the time of the trial. I overheard the other girls in the barn, talking about how Reed should go free, that what was happening to him was wrong. Maybe Kate will tell you something. She was still around then."

"Kate?"

"Kate Spellman. Marnie's mother."

"Where can I find her?"

"Believe it or not, she's at some campground south of Bellingham. I never liked her. I might have, if Marnie had. Marnie had a way of transporting you into her own heart, her way of thinking. Kate was persona non grata."

Dina Marlow didn't get out much, it was clear. She was a storyteller with no one to tell them to. Now here was Lindsay, actually *asking* for them. Though as it turned out, these weren't stories Lindsay was interested in. These were all about Hollywood, and its mistreatment of Dina Marlow.

She wound things up with what she clearly considered the most tragic tale of all.

She knew, she told Lindsay, that she had become the embodiment of the most banal Hollywood cliché. She was washed up. Her fans had aged their way into retirement centers and cemeteries. When her official fan club leader died, no one came forward to take the unpaid job. When she went to fill a prescription at Rite Aid, the counter pharmacist didn't even do a double take. No one under thirty knew her name.

The nadir of her decline, however, was the final round of an episode of *Jeopardy!* The category was "Former Leading Ladies."

"The star of *Along the Frontier* who was nominated for an Emmy six times but never won."

The contestants' answers were "Who is Cybill Shepherd?"; "Who is Dinah Shore?"; and "Hi, Mom!"

Dina wondered if Cybill felt terrible.

She hoped so.

When Lindsay finally extricated herself, she pulled over a mile away from Dina Marlow's sprawling home—or rather, her estate—her mind overflowing with thoughts about what Dina had said about God, about herself, about Marnie and Calista and Sarah Baker, too. She filled a page in her notebook and then half of another, ending by wondering if Sarah had made a visit to Kate Spellman, too. Lindsay knew that *she* would have, if she had been trying to investigate what had happened all those years ago.

Which, as it happened, she now very definitely was.

After Lindsay finally left—the poor thing had lingered like she didn't have a home of her own to go to, or perhaps she was just starstruck—Dina poured herself some gin and replayed the encounter with the detective, which, in turn, led her to recall her talk with Sarah Baker. Toward the end of the interview, Sarah had broached the subject of Dina's relationship with Marnie.

"For a time, we were very close friends," Dina had told her. "She was my teacher, my mentor. I am the woman I am today because of her."

Those words were a smoke screen, and she nearly choked on each syllable.

"So you say you were 'very close'?" The girl leaned heavily on the air quotes and failed to fully suppress a smirking little smile.

"I told you. Yes, good friends."

Sarah shook her head as though saddened. "Come on, Dina. Times have changed. The world is more open now."

Abruptly, Dina had dropped the curtain on the interview. She swept to the door and flung it open. "You," she said, "need to go."

The girl laughed at her. Tried to speak, then laughed again. "You *are* an actress, aren't you?" she said as she got to her feet. After she'd pressed past Dina, out the door, she whirled and delivered a rather impressive exit line of her own.

"For someone who's supposedly living a fully actualized, authentic life, you sure are a phony."

After young Sarah Baker drove that dagger into Dina Marlow's heart and exited the stage, Dina had hurried to her bathroom and vomited into the toilet. When she got to her feet, she spent several long, bleak minutes looking at her ashen reflection in the mirror, wishing she'd never opened her door to that reporter.

And never laid eyes on Marnie Spellman in the first place.

She started drinking, fuming, her anger rising with every tick of the clock. That bitch of a reporter! Dina knew ambition when she saw it. By dredging up the past, Sarah Baker was bent on tearing Dina's legacy to shreds.

There would be no star on the Hollywood Walk of Fame. No revived career. No nothing but . . . *nothing.*

Dina found the phone number that Sarah had given her. It wasn't even a business card, rather a scrap of paper pulled from her purse! She probably didn't have a thing that could pass as a press credential, either. How could someone like that ruin her?

She picked up her phone and jabbed in the number. She had to do it a second time to get it right.

It went immediately to an automated voice mail.

Not even personalized!

"Look, please don't include me in your article. It will destroy me. I don't care that times have changed. My fans haven't . . ."

What was she saying? And what was this wheedling, conciliatory tone? She was drunk, sure, and she was also angrier than she'd been since she was cruelly informed by her agent that she needed to go up for more mature parts.

The grandmother! The friendly aunt!

She was only thirty-seven at the time.

"Sarah Baker! You are a nothing," Dina railed into the phone. "Don't you know who I am? You don't know what I can do. I swear to God that if you carry on with your story, you'll be sorry."

Satisfied, Dina ended the call, disciplined her breathing, and let the heat drain from her face. She opened a bottle of wine, filled and half emptied her glass, then placed it out of easy reach on the enormous walnut table she'd had custom made.

She thought of how Marnie told her that nature, even wood, spoke to her. Even now, all these years later, Dina couldn't pin down whether Marnie Spellman was a supreme liar or the only woman with a direct pipeline to nature—something otherworldly.

She recalled one time watching Marnie run her fingertips over the wood surface of her enormous desk, back and forth, back and forth. Dina had felt this surface herself, knew it to be smooth, but not so smooth that its grain couldn't be felt under its satiny gloss. Marnie let her nails follow the grain, which had an inner glow like topaz.

Marnie regarded wood as extremely sensual. "I feel the grain like a sightless person would roam a page written in Braille," she said while Dina looked on, transfixed. "The wood, like the bees, talks to me. It discloses the world's seasons of long ago. It discloses secrets of the presidents, the kings, the men who have ruled the world since the tree rose from a seedling."

Marnie said her fingertips felt electric. The vibration moved throughout her body. She wanted to cry out, stop the ecstasy from taking over her brain. It was if she had no choice. She said she wanted Dina to feel what it was like to have the power of a millennia run through her, an endless, electric stream. Her breathing accelerated. She said that humming current was what God wanted her to feel. That there was complete and undeniable joy in sharing all that she had to offer. That she could unleash the power of nature. Not just for herself, of course. For everyone who would dare to dream it. One hand left the table and found its way to where Marnie wanted it to go.

Dina melted under her touch. Melted under her own touch now, remembering it.

CHAPTER 21

Saturday, February 6, 1997
Lummi Island, Washington

In the early days especially, whenever Marnie invited Dina to Lummi Island, it came with a definite hitch. Dina knew that Marnie would parade her around as a kind of walking, talking advertisement for what she was doing. The groups were small then. Later, when Marnie's own fame grew, she didn't use Dina in that way.

Marnie had been on the shopping channel a dozen times by then, and her product line was growing. Her hairstyle was more refined, and the makeup she applied so expertly was what some critics considered more appropriate for evening than for daytime. Marnie didn't care. She was always a woman with the smarts to see that her look had every bit as much to do with her growing success as anything. Especially on TV.

The number of women helping on the farm had nearly doubled since Dina's previous visit earlier that month. And ever the actress, Dina noticed that most of the men were in supporting roles. The women were center stage. Marnie led her to an upstairs bedroom.

She paused before its closed door.

"I had this made especially for you, Dina. I think of you as a long-lost sister, and well . . . I just wanted to create a space that would always be yours. Always ready for whenever you come to visit."

Marnie opened the door with a flourish.

The room was magnificent. No expense had been spared. The walls were covered with ecru silk, and the furnishings were antique.

"The bed is Louis XIV."

"I love that style."

"Not style, Dina. It was Louis XIV's. His bed."

"You can't be serious."

"Oh, I am."

"It must have cost a fortune."

Marnie gave a self-deprecating shrug. "God gives me the ability to send love where it needs to go. I prayed on it. And it came to me in a dream. You were there, Dina, alongside kings and queens."

Dina sat on the bed, her feet unable to touch the floor. She brushed her hands over a bedspread of yellow, white, and black.

"I had that made, too."

Dina looked closer at the fabric. The black stripes were a chain of bees.

"I adore it."

Marnie smiled and sat down next to Dina. "That makes me happy."

Dina set her hand on Marnie's. "You need to be careful, Marnie."

"How do you mean?"

"With your money," Dina said. "I've been there. I thought the income stream would rush forever. If I hadn't done TV, something that I considered a great humiliation at the time, I'd have never been able to survive."

"I appreciate your love, your concern, and I understand all of that. Right now, I view things differently. I see the world through her eyes. I hear from her. She tells me that the pie is infinite and that I can have as many slices as I want. Of course, everyone can."

Dina knew that there was truth in her words. At least, she desperately wanted to. In her insular Hollywood life, she'd always felt that she was good enough to win an Academy Award, that fate had conspired against her. The other women who got those award-winning roles weren't more talented; they were just lucky. In the world according to Marnie Spellman, nothing would stand in the way of ambition. That God wanted success. Infinite success. Endless power.

Dina and Marnie had talked about it.

"You'll get that award you covet," Marnie had said. "When you do, it will only be proof that you didn't need it after all."

Conversations often went that way. Marnie telling Dina that in reality, she was a brighter star to the world, to humanity, than she was to Hollywood.

"You are the brightest light," Marnie said.

Dina, divorced five times, was alone. She'd had no children. Her friends were always in a constant competition with each other. She knew she didn't belong in Hollywood. It was her unlikely friendship with a woman she bumped into on a home shopping channel who had become her mentor, her mother, her ally.

It was at a celebration dinner in the barn that night that Dina met Calista Sullivan. Marnie had announced that she was close to her breakthrough on her antiaging serum and that she had a new product launch in the works. Her brand was about creating the most perfect, most beautiful you, from the outside in. That meant ensuring that when one presented herself to the outside world, she projected radiance and confidence. She'd already sold a hundred thousand CDs, a book, and affirmation cards that nurtured the spirit inside.

"I've been offered my own TV show," she told the small group. "It's going to be called *The Marnie Way*, and it's all about helping other women with body, soul, and spiritual teachings."

Dina couldn't believe her ears. She'd been vying for a talk show that would reinvent her as a thoughtful, Jane Pauley type. She wondered why Marnie hadn't mentioned she'd been pursuing a TV endeavor of her own.

Marnie raised a glass of wine.

"Dear Dina," she said, "I really owe this opportunity to you. Your agent said that I'd be perfect for it."

"I'm thrilled for you," Dina said, while she made a mental note to fire her agent. "This is so out of the blue."

"See," Marnie went on, "you don't know what you will be in this life from day to day. You only know that you, and you alone, set the course." She tilted her gaze upward. "She, of course, had her hand in it, too."

CHAPTER 22

Fall 1996
Seattle, Washington

Marnie Spellman was already a star when Greta Swensen first met her. There was a long line of women—a hundred or more—snaking out the front door of the bookshop in Seattle's Pioneer Square. Marnie had been on a local talk show, *Northwest Afternoon*, the day before, and the shout-out of her signing had brought a decent mix of admirers and the curious to the event.

"Would you sign my rather beat-up copy?" Greta said.

Marnie, seated behind a table next to a pile of her books, nodded, and took the dog-eared hardcover with its foxed pages and folded corners. "Looks like someone's been tossing this in a paint mixer or something," she said as she signed, her pen making a catlike scratching sound on the paper.

Greta felt her face grow warm. "Oh no. It's just been loved a lot. Sorry. I guess I should have bought another copy."

Marnie looked up and smiled. "Don't be ridiculous. It isn't the words on the pages that matter. It's what you do with them."

Greta nodded. "Right. Of course. I swore I wouldn't say this, but I'm here because you changed my life."

"Name?"

"Greta."

"Lovely. What do you do?"

"Nurse. Wanted to be a doctor."

"What stopped you?"

"I don't know. I guess I wasn't as sure of myself as I needed to be."

"Setting a compass is tricky," Marnie said.

Greta wanted to say more, but the woman behind her nudged her away.

"Thank you, Ms. Spellman."

"Marnie, please."

When she stepped outside, she opened the book:

> *For Greta,*
>   *I see you. I know you. You are on the way to becoming everything God has in store for you. She loves you. Come to my farm anytime.*
>   *Love,*
>   *Marnie*

Next to her name, as was her custom whenever she signed anything—a book, a sweatshirt, a lotion bottle—Marnie had sketched a simplified depiction of a honeybee.

Three days later, Greta drove out to Lummi Island. She'd done everything she could to resist the impulse and not make the trip so quickly, but she couldn't. She had moved to Washington State from Nebraska after discovering Marnie on TV, and now, after finally meeting her in person, she had to see Spellman Farms for herself. At the time, she thought she was heading in the direction of the most beautiful flower. She was the bee. In time, she found out otherwise.

She wrote a letter to her parents shortly after.

> *Dear Mom and Dad,*
>
> *First off, things are going well. Don't worry. The truth is that I just wanted to write to let you know that I love you and my sisters. I've put my nursing career on hold and am working in a kind of women's co-op on an island in Washington State. I don't want to be mysterious about it, because it really isn't mysterious. I'm working with Marnie Spellman. You might have seen her on TV, Mom. She's the amazing woman who put together a line of products that nourishes both the body and the mind. I'll send you a sample of her bee pollen elixir, and I know you will agree. Anyway, while I'm not a nurse at the moment, I feel as if I'm doing something special, something that heals women (and men) in ways beyond the physical. I hope this makes sense to you. I'm not asking for your support in this endeavor but rather just a basic understanding about me that I've tried to tell you over and over. I am more than just a daughter or a sister. I have more to give.*
>
> *Love,*
>
> *Greta*

Pamela and Frederick Swensen sat in silence after reading the letter twice. Fred was ten years older than his wife. He was broad shouldered with sinewy arms and hands, and she had brilliant green eyes. She was forty-five, her hands mottled with spatters of freckles and her fingertips the same length as her husband's. The Swensens had never known a workday that didn't end after sundown and start at first light.

"She's not one of those lesbian gals now," Fred said. "Is she?"

"Oh no," Pamela shot back, giving her head a shake. "She had four boyfriends in high school. I thought she'd be one of the girls to end up having to get married."

Fred looked over his reading glasses. "Then what?"

"She's finding her way, Fred."

"That's it?"

"That's what I want to believe."

"Fine, Pam. You know the girls better than I do. Seems strange to me that she'd give up her life in Omaha to follow some gal who makes hand lotion on the other side of the country."

Pamela Swensen folded the letter and returned it to its envelope. "Honey," she said, "Marnie Spellman doesn't sell lotion. She sells something else to those who are looking for it."

"Oh, really? What's that?"

"Hope," she said. "Possibilities."

Fred blinked at her, then turned back to the TV they'd been watching before the mail arrived.

Pamela returned to her crossword puzzle. She loved her husband more than anything. She loved her life. Her girls. Farm living. Being the center of attention at a wedding because you're the mother of the bride. At the same time, she couldn't help but look at her own life and wonder if her middle child—the one who never played by the rules—had been the one with all the right answers after all.

She wrote a letter back the next day.

Dear Greta,

I miss you. Dad does, too. Your sisters also. I want you to know that I understand where you are coming from. I have thought about my own life, too. Remember when I used to tell you that I wish I had been a writer and had gone to New York? How I didn't have the courage to leave something comfortable for something unknown? You did that, sweetheart. You did what I wish I had done all those years ago. Do not get me wrong. I would never regret the life that I chose. How I love my girls and their dad. That's separate. I know you will understand me because you, Greta, are the one most like me. I love the life I had. I mourn the life that I could have had. Write back when you are able. Keep believing in yourself.

PS. Thank you for the lotion you sent last month. It smells good, but it gave me a slight rash. I'm fine now.

Greta corresponded with her mother over the next few years. All the missives were positive. All were steeped in love and regret. When her dad finally passed, she sent flowers. When her mother died the following year, she sent flowers once again.

"Why don't you go back to Nebraska and see your sisters, Greta?" Marnie asked not long after Pamela Swensen's funeral.

Greta didn't hesitate a second. "This is where I'm needed," she said.

Marnie reached out and put her arms around Greta.

"I know," she whispered. "You are ascending now, becoming all that you can be. Hold this thought, like I'm holding you right now. The past is a memory album that stands open for the weak, for those who aren't growing, those who are stuck in lives that only serve to make people like us stand out."

That moment was a turning point for Greta. She knew it even then. She'd become something that a Kearney, Nebraska, girl didn't even dare to dream of being. She'd found her way to a light so bright, so full of promise. She'd found her way to her destiny.

Marnie let go and held Greta in her gaze with those blue, penetrating eyes of hers.

"Now," she said, "let's get to work and see what we can manifest for others."

Chapter 23

Wednesday, September 18, 2019
Chuckanut Drive, Washington

Stone guardrails installed by the Civilian Conservation Corps in the 1930s kept vehicles from a precipitous drop into the cold waters of the bay as Chuckanut Drive careened through the deep, dark green of second-growth timber. Driving along it now, ninety years later, was still akin to passing a green curtain that opened and shuttered, the trees giving way to incredible views, including glimpses of Washington's famed San Juan Islands.

Greta Swensen, now nearly twenty-three years removed from that starry-eyed Nebraska girl who'd followed Marnie Spellman to Lummi Island as if she were a lodestar, did what most people say they'll do when they own property with expansive views but seldom do. She sipped her coffee and watched the gulls as they glided in the air currents, which were frequently formidable.

Not today. At least so far, the winds were just strong enough to keep the gulls lazily turning as though suspended from a mobile.

The shoreline in front of Greta's house was tucked snugly between a pair of cedars. The property was rugged, quiet. Unspoiled. As Greta looked out across the water, dusky clouds swelled in the distance. She glanced at her phone. It was almost 10:00 a.m. The promised storm would be on her by noon, supposedly, about the time Lindsay Jackman had said she'd be there.

Prophetic?

Possibly, she thought.

Dangerous?

Maybe so.

Only time would tell.

The detective said that she wanted to talk about an old case and a new one. Greta didn't ask which ones. She just said yes to the request for a meeting. Stupid mistake. Better to ask. Then, she thought, why should she? She already knew the detective was going to ask about Calista Sullivan and Sarah Baker.

Lindsay parked her SUV in a graveled space above Greta's house, a modern glass-and-steel structure that, while clearly made of the finest materials, was surprisingly small. No larger, she thought, than her family home. Modest yet luxurious. It looked like a cubicle made of glass had fallen from the sky and landed among the trees. As Lindsay approached the door, also glass, she could see, through the floor-to-ceiling windows on the other side of the residence, glittering silver-and-blue salt water.

Greta answered before Lindsay could knock, an advantage of living in an all-clear abode. Greta was a beautiful woman with sharp, striking features. Her red hair had softened some, like cream in coffee. She had the kind of eyes that pulled people closer. Even without saying a word, she was a friend. She was a confidante. She was the woman in the checkout line who smiled at the person in front of her and said, "Have a nice day," not as a throwaway line but as an obviously sincere wish, a hope.

"Detective Jackman," she said, easing the door open.

"That's me," Lindsay said.

"Come in. I just started a fresh pot of coffee. Want some?"

Lindsay stepped onto a travertine-tiled foyer. "Yes, please. I haven't had my usual three cups today."

Greta motioned for Lindsay to follow.

"I thought the storm would be here by now," Greta said. She pointed to the horizon. "Winds shifted to the south."

"You seem disappointed."

"Nothing like watching a storm," she said.

"I guess that's why I'm here, Ms. Swensen."

"Greta, please. Now, about that storm," she said, pouring the coffee into bright-yellow cups. "A metaphor, I'm guessing. You want to talk about Calista Sullivan. That was forever ago. Why now?"

"Just following up."

"After all this time?"

"Looking into another case, too. Recent and possibly related."

"The girl they found out in Maple Falls? I read the paper. In fact, I subscribe to three newspapers. A bit of a news junkie."

Greta was just as easy to talk to as she'd seemed, and as apparently forthcoming as Lindsay could've hoped for. For the next half hour, she talked about her former friend and the loss she'd felt when she went missing.

"It was unthinkable. A betrayal."

"Betrayal? How so?"

"Calista was an amazing woman," Greta said, selecting her words with great care and almost a wistfulness. "She was growing in so many ways. We all were. We were together, united in purpose. We had given up so much to find so much more. Calista had made a huge sacrifice, giving up her children the way she did. She was in the group with both feet planted firmly."

"The group. The group as a whole, or the Hive?"

For the first time, Greta fell silent. Her eyes watched the gulls, then shifted back to her coffee.

"All of us working on Spellman Farms. We were close, almost like sisters. No, I take that back: we *were* sisters."

"I need to know what happened to her."

"You already know."

"No. No, I don't think I do."

"The law settled it all."

"I don't think anything feels settled about any of it. What do *you* think happened?"

"Reed Sullivan killed his wife. He was angry and jealous. He despised the woman she was becoming, and when he couldn't force her to come back to him, he took her. Killed her. Tossed her to the curb like garbage."

"He wasn't found guilty," Lindsay said flatly.

Greta pushed back. "He should have been. I know it, and I think you do, too."

Lindsay didn't blink. "His alibi was tighter than tight."

"All right, so you say."

"I do, Ms. Swensen."

This time, Greta didn't correct Lindsay by reminding her to call her by her given name.

"You and Calista were in the Hive. Did you two work together?"

"We did."

"What did you do?"

"Lots of different things."

Now Greta was being evasive. Lindsay pushed a little. "Like what? I really can't get a handle on the goings-on at Spellman Farms."

"I can't talk about Marnie, if you're looking for something along those lines."

"You can't?"

"Confidentiality agreement. You understand, right?"

"Your friend was murdered. Don't you want to find out who did it?"

"I told you," she said, "I already know."

"Well, how about if you just tell me about Calista? How you met. What you thought of her."

February 1999
Lummi Island, Washington

Greta Swensen had arrived on Lummi Island more than two years earlier than Calista Sullivan. Calista was California through and through. She was beautiful and athletic and wore mostly high-end running clothes, although no one saw her actually run anywhere. Greta met Calista in the dining room of the big house with others who'd come north for the same reason. At any one time, there were a dozen or so women and the occasional man who had ditched the mundane world for the one Marnie Spellman offered.

Above the sleek fireplace in the Spellman house was a mosaic, flames shooting through chunks of black and yellow glass and the words TO BE THE BEST YOU KNOW.

"I don't get it," Calista said, studying the art on the wall.

"You don't?" Greta smiled. "I didn't get it right away, either, and I remember being bothered by it, too. Until it came to me that maybe we're not supposed to 'get it,' not supposed to understand it in the way that we processed things in our lives before coming here."

The two of them just looked at each other for a long, long moment while the dining room buzzed around them, and then both burst out laughing at once. Watching this beautiful girl laugh was like its own religious experience for Greta. Such warm, dancing eyes.

"Well, I don't get *that*, either," Calista said when she could finally get the words out.

"No? Well, I'm not Marnie. And you're new. We all were new once." Calista gave Greta a nod.

"I think I've made a mistake," Calista said.

"That's the old you speaking now," Greta told her. "The new you, the you that you are becoming, is a perfect human being. That's why you're here, Calista. That's why you left your old life behind."

Greta looked at Calista's hand.

"Arizona? California?"

"California. How did you know?"

"You're tan except for right here." Her fingertip gently brushed the white skin left from Calista's wedding band.

"Oh," she said, this time allowing a smile to cross her face.

"Children?"

Calista nodded. "Two boys."

"That must be very difficult."

"Yes," she said.

"Husband? . . . Difficult, too?"

Calista shook her head and looked around the table. The others there were listening, though pretending not to.

"No," she said. "We'd grown apart."

"That means you grew, and he didn't."

"Something like that. Yes, that's how it went."

"Where are you living?" Greta asked.

"Nowhere, really. Just got here. Wanted to meet Marnie."

"That's not going to happen. We only see her on Saturdays when she teaches or lectures."

"Oh," Calista said, crestfallen. "I didn't know that."

"That's three things you don't know, Calista. See how helpful I am? I'll flush out all of them for you, and then Marnie will help you find the answers. You just need to be patient."

Wednesday, September 18, 2019

"Calista sounds great," Lindsay said, thinking of Marnie's power over her group. Smart people. Women who were bright, attractive. Women who were searching and determined to close the gap between who they'd been before Marnie and what they'd become. It dawned on Lindsay just then that each of the women was also more than a little bit broken.

"She was great," Greta agreed.

"And so are you," Lindsay half expected her to say. Rolling on in her cult-member script. Greta didn't do that, however. She just fell silent again, appearing sad and lost in the endless view afforded by her stunning house's invisible walls.

The oddest thing was, Lindsay felt a little sad and lost herself. Almost as if she were disappointed that Greta hadn't tried to convert her.

Ah, but there wasn't anything left to be converted to, as far as Lindsay could see. Marnie Spellman was just another woman these days—well, just another mini corporate titan, shilling her lotions. And the Hive was no longer the Hive, apparently.

"Tell me about them?" Lindsay asked.

"Who? The Hive?"

"Yes. The Hive, and all of the people who came to Marnie."

"They were just people interested in what Marnie was telling the world. I know why you're asking, because everyone does. Marnie's world was not a cult unless you consider your own world a cult."

"I don't follow a supreme leader," Lindsay said.

Greta gave a slight shrug. "You think you don't, but most of what you do is follow a path charted by someone other than yourself. That's pretty much it for everyone on the planet. Marnie tells us that we are free beings, that we can and do chart our own destinies."

"Marnie *tells* us," she'd said. Present tense. A true believer, still.

Lindsay pushed back. "Marnie sells cosmetics," she said.

"It may have started that way. The idea of looking your best to feel your best isn't so hard for anyone to really comprehend. It makes perfect sense. Like if you lose five pounds and someone notices, it makes you happy."

"Sure. But it's quite a leap from that kind of happiness to 'charting our own destinies,' isn't it? It's only face creams."

"You say that, and you should know better. You know that whatever products Marnie sells, it comes with so much more. She exists only to help women to become all that they can be spiritually . . . not physically."

That part baffled Lindsay. It was the antithesis of the way she tried to live her life and how she approached her work. How a person looked didn't define their character. A person with bad breath and bad teeth might have the biggest heart. A gorgeous redhead in a multimillion-dollar home might be a killer.

Or at the very least, a liar.

"Then why all the focus on the exterior?" Lindsay asked.

"Our coating, our shell, our packaging—however you want to think of it—is the first thing we see when we wake up. It's the first thing we bring into every interaction. People look. Judge. A split-second determination is made that can and does impact who we are and what people make of us. Being who you are starts with the physical."

"What about those who could never fit society's conventional wisdom of what beauty is? Marnie's teaching struggles to address that, doesn't it?"

Greta gave the detective a hard, cool stare. "I feel an agenda behind that question. That was one misunderstood incident. That was a long time ago."

"Right. It almost ruined her."

"And that's why you and I will never talk about it. I don't work for her anymore. I don't support her products in any way. Even with all of that, I will never talk about that."

"Out of respect for Marnie?"

"Out of respect," she said. "Let's leave it at that."

After an extended silence, Lindsay decided they had indeed come to the end of their conversation and gathered herself to rise, when Greta spoke up.

"Are you going to talk to the other women?" she asked.

"Talked with Dina, made calls to Heather's office, can't find Trish yet."

"What about Marnie?"

"I always work from the outside in," Lindsay said. "I'm saving her for later."

As the detective's SUV retreated from its parking spot at the top of the hill, Greta went straight for her phone and dialed Dina's number.

"It's me, Greta," she said. "I'm worried."

Silence.

"Did you hear me?"

"I heard you. You're worried. Why would that be?"

"You know why."

"Look, we haven't talked in eons, and you're calling me because you're in the middle of a problem you can't solve. What is it? Your dog's sick?"

"Not even funny," Greta said. "Why do you have to be such a bitch?"

"See how easy it is to slip back into old, bad habits, Greta? Except you were the bitch, as I recall."

"I'm calling about that detective poking around. She came to see me just now. She wanted to know everything I could tell her about Calista and what happened to her. She also mentioned Sarah Baker, a reporter I know you talked to. She called me and said so."

The phone went silent again. This time, Greta waited her out.

"What did you say?"

"Nothing. How could I?"

"Have you told anyone else?"

Greta faced the blackening water and wished the storm would come and beat the living daylights out of her house, out of *her*.

"No," she said. "And I have no intention of telling anyone."

"Good. It will be all right."

"Are you sure?"

"Yes. Just do me one favor."

"What?"

"Don't ever call me again. Not for any reason."

Greta held the phone to her ear, listening to the silence as her thoughts took over. Marnie Spellman had been wrong. The way Greta looked at herself and the others had changed. They weren't invincible; they were just a cadre of fools who thought a pact of silence would stop someone from revisiting what had happened on the farm.

She went to her bedroom for a cable-knit cardigan. A chill from the past had wrapped itself around her. Not a warm hug, rather a cold choke hold.

Nothing, she knew, was ever really over.

Chapter 24

June 1999
Lummi Island, Washington

Amplified, the sound of an active hive is like that of an approaching tornado or even a freight train. Pulsing noises lay atop each other as drones bring nectar stolen from the clouds of blossoms that hover over blackberry brambles that line the roads on Lummi Island. It could be comforting like white noise, when dialed down. Marnie had a recording that she played in her bedroom upstairs in the big house. It was on a speaker system that her brother had set up when he came back from rehab. One time when Greta was passing by the master bedroom, she saw Marnie lying on the floor between the speakers. Her eyes were closed, but her lips were moving. Her feet twitched and then smacked together.

For a second, Greta thought Marnie was having a seizure of some kind.

When Marnie opened her eyes, she nodded in Greta's direction and mouthed for her to leave her alone, close the door.

Later that evening around the kitchen table, Greta waited for Marnie to say something about what she'd witnessed, but she didn't. Greta didn't bring it up, because no one dared to ask Marnie a single thing about her methods.

They were not to be questioned or analyzed.

The summer air was warm later that night, and Greta found a place on the front porch. She could hear the squawking of the neighbor's chickens, and by the sound of the ruckus, a raccoon or coyote had managed to make a meal of a hen or two. A gun went off, and silence took over.

"Join me."

It was Marnie. She was wearing a T-shirt and shorts and holding a pair of wineglasses in one hand, a bottle of Syrah in the other.

Greta took a glass while Marnie poured.

"I want to talk to you about something important, Greta. You know how the swarm visited me when I was a girl?"

"Of course. Everyone knows."

"Did I ever tell you what I heard?"

"I thought it was a message—not words, a feeling."

Marnie's glass was already empty. She filled it again, this time nearly to the brim.

"It was words," she said. "They spoke. They told me specifically what to do. They told me that I was going to do something important. Something that no one else had done. They anointed me, Greta. They said my products would be a gift to the world."

Greta wanted to believe. She really did. She *always* wanted to believe. Sitting in church next to her sisters, who seemed to soak in all the pastor had to say, had only made her feel inadequate. Like she was missing some component that God handed out when she was deciding who would have what gifts. She knew that what Marnie was saying was either a great big lie or she was insane.

"I believe you, Marnie," she said.

Marnie put her head on Greta's shoulder.

"We will do great things together. The world doesn't know it yet, but things are going to change. The era of men deciding what we will do, how we will be paid, where we will nurse our babies, is over."

They quietly clinked their glasses and sipped some more.

That was the part that Greta wanted to believe. More than anything. She wanted to truly recognize that she was part of the solution, a leader in a quest to do what others had tried though ultimately failed at. She didn't know how Marnie intended to bring about this new era—what the bees had told her that would, apparently, help her do that—but she did know she needed to be a part of it. And she did believe that Marnie possessed *some* sort of extraordinary power, even if it was just the force of her personality, the force of her colossal self-belief.

"Be beautiful," Marnie said as a wall of clouds moved in from the water. "Be powerful."

The house was in the midst of its umpteenth renovation, and Greta slept in Marnie's childhood bedroom down the hall from the master. It was strange, she thought. Not a single thing had been altered in the room, save for the addition of a little brass plaque Calista had made for her. It hung under the window like the room was of historical importance.

Greta struggled to sleep. Was everything Marnie said true? Or was there something else at work? Mental illness?

Maybe even something dark?

In the morning, she thought, everything would be fine.

CHAPTER 25

Thursday, September 19, 2019

Greta checked her makeup in the rearview mirror and psyched herself up. *I can do this. One, two, three.* It had been years since she'd seen Trish Appleton. She'd rehearsed what she'd say on the drive over from her glass cube house on Chuckanut Drive, utterly blind to the gorgeous afternoon. She would be broaching a delicate subject, and things were not good between them.

She found Trish's place—a dowdy little suburban ranch house— took a deep breath, and knocked on the door.

Trish answered and stared flatly at her. "What are you doing here?"

"I should have called," Greta said, her tone somewhere between irritated and apologetic. "I know. Of course, I should have called. I just didn't think you'd see me."

"You're right about that."

Trish started to close the door, but Greta's foot was lodged in the doorway.

"Do you mind?" Trish asked.

"As a matter of fact, I do. Look, we really need to talk. I wouldn't be here otherwise."

Trish kept her eyes narrowed on Greta's. Though they had been absent from each other's lives, Trish would have recognized her anywhere. She looked good. *Money can do that,* she thought. Her clothes were designer, though not new. She'd seen a celebrity wearing the same white-and-black blouse in *People* magazine the previous year.

"You always worry, Greta. It's what you do. Worrying might be your one true talent. Oh, and being a bully—that's another talent of yours."

"Can't we make peace? We need to talk."

If what she was offering was an olive branch, Trish was sure the fruit was rancid.

"Please," Greta said, the word sounding so odd coming out of her mouth it seemed as if it were in a foreign language.

Trish wasn't having any of it. She shared a history with the woman with her foot in the door, and it wasn't a happy one. "Greta," she said, "there was a time when I hung on your every word. I think I lost part of myself back then. You swallowed me up. Like Marnie. Like Dina. All of you and your crazy ambitions."

"I own that," Greta said. "I'm sorry. I really am. What's done is done, though, and none of us can turn back the clock." She drove her hand into her hair and gripped it. "You need to listen to me. Hear me out."

Trish hesitated, then said, "Okay, come in. I just made coffee. You can have one cup and go. That's about all I can take—and you know it's more than you deserve."

Greta followed her into the kitchen. She noted the knife block with the handles of six chef's knives protruding from the amber wood like the quills of a porcupine. A pot rack with cast-iron skillets hung overhead.

"Your kitchen is charming," Greta said.

"That didn't take long."

"What didn't?"

"You, judging me like I'm a quaint commoner and you're the Duchess of Whatcom."

"Sorry," Greta said, suddenly embarrassed. "Didn't mean to."

"I know about your life, Greta," Trish said. "Hope you are happy in that beautiful house."

Greta looked around once more, taking in everything that had eluded her. Greta's own house was lovely, the envy of many. It had the kind of style and presence that announced, in a very loud voice, that whoever lived there was special.

Trish's place was worn, comfortable. People lived there. Loved there, too.

"I'm lonely," Greta finally said. "I stayed with Marnie too long to make a real life of my own."

"I doubt you are that regretful, Greta. You have all the money in the world. You finagled that out of Marnie. Don't know how. Don't care. In any case, I bet you sleep just fine at night."

Greta's eyes returned to the knife block.

"Money isn't everything," she said. "It's really true."

"You could always go back to nursing. Do something for others. Just a wild idea."

"That was never an option for me."

"I did for a while."

"Right. I knew that. Really, Trish, how long did you stay? Hard to backtrack in life, especially when you know everything we did was wrong."

Ultimately, Trish decided not to serve the coffee after all. This visit wasn't going to do her any good. Tripping down memory lane with a former friend shouldn't feel this way. It shouldn't make one sick inside. The shared memories shouldn't cause one to blink hard.

"Why are you here?" Trish asked. "Can we just skip everything else?"

"Fine," Greta said. "I'm here as a friend."

"Right." Trish knew a lie when she heard one. "I thought we'd established that we weren't friends."

"You can think whatever you like," Greta went on. "I'm here to tell you that a detective has been by asking about Calista."

"That's a lifetime ago."

"A reporter was poking around, too."

"Why are you telling me this?"

"The reporter was the girl found out at Maple Falls. The detective is trying to link what happened to Calista to what happened to her."

"What's the connection?"

"I'm just warning you. We need to stick together. Something could be coming."

It sounded like the language in one of Marnie's old CDs, ominous and un-pin-downable.

"If that's all . . . ," Trish said, indicating the door.

"Fine, then. You're on your own, Trish. Live with the consequences."

As Greta turned to leave, Trish noticed that her expensive blouse had a long thread coming from its seam. It took everything she had not to pull it.

"Goodbye, Greta. Don't come here ever again. Not ever."

Trish shut the door behind her, turned the dead bolt, and hooked the chain. Greta could always get the best of her. She'd forgotten Greta's talent for jiggling the knife after piercing a vital organ. She found her way to the kitchen, where she poured herself a glass of wine, knowing that she'd finish the bottle.

Greta was right about one thing.

She was, in fact, on her own.

When push came to shove, Trish intended to be the last woman standing.

CHAPTER 26

Thursday, September 19, 2019
Bellingham, Washington

Marnie Spellman was, as TV people liked to say, a big "get."

And at the time of the Sullivan trial, impossible to get.

She had retreated from public life during that time. She'd be seen around Bellingham, but such sightings were rare. Tedd McGraw's interview was hardly definitive, and Lindsay imagined if he'd known that it was the last interview she'd ever give after a *60 Minutes* piece skewered her, he'd have pressed for a much larger story. Perhaps even bypassed the *Seattle Times* for another media outlet.

Lindsay read the article a second time while she sat outside the Whatcom Museum, a looming redbrick and sandstone structure, the old city hall, that had become the repository for objects, records, and other ephemera that told the story of Western Washington's northernmost county: logging, wood pulp and paper production, fishing and canning, and farming.

Tedd McGraw worked at the museum now. His dreams of rising in the ranks of the journalism world had collapsed along with the logging industry. The *Times* closed its bureau in Bellingham after two years of trying to make it work. Tedd bounced from PR to retail before landing on his feet—or at least his knees—as the director of the museum. The job didn't pay as much as he'd hoped, but by then he had learned the reality of the world.

Nobody gets paid what they think they're worth.

And that went double for journalists.

Maybe even triple.

She didn't have to look hard to spot the former reporter when she entered the museum. He was the only one there. He wore a white shirt with a brick-colored puffy vest and black jeans. Lindsay noted that his sartorial selection looked like a uniform, very similar to the color of the building or even the clothing mandated by Target shift bosses.

"May I call you Tedd?" she asked as she followed him into his office.

"Of course," he said. "Just remember I'm a double *D*."

She gave him a funny look.

"Tedd. Double *D* on the end. Consonants. Just a joke that used to get laughs."

She admired an enormous poster, really wallpaper, that covered his office wall. It showed a group of ten men, early loggers, wrapped around a mammoth old-growth western red cedar.

"One of Darius Kinsey's glass negatives," he said. "Photographer who traipsed through the woods along with his brother, Clark. Fantastic record of early life in the logging camps of the Pacific Northwest."

"Detail is amazing," she said.

"Great negative, even better scanner and printer. Last decent acquisition here. Gift from Microsoft."

An antique Underwood occupied the space on the desk, blocking his view of his visitor. He struggled to lift the typewriter to move it to the side.

"Heavy machine," she said.

"Cast iron, I think."

Small talk. The kind of talk that eases people together.

"Tore a rotator cuff last year," he said. "No insurance at this job. Anyway, we have about ten of these." He slapped the hulking machine's side. "All different ages, different uses. This one was in the mayor's office. A secretary who'd been there forever used it to type correspondence up until five years ago. Staff gave it to us the day after her funeral."

"I see," Lindsay said. "People do move on. You know, when the time is right."

He studied her, as though wondering if that comment was about him or the secretary. She couldn't have told him. Maybe it had been about her husband.

Ex-husband.

She pivoted to the purpose of her visit. "County archives say you have the Reed Sullivan court case files out here."

He leaned back in his chair. "Yeah. Such as it was. I was pretty sure he was guilty."

"I read some of your articles," Lindsay said.

"Right," he said. "They're out there, too, and I look pretty stupid, I guess. I quit following my gut and trying to be the next Woodward and Bernstein. Well, not both. One or the other."

"I'm sure you did your best."

He flicked that away. "That's nice, but no. Not really. I see Sullivan now and then around town, and he shoots me a look that makes me turn away every time. I have it coming. Blame myself for fanning the flames."

"Can we take a look at what you have?"

"Sure. Follow me," he said, getting up. "I have it all. Good thing; the county destroys originals after ten years. Microfilm doesn't do things justice, in my book."

"Mine, too," Lindsay said.

Tedd led her down the stairs into the basement.

"We keep some rotating exhibits down here, and some of the oldest, most valuable records. As you probably know, this was Whatcom County's first city hall. Built in 1892."

He unlocked a door and pulled the switch, sending the sputtering old fluorescents into active duty. One strobed for a few seconds before finally conking out.

Metal racks with legal boxes stacked to the ceiling lined the edges of the space. In the center, an empty oak library table. A pair of white gloves rested under the glow of a green-glass-shaded banker's lamp.

"No gloves needed," he said. "This isn't the Declaration of Independence. I'll get you the first two boxes."

"How many in total?"

"Two are the trial and two are Marnie Spellman specific."

"Can I help?"

"Got a cart. Just a minute, and I'll get you started."

After wheeling in the loaded cart, Tedd went back upstairs, and Lindsay started on the Marnie-centric boxes. Video tapes, newspaper clippings, magazines, pamphlets, even an early catalog of her products.

Bits and pieces of her life and philosophy emerged among the ephemera. Some things were easy to admire. As Lindsay had already discovered, she'd been a kind of holistic Martha Stewart of her day, maybe even a pre-Goop Gwyneth Paltrow.

"What do you think of our girl?"

It was Tedd, carrying two cups of coffee. A little more than an hour had passed.

"Marnie? It's hard to decide what to make of her," Lindsay said, taking the coffee. "I can see why people are so divided."

"Right. She's a love-her-or-hate-her kind of figure, that's for sure. The philosophy behind her products seemed pretty shallow to me. I understand about looking better to feel better, but she went off into woo-woo land."

"Seems so," Lindsay said. "This isn't the start of my deep dive into Marnie Spellman."

"Why?"

"Curious. Nothing concrete." She shrugged. "Weirdly compelling stuff."

She couldn't tell him any more even if she wanted to.

Tedd's days as a reporter were over. So, it seemed, was his penchant for sharp, invasive follow-up questions.

"Well, I have a reading copy of her autobiography. Some CDs, too. You can take them with you. The whole lot is a mix of self-help, science fiction, and a cookbook all rolled into her life story. Hard to find a signed first edition of her book. Saw one go for more than a grand on eBay. I'd file it under fiction, but that's me."

She thanked him for the coffee and the offer of the book and went back to the materials, taking photos of pages that she planned to read later.

Next she skimmed through the court records—transcripts, depositions, witness statements, letters on behalf of Reed Sullivan. It was a lot to take in, especially for a case that ended in an acquittal. It appeared that Marnie and/or her minions had engaged her fan base in a letter-writing campaign. One box contained more than a hundred such missives defending her and debasing Reed Sullivan. She wasn't even on trial, but—based on what some of Marnie's followers had written—the source of their outrage wasn't a belief that Reed was truly guilty.

It was that Marnie's name was being dragged through the mud by association.

She took pictures of the letters, including some that were still sealed in their original envelopes.

On her way out, Tedd gave her a copy of *The Insatiable Heart.*

"The DNA evidence was certainly problematic," she said, taking the book. "If he was away at camp, how did he put it there? And how in the hell could it have survived in the water, even if he'd managed it?"

Tedd went quiet for a moment. He looked at Lindsay, sizing her up and wondering if he should tell her what he'd never written yet always suspected.

"Planted," he finally said. "Of course. Had to be."

"Well, yeah. That was why he was cut loose, I presume. Who did the planting?"

"Look, I don't know. I don't get paid to speculate anymore. Hell, barely got paid for it then. And besides, it was twenty years ago," he said, his face turning a little pink. "We didn't know as much about DNA as we do now."

He was defensive and embarrassed.

Good. He should be. His article had fanned the flames of public opinion against an innocent man. But then again, he was working at the museum now. That was plenty penance for a man who wanted nothing more than the spotlight for himself.

"The only people who had access to the morgue were the cops and pathologists," he finally said. "They were all questioned in chambers, and the judge ruled the evidence admissible. It was a crock."

"Why didn't you write that? I didn't see it in any articles."

"Look," he said. "You don't burn sources in this town. If you do, you will be looking at a blank computer screen all day long."

CHAPTER 27

The reading copy of *The Insatiable Heart* Tedd McGraw provided beckoned Lindsay from the passenger seat of her car. She'd already skimmed it once, in the museum parking lot, with so many eye rolls that her pupils hurt, and yet she continued to find something oddly compelling about the mix of hokum and healing that Marnie promised her followers. The Spellman story was a strange blend of mystical and self-help, written at a time when the New Age movement was gaining converts. People were wearing pyramids. Gathering healing stones. Marnie Spellman's take, it appeared, was to grab a piece of that and then draw in the very real hopes and dreams of an entire generation of women who'd found themselves unable to get where they wanted to go.

The fantastical was the kind of thing that Lindsay rejected. It was who she was. She was raised in a casually religious home but always wished she'd believed as deeply as the rest of her family. She just couldn't get there. She loathed fantasy films in favor of documentaries and, of course, crime thrillers. She considered Muggles and magic and fantastic beasts far beyond the construct of reality.

Stupid. Ludicrous. And now, she wondered, if *dangerous* also applied.

Lindsay ordered a Dr Pepper and a burrito from the Taco Bell drive-through and pulled into a shady spot in the parking lot to eat. And she started to read.

Skeptics always ask me how is it that I think my way of healing body and soul could possibly be better than Western medicine. I point out to them the cases of those who no longer feel pain by way of acupuncture treatments. I tell them that if you are hurting right here, right now, would you allow me to stick a needle in your eye if I promised no more pain? If you hurt enough, then you would. Even though a needle piercing the eye has nothing to do with any remedy—Western or Eastern—you'd still allow it. Desperation makes people grasp at straws in order to find what is inside of them already.

Love is the only answer.

It is the only cure.

Years ago, when I worked as a nurse, I saw first-hand how the slightest improvement in a person's appearance affected their eventual outcome. One woman I was assigned to refused to get out of bed. She'd been in the hospital for a while, but she just wouldn't cross over that line that would have allowed us to set her free.

Yes, I view hospitals as prisons of a sort. More about that in another chapter.

I'd been working on my royal jelly face cream at that time, much to the chagrin and continued irritation of my charge nurse. I tried it out on patients who would give it a go, with marvelous and magical results. The patient who refused to get out of bed was a woman named Wendy, and she'd been in the hospital dealing with various health problems, most notably a perforated uterus. I told her about my cream and how I believed that beauty attracts possibilities, admiration. Even love. I told her that how others see us reflects a genuine energy in our direction. If you feel beautiful on the outside, you are bolstered. You are able to face the world and all that is in it. Not only that, you are stronger in your own beauty.

After all of that, she took the cream but didn't put it on. I asked for it back, and she declined. I was absolutely certain that she was going to turn me in, call the police, maybe even call the FDA. Instead, she started to cry. I will never, as long as I live, forget what she told me.

"There was a honeybee bouncing off my window today. Just bouncing up and down, and I watched it, and really, I thought it was watching me."

She stopped and looked down at the jar I'd given her.

"If there is something in there that will give me back what I've lost . . ."

"There is."

She twisted the lid, and I helped her apply the thinnest application.

If you are a believer and you know the power of her love for all of us, then you know what happened next. Wendy was healed. It's true. And if you don't believe, I doubt you ever will. The truth is that what was in that jar was the start of a journey for Wendy. It was also the beginning of a journey for me.

Lindsay finished the rest of the chapter. Wendy, the woman who used the cream, left the hospital the very next day. As Marnie saw it, this woman who'd lost herself had been reborn by virtue not of the cream but of the truth behind it. It was purportedly a pivotal moment in Marnie's life. As Lindsay saw it, though, the whole thing smacked of a fairy tale. It was the kind of story for which there was no basis in reality. She was a detective. There was no such thing as taking anything at face value.

And this memoir, she thought, was as farfetched as anything she'd ever read.

She picked up where she left off:

> *I quit nursing a few days after the encounter with Wendy. I had no choice. I knew very clearly that my time attending to one person at a time was a losing proposition. I had so much work to do. I had a vision that I just couldn't shake. In my mind's eye, I could clearly see that my hand—through hers, of course—could change the world. That the world desperately needed what I had created with her all-knowingness as my guide. The bee that had been rapping at Wendy's window wasn't a message to her but to me. It was what brought me back to Lummi Island. It was not only home; it was the place where everything started.*
>
> *It would also be the place where I would begin.*

Lindsay flipped to the photo section, eight pages of bright-white glossy paper with grainy black-and-white photographs from various stages of Marnie's life. A cute baby. A darling little girl. The farm on Lummi. The old barn before it was razed for the new one that served as production studio and packaging center. Pictures of her mother and father. Her brother posing on a hillside, pointing to where the swarm came for his sister. A group photo from her nursing days. Most of the photos were of Marnie with celebrities, including her number one, Dina Marlow. In some of those shots, they looked like the Doublemint twins.

Lindsay set down the book. She wished she could phone Alan just then, tell him what a load of bullshit this Marnie stuff was. He'd listen. He'd laugh. He'd agree.

At the same time, she couldn't deny that other women truly embraced what Marnie was teaching from the labels of all her products. *What she was selling.*

Was she the greatest saleswoman of all time, or was it possible she really did have something that no one had? That no one else dared to promise was possible.

Her message? It seemed to be that, though the modern world made such a show of promising women a seat at the table, paid such grand lip service to their ability to chart their own destiny, there was an obstacle that kept them locked just outside of their dreams.

And it wasn't men, Marnie suggested.

It was the women themselves.

They just didn't believe enough in themselves.

This notion lifted Lindsay's blood pressure—*That's right, blame the victims. Even* this *is our fault!* It also niggled at her, scratched like the neighbor's yowling Siamese at her door.

Why had she stayed with Jack so long after she knew he'd been having an affair with his secretary? What made her hang on to someone who'd done nothing but hurt her?

Why had she thought so little of herself?

Lacking answers and wanting nothing at all to do with these dark questions, she turned her investigator's light back on and found illuminated there her next task.

She needed to find out why all these true believers, these women of the Hive, were no longer in the fold.

Alan would offer up a lame one-liner: "Just why, Lindsay," she heard him say, "did they all buzz off?"

As if on cue, her phone buzzed. It was the university reporter Carl Flanders.

"Carl," she said, turning the ignition over and moving on to the roadway.

"Detective. I was hoping we could work together. You aren't returning my calls."

"I'm sorry," she said. "We're in the middle of a murder investigation, and we don't work with the press."

"Then you won't want to know what I just found out. I guess you'll have to read it tomorrow morning when it goes online."

"Fine," she said.

"I'm going to tell you, anyway. Sarah was working on some story about that bee lady on Lummi Island."

"How do you know that?"

"Anonymous sources. I checked 'em."

"I'll read the rest tomorrow. Goodbye, Carl."

He was only being helpful, she knew. Alan would insist he was being too helpful. They'd argue over that. He'd say that being overly interested in a case suggests involvement. She'd tell him that he was only a skinny kid journalist looking to make a name for himself.

She'd finish the conversation thinking that the life she chose only connected her with people who were either the criminal or the do-gooder whose motivations were truly about what they could get out of the experience. At least Carl was clear in his motivations.

Carl Flanders stayed hunched over his laptop. He'd hacked into Sarah's staff folder at the *Western Front*. It was password protected, and he'd worked every angle he could think of to open it. Called the help desk for the manufacturer. Told a computer science geek from Vancouver that he'd publish his science fiction in the paper. He clicked on a folder named "Marnie Spellman." Inside were pdfs of articles and links to YouTube videos and various bulletin boards.

He posted a short but *tantalizing* article—his word to other staff members later—on the *Front*'s website.

> Murdered WWU student Sarah Baker was working on an exposé related to Marnie Spellman, the Lummi Island woman who led a kind of women's empowerment movement back in the 1990s.
>
> "She never mentioned Marnie Spellman to me," said roommate Zoey Carmine. "She just told me that it was hush-hush and I'd find out about it later."
>
> Others in the journalism program confirmed that the story was about Spellman.
>
> "She told me it was explosive, that it would make some high-powered people very, very nervous," said Carl Flanders, editor.
>
> Calls to Spellman Farms went unreturned this evening.

CHAPTER 28

Lindsay kept sneaking in time for the damn book before forcing herself to put it away until after she'd finished her work at home that night. Even if she had someone to confide in—and since Alan was gone, she didn't—she wouldn't have told a soul about how weirdly drawn she was to Marnie Spellman's story.

This was beyond the fact that Marnie and Spellman Farms were central, she thought, to what had happened to both Calista Sullivan and Sarah Baker. She hadn't yet really begun to figure out how, but she felt certain Marnie was a bridge between the two cases and intended to keep pushing until the pieces fit. If anyone were to ask her about it, she would have copped to that. Would have laid out her reasons for believing it, justified without much effort her continued digging.

What she would never try to justify or even fully admit to anyone (even herself, frankly) was the way in which Marnie's ideas kept seeping into her thoughts, like the first tendrils of smoke curling under a door. Even while she told herself it was all nonsense, if not flatly offensive, the more time she spent with it, the more Lindsay found herself wanting whatever it was Marnie was selling.

If she'd had her wits about her, she might've known how perfectly primed she was to receive these messages, delivered in just this package. Her own barren personal life, her husband's humiliating betrayal, her partner's suicide—all of it had left her bereft and empty inside.

Marnie's concept of looking good outside as a means of making one feel better inside seemed hideous at first. Yet Lindsay knew that plastic surgeons, cosmetic dentists, and hair replacement purveyors made fortunes promoting the same point of view.

Lindsay was attractive, with big eyes and honey-blond hair that curled in high humidity. For work, she wore it up, caramel tendrils falling as they pleased. She wasn't vain. Neither was she blind to the fact that even now, in her depleted state, when she wore a nice outfit or did her hair in a certain way, she'd receive a spate of compliments. And that, in turn, would fuel an elation bordering on euphoria. It was ridiculous and probably sad, but it was undeniably a fact.

How powerful must that feeling be for the truly beautiful? For Marnie herself? Marnie was stunning. No one could say otherwise. In fact, of the two highest-profile members of the Hive, Marnie herself and the movie star Dina Marlow, Marnie was the more beautiful of the pair. Again and again, as Lindsay pored over online images of her (researching her case, she told herself), Lindsay marveled at her. Her beauty really was a light, a radiance that came from somewhere deep inside her.

How could she *not* have drawn people to her?

Lindsay wondered if in another time, she'd have followed Marnie, too.

Crazy, she told herself, but after folding up her laptop for the night, exhausted after scratching her way through the Sullivan file for the umpteenth time, she nonetheless found herself pouring a half glass of white wine and slumping into bed with *The Insatiable Heart.*

I knew everything was at stake as I checked myself in
the mirror in the greenroom of Home Buyers Club in

Hollywood, Florida. The makeup artist had overdone the White Rain. My hair was so stiff my head was bullet-proof. I put my fingertips to the dome that was now my hair and crossed my fingers that I wouldn't melt under the klieg lights of the set.

Five products, all honey and pollen based, were on the line. I was on the line. The producers had low expectations, telling me that I was there on a trial basis. I assumed that everyone who pitched a product had taken a seat in the same boat. A weak sell-through meant no return trip. The boat would sink.

The set was blindingly bright. It was as if there were five suns hovering inches away from the long white counter that a production assistant led me to. Another fussed with my hair; yet another adjusted the lighting.

"Remember to look at the host," someone said.

"Where is she?" I asked. I felt silly standing there, baking in the lights, wondering when the whirlwind they'd promised would materialize.

A second later, Connie Dryer, the top-selling host for beauty products, came at me in a wheelchair. I was completely stunned. I'd seen her show a hundred times. I had no idea she was unable to walk.

The production assistant pushing her stopped right in front of me, and Connie stood.

"The look on people's faces never gets old," she said with a cheeky grin. "The wheelchair is our clever way of getting me from one set to the next in record time. These heels"—she indicated six-inch spikes—"weren't made for running."

We chitchatted a moment. Connie said that I'd have fifteen minutes to make an impression and sell a quota— a figure the network bigwigs refused to disclose.

"No pressure," Connie said, again with a disarming but ultimately terrifying smile.

Before I knew it, more lights powered on, and Connie was telling her viewers about me.

"Marnie Spellman has created all-natural products that not only make you look luminous but make you feel great, too."

I wanted to tell her that anything would look luminous under the scorching wattage of the studio lights, but I didn't. Instead, I thanked Connie for the compliment and pivoted to the reason behind Spellman Farms' growing success.

"You know, Connie," I said while holding a bright-yellow jar of face cream to the camera, "the bees make all the difference."

"Bees?" she asked, as though she hadn't noticed my logo with the honeybee.

"That's right," I told her. "Bees not only pollinate the world's food source—without them, we'd all die—they also create honey, and the magical royal jelly."

She asked about royal jelly, and I told her how nurse bees secrete the protein-rich liquid to feed the larvae that will grow into queens. How the substance is so powerful—and, yes, magical—that it alone can turn an ordinary larva into a queen bee. While I was explaining everything, a videotape rolled on the screen. It featured beauty shots of my farm and the hives before going into the process for collecting the royal jelly from a hive.

Connie remarked that she'd heard "wonderful" things about the product and only started using it the day before the show.

"I'm getting results already," she said.

I made my move then. I knew that there were a million people out there who would kill for a single chance to be on the channel, but I was thinking beyond that. I thought about what to do to make sure that my one shot was watercooler-conversation material. I needed to do something that would move my brand away from the clutter of other natural products.

Luckily, I knew I had something few, if any, of those other million entrepreneurs had to offer. I talked about how Spellman Farms products can change your life.

"Look, beauty is only skin deep, Connie. What's inside is what makes a woman radiate confidence and power. But at this moment in time, beauty is what gets us into the conversation. Not always, but most dependably."

I turned and faced the camera.

"Ladies, you know that when you feel better about yourself, you are able to take that extra step, the step that moves you from being someone's possession to being someone's equal. At home. In the office."

Connie blinked a little. None of what I had said was on the card she held. I saw her looking for her next prompt.

I took my chance.

I removed a cotton ball from the display counter in front of me, dabbed it with mineral oil, and started to wipe off the makeup applied by the same woman who had oversprayed my hair.

The cotton turned color, the beige tone of the foundation.

I turned to the camera.

Even the cameraman looked around his viewfinder to see me as I was, not through a lens.

Connie was completely dumbfounded.

"Oh my," she said. "Your skin, Marnie . . . it's flawless."

"That's the real secret of Spellman Farms, Connie. Our products don't cover your face in a mask. They make your skin luminous, clear. They reveal it for what it is. A little lip color and a touch of mascara, and you are set."

Connie came closer, her fingertips nearly touching my face.

"This is truly remarkable."

"Royal jelly, bee pollen, and nature's herbs do what no man-made product can. Spellman Farms was founded on the principle that Mother Nature knows best, and we prove it each and every day, with each and every product."

Everything we had in inventory sold out that day. Probably within that very hour. It was hard to say because there was such a flurry of attention. Interest from outsiders can distract.

When the media picked up the story of the entrepreneur from Lummi Island, Washington, it wasn't about the products. Not really. It was about my belief that all women were entitled to live beautifully and free of the mask of conventional makeup. I was no longer leading a cosmetics company. I was the vanguard of a revolution.

When I look back on that time, I think about how many would come to depend on my support, embrace my mission. I go back to that time when women started lining up to work at Spellman Farms. No one did anything to make money. To be rich. To get attention. We were all there to help others find the way to be the very best they could be. We put a sign out at the ferry landing on the mainland that indicated all our jobs had been filled, yet they still came. They wanted to be close to me. Some

called me the queen bee of Spellman Farms, and in turn,
I would think of my closest allies as "the Hive."

Lindsay set the book on the nightstand. It was after one in the morning. Her brain had reached the Marnie saturation point for one night—but all too predictably, when she turned off the light, her investigative mind snapped on.

It was Marnie Spellman she thought of then, too. Or more accurately, her Hive. Whatever had happened to Calista, and perhaps later to Sarah, was known by those women.

As she drifted off to sleep, Lindsay shuffled through the mental afterimages of her interviews and research and wondered which of them would break from the group and tell her the truth.

Greta Swensen was still fresh in her mind. So engaging and open (or at least seemingly so) during their talk in her fantastic glass house. A hospital administrator after leaving the Hive, she was still a natural beauty. In her photos, she was a pretty young woman—reddish hair, freckles, and a gaze somehow both warm and cool at once.

Dina Marlow, the actress. She dyed her hair blond like her mentor/ guru, Marnie. In nearly every photo, she would turn slightly sideways, her arm hooked. Lindsay knew the Instagram-ready pose well. She wondered if Dina was the originator. Lindsay had left their interview feeling sad for Dina, who'd fallen from the top with no safety net.

Heather Jarred, a tall, impressive brunette with dark eyes and a slight overbite, was a stunner, too. All the women who surrounded Marnie were lovely—though not as lovely as she. By design, no doubt. She was Beyoncé, choosing backup dancers who added to yet never dared distract from her. Heather certainly hadn't hidden herself away after the Hive, though: she'd gone into politics and prospered. A two-term congresswoman from Western Washington, now running for the US Senate. Lindsay had phoned the congresswoman's office but was told that her schedule was on overload.

"Maybe after the election?" the young woman who answered said.

And Greta. Tough. Smart. Lindsay could see why Dina and Greta would pit themselves as rivals. Dina had Hollywood clout, but Greta had the business sense that was sorely needed to keep the enterprise going. Especially after the home shopping debacle.

And then there was the elusive Trish Appleton. She was an apparition, it seemed.

She testified at trial and then was gone. No trace in any of the police databases, court records, or even a hit at the DMV.

She thought how Alan would pipe up just then to remind her that it's hard work to truly vanish. She could hear him: "If you want to stay gone, all you have to do is change your social security number, change your name, and never tell anyone why you're on the run. Good luck."

Forget all the tools of law enforcement. Lindsay went to Google and searched on the Internet.

Bingo.

She immediately found a tiny mention, a news item in a weekly newspaper in Omak, Washington. Three months after the Sullivan trial, Trish Appleton, twenty-seven, was killed in a boating accident on Lake Okanagan. A man on the shore saw the boat flip. Her body wasn't found until two weeks later.

Scratch Trish, the second member of the Hive to die.

The way Lindsay began to see it, Marnie was not just the leader, the queen bee, but also a member of this collective of the beautiful and brilliant. Counting Calista, that meant the Hive had once had six members.

And then five.

Lindsay would work her way up to the queen. First, she thought she'd seek out the queen mother.

After all, who would know more about her?

CHAPTER 29

The last time Kate Spellman saw her daughter was a few weeks before Detective Lindsay Jackman appeared outside her motor home. Kate had taken her Winnebago on the ferry to Lummi early one morning. She'd thought that enough time had passed that there might be a chance at reconciliation. At least that was the hope. Ten years was a long time, wasn't it?

She also brought a serious concern with her.

Kate parked by the barn, in the spot where she always did. Or had, anyway. It felt so strange, so sad, to be back on what still felt like her own farm.

She found Marnie outside with her hives. She was older now. They both were.

Marnie didn't say hello when she saw her mother. "What are you doing here?" is what she said instead, her eyes grazing over Kate, no doubt taking in the lines on her face, her graying hair, the stoop of her shoulders.

Kate also sized up her daughter's appearance. Behind Marnie's ears were thin white lines, a telltale marker of a face-lift. She knew her daughter gave herself bee venom injections, and rumors from haters hinted that she had just enough fillers to keep the sagginess at bay.

Even so, she looked as lovely as she did the day *Smithsonian* took her photo out in the honey orchard.

Kate recalled the fallout from her daughter's remarks on the shopping channel in the late 1990s. Kate was there the week the world turned its back on her. A week after the debacle, Kate watched Marnie take a sledgehammer to hive number one, smashing the honeycomb and bees into a writhing amber goo. It was a frightening display of unbridled rage. It came from some dark place deep inside, and it came with a force that Kate hadn't seen come from her daughter before.

Kate was unsure what daughter she'd find today. The one who preached helping others, or the one who'd condemn any enemy. Perceived or genuine.

"What do you want, Mother?" Marnie asked.

"I came to see you, honey."

"You saw me. Now go. Take that hideous shack on wheels with you."

It was *that* Marnie. The one who suffered no one.

Marnie went about what she'd been doing, acting as if her mother were an annoying fly to be swatted away. Kate followed her into the dressing room, where Marnie put on her beekeeping suit.

"Make yourself useful for once, Mom. Bring the smoker."

Kate picked up the tin smoker and followed her daughter into the apiary, or honey orchard, as Marnie preferred to call it. She handed Marnie the smoker and watched as she unlatched and swung open the door to hive number two. She let the smoke down like a wispy white blanket.

Marnie took off her mask, stood still, and let the bees buzz past her face. As Kate looked on, her daughter's demeanor changed. Her face, just a moment before hard and angry, had softened. Now it glowed. Joy. Elation. Tears streamed down her face.

Kate's heart raced, and her eyes softened with concern.

"Are you all right?"

Marnie gave a start. She'd forgotten her mother was there and was not happy to be reminded of that fact. Instantly, her euphoria was gone. "I'm fine, Mom," she said. "I'll be even better when you leave."

"I'm here to try to fix things, Marnie."

This elicited a harsh laugh from Marnie. "Really? That's pretty funny, Mom."

"I love you."

"Now that's *really* funny. You only loved Casey, and you know it. I was competition for Dad's attention, too. You hated that. Now Casey's gone. Dad's gone. And we have nothing other than biology between us."

"But we do have more, a deeper connection. I'm here to help you. Something's going on."

"What?"

"A girl came around asking about you."

Marnie set down the smoker. "So? A fan. I have millions of them."

Kate seriously doubted that number, but Marnie always had a flair for the grandiose. Kate also knew that to challenge Marnie on such things was to come up on the losing end of an argument.

"I know," Kate said. "She wasn't just a fan. This girl was a reporter. She was asking about the Hive."

Kate waited, but Marnie said nothing.

"She was asking about Calista, Marnie."

"What did you tell her, Mom?"

"Nothing."

"You promised that you'd keep your lips zipped. Our confidentiality agreement requires that."

"I didn't say anything."

"I want you to go now."

"I want us to start over, honey."

Marnie looked at Kate with a cold stare. "Fuck off, Mom. And don't ever come back."

"Don't talk that way, Marnie."

Kate stepped back as Marnie let the wind carry a veil of smoke over rows and rows of hives. Nearly a graveyard now, Kate thought, the honey orchard looked like a smaller version of the Arlington National Cemetery.

She watched Marnie take it all in as the hazy sun moved slowly overhead. A hummingbird brushed by Marnie's face. A sign. Always a sign. Marnie's fingertips lingered over the Spellman Farms logo embroidered over her breast. She stood motionless.

"You are my daughter," Kate said. "I want to be in your life."

"I don't need you. Want you. Or care about you. I can handle any reporter on my own." With that, Marnie walked away, without so much as a backward glance.

Her pleas futile, Kate felt sick to her stomach, bereft. Marnie would never let her back into her life. Kate's thoughts pivoted toward anger. She wanted to yell after her, tell her off. Remind her that Kate had fueled her interest in herbs, honey, bee pollen. It was she who'd made the first products to sell from the hives—beeswax candles. She ached to tell her she was an ungrateful brat and always had been.

She didn't, though.

Persuading her daughter was a losing proposition. Marnie is as Marnie does. That had been true since she was a little girl.

Her heart still pumping and her hands shaking from the encounter, Kate didn't cry. She wasn't much of a crier. Maybe it was because she'd already cried all those years ago and there was nothing left anymore. She wondered once again how it was that this place, this life that she'd loved, had been erased so completely.

Instead of going straight to her motor home, Kate decided to take one last look in the house.

The bones of the old farmhouse were barely evident. The interior—including a massive addition in the back—now spoke of money and good, albeit bland, taste. *Understated*, at least for her daughter's generally grand sense of style, was the word that came to Kate's mind as she took in each room. The kitchen was a pristine white, with a gleaming island that seemed large enough to skate on. Only the knobs hinted at the owner's interests—black in a hexagon shape, suggesting the form of a honeycomb. Two white leather sofas faced each other over a glass coffee table that reflected an enormous Chihuly chandelier in the living room.

Above the fireplace was a Picasso, a blue figure of a woman. It was Marnie's first purchase when big money started rolling into her burgeoning empire. Kate loved the painting, but at the same time, her daughter's purchase surprised her. She had asked Marnie about it when it was delivered by armed guard.

"I didn't know you were a fan, Marnie."

Marnie gave her mother a side-eye at the time. "I'm not. I bought it because it matches the couch."

The new couches, however, were white, and their accent pillows, yellow. No more blue.

Her heart rate accelerating, Kate visited each room as quickly as she could, taking everything all in for what she was sure would be the last time. Each chamber was a vignette out of *Architectural Digest*. She marveled at what her daughter had accumulated over the years since her banishment. Beautiful antiques. Gilded wallpaper. A tapestry of an ancient hive that had to be four hundred years old. Possibly older.

Marnie had surrounded herself with the best money could buy.

Money that had come from followers and their now-empty bank accounts.

Not bad for an ambitious girl who deigned to match a Picasso with a sofa, Kate thought.

It was as if her daughter had been trying to blend into a beautiful environment, like a chameleon. Trying to hide among the hibiscus before attacking the fly with a flick of a long, sticky tongue.

Kate poked her head into the cavernous master bedroom. The huge antique bed—Marie Antoinette's?—with its eight-hundred-thread-count sheets was unmade. She ran her fingers over rows of designer clothes, many still with tags dangling, in a showroom closet.

She has everything and values none of it, Kate thought. *How did I raise a girl like that?*

Next, she swung open the door to Marnie's childhood bedroom.

At first, it seemed untouched in the way that some moms never change a thing when a child goes missing. Kate stood still, scanning the room. Something wasn't right. It wasn't the same. It had been styled to reflect a better version of what it had been when Marnie was a girl. Dolls on a shelf were beautiful antiques, not the grimy Raggedy Ann and Andy that Marnie dragged around the farm. A mural of bees and butterflies had replaced vining rose wallpaper. Marnie's original pineapple poster bed, a vintage chenille spread in lavender layered over it, fit snuggly into a corner near the window.

That window.

It was the only one in the house that had not been replaced, repainted, or even washed. It was as it had always been, except for the addition of a yellow velvet rope, a barrier from the rest of the space.

Kate moved closer to read a small engraved brass plaque that hung under the sash.

THE BEES FIRST CONTACTED MARNIE SPELLMAN THROUGH THIS WINDOW. IT WAS THE BEGINNING OF A CONNECTION BETWEEN WOMANKIND AND NATURE THAT WOULD CHANGE THE WORLD.

Kate had seen enough. She'd believed in the swarm. She'd thought her daughter was given a great gift, but this? The room was all about ego, a phony shrine designed to bolster her story.

Kate's curiosity turned to bitterness.

Had she been scammed, too?

She hurried from the bedroom and made her way back to the living room. The Picasso beckoned. Without a bit of hesitation, she found herself taking it from the wall. She didn't have accent pillows to match in her RV, but she figured her daughter would barely notice.

And when she did, she'd never come after it.

As she turned the ignition on the Minnie Winnie, Kate took a quick look at the painting, now in the passenger seat. She couldn't believe that she took it. Or determine exactly why she had. It was worth millions.

Pulling out of the driveway, she caught a glimpse of Marnie standing by the front porch, a hard stare fixed on her face.

One thought floated above all that was running through Kate's mind.

Marnie hadn't asked the name of the reporter who had been poking around her past.

The RV followed the road to the ferry landing, past the spot where Calista's body had been found by the beachcombers.

Marnie hadn't asked for Sarah Baker's name because she already knew it.

Chapter 30

Friday, September 20, 2019
Alger, Washington

Lindsay drove south on I-5 to a campground just outside of Alger, a speck of a place off the highway in Skagit County, not far from the cabin her family owned at Lake Samish. Marnie's mother, Kate Spellman, had been living there while working for a chain of camping resorts designed for the RVing set—those who mistakenly thought a one-hundred-thousand-dollar motor home was a smart way to save money on hotels and dining out. For the female half of most couples, Lindsay had heard from too many sources, the RV life was hardly a vacation. They had to cook with mini appliances and clean tables that morphed into beds. The men mostly sat around and drank beer and poked at campfires with sticks they'd whittled to spear a marshmallow or hot dog.

Even as Lindsay pulled onto the shoulder before space number one, she knew she was looking at Marnie's mother. Kate Spellman had the same high cheekbones and beautiful features as her famous daughter.

She waited as Kate directed a couple towing a trailer to their campsite. "Just turn right at the second curve; you'll find your spot in the middle of the loop. It's a pull-through, so you shouldn't have any problems." The new Airstream reminded Lindsay of the lunch box that her father used to take to work at the paper mill.

As Lindsay stepped out of her SUV, Kate turned around and fixed her eyes on her. "You don't look like a camper."

"I'm not," Lindsay said, approaching. "I'm a detective with the Ferndale Police Department. I'm investigating a death."

"No deaths here. Some rowdy campers from Marysville that I'd lose no tears over. That comes with the territory."

"I'm looking into the death of Sarah Baker."

Kate reviewed the contents of her clipboard. "No Bakers here," she said, looking up.

"I'm here to talk to *you*."

"Me? I don't know anything about any death. I've never heard the name in my life."

Kate stepped closer. Her hair was a silky gray, her eyes faded blue. Her back was very slightly stooped, and she worked hard to hold her head up. She wore brown pants, black boots, and a chambray shirt with her first name and "Camp Host" stitched on the pocket. A gold chain fit snugly in the soft folds of her neck. Again, Lindsay was struck by what an accurate—albeit older, more weathered—replica she was of her famous daughter.

"I'm here because the death, a homicide, is similar to a death on Lummi you might know something about," Lindsay said. "You were interviewed by the tribal police at the time."

A look of recognition came to Kate's face.

"Calista," she said. "Years ago. Nice girl. Terrible what happened. I figured the husband for her murderer. I guess I was wrong. Police exonerated him."

"Can we go somewhere to talk, Ms. Spellman?"

"Kate. I don't mention my last name. Too many of the curious still around here. Anyway, I'm pretty busy. Three trailers and four motor homes are due in on the schedule. And I've got to check the restrooms."

Lindsay regarded the rows of mostly vacant campsites. "It doesn't seem that busy right now."

"Not at the moment," Kate said. "But trust me, they all caravan in at once after school starts. Not planned, mind you, just the way it seems to work out."

"I'll go with you. We can talk on the way."

"Suit yourself."

Lindsay followed Kate, who by anyone's estimation was a very fast walker. Campers waved and called over to her, inviting her to coffee or to play cards that night.

"This is really about my daughter, isn't it?" she asked, looking at the gravel road. Her voice was low.

"Yes."

"Do me a favor, Detective, don't tell anyone here who I am or, really, who she is. I don't want any trouble. I've been here awhile, and I like it. I don't want any of her disgruntled followers to track me down. I had a nice place up in Blaine. Ran a little gift shop that sold Marnie's beeswax candles. One day, a woman comes in and makes a big scene. Says that I ought to be in prison for what my daughter did to her mother and the like. I didn't fight back. I didn't really blame her. Stopped using my last name. Go by my maiden name now. Stratton."

"That must be difficult."

"Difficult is having two children you never get to speak to, for one reason or another. *That's* difficult. Well, to be honest, one I don't mind that she doesn't talk to me. I pine for my son, however. Always will. I failed him. I know it."

"How did you fail him?"

"You're not here to talk about Casey. Why would you be? He's dead. You're here about Calista and what happened on the island."

"You brought him up."

"My mistake, then." Kate opened the door to the women's restroom. The place was small, two showers and two toilet stalls. Lindsay watched while Kate made a face and flushed a toilet by pressing the lever with the tip of her boot.

"People are pigs," Lindsay said, trying to find common ground.

"Sometimes it does seem that way," Kate said, nodding. "Wait until you see the men's lav. Ten times worse."

Kate put her initials on the card taped to the inside of the door. She also noted the time.

Lindsay watched over her shoulder. "You keep quite a strict schedule."

"How's that?"

"You are here at a quarter past all day long."

"Time is important. So is commitment. Can't live properly without managing both."

Lindsay didn't say a word. The sentiment was the same as one expressed by Marnie in *The Insatiable Heart*. They went to the other side, the men's. Kate was right: It was worse. Apart from the hygiene issues on display, which Kate made brisk work of cleaning up with materials drawn from a locked janitorial closet, vulgar graffiti decorated the space above the trio of urinals.

Kate saw her looking at it and shook her head. "These guys are all on Viagra and think they are hot stuff. Sowing their droopy wild oats in my campground turns my stomach."

Kate washed up, noted the time, and initialed the card. "Maintenance will take care of the graffiti before I get back here."

Lindsay motioned to a picnic table next to a slow-moving creek. "Can we sit for a minute?"

"A minute. Really, I can't help. I tried to get Marnie out of one mess after another when she was growing up, but she found a way to mischief. Her dad said that's what made her special. He always took her side over me and Casey. It was the two of them against us."

"Special?" Lindsay asked. "Like the swarm?"

Kate fastened her eyes on Lindsay's. "Right. The swarm. It changed her. It changed all of us. That's God's truth."

Lindsay had read about the swarm in *The Insatiable Heart*. It was fantastic, scary, and about as believable as a 1970s disaster movie.

"You didn't see it happen, did you?" she asked.

"I'm not really comfortable talking to you about this. Besides, it has nothing to do with Calista."

"Are you sure?"

"Yes."

Lindsay persisted. "Please. We have two dead women. Families who need answers."

"Talking to anyone never did me any good. But fine. I'll talk. Come back to my motor home. We can talk privately there. You said two women?"

"A college student, Sarah Baker, was found murdered up at Maple Falls. She was a reporter for the campus paper working on a story, we think, about Marnie and Calista."

"Can't help you with the college kid. Never heard of her."

Tucked in behind an especially gnarly madrona, Kate's motor home had subtle and not-so-subtle nods to her life prior to the one that had her checking campground bathrooms and organizing abandoned camping gear. It was a Minnie Winnie, older model, though immaculately maintained. The dining table had been modified with a wood top, rather than the standard Formica. Along the large window was a row of herbs in terra-cotta pots. When Lindsay sat down, her elbow brushed against the mint plant, releasing the essential oils and filling the space with a pleasant freshness.

On the wall opposite the dining table was a small abstract painting.

Lindsay craned her neck. A Picasso. Really a remarkable reproduction.

"Picasso, all right," Kate said. "Real deal. I took it from my daughter the last time I saw her. She only purchased it to spite me, anyway. I'm sure she reported it stolen and pocketed the insurance money. That's just like her. Sometimes I wonder if money is her sole driver."

"Aren't you afraid someone will steal it?" Lindsay asked.

Kate slid into the seat across from Lindsay.

"Are you kidding? The crowd that comes here is more Thomas Kinkade than Picasso. I'll tell you about that day of the swarm. And after that, I'll have a question for you, Detective."

CHAPTER 31

Kate and Johnny Spellman had been away all day when their lives and their children's lives were rewritten by the incomprehensible. They'd been to Bellingham to scope new restaurants for their organic produce and, of course, their honey. The bees had been spectacularly productive that year. In truth, there was no way they could sell the entirety of the harvest to their existing accounts. Honey, especially organic honey, hadn't found its way into the cupboards and pantries of the average person at that time. It was a specialty item, which meant the price could be higher, limiting sales. With her son and daughter by her side, Kate had been experimenting with different uses for the honey. She'd produced beeswax candles, soaps milled with honey, and had even created a hand cream.

When she and her husband drove off the *Whatcom Chief*, one of the farmhands stood by the ferry dock, waving frantically to get their attention.

"What is it?" Kate asked from the passenger window.

"Marnie is okay" were the first words out of his mouth.

The hair on the back of her neck lifted.

"What happened?"

"She got stung. She's fine now. Got a doctor from the Wildwood Inn. A good doctor."

"Hop in, Mickey," Johnny said.

Johnny floored the gas pedal, and the Spellmans' car, tires squealing, sped along the road skirting the beach, which was littered with driftwood.

"Brother's okay," Mickey said. "Saw it happen."

"Saw what happen, Mickey?" Johnny asked.

"A swarm. I've never heard anything like it. A swarm, Mr. Spellman. A swarm picked her up. It lifted her. Carried her. Brother saw it all. It was like the hand of God lifted her."

Marnie lay in a bed surrounded by white ruffles and a collection of plush animals. Her brother sat in the corner, silent and frozen.

The girl's eyes were clamped shut.

Kate leaned over her daughter. "Marnie," she whispered. "Momma's here."

No response.

Kate looked at Johnny. She wanted to speak. Nothing came out. She looked back down at Marnie, and a tear slipped down her face and landed on her daughter's cheek.

Marnie's eyes opened.

"I knew you'd be all right."

Marnie nodded.

"Casey says you were caught in a swarm," her father said.

She nodded a second time.

Kate was on her knees, smoothing the light coverlet on her daughter. "How do you feel?" She brushed her hand gently over her daughter's forehead. "You feel warm."

"I'm fine, Momma."

Hearing her speak these words so calmly and clearly was a confirmation of that.

God had saved her.

Her father spoke. "The hives will be burned tomorrow morning."

Marnie pulled herself into an upright position and started to cry. "Daddy, you can't do that."

"Honey, they attacked you."

"They didn't."

"Casey says they did. Mickey says so, too."

"Daddy, please leave the hives alone. The bees didn't hurt me."

Kate pulled back the sleeve of her daughter's nightgown.

She looked at her husband. Her mouth hung open.

"What is it, Kate?"

"She wasn't stung."

"I was, Momma, but only a few times. It was my fault. The swarm told me to be still."

Friday, September 20, 2019

Kate was eyeing Lindsay, nodding.

"That's right. The swarm *talked* to her," she said. "That's what she told me, and I believed her. Still do, though sometimes that varies day by day." She leaned back in her seat. "I know what you're thinking. Everyone does. That I'm an idiot hick and that I ought to have my head examined. That's what you're thinking, isn't it?"

"It's a lot to take in," Lindsay allowed. "A lot to believe."

Kate waved through the window at a camper walking a schnauzer in an unneeded raincoat.

"Look," she went on, "like I said, I wasn't there. I didn't see it. I want you to know more than anything I believed it to be true. Believing is enough to make it true."

Another one of Marnie's riffs.

"I can't quite get there with you, Kate. But that's okay. You said you had a question for me when you were done. What is it?"

"Not just yet. I'll need to tell you a bit more."

Kate had been happily playing nurse to her daughter all day. Marnie seemed fine and, truth be told, probably didn't need to convalesce. However, the doctor from the Wildwood Inn had returned to the farm and told them that she should stay in bed, so that's where she was.

"Rest is the only treatment here. Fluids, too. She's fine physically, although obviously there is an emotional issue here," he said.

From the kitchen window, Kate watched her husband and son walk the rows of lavender, close to harvest, but not quite ready. She could smell the perfume of the spikey blossoms even inside the house. Fussing over increasing their profits by selling to more restaurants seemed so foolish at that moment. So completely distant and unnecessary. Home was what mattered. She reveled in the heady scent and poured herself a cup of tea. A golden orb of honey slipped slowly from her spoon and landed in the teacup. She swirled it into the tea, her own blend of peppermint and spearmint.

She added another ingredient to the brew, never telling anyone what it was.

"The unknown," she had told her daughter one time, "is a powerful motivator. People will either avoid or gravitate toward things they don't understand."

The thought of the conversation made her smile.

As her husband and son disappeared from view, she scanned the property in the direction of the hives. There were twenty of them. They had been placed in structured, neat rows. It passed through Kate's mind, not for the first time, that they looked like headstones at a military cemetery.

Crisp.

Organized.

Attention!

The tea was sweet, the way she liked it.

She heard Marnie call out. It wasn't an urgent call—not a scream—but it startled her so that she dropped her cup, which shattered on the floor. Without bothering to pick up the broken pieces, she hurried to the bedroom.

The room was dark, which was odd. It was a sunny day. Kate had been in the room only a moment earlier. Ten minutes at most.

"Momma, the window."

She turned to look, and let out a scream.

Friday, September 20, 2019

Kate stopped telling her story, and Lindsay watched her get up and then sit back down. She held on to the edges of the redwood tabletop. The veins on her hands pulsed perceptibly. The color had left her face. She was as pale as the bark of the alders that crowded the space around them, letting only slivers of light fall onto the damp campground.

"What did you see, Kate?" Lindsay asked. "What was going on outside?"

"I couldn't see anything. Not a thing. Not at first. It was like my mind couldn't make sense of it."

"What did you see?"

Kate's eyes bored into Lindsay's.

"The swarm," she said. "It had massed over Marnie's window, like a moving curtain. I could actually feel the vibration coming from it. It was like the bass turned on full in some kid's car. You know, when you're stuck at a traffic light and then you feel the thump? It was like that, but a buzzing. The sound was fascinating, mesmerizing. Calming. Scary. It was everything all rolled into one. Even after all these years, I have never heard anything exactly like it. And though it didn't—"

Kate stopped, gathered herself.

"This is the hard part, the part that I have never really told anyone other than my daughter."

"What was it?"

She let the question loiter for a beat.

"It was like the buzzing noise—you're going to think I'm crazy—the buzzing noise was talking to me. Not in words. Not specifics. I just felt that it was telling me that everything was going to be fine, that my daughter was fine."

A breeze blew through the old madrona just then, sending a flurry of yellow and green leaves to the picnic table outside.

"No words," Kate repeated. "It was just a feeling. There was something about that swarm that seemed—and I'm sure you could never understand—that it was not from this Earth. That it was telling me that Marnie was special."

"All children are," Lindsay said.

"Of course. But not all children lead. Most follow, and that's what the swarm told me. That she was beyond what I was, beyond what our family had expected her to be."

"Blessed?"

"Yes . . . blessed. Then you understand after all," she said.

Lindsay wasn't sure what to say, how to encourage this woman and get at the truth at the same time. She didn't understand anything. Not really. Kate Spellman gave off such a no-nonsense vibe. She was a pragmatic woman who had organized her daughter's hives at the farm, kept up with the lavatory checklists at the campground. She hadn't heard the swarm speak . . . she'd felt it. And she'd seen the swarm blacken her daughter's window, felt it rumble like a gangbanger's ride.

"I don't know," Lindsay finally said. "I want to. But mainly I want to do my job. And that's going to start with understanding why Calista ended up on a beach dead twenty years ago. I want to understand a feeling *I* have. I want to know why Sarah's death at Maple Falls seems to be a bridge to Calista and that time."

"Let's get to that," Kate said, getting up and offering an iced tea, which Lindsay declined, "after you answer my question first."

"Yes, your question. What is it?"

"Are you a believer?"

"In God? Yes. Raised in the church."

"Not God. My daughter?"

"Like I said, even if I might want to . . . no. Not at all."

"But you're interested in her. Let's be direct. You're following a case from two decades ago and digging into my daughter's life. Is it interest in her? A fascination?"

Lindsay shook her head emphatically. "No. Not a fascination. Just follow-up on a case that was never fully resolved."

"All right," Kate said. "If you say so."

"That's right. I do."

"In any case, I can't help you. I don't know anything about any murder. What I do know is my daughter had nothing to do with it."

"Yet you and your daughter are estranged. How can you be so sure? Why would you defend her?"

"Because I have a knowing inside of me, Detective. People who are without that knowing are servants to the whims of fate. I know my purpose. I have lived a life that I own completely."

"Your daughter lives on an estate. And you—"

"I live in a Winnebago."

A feeling of awkwardness hung in the air between them.

"I'm sorry. That was mean."

"You're not sorry. You're just doing your job. I understand, and whatever you say can't hurt me. If you think that someone associated with my daughter's movement is a party to murder, then I hope you find the perpetrator. God would want that. She appreciates both love and justice."

Kate's words were an echo of her daughter's theology. How could this seemingly pragmatic woman embrace those concepts? Lindsay couldn't fathom it.

She switched gears. "Did you tell your husband about the swarm and what you saw . . . what you felt?"

That stopped Kate. She regarded Lindsay with interest, maybe respect. "No, Detective. I didn't."

"Why not?"

"The same reason I probably shouldn't have told you. You don't believe me because you're just like him."

"And how's that?"

"You're a skeptic, Detective Jackman. That's probably why you have chosen this path in life. That's fine. You'll learn. And maybe next time we meet, if we do, it will be on another plane where we share equal footing and equal knowing."

"Fine. Then tell me about Spellman Farms. It is a bit of a mystery."

"It's supposed to be. That's the way she likes it."

"'Supposed to be'?"

Kate averted her gaze. "I've said too much already," she said. "I think you should go now."

With that Marnie's mother stood and escorted Lindsay out of the motor home and to her car.

"Are you sure you can't help me?" Lindsay asked.

"If you keep looking into things that are dead and buried like Calista Sullivan, you'll find yourself in bad company."

Kate watched Lindsay drive away and returned to her motor home. In the junk drawer next to the tiny stove, she retrieved a scrap of paper with a phone number and Sarah Baker's name. She wadded it up and tossed it into the trash.

CHAPTER 32

On the way back from Marnie's mother's campground, Lindsay slotted one of the CDs Tedd McGraw had given her into the SUV's player. It was one of Marnie Spellman's first recordings. Her voice filled the vehicle with a kind of sweet, tremulous timbre that made each word feel intimate, authentic. There was no TV preacher shouting to get the point across. Just a woman telling an amazing story.

> *The swarm and the time God healed my brother's burns with Her loving hand are well documented and, indeed, witnessed by others. Even with that kind of unyielding corroboration, I have been the target of vicious attacks in the media.*

Interesting, Lindsay thought, thinking of what she'd say to Alan if she could.

"Most of the people who could corroborate any of her claims about the swarm are dead," she'd say.

"Dead men tell no tales," he'd say.

Or something like that.

So even as I sit here, classical music playing softly in the background and a view of the Salish Sea in my gaze, I have no fears in telling you something that I have never talked about outside of my very close circle of friends, the girls who make up what I call the Hive.

It is the reason I have never married, nor have I ever let a man dominate me in life or in bed.

I was nineteen and in college when the swarm materialized for the second time. It was impossible, yes, but in my heart, I just knew it was the same group of bees that had lifted me to the sky. This time we weren't outside but in, of all places, a bathroom in a college library. Even more striking, it was late at night, when bees are not active.

Again, no one else was there! *Smart,* Lindsay thought. Her everyday details made the story seem authentic.

It was a few minutes before closing time, and I had made a quick trip to the restroom. I was completely alone in there, doing what must be done after drinking tea all evening as I prepared for an exam the next day. As I sat there, I heard a buzzing noise, and my attention went directly to the fluorescent tubes that hung over the space. One was acting up, flickering. Not quite off, yet not truly on, either. When I finished, I noticed that the sound wasn't coming from the lights but from the stall next to me. I bent down and saw no feet.

Yet the buzzing grew louder.

I flushed and found myself going to the second stall. I pushed the door open and was immediately confronted by the swarm. The same one. I was certain. I stood there watching as the mass of honeybees morphed from one shape into another. It was an undulating movie. Some were imagery from my life. My father. The garden. The farm. The swarm didn't speak in the way we speak, of course, but the bees were talking to me about my life. Not only about the past, about the future, too. The swarm morphed into a cylinder that I recognized as the shape of a face cream my mother had used. As it moved, it showed me that it was my destiny to bring hope, beauty, and prosperity to the women of the world. Although I belong to no organized religion, I have never doubted God's hand. In that bathroom stall, she had come to me once more, showing me that my purpose was by her design.

She was shrewdly, cunningly mixing nature and religion, binding them together as a single force. And careful to use the female pronoun for God, amplifying her message of female empowerment.

I stood there. Frozen in a way. I didn't move an inch, because I didn't want to. I was transfixed. I was a sponge and the bees were dousing me with holy water. One by one, they formed a chain and started for what I noticed for the first time was an open window. Hundreds of scouts whisked themselves away into the night sky. In less than a minute's time, only six remained.

Five bees formed a circle around the queen. She dominated them all in size and beauty. Her wings were iridescent, even in the flat light of the fluorescent tubes. I was mesmerized. It wasn't that I heard her say actual words to me. I wish I could tell you that she did. I can only say that I felt a feeling coming from her. The feeling made my eyes flood, and I started to cry. It was a rush of emotion, both joy and sorrow. My knees buckled, and I held on to the doorway so I wouldn't fall.

Lindsay reversed the CD to the lines she was looking for: *Five bees formed a circle around the queen. She dominated them all in size and beauty.*

Marnie saw herself as the queen, of course. There were five bees to protect her. Five to do her bidding?

CHAPTER 33

Lindsay interrupted Patty Sharpe with a call that afternoon. The lieutenant confirmed that the state insurance policy covered Alan's suicide, a question Patty had asked after the memorial.

"Lieutenant Madison wanted me to let you know that the death benefit has been processed."

"Thanks, Lindsay," Patty said. "I'm glad you called. Need a bit of good news. Going through Alan's things now. Just killing me."

"Can I help you in any way?" Lindsay asked.

"No. Not really. Just need some time to process."

"Can I call you later? Maybe stop by?"

"That would be nice," Patty said.

Lindsay hung up and looked over at Alan's empty desk through the doorway. For a second, she imagined his laugh, the sound of the chair as it rolled across the linoleum floor. His quick take on things—right or wrong.

God, how she missed him.

Patty went about the business of organizing her husband's clothing into two categories: what she thought could be dropped off at Goodwill and what should be disposed of in the trash. She had high standards. She didn't want to give away anything of Alan's unless it was perfect. He deserved respect.

She listened to an oldies radio station as she went about the business of disassembling Alan's life. Sometimes the music reminded her of her husband and their life together in the way that only music can. A Linda Ronstadt song took her back to a vacation they'd taken when Paul was four, to Cannon Beach, Oregon. They'd rented an old, musty beachside cabin, eaten hot dogs, had s'mores, and walked the wide, sandy beach past Haystack Rock every morning and early evening.

She closed her eyes to halt the tears.

They'd been so happy then.

They'd been free of all the things that had weighed them down. She still worked at the hospital at that time with a reduced schedule. He'd moved from a small five-person police department on the reservation to a new job, promoted to lieutenant—one of the youngest in the history of the Ferndale Police Department. Not long after that, he moved into the detective ranks, which consisted of only two people at the time.

And yet, as good as their life had been, and despite being blessed with a son, Alan fought through the high walls of depression that surrounded him over the years. Sometimes when he was silent, Patty knew he was thinking about things that haunted him. He'd been a hero. He'd done what had to be done. To be sure, those same things haunted her, too. Yet not in the same way. Sometimes it made her wonder why it was that her husband, who fought real monsters on the job, couldn't vanquish the ones that inhabited his memory.

Like she did.

After sorting through his clothes, Patty went to work on Alan's desk. First, the little things that were reminders of life and work events that held meaning only for the owner. A framed black-and-white photograph of the family. Paul was seven in the photo taken by a stranger at Six Flags in Southern California. He wore a pirate hat and was making a silly face. His parents were young and full of joy at the moment a woman snapped the image for them on Patty's old Hasselblad. Patty remembered how, before printing them, she'd pored through the negatives, looking for the perfect reminder of a time she'd thought might never come. A medical condition when Patty was a teen had led her to believe she'd never have a child. Her doctor told her she shouldn't worry; she should keep trying.

Paul was their miracle baby.

Alan had assured her that it would work out, that God would not let them be childless.

"Especially you, Patty," he'd said more than once during those early days. "You are the kindest, most loving woman in the world. He won't let you miss a chance to be a mother."

Patty set aside the photo. It was from a large-format negative, processed in her own darkroom. She'd keep the photo, of course. Though she didn't need it as a reminder. Paul himself was proof that her husband was right. No matter God's missteps along the way, she and Alan were destined to have a beautiful son of their own.

She tried squeezing her eyes shut to stem the tears. When they stopped flowing, she wiped them away, scanned the desk, and continued with her work.

Alan's datebook with his last appointments written in green ink. The mug Paul, age twelve, had given him for Christmas—hand thrown on a potter's wheel at a day camp in Blaine—was another keeper. She flipped through the papers as she'd done with the officers the morning he'd died.

She put the odds and ends into a black plastic bag and cinched the yellow tie tightly.

The space had been both an office and a nursery. The house was big enough that she could just leave it as it was, a cleaned-up, more organized testament to her husband's life in law enforcement. She didn't have need for a craft room. She wasn't the artsy-craftsy type. In fact, the only thing that occupied her time was thinking about how she could make things better for her son. Their shared hurt over the suicide was out of balance.

She'd always expected it might happen one day.

Paul, she knew, had no such inkling.

"How could we let this happen, Mom?" he'd said when his mother told him the terrible news. Paul couldn't stop crying, couldn't even speak while his mother tried to console him.

Patty was firm. "It will be all right, honey. Your dad has had those tendencies since before you were born. Suicides are tragic, and we can never know for sure what's truly behind the act."

Nursing a hangover and washing his eyes in Visine, Paul Sharpe drove to the Ferndale Police Department the next day, a Saturday, to collect his dad's belongings. He'd called Lindsay the night before to make sure she'd be there.

"I gathered a few things for you," Lindsay said, walking him into his father's office.

Paul brought a transparent plastic tote from home. Lindsay left him alone for a while, as though she saw it as something private and didn't want to intrude. Paul stayed quiet as he sorted through what Lindsay had collected and other desk bric-a-brac, including the previous year's softball trophy. His dad hadn't played; he coached. The ball was signed by everyone on the team.

"I was careful with the files," he said when Lindsay returned, noticing how her eyes lingered on them. "Want me to take everything out?"

"Oh no. It's not that." She pulled back a little. "Just so sick about your dad. I miss him so much."

"Me, too. My dad was my rock. He was there to back me in everything I wanted to do."

"He loved you so much. I know you know that. That's why I just don't get why he would take his life. Yes, I knew about his 'moods,' as he called them, but still, at least to me, at base he was never anything if not optimistic."

"Sometimes people just get fed up with it all. Or they snap. My dad was probably optimistic that he'd be successful in his job. He pretty much was like a dog with a bone when working on a case."

"Amen to that, Paul."

"Been meaning to ask, how are things with the Maple Falls case going? Dad would have been all over it."

"I wish he were here," Lindsay said. "It's moving along. In fact, a lot more moving parts than I realized."

"What was the girl doing out there, anyway?"

"Dump site," she said.

"Not the scene?"

"As far as we can tell. No sign of her clothes. No struggle."

"Dad said those are the toughest cases to solve. You know, not knowing where the crime scene really is. He'd play out different scenarios over dinner. Mom hated it. I was all over it. Even as a kid. He called me his partner. Kid detective."

CHAPTER 34

Lindsay made good on her promise to stop by, and she and Patty sat that night in the Sharpes' living room, a cozy space with a gray velvet couch, a leather recliner that had Alan's name all over it, even a slight indentation where his head had rested. The room, however, was dominated by the blank, black stare of a flat-screen TV Patty said Alan had purchased a couple of weeks before his suicide. Although Patty didn't mention it, Lindsay wondered why Alan would go to the trouble of buying a TV and not hooking it up. Or why he'd even buy one at all if he'd been mired in a deep depression.

"It about killed me when Paul came and gathered Alan's personal belongings today," Lindsay said.

"I did the same thing here at home. Just makes me feel closer to Alan, you know?"

"Right. I can see that. How is Paul doing?" Lindsay asked.

"He blames himself, you know. I blame myself, too."

Patty opened a bottle of red wine and set out some stone-ground wheat crackers and a wedge of brie. Neither woman was hungry. The wine was another matter.

Sips filled stretches of silence.

They were on their second glasses after twenty minutes.

"How are you holding up, Patty?" Lindsay asked.

"I must look awful," Patty answered. She wore a yellow top and white jeans. She wore no makeup except for a touch of blush.

Lindsay gave her a warm smile. "You look fine. What can I do?"

Patty drank more wine. "I hate to say I'm fine. I am. I just am. I know that Alan is in a better place."

Lindsay waited quietly. She wanted Patty to fill in the empty spaces in the conversation.

"Everything reminds me of him," Patty said, looking around the room.

"Me, too. I thought I saw him today, but of course, it was just a stranger with the same blocky body."

Patty let out a little laugh. "Sometimes I can feel him like he's in the same room, and I have things I want to tell him. And I guess I'm doing that. Not aloud, but in my heart, in my head." She noticed Lindsay's empty wineglass. "Another? The couple next door brought a bottle of white wine over, which I thought was odd; then I thought better of it. They were just trying to be nice."

Lindsay put her hand over her glass. "It has been a long day, and two are more than enough. Still have work to do."

"How is the Maple Falls case?" Patty asked.

"I wish Alan were here," Lindsay said. "That kind of goes without saying, I know. As a practical matter, I know he'd be able to steer me in the right direction. That was his gift, you know. Letting me figure things out, listen to my heart, allow things to be peeled away. He was an awesome mentor."

"You can talk to me about the case, Lindsay," Patty said. "Maybe I can help? I was married to the man for twenty years and have a good idea how his mind worked."

"No, that's fine."

"I'm here if you need me."

It wasn't Maple Falls that she wanted to talk about. And Lindsay hated to bring it up, but she knew she had no choice.

"Patty, I need to ask you about Alan's suicide."

Patty gave her a quizzical look. "Are you investigating it?"

"Oh God, no," she said. "Like I said at the memorial, I never caught even a whiff of major depression. I feel like an idiot. I should have seen the signs. I should have been able to intervene."

Patty's eyes puddled, and a second later, tears slipped down her cheeks.

"We can't know everything about everyone, Lindsay. I knew that he was struggling with something. I never saw this kind of an outcome."

"I feel so stupid. I should have noticed."

"Alan was a complex man. You know that. He was gregarious, that's true," Patty said, reaching for a tissue. "He was also very, very private. I know that he let you inside because he loved you, Lindsay. Yet at the same time, he couldn't share certain things with you."

"I guess so. I certainly told him a lot about *my* life. I leaned on him. Needed him as a friend and adviser."

"I understand. I do. I really do. You're just going to have to hold him in your heart and think about how you can take all of what he was and use it to love yourself more, love others more."

The phrase felt familiar.

"Alan was so meticulous and conscientious," Lindsay went on. "When I first started at the department, he always flagged salient points in reports with Post-it notes so that I would get up to speed. And what a memo writer. He lived to tap away on that old Dell we have in the office."

Patty looked at her quizzically and finished her second glass.

"It's just, being such a writer, I guess I thought he might've left a note," Lindsay said. "He seemed like the kind of man who would tell us why he did what he did."

"There was no note, Lindsay. Believe me, I've looked high and low. It would have made things so much easier for all of us. We just won't ever know. And that's what we're all stuck with."

"Sure," Lindsay said. "Of course." She sighed. "Any idea what he was struggling with? If it wasn't too personal?"

Patty shrugged. "A case. You know how he took them to heart. He was that kind of cop."

"Right."

Patty took their empty glasses to the kitchen. The conversation was at an end. Lindsay needed to leave the poor woman alone.

Yet at the door, after Patty embraced her, Lindsay heard herself asking, "Do you know which one, though?"

"Which one what?"

"Which case he was struggling with. Any idea?"

"Never said. And after nearly twenty years of marriage, I guess I've learned better than to ask. If you open up that door, you become a sounding board to things, sometimes very ugly things, you'd rather not know about."

Patty shut the door after her and set the wineglasses in the dishwasher. Then she went down the hall into her husband's office and sat down at his desk.

Lindsay knew Alan so well. They'd truly been more than just coworkers, nearly father and daughter.

And she was right.

There had been a suicide note.

In fact, there had been two.

CHAPTER 35

The dog next door barked that night like it was making its last stand against a legion of opossums. It yapped at everything. And every bark was directed at Lindsay's house. The owners were nice enough, claiming that they had no idea why the Maltese mix was such a nuisance where Lindsay was concerned.

"She's usually just a sweet little puffball," the neighbor said. "Gets excited. Piddles. And that's about it."

So I'm the problem, then?

Lindsay knew better than to argue with a dog owner, especially one with a sweet, annoying little puffball.

Instead, she had casually revealed her shoulder holster.

Not that she would ever hurt an animal. She just wanted to let the folks next door know that she was a cop.

As if that mattered anymore.

In fact, it clearly didn't. Witness the incessant yapping.

To escape the noise, she took her laptop to her bedroom and shut the door. This house was far from the place she and her ex-husband had built overlooking Lake Whatcom. It didn't have the view or the brushed-nickel fixtures. But it was hers. When she'd unpacked the bedroom boxes from the move, she found a wedding photo and shoved it under some blankets in the bottom drawer of the dresser.

It was always there, reminding her of her husband's betrayal.

At least it was all for nothing.

At least he'd been dumped by his lover.

And now they were both alone, which made her smile.

Lindsay undressed, slipped on a nightgown, and adjusted the pillows on the bed . . . and searched YouTube for more on Marnie. She was obsessed, that much was clear to her. What was fueling that obsession—dedication to her job or a growing, worrisome compulsion to know more about the woman and her message for reasons that had nothing to do with either Sarah Baker or Calista Sullivan—she chose not to dwell upon.

There were dozens of videos posted by fans and media outlets over the years. The one that caught her eye tonight, deep, deep down the list, had Reed Sullivan as its featured image. It was uploaded by BeeHappy, likely one of Marnie's legion of supporters. The source of the clip was *Northwest Afternoon*, a talk show broadcast by KOMO-TV, the ABC network affiliate in Seattle.

The theme of that particular episode was "justice wanted." Three stories of men who'd been falsely accused and ultimately proven innocent took up the hour. First up was Reed's vignette, a montage of photographs of Calista mostly taken by Reed himself in California; only a handful of images were from her time in Washington.

In one picture, she was shown hugging Marnie Spellman at a book signing.

> Host: Reed Sullivan, welcome. We appreciate having you here today. You've been through the wringer, to say the least. How are you and your sons coping these days?

Reed: We feel like we got our lives back—and we're very appreciative of that—at the same time we also feel that the culprit who murdered Calista is out there, enjoying life and freedom. We are never going to be the same.

Host: Of course not. Have there been any developments in that regard?

Reed: No. Whatcom County was carved by the glaciers of the last ice age, and the courts move about as swiftly now. It takes them a while to get where they need to be.

Host: Yes, but ultimately, as in your case, they did get where they needed to be.

Reed: Correct. Pretty much ruined my life in the process. If you want to call that "where they needed to be," that's your prerogative. I was thinking that getting where they need to be means finding my wife's killer.

Host: Sorry. I see that. Of course.

Reed: Thank you. Few seem to.

Host: I read where you think that Marnie Spellman has some kind of role in the case.

Reed: She wields great power in the county. I'll leave it at that.

Host: I understand Spellman reached out to you after your release?

Reed: I thought we weren't going to talk about that. About *her*.

Host: I know people want to know.

Reed: She sent me a card and a gift basket of her products.

Host: That's a little strange. What did the card say?

Reed: She wrote, "Calista will always be in my heart."

Host: That's nice. What's so strange about that? You said you were put off by the gesture.

Reed: You don't know Spellman. You can't conceive of why a beautiful woman could be so dangerous. Can you? The reality is that Spellman is a predator. Her affinity is more akin to spider than her much-lauded honeybee. She spins a web, that one. I know she knows what happened to Calista. She wrote that my wife will always be in her heart, not as a memory or a dream, but as a possession. That's the kind of person Marnie Spellman is.

Host: Well, Reed, you certainly didn't hold back. Let's break for a commercial now. When we come back, Reed will have more to tell us.

Despite the promises of more to come, the segment ended. When the host cut away for the commercial, Reed apparently unhooked his mic and left the studio.

Calista's husband never said another word about the case. When reporters would phone for an interview, he told them, on advice of counsel, he wouldn't be saying anything more.

He stayed quiet for almost two decades until Sarah Baker's body was stumbled on by a young mother pushing a baby stroller at Maple Falls.

And then he phoned Lindsay.

She powered down the laptop and noted the late hour. She was exhausted from the long day, the visit with Patty. The unanswered questions of what had taken place circled through Lindsay's mind as she finally drifted off.

CHAPTER 36

Fame was a kind of resplendent cocoon.

No, a straitjacket.

A gag.

A combination of all three.

Dina Marlow took her wine out to the swimming pool and wondered why she'd even had one installed in the first place. The weather in Washington made it usable only for the three months of summer at best. Maybe only two. The reason was obvious, of course. She had a pool because not having one would signal to the world that she was just like everyone else. It was silly. Stupid. She looked at her reflection in the water and then turned away.

She'd come north to grow as a human being. Her California friends had thought she was crazy to move to a part of the country where it rained all the time and there were so few good restaurants. She went, anyway. It gave her a feeling of superiority that they were stuck in the phony construct of fame and adulation, that they didn't seek enlightenment.

She was such a liar.

To everyone.

To herself.

Her arrival hadn't been an escape to something, but rather a retreat springing from an urgent need for reinvention. She was disappearing from the pages of the magazines that had once featured her on their covers. Her time in Hollywood had started to wane, then poof! Vanished. Hardly an uncommon phenomenon, of course. Very few of her contemporaries had been able to make the leap from headliner to character actress. The transition from child star to adult was just as arduous. She'd done that. She'd been a successful child model and teen actor.

She drank the rest of her wine and returned for the bottle. It was empty, so she opted for the box wine she kept in the pantry.

Dina wandered her huge house, wondering where she'd gone wrong with Marnie. How something so great could have turned so ugly. She'd been a die-hard supporter following the shopping channel debacle. The two of them had commiserated on career stumbles. Dina's was a part she'd turned down that became a Golden Globe–winning role for another actress. Marnie's was hardly in the same league. She'd never been knocked off the pedestal of being one of America's sweethearts—at least, not at that point.

There was a time when Marnie was a tireless coach and mentor. After the Golden Globes disappointment, she'd urged Dina to get back into the game.

"Not taking that part was one of the biggest mistakes of my life," Dina had said.

"A blip," Marnie soothed, pouring them each another glass of wine. "What matters now is that you persevered. And look at you. Stronger than ever."

This was overstating things, Dina knew. She no longer had a career. But she had good skin and, most days, hoped that her luck could change. Some days, she even felt it *would*. "If that's true," Dina had said, misting up, "it's all because of you."

"Nonsense," Marnie insisted. "It is because of *you*. I've given you only the softest push. The real power has come from inside you, Dina."

Then it was Marnie's turn. Dina listened as her friend and mentor replayed how harshly she'd been treated after her misstep on the shopping channel.

"No more forgiveness in this country," Marnie said. "People seem to thrive in the dark now, looking at any little fissure to slip into and do harm."

As if to punctuate this remark, still darker news chose that moment to find Marnie, via her ringing telephone. She looked down at the caller ID. "My agent," she said. "I'd better take it."

Dina drank her wine while Marnie put the call on speaker.

"Foxwood is dropping you, Marnie."

"What do you mean by 'dropping' me?"

"They aren't going to publish the paperback of *The Insatiable Heart*."

"They can't do that, can they? It was a mistake. I misspoke. What I said on TV isn't me. You know that. They know that."

"Correct. We all know that, Marnie. Nonetheless, you've put yourself in a shitstorm, and you can't do anything, at least at the moment, to fix it."

"I went on every TV and radio outlet that would have me. I'm about helping people, not hurting them. I think that came across."

"I'm sorry, Marnie. I know it was heartfelt. However this is business, and Foxwood won't budge. It turns out one of their senior editors has a brother with special needs."

"Good God," she said. "It was one mistake."

"I know. I have to go into a meeting. My advice is lie low. Ride this out. It's all you can do at the moment. And, Marnie, I'm not promising anything. Just know I have faith in you and your message. I know you can overcome all of this, too. Bye, now."

The line went dead.

Marnie took a breath and faced Dina.

"I'm down, Dina. I'm far, far from over."

"You'll rise up, Marnie. I know it. We both will."

It had been a while since Dina had any kind of a real offer, or hope, to jump-start her mothballed career. So much had changed. Indeed, the industry that had made her famous had transformed. She'd had her biggest success in the last days of Hollywood glamour, the time when the female star was called a leading lady. Now everyone was an *actor*. No longer even an actress, a moniker she'd considered a much better descriptor than the blanket, denuded, dull *actor*. Her agent's office told her that there was serious interest in her return to acting, albeit with a hitch.

She met Santiago Phillips at Craven, a Santa Monica restaurant that had been her favorite before her move to the Pacific Northwest.

Dina was already seated at an outside table, enjoying the pleasures of a marine breeze from the Pacific.

Santiago, her agent's daughter, had recently taken on some of her father's clients, a move toward the day when she'd manage his very full and eclectic "stable of stars." Barely in her twenties, she wore a Versace top that Dina knew had to be genuine, but something about the fabric seemed suspect.

"I love your blouse," Dina said, getting up to embrace the young woman, feeling the fabric. Versace would never have approved of that fabric. "You've certainly grown up," she went on. "The first time we met, you were barely able to walk."

Santiago, her long black extensions swept back and her eyes shielded by sunglasses with oversized white frames, looked more the star than Dina, who'd agonized that morning about what to wear and finally decided on a Chanel shift that she was nearly certain she'd only been photographed in once.

"You're ageless," Santiago purred, pulling her shades down, then popping them back in place on the bridge of her new nose.

"Not everyone thinks so," Dina said, waiting for Santiago to confirm the compliment. It never came.

The waiter took their drink orders, and again Santiago's glasses came down so she could check him out. Nothing special, apparently, because she ignored his final pleasantries. "I've never been here before," she said to Dina. "How'd you find this place?"

Her tone felt a little disdainful. Possibly bait.

Dina thought just then that Santiago took more after her mother, a climber from Des Moines who had acted three times in *All My Children* before snagging her first husband.

"How's your mother?" she asked.

Santiago forced a quick smile. Maybe a smirk. "You know how she is. Always reaching for something new."

Or someone new, Dina thought. She swallowed her gin and tonic and got down to business. "You have news."

Just then, Santiago's phone pinged.

"I do," she said, giving Dina a little nod without looking up from her phone. "Just a minute." She rose and started for a quiet spot to take her call, then stopped and turned to Dina. "If the waiter comes while I'm away, order a Caesar salad for me, please. With shrimp, only if it's wild caught."

"Of course," Dina said, spotting a photographer on the street outside. She adjusted her body, affording him a good angle. It had been a while since she'd made the papers, and the last time had been for all the wrong reasons.

Santiago returned just as the salads were delivered. She seemed annoyed, maybe angry. Her face was so smooth, it was impossible to really tell.

"Is everything okay?" Dina asked.

"Just the business. I know you know this—and thank God for it—as the most seasoned and reasonable client in our stable."

Seasoned. Fine for a steak. For a person, however, it just meant old. And again with the *stable*.

"Right," Dina said, still hoping that the photographer would notice her. "Tell me about the part."

"It's not the lead," Santiago said quickly, darting a look across the table. "Just need to get that out first."

Dina speared a wild-caught shrimp in her salad. "That's fine," she said. "I'm so busy up in Washington that I doubt I could free up the time for a major part, anyway."

She refused to allow Santiago to see the disappointment that had dropped over her. She was not going to give anyone, especially this kid agent, the satisfaction of seeing her crestfallen.

"It's a reboot of *Dragnet*. Have you heard about it?"

"Yes," Dina said, though she hadn't.

"They really like you, of course. They think you'll be marvelous in the role, and your part could expand if the numbers are good."

Dina brightened. "Sounds intriguing."

Santiago motioned for more sparkling water, and the nothing-special waiter hurried over with another glass.

"What's the part?" Dina asked.

Santiago checked her teeth for bits of romaine before answering.

A delay tactic.

Just wait for it.

Here it comes.

"It's really exciting, Dina," she said, back in control of her teeth. "They are considering you for the part of the dispatcher, Kay Lee."

Dina didn't blink. "Series regular?"

"In almost every episode, Kay Lee will direct the leads—still not cast—to head to the crime scene."

It sounded like a thankless part, the kind of part that only a beginner would covet.

"I don't know," she finally said.

"What do you mean? You'd have a chance to return to the spotlight, even if only for a limited basis."

"Look, I appreciate the offer. I'm just not sure."

Then the other shoe dropped.

A fake Jimmy Choo, most likely.

"I'm sorry, Dina," Santiago said, again lowering her glasses. "They are only *considering* you. You'd have to audition. Tomorrow. You're up against one of the *Three's Company* girls and another from some other old—I mean, *classic* show."

Dina felt sick. Discarded. Used up. She bit her lip and spoke up brightly. "I'm absolutely interested. Excited. Let me know the deets when you have them."

Did she really say *deets*?

Santiago paid the bill with the flash of her American Express Black Card.

Dina returned to her favorite bungalow at the Chateau Marmont, next to the one in which John Belushi had overdosed all those years ago when she was someone. She'd been there that day, in fact. Her heart was broken for John, his family, his fans. She'd seen him in the Polo Lounge just the day before. He was laughing and playing to the hangers-on who had encircled him.

Like vampires.

Sucking the life force from his body.

Making sure they got every bloody drop.

She cried into her hotel pillow, her mascara leaving a cavern's worth of bat wings on the satiny-smooth linen. She fetched some gin from the minibar and made herself a dry room-temp martini. No olive. No nothing. She lined up the cute little bottles of Tanqueray in a row that grew to four.

All right. Five.

Santiago texted that while she'd planned to be at the audition, something had come up and she'd be unable to make it after all. That was perfectly fine with Dina. Actually, she preferred it. A car service would pick her up at 2:00 p.m. for the Paramount lot, which would be home to the show if it was picked up as a midseason replacement. Dina selected black palazzo pants and a cream-colored Marc Jacobs top. Simple, elegant. She had nothing to prove, of course, but considering the part was a dispatcher named Kay Lee, she thought simple and elegant was in order.

A production assistant named Inga met her at security to escort her to the audition. Inga's beautiful brown eyes didn't even flicker with the slightest bit of recognition when she extended her hand. She was young, of course. Quite, quite young. Dina always liked it when someone said that they loved her in something she'd done on film, especially. TV not so much, but film. She was of that age group of actors that considered TV a kind of convalescent home for the aging, overly nipped, and no longer fuckable group of actors and actresses who'd started their careers around the same time she did.

Inga introduced Dina to three men and a woman behind a table nearly encrusted with script notes, Starbucks cups, and Twix wrappers.

A half hour later, it was over.

Dina was in the Town Car when Santiago phoned to check in.

"They loved you!"

"I had four lines."

"How did it feel?"

"I don't know. The part or the audition?"

"Either. Both."

"The audition was fine. The part probably isn't right. Doesn't give me anything to do."

"I'm so glad you said that."

Dina's stomach went heavy as lead. "Why's that?"

"I think they are going to use someone else."

"Oh."

"They just told me. There will be other parts. There will be better and bigger opportunities to flex those acting muscles."

"Right."

"Maybe you should write a book or something."

"Maybe so."

Dina ended the call and asked the driver to go past her old house in Bel Air. As she watched the palm trees go by the window one after another, it almost seemed as if they made a sound like the playing cards that she and her brother affixed against the spokes of their bikes with clothespins. Nostalgia wrapped its arms around her just then. Everything she'd ever wanted as a girl was gone or never existed. Becoming a star had seemed an unattainable ambition, yet through hard work and the fortune of beauty, she'd somehow managed it. She wasn't sure which had been more important, her work ethic or the face and body that the lottery of biology had bequeathed her.

She still looked beautiful, and she was willing to work hard, but the ship had sailed. Or rather, foundered.

The driver parked in front of the sprawling pink château that had been her home, and she rolled down the window. Dina wondered if she'd made a mistake by following Marnie Spellman. Had she given up everything she'd ever wanted for something that would always be out of reach?

Greatness.

It was all she wanted.

Dina turned on the steam and slipped out of her pale-rose robe. She didn't really care for the color; the costume designer on her first film put her in the hue and pronounced it her "signature." From then on, she wore it all the time, although she felt the "just-under-carnation" hue made her look washed out. As the steam rose from the glass-enclosed shower, she studied her body. She'd fought off aging with every single trick in the book. She'd had more touch-up surgeries than she cared to admit, even to herself. There was nothing left to be done—not really. She was older. Old. She'd be lucky to get the grandmother parts at this point. Maybe even a cameo now and then when the prying eyes of viewers could subject her to scrutiny from the comfort of their living rooms. She'd played a nasty trick on herself. Aging was a battle that no one could really win. She wondered, as the steam rose and layered a light fog over the mirror, if she'd gone too far. If she'd been better off giving in to the process.

Her last conversation with Marnie, at the Bellevue home of one of the Microsoft millionaires who followed her, had rattled Dina a little.

"Women can be so catty," Marnie had said after returning from the bar.

Dina wanted to just let that sit. Fade away. Longed to be the kind of person who could do that.

"What do you mean?"

Marnie handed Dina her drink. "Never mind. Not important."

It was a trick. A way to open the lid on a box of jealousy and allow it to seep into the room of the beautiful and rich. Just a thin vapor of vileness that could be detected only by the target.

Of the two of them, Marnie was the more intelligent, the more beautiful. Dina was convinced of this—and knew Marnie was, too. It ate at her that whenever the two of them were in a room, Dina'd play the supporting role.

"It's just . . ."

Marnie was going for it.

"What?" Dina asked.

Marnie took a long sip of wine, smudging her lipstick in the process. "I think you are the most beautiful woman here," she said. "Just leave it at that."

Dina hadn't said a word about the smudged lipstick. She'd let her closest friend work the room with the smeared face of a clown.

Before stepping into the shower, she locked the door. The locked door was a habit. It was what she'd done when the casting director came for her before filming, or when her mother went looking for her to go on one more audition.

Slumping onto the marble bench, steam rising all around her, she let her tears mix with the hot vapor. She screamed out, not words but wounded animal sounds, all the pain that had been foisted on her by others.

Dina had talked a good game around Marnie and the other members of the Hive. They saw her as composed. Clear on where she was going. Yet it had all been a lie.

Indeed, everything about her was a lie. From the way she looked to the way she feigned a certain kind of intellect—curious, full of wonderment. How she followed the teachings and embraced the idea of a no-limits world. Such a phony. She was as one-dimensional as a stack of photos waiting for her autograph. The whole time, she was scared she'd be unveiled as a fraud. She knew she wasn't as good as Glenn, Meryl, Helen.

Steam billowed from the shower, and her fingers found her razor. She wondered if it was true that suicide in hot water was painless. That if you didn't look at the blood as it curled down the drain, you wouldn't even know what was happening. Eyes closed. The sound of water. The ebbing of your life as it follows the water to the drain. It would be better than overdosing, that's for sure. She didn't want forensic photos of her lying in her own vomit. She didn't want to die on the toilet and have her whole life be made into a punch line.

She held the razor in her fingertips and tried to relax. She studied her wrists, among the only parts of her body that she'd never altered by surgery. Her flesh was a virgin snowfield. It passed through her mind just then that when they found her, they'd see the telltale scarring from the breast implants. Breasts were not her calling card like some actresses. She did the augmentation only to ensure that her clothes fit properly. They'd find out that her confidence had been an act, that what she'd preached as natural beauty—the beauty of bees—had been a fraud.

The scream came from deep inside, a plaintive, guttural sound of no words. Just anguish released from a punctured balloon. The razor fell to the drain, its pink plastic form spinning like a minute hand gone berserk.

She didn't have what it took. She couldn't even make a proper exit from the living.

It was true that Marnie had used her. She had used Marnie, too. It seemed as though they should be equal, but somehow the balance of power in their relationship always tilted in Marnie's favor.

They'd had it out on her last visit to Spellman Farms.

Marnie was on a high that particular day. She'd been in talks with her distributor in Europe, and it appeared that things were heading toward her biggest-ever product launch.

"Worldwide," Marnie insisted. "Truly. I'm doing it."

There was something in the way she had said it that felt to Dina like a little dig.

"I've been there," Dina said, unable to resist setting the record straight.

"Not the same, Dina. You were there selling your looks. I'm selling female power, choice."

Dina pushed back, something she rarely did. "You're selling a promise in a jar."

Marnie's eyes flickered, while her expression remained cool. "Oh, wow, did someone really just say that?"

"Not someone, Marnie. Me. Everyone."

"You're full of shit, Dina."

Dina gave her a look—the same look she used on TV when pretending to be surprised in a scene. "Really? You're telling women that in order to get what they want, they have to be beautiful? That's the oldest line in the book. Men have been doing that to us for as long as there have been men and women."

Marnie waved this away. "You know that's not it at all, Dina. Or you should, by now, unless you've been too busy gazing into the mirror. Yes. I think you're just talking about yourself, Dina. You are your own biggest fan, you know."

No one was yelling; instead the two were speaking in a quiet version of all caps.

"I might have to be," Dina said, refusing to back down. "You've taken away my career and made me look the fool, going after that stupid bit part on that insipid *Dragnet* reboot."

Emotion leaked from every word.

Marnie, for her part, simply maintained her composure.

"I wanted you to succeed," she said.

"You wanted me to fail! You have this insatiable need to be the queen bee, literally, and there's no way you'd ever let anyone be held up higher than you."

"You, Dina, just have to face facts. You've had your time in the spotlight. Nothing lasts forever. I would have thought you've become reconciled to that by now."

"You used me, Marnie."

Marnie shuttered her eyes and shook her head dismissively. "That again? Seriously? Why do you feel the need to trot that out whenever you are angry? Or when you've had too much to drink?"

"I'm not drinking now," Dina said.

Marnie persisted. "All right, then. Let's get it all out, once and for all. I don't want to have this conversation again. You need to get your shit together. You are a has-been in Hollywood. You can still be something here . . . but no, maybe not. Frankly, I'm not sure. Your attitude is giving me a headache."

Dina just sat there. It was like her mother telling her to lose weight. Or the agent who made her undergo breast augmentation twice because the first time was not the "eye-popper" he'd felt was necessary to attract more substantial roles.

She tried to rally, tried to stand up to Marnie. No words came to her. She knew that Marnie was ascending in her own star power while Dina's was only a dying ember.

"Oh," Marnie said. "Looks as though we *won't* have this conversation again, Dina."

Dina stayed mute.

"Fine," Marnie went on. "You're here. And as long as that's still the case, we have things that need to get done around here. Do your goddamn part."

Now, years later in her beautiful, empty house, Dina attempted to jettison these memories by sheer force of will (and long practice) and took her wine back to the pool. She knew where she stood. She was never going to be back in the spotlight in the way she had been when she was younger. If she were ever mentioned at all, it would be in conjunction with something that Marnie Spellman was doing.

Trusted friend.

Confidante.

Adviser.

As she finished drinking, a faint smile crossed her lips. She was none of those things.

She hated Marnie Spellman as much as she loved her.

Some saw their relationship as sisterly. Some saw more. While Dina knew that she was older than Marnie—although Dina lied about it on Wikipedia—Dina always saw herself as subordinate. Marnie was a woman fully realized, in control of her body, mind, and career. She was powerful, and she had a purpose. Dina's life had been charted by others. Men, almost without exception. Most of whom just wanted to take advantage of her.

Dina found herself on the move again, haunting her own wildly oversized home. Back into the kitchen she went, to drop off her empty wineglass and pick up a bottle of water from the refrigerator, which she took across the hall to her office. From deep in the back of the closet, she retrieved a scrapbook her mother had made when she started out in the business. She remembered how her mother had told her how much she had loved modeling when she was young. *Loved* it. *Lived* for it. This had confused Dina. What was there to love about it? She didn't care for any of it. She could see, however, that it mattered to her mother.

The newsprint affixed to the pages of the scrapbook had yellowed, the clippings held in place by ghosts of cellophane tape. There she was at age two, in an advertisement for Snowy White, a laundry detergent. She touched the frayed edges of a photograph that her dad had taken when she was Fiona in *Brigadoon*. Page after page. Back and forth through time.

Dina returned to the *Brigadoon* picture. It was as if her eyes were magnetic and the black-and-white photo was a sheet of iron.

Marnie had told the story behind that photograph at a gathering at Spellman Farms—told Dina's story as if it had happened to Marnie instead. She frequently shared a little something from her own tragic and mysterious background to loosen the tongues or wallets of devotees who held back something valuable that she might be able to use.

She'd long ago made up the ground she'd lost since her apology tour. In many ways, those who adored her loved her even more, respected her for her candor. And as for those who didn't believe a thing she said, who cared? They were never going to be of value, anyway.

"I was so frightened and so weak that I just let it happen," Marnie explained that night. "It was the church janitor. I liked him. Everyone did. He asked me to help him with some equipment during a break from a program we were practicing. I gladly went. It was such a small, little decision. It changed me. It really did. I vowed right then and there that I would never, never let a man take advantage of me. Tables turned."

Dina never confronted Marnie about how she'd appropriated her story. In fact, she never even mentioned it to anyone. It was another lesson, though inadvertent, that the woman who held herself to the highest standards was more than just a liar.

She was also a thief.

Dina closed the scrapbook.

For the first time, she wondered what Marnie had done to Sarah Baker.

CHAPTER 37

Wednesday, September 4, 2019
Ferndale, Washington

Alan Sharpe was in the living room with the cable news channel buzzing about something terrible. He couldn't keep his mind on it. On anything. His thoughts kept dipping—no, plunging—back to memories of what had happened on Lummi Island all those years ago, stirred up by a girl his son, Paul, had started to date.

Sarah Baker had shown up at his office the day before and said she was working on a story about an unsolved murder. She was pretty, smart. Inquisitive, too.

"Calista Sullivan," she said.

Alan let the name sink in. "Let me think. Seems familiar."

Sarah suggested that maybe they should shut the door.

"That's a good idea," he said.

Once he was seated, Alan stayed mute, folding his hands on his desk.

"You look like you're trying to remember," Sarah said, playing it as coolly as she could. "It has been a while. Body found on Lummi just after you left the tribal police there."

He held his tongue a bit longer. He'd thought that he and Patty were free and clear. That nothing would ever come back to destroy the lives they'd made for themselves.

That the past would never come back to haunt them.

"Yes, I remember. Husband was acquitted. Never found the real killer."

"Never found her baby, either."

"What baby?"

"The one she had the night she died."

"I don't know anything about that. Wasn't mentioned in the papers."

"No, it wasn't. But her coworkers thought she might be pregnant, though no one was sure. Didn't ask her. She was always with her Marnie Spellman clique. In fact, she quit her job three months before she was killed. Said she was working on some issues with her ex."

"As I said, I don't know anything about that," he said.

"I think that you can help me figure it out."

"I was the most junior officer on the island. I had nothing to do with the investigation."

"I know that. I'm not talking about what you did. I'm talking about your wife. Sources say she was at the farm the night Calista Sullivan died."

He leaned back in his chair.

Breathe evenly.

Telegraph no worries.

"She most likely was," he said. "Patty worked there on some weekends. Probably that weekend. I can't recall specifics."

Alan had conducted hundreds of interviews in his years in law enforcement. This young woman was using one of his own techniques on him. She had dropped a bomb and somehow managed to keep it suspended in midair. No threat, just a combination of words that felt like one.

"Look," he said. "We'll need to do this another time. I want to help you with your story, but I have to speak at Rotary in ten minutes."

It was a lie. A lame one at that.

"All right," she said. "I wouldn't want you to miss that. My uncle was in Rotary, and I know how important those meetings are."

Her words were cloaked in sarcasm she made no effort to conceal.

He got up and looked at the Salish weavers calendar that hung on the wall next to his desk. "Let's catch up again, say, a week from today?"

"Fine," Sarah said. "I'm still piecing things together, and maybe I'll know more by then."

She already knew everything, he thought. Or enough. She was just seeing how far things might go.

"One last thing," she said, getting up to leave. "Have you ever heard of Marnie Spellman's group of women called the Hive?"

"Can't say that I have," he said.

Another lie.

CHAPTER 38

May 1999
Lummi Island, Washington

Marnie's clothes closet was the stuff of legend. When she was on top, bloated and bloviating TV presenter Robin Leach featured her sartorial display for one of his shows. Even Dina was envious of the array of designer outfits that hung facing outward, not crammed together like a bunch of Donna Karan pleats. Her bees were her love; her clothes were her passion.

The first time Marnie and Dina made love was in that closet, under the fringe of cream hemlines in the Chanel section. It was sudden. Unexpected. Dina had never been with a woman, although she nearly succumbed to a Hollywood casting director who sized up vulnerable girls to "take under" her clutching wing. She'd been trying to get a part on a TV series set in Boston. That's all she knew about it. The casting director, thirty years her senior, was a predatory woman who tested girls in her apartment in Studio City. Her line sounded like a practiced one.

"You have amazing cheekbones," she'd said. "I'll need to see the rest of you. Sorry. I know. That's the way things work, dear. I want. You have. You give. I get you the part."

When her career sagged and she sought a boost in the media, Dina recounted the story on *Access Hollywood*.

"I just want everyone to know that there are more predators out there than you can imagine. They can be beautiful. They can be ugly. Most are male. In my case, however, it was a woman."

The host probed for how far it went.

"Some awkward and embarrassing touching, but that's all."

The host attempted to lift her Botoxed brow.

"Really?"

Dina gave her an unconvincing stare. "That's all."

It was more than that, of course. Dina didn't want to tell the host that she'd done everything the casting director wanted and it had left her in tears. She felt lower than she ever had. Ashamed. Foolish. Dina wasn't sure if her relationship meant she was bisexual or what. She knew she preferred men. Yet somehow, being close to Marnie in any way— mentally, emotionally, and, yes, even sexually—was beyond any kind of joy she'd ever felt. In the outside world, she was the star. At home, with Marnie, she was the submissive one. She acquiesced to Marnie's needs. Her whims.

Dina had always kept a journal, especially during turbulent times. She never seemed to have anyone to talk to about the most important things, so she talked to herself. Marnie, of course, figured heavily on its pages—as Dina tried her best to sort out her life. Her feelings. Her unrelenting fascination and, yes, she admitted to herself when she'd had a few drinks, her obsession with Marnie.

She revisited a representative late entry in the leather-bound folio that she'd told her mother was a gift from Kate Hepburn.

A lie, of course.

Acting was a lie.

She drank and read:

I've never been able to figure it out. God knows I've thought about it. A lot. Tried to wrap my brain around the idea that I loved this woman more than anything, but I was not in love with her. It wasn't like that in the least.

So what was it like? Our relationship was purely about friendship, advancing the agenda. Trying to make the world a better place. That was it, wasn't it? And oh, she has this way about her that . . . I don't know . . . that somehow transcends being a person . . . almost like a deity.

That sounds crazy. I know it. But that's how I've felt at times.

I'm sorry for the way things turned out, for all of us. I did love her. She was special. And that's a truth that the rest of the world would just have to come to grips with, if it ever decided it cared about me again. (Not too likely!)

And I was of use to her. And happy to be so.

I became a fixture around Spellman Farms, and since I was a celebrity, Marnie garnered a lot of attention she would have had to struggle to attract, otherwise. At least for a while—never underestimate her!

I was fine with that. I loved it, in fact. It was an exciting time, and it came when I'd thought—feared—my exciting times might be over.

Which, as it turned out, they soon were. Ironic, I suppose. Marnie's excitement with me, mine with her, excited the jealousy of the other members of the Hive. They didn't even bother to hide it, at least among ourselves. Heather was especially hostile. She'd been the favorite of their mentor, their guru, until I arrived.

Jealousy is a terrific motivator, it turns out. Marnie would've lost interest in me soon enough without help, especially as my star continued to fade, but my Hivemates surely moved the timetable more swiftly forward. My only solace: they didn't have much time to enjoy the cleared field once I was gone.

CHAPTER 39

Among the volumes in Greta Swensen's home library was the copy of *The Insatiable Heart* that Marnie had personalized to her. She'd been free of Marnie World for years, and then, all of a sudden, she'd found herself, unwittingly, being put back into a place and time she thought she'd set aside forever. She'd done things that no one could ever know. She wondered if Detective Jackman was digging deep enough to find out the secrets that bound the members of the Hive together. She took the book to her desk, a seventeenth-century French antique that her arrangement with Marnie had made possible.

Her promise to never tell what they'd done at Spellman Farms in exchange for a half million dollars.

Marnie bitterly complained that the payoff was extortion, but Greta didn't see it that way. She considered it a reasonable exchange.

A necessary one.

Greta sat down and started to leaf through the foxed pages of the book. Her eyes landed on a passage, and she found herself reading.

As my father had told me on his deathbed, Spellman Farms passed directly to me, along with a considerable amount of money. There was a provision for Casey, too. A substantial one, left in a trust indicating that if he were to maintain sobriety for a specific amount of time, he'd get a share of the cash. I was fine with that, of course. I had often meditated on my brother, hoping and praying that he'd find his way back to health. Until then, I would go full-on "Marnie mode," as my first employees liked to say. My vision was that my apiary-based product line would feed the souls of millions.

My outside-in philosophy was met with skepticism at first. I was prepared for that. My father's words on his deathbed echoed over and over in my brain.

"Change the world!"

It was a monumental task that many would deem impossible to achieve. Not me. I understood then, as I do now, that changing the world can be done only when you can change the misconceptions that people—some bitter, some angry—cling to with C-clamp tenacity. They hold tight only to what they know, because they haven't had a glimpse of what was really possible.

The time was right to talk to the world.

And so I did.

"Placing such importance on a person's appearance diminishes what they have to offer," said the first reporter sent out to see me. I'd been in business eight months. Even in that short time, I'd struck a nerve.

Her name was Daria. She was from the Seattle Times.

"Let me put it this way," I answered. "How do you feel when someone compliments you on a new outfit?"

Daria was in her midthirties. She had a lovely face and silky brown hair that she wore in a ponytail.

"I feel good," she said, before pulling back. "But that's not the same thing as elevating appearance above all else, Ms. Spellman."

"Does their compliment make you feel good? Yes or no."

"Well, yes. Of course. It's human nature."

"Nature. Right. So when you feel good about yourself, do you attract more compliments or fewer?"

"More, I guess."

"Correct. That's the point. When you look the best that you can, you feel better. Feeling better can be transformative. You absorb more positives when you are more attractive."

"'Positives'?"

"Praise. Invitations to participate in something. Dates. More money. A better life."

"That's a pretty big promise for a line of soaps and lotions."

"I don't think so, Daria," I said. "Neither do my customers. They are absolutely devoted. And for good reason. The reason they feel that way about me, about my products, is because they work."

Greta closed Marnie's book. Reading it all these years later, she wondered how it was that she'd fallen for it. How she'd compromised herself, forsaken her family, and then turned around and been so ruthless as to ask for money—extort, really, because now she could admit that's what it was. That Marnie had acquiesced shocked her now, but at the time, Greta had been dead certain of her calculations.

And she'd been right. She'd left Marnie little choice.

But what a risk she'd taken.

She'd never forget the cold light crackling in Marnie's eyes that day. It had iced the soul of even that younger, harder version of Greta. It chilled her even now. "If one of us goes down," Marnie had said when Greta provided her the information for the offshore bank account, "we all do."

Greta took the book to the fireplace and doused it with lighter fluid.

She watched as the flames licked at the dust jacket and Marnie's face began to disappear.

Everything she'd ever wanted—money, a beautiful home, the prestige that came with her role as chief hospital administrator—could still be erased.

She was glad that Sarah Baker was dead.

CHAPTER 40

Lindsay waited for the advertisement to reach the point where YouTube would allow her to skip it. Ten seconds seemed an eternity. At last, the grainy recording began playing.

It had been uploaded by a bitter husband from Cleveland, leading a tireless, lonely charge to expose Marnie for what he was certain she was. It wasn't much of a movement, as it turned out. Gordon Carlton's subscriber base was fewer than three hundred.

Even so, he had remained a thorn in Marnie's side.

Nothing he'd tried to this point—letters, postings, news conferences—had amounted to anything. Marnie Spellman was Teflon, he said, and just as deadly.

This video clip, however, had legs with more than thirty thousand views.

Lindsay watched Marnie on the set at the shopping channel, some-how looking simultaneously glamorous and approachable. She wore her hair up, with a pair of ringlet strands that trailed softly in front of her ears, which were adorned with citrine diamonds, yellow being her signature color. She was beautiful and serene. The lights didn't wash out her features the way they did her host's. Brett Freeman, a straw-slender man with an Adam's apple that protruded so much it could support a scarf, seemed halfway in love with Marnie, insisting that she'd been his discovery and that no other host, male or female, would ever get to work with her on set.

Forget Connie, who'd been the first. She'd somehow been pushed into the Christmas in July slot, midnight to 4:00 a.m.

By then, Marnie and another entrepreneur who cheerfully sold whimsical jewelry featuring cherubs and hearts were the unabashed stars of their respective time slots. The hosts were there only to keep things moving along when there was any lag in conversation or, more importantly, sales. When it came to Marnie and Spellman Farms, there was never a problem in either regard.

All of that changed with what Marnie would later insist had been an "unfortunate slip of the tongue" and that in no way had she meant any animosity to anyone whatsoever.

Brett: Marnie, you look amazing.

Marnie: Oh, Brett, you say that every time I'm here. And by the way, I'm absolutely thrilled to be here with you tonight.

Brett: I remember when you first appeared on our air.

Marnie (laughing): Don't bring up that ridiculous vest I wore! Oh my, you must have thought you were watching someone from Hooterville!

Brett (somewhat coyly): Now, now . . . you know better. Tell us about what you have in store for us today.

Marnie: Well, we're definitely going to make history tonight. Today, we're launching our first-ever quad pack. That means you get four Spellman Farms products that will absolutely change the way you look and, as I say all the time, also address the you inside.

Brett: The you inside. That's really what you do, Marnie. You help people become better inside and outside.

Marnie: Yes. That's the gift that I freely give. I give everyone the chance to be beautiful through and through. Really, isn't that what everyone wants?

[Before Brett can answer, Marnie begins going over the quad pack, its cleanser, scrub, toner, and elixir cream.]

Marnie: Every single product is all natural. One hundred percent. Kelp from the sea right off the coast of my home on Lummi Island, Washington. Hazelnuts from Oregon. Bee pollen and honey, of course, from the hives on my farm and from reputable, sustainable beekeepers all over the Pacific Northwest.

Brett: The Pacific Northwest is crucial. I understand many of your fans have moved up there. What is it about the region that you think draws them?

Marnie: That's kind of a rumor, Brett. I've met a few people who enjoy my products and my theories about life and beauty, but no real fans or followers.

Brett: Andrea from Rapid City is on the line. Hi, Andrea!

Marnie: Hello, dear Andrea!

[Andrea nervously chats about the enormous improvement of her complexion since she adopted a regimen of Spellman Farms products.]

Andrea: My husband says I look twenty years younger.

Marnie: That's wonderful, sweetie. Be sure to remember to feed your spirit, too. Your husband can't see what's inside, and remember, that's the most important thing about Spellman Farms products. Inside. I have a new book out, *The Insatiable Heart*, and you'll just love it.

Andrea: Already ordered. You changed my life, Marnie.

[The pair thanks Andrea for the call, and a model named Geneva comes into view. She's in her early forties, with the soft edges of age on her face, her neck, and her ears. Her skin is only slightly marred by age spots. With all of that, Geneva is very attractive.]

Marnie: Geneva here is as lovely as she could be. Or is she? I want to show you how using the elixir with bee pollen and royal jelly can work miracles.

[She glides over to the model and gently applies the product to the woman's cheeks, under her eyes, and over her forehead. Almost instantaneously, the product sharpens Geneva's features.]

Marnie: Brett, look at the way her skin is responding. Her face is looking younger already.

Brett (his eyes wide): This is remarkable!

Marnie: No, it's reality. It's Geneva's reality.

Brett: How does it feel, Geneva?

Geneva: It feels good. Fresh. Not sticky. After being up all night with a new baby with special needs, Down syndrome, this feels good.

Marnie: I'm sorry about your baby. God sometimes makes mistakes.

[Silence.]

Geneva (blinking): I'm sor—What do you mean by that?

Marnie: Oh. Nothing. Just . . . well . . . if she didn't make mistakes, we wouldn't know how perfect the rest of us are.

[Geneva is no longer lovely. Her mouth hangs open, then tightens into a warlike grimace as she steps toward Marnie. Brett, who's been standing there, stuck in cement, looks off camera and then pivots.]

Brett: Today's awesome accessory—our TAA—is selling out. Take a look.

And that was it.

After that, Marnie was never asked back. Turned out, the head of the channel also had a child with Down syndrome. Marnie tried to dig herself out of it by going on one of the first apology tours in a country that in time would become overrun with them. She told radio and TV talk show hosts from coast to coast that she'd been misrepresented or misheard.

Of course, she had been neither of those things.

Two months after the show, Marnie retreated to Lummi Island. Her business nearly foundered completely. She fought harder than she ever had to get things back on track. She believed that her products were good—good enough for people to forget what she'd said.

CHAPTER 41

July 1999
Lummi Island, Washington

The day after the tabloids published a story about Dina Marlow's drunk-driving incident, six months after her humiliating trip to LA to have the death of her career confirmed, Marnie recorded a video message for her followers. A big, gold barrette held her hair in place. She pulled back a little from the lens, having seen her last video and noting that the slight, exceedingly fine, nearly nonexistent lines on her face were somewhat evident.

"I'm reaching out because unkind things have been reported about my dearest friend, Dina Marlow. She's been the subject of nasty rumors. I won't dignify the rumors by detailing them here. You probably know them, anyway. Dina is among the most beautiful and enlightened women I have had the privilege to know. She's not perfect. No one is. She's made mistakes. But believe you me, she is the victim here of a bitter agent with his own sour agenda. This man has used her for income, and now, he seeks to destroy what he can no longer control."

When the video went out, Dina was among the recipients. She didn't even have a chance to view it before her phone started ringing with calls from reporters and friends. The reporters wanted more details; friends feigned caring, so they'd be able to tell others that they'd spoken with Dina.

Dina was livid. Hurt. Marnie had made the video under the pretense of defending her, even though she knew her mentor also had an ulterior motive—she lusted after attention and fame and saw this as perhaps her last opportunity to milk her connection with Dina. A young star with a drinking problem elicited sympathy, whetted the public's appetite for a comeback story, evidence of the beautiful but troubled young person's hard-won maturity.

An old, fading star with a drinking problem?

Nothing but a drunk.

Dina got Marnie on the phone.

"I wish you hadn't done that," she said, right away.

"What?"

Marnie could be so exasperating. Answers so often came in the form of a question.

"The video."

"I couldn't just stand there and let them say those nasty things about you, Dina."

"Actually, Marnie," Dina said, "you could have. Or rather you *should* have. My phone has been ringing nonstop."

"You're a star. People adore you."

"Right, Marnie. Sure. But that's not the point."

"Is there anything greater than love?"

Dina gnashed her veneers. She hated when Marnie asked questions that elicited obvious answers. There was a tactical point to it, she supposed. It was Marnie's way of shutting down the other party. It was a technique employed to inject her philosophy and her need for control into any conversation.

"No, Marnie. Of course not. There is nothing greater than love."

"Love is the reason I back you all the way."

The call was getting her nowhere.

Dina hung up, dug for a pack of cigarettes in the kitchen, and lit one with a nearly dead disposable lighter. As she inhaled, she noticed her hands were trembling. They hadn't really fought, but her nerves were frayed. For a moment she nursed the hope that Marnie might be as upset by their call as she was. Yet only for a moment. Marnie was, as far as Dina knew, an utter stranger to regret. Whereas Dina was a connoisseur: Why in the world had she acquiesced to Marnie when she'd meant to call her out?

For of course, that evening, the narrative was transformed. No longer was the leading story about her drunken mishap; it was about how Marnie Spellman had nobly defended Dina and had put down men in the process.

The following morning, Marnie looked at the framed screenshot of the first order she'd ever had from her days with the shopping channel. It hung in a Tiffany frame presented to her by the man who ultimately would fire her and try to ruin her. It hung next to a vanity that she had custom built in an alcove between her bedroom suite and bathroom. When she first got home after the TV debacle, she'd wanted to hurl it into outer space. She even took it down once because the reminder was so painful. In time, however, she returned it to its most powerful position: in front of her face. It was always there, telling her that no matter what obstacles got in her path, she'd find a way to either plow right through them or leap over them. Nothing, she'd vowed after her failed apology tour, would stop or even slow her.

The world, she knew, needed her.

Still.

Chapter 42

With the exception of the cigarette she bummed at Alan's memorial, Lindsay hadn't smoked since her divorce, and that was more out of defiance than stress. As the Baker case, and by extension the Sullivan case, drew her deeper into Marnie Spellman's world—one of missing people, bitter charges from ex-followers, and the increasingly dark events that shrouded all the key players—old habits brought false comfort. She stopped at Circle K and bought Marlboro Lights and a six-pack of Bud Light.

God, she thought, *I'm turning into a teenager.* The idea made her smile a little, though briefly.

By the time she got home, she was ready for a smoke, a beer, and a call to Calista's mother, Cheryl Furlong, who Reed had said was in her nineties, still sharp and living in Southern California.

Lindsay snubbed out her cigarette and dialed.

"Mrs. Furlong?" she asked when an elderly voice answered.

"I'm capturing your number and putting you on my do-not-call list."

"Wait! I'm a detective. I'm looking into your daughter's murder."

The old lady on the other end of the line stayed quiet before snapping out a response.

"Look, Detective, what's your name?"

"Jackman. Lindsay Jackman. I'm with the Ferndale Police Department."

"Look," she repeated, "my daughter was murdered twenty years ago, and I've made peace with the fact that we'll never know who exactly did it. Though I have my ideas. It wasn't Reed. I know that much."

"Who was it?"

"I don't want to be involved. I don't want to end up like the others."

"What others?"

"Karen Ripken, for one. She and I talked. And then she was gone."

"Tell me about that. It could be important."

"Fine. My show starts in twenty minutes. I'll give you that much time."

April 2000

Cheryl Furlong was in her early seventies, although most would have thought her to be much younger. She had high cheekbones; soft, beachy blond hair; and perfect posture. Calista had been a younger version of Cheryl—except for the inexplicable belief in Marnie Spellman. Cheryl thought it was a bunch of hooey.

Deadly hooey, at that.

After Calista's body was found by the beachcombers, Karen Ripken phoned Cheryl at her home in Southern California. They'd connected through Karen's support group by way of Reed Sullivan. Cheryl had been rocked to her core by her daughter's decision to leave her boys—and even Reed, for that matter.

"Marnie has that kind of effect on people," Karen insisted. "My mom let me and my little sister go, too."

"I will never understand any of this, Karen. My daughter was smart. Kind. Loving. And now she's gone."

"We have Marnie Spellman to thank for that."

Normally a woman known to speak her mind, Cheryl hesitated.

"Do you think she had something to do with Calista's death?" she finally asked.

"Uh-huh. I mean I wouldn't put it past her."

"Police think Reed might be behind it. I told them that was a crock. Reed would never, ever hurt her. He loved her despite what she did to him and the boys. He wouldn't hurt a fly."

"I'm telling you, Cheryl," Karen said. "Just like my mom, Calista fell into a viper's nest the minute she started listening to those CDs."

"Oh, I know it. Those recordings are a big lie. Only empty promises. Garbage."

"Yeah," Karen said, then sighed. "We're both just preaching to the choir, aren't we?"

"Yes, I guess we are. It's good to have someone to talk to about it."

"Yes. Yes, it helps. A little, at least, and for a little while."

When Cheryl spoke again, it was as if her voice had been torn down the middle. "And Karen, I think the worst of it . . . the worst of it is that Calista was almost free of them."

"What do you mean?"

"She didn't outright say it, but by the end, she hinted that the whole supposed movement was bullshit. Forgive my French."

"What did she tell you?"

"Never anything specific. She just said she'd found something that made her rethink everything she'd believed. I think she wanted out of there. She called me a few weeks before she was killed."

January 2000

Cheryl had been deadheading geraniums on her back patio. She had foolishly planted white ones that year, a floral scheme she'd never repeat. Every time the Santa Anas kicked up, the blossoms would curl at their edges and turn brown. Red was a much better choice, more forgiving of the hot wind, more resilient.

She was ready for a break when her daughter phoned.

"What a great surprise, Calista. Perfect timing, too. I've had it with these darn geraniums. I might even go plastic next year."

"You'd never do that in a million years, Mom."

"I don't know . . . How are you? Is everything all right?"

Cheryl sat on a wicker chair and waited for her daughter to respond.

"I don't know how to say this," she said. Her voice was tentative. "I don't even know if I should say it. It's really bothering me."

"You can tell me, honey."

A long pause.

"I don't know, Mom. It's just that I'm not sure about things here."

"'Not sure'?"

"I don't know," Calista said. "They are doing things that feel wrong to me."

"What kinds of things?"

"Researching new products at the farm. They've crossed a line." She fell silent. She was thinking, working things over in her mind. Cheryl knew to let her do it. Trusted her daughter to get where she needed to go; knew she hadn't called to be told where that was.

Cheryl would have the rest of her life to regret not stepping in, demanding details, begging her only child to come home to her.

Instead, she'd let her think it through, and when Calista said, "You know what, Mom? I've said enough already. Really, I just wanted to call you and hear your voice," Cheryl had melted a little inside and smiled into the phone.

"You know I'm always here, honey."

"I know that, Mom. And I'll have some happy news for you soon. I'll leave it at that for now."

Cheryl had no idea what the happy news was.

They never spoke again.

Sunday, September 22, 2019

"*Wheel* is on in a minute," Cheryl said. "My guilty pleasure. We're done here."

"Good show," Lindsay said.

"You're right it is, Detective. Not a mystery. Not like law enforcement and the constant guessing games about what happened to my daughter. A puzzle is solved and you win. Done. Game over."

"I'm sorry that no one paid a price for Calista's murder, Mrs. Furlong."

"I'm ninety-two," she said. "I know it's just a matter of time and I'll be done with this earth. Same thing will happen to whoever killed Calista. Only difference is that I'm going to heaven."

With that, she thanked the detective and hung up.

CHAPTER 43

December 1994
Lummi Island, Washington

Marnie had set up a studio in the barn to record her self-help tapes. When it was new, it was truly state-of-the-art. At one time, she even had a small staff associated with that part of her empire. One girl was assigned to put the stickers on the CDs, and another packaged them for mailing. She even had a sound engineer on call, a Lummi man who worked for KVOS-TV in Bellingham.

She poured a glass of Syrah, her favorite, as only the deepest reds would ever do, and sat down at the once-pristine table. She moved aside the lavender bunches that she'd harvested herself the day before. The air was fragrant, and she closed her eyes to breathe it all in and remember where it had all started. She could imagine the sun on her face the day the swarm came and spoke to her. She could feel the vibrations of hundreds of thousands of bees' wings as the insects lifted her and spoke to her.

She needed money. She maintained a mailing list of two hundred thousand in seventeen countries. In Marnie's mind, those who were on her list—those who wanted enlightenment and perfection—would welcome a message in a world that was becoming increasingly unhinged.

She sipped more wine and inserted a tape into the recorder.

She started slowly.

"It's me. It's the one who knows you are hurting now and you are confused about the world and where we are going. I'm calling on you right now. I'm here to tell you that you are beautiful. You own your place in the world, and it is an ownership that no one can wrestle away. People have tried to harm me, people have misinterpreted things that I've said, I still remain steadfast. Undaunted. It is because of you. All of you. No matter where you are, I feel your love pour over me. I am nourished. I will survive. And so will you.

"When I was a girl and the bees lifted me, I wasn't afraid. I think now that if I had screamed, if I had tried to wriggle out of the swarm, the bees might not have selected me for this life that has brought us together. Indeed, they might have stung me to death. So I'm asking you, I'm telling you: Be your most perfect and beautiful self. Never be afraid of what is to come. Because what's to come is your destiny—a destiny created by you and our Heavenly Mother.

"I have a small piece of paper I saved years ago. I tucked it into an envelope that I will open for the first time since that day. It was a message from the swarm. It was written by the bees themselves in the yellow of fireweed pollen."

(The sound of paper rustling.)

"It says . . ."

(The sound of tearing now.)

"It says this: Help her."

(A long pause.)

"When I first saw this, I thought it was just for me. For me to help our Heavenly Mother as she fights against the male status quo, but I think otherwise now. I humbly ask you now: Help me. Help me continue my work. Send me what you can afford. Ask your friends to help."

Marnie pressed the button to stop the recording. Tears streamed down her face as she sat looking at her image reflected on the shiny surface of the table. She finished her wine, then composed a brief note on her personal computer and included a link to transfer money to her account. It wasn't subtle, but she didn't come out and ask for money. It was implied only by the link—and the words sent to her from the bees. She uploaded the audio file and sent it out into the world, to those thousands of people who loved her. She didn't even think about the response rate, a crucial measure of her past sales endeavors. Instead, she waited for the first person to answer her call.

It was, not surprisingly, Gina Krause from Casper, Wyoming, who answered first. A stalwart fan from nearly the beginning, Gina not only lived facing her computer screen, but she'd been the first to start a local chapter of promoters for Spellman Farms products. No one was paid to go door to door or to post notices on office bulletin boards. No one even asked for anything of the sort. Marnie's army was on a mission.

She opened Gina's email.

> I just listened to your message, Marnie. I hear you.
> I'm not going to let you down, as you have always
> been there for me. I'm sending $200 right now. I'll
> send more after payday next week. Sending my
> love and commitment to the most amazing woman
> on the planet.

Marnie pushed herself away from the table as her email inbox flooded with responses. The pinging mimicked an old pinball machine. Or music. She had gone to the well before, although never with such need. Never with such urgency.

Marnie would not give up on her dreams.

She reached for the blank paper, the purported missive from the bees, and threw it into the trash.

CHAPTER 44

Monday, September 23, 2019
Lynden, Washington

Lindsay considered Marnie's life, her philosophy, a veritable train wreck, and yet a compulsively interesting, almost eerily compelling one. How was it that even Kate Spellman, a no-nonsense woman among no-nonsense women, had gotten caught up in her daughter's scheme, her woo-woo philosophy? What was it that drew accomplished women like Heather, Greta, and Dina into the Hive?

That everyone was looking for something to make themselves whole would likely be the guess from any armchair psychologist. Surely, there had to be more to it than just that common need alone, though. Marnie Spellman was almost certainly a self-serving, self-mythologizing, once-in-a-generation charlatan—but there was no denying that she had a gift for seeing the hurt inside the women who flocked to her and for appealing to them with the promise of something better.

Predators do that, Lindsay thought. *They find the weak—even when the weak seem as though they aren't weak at all—and they have an innate sense for whom to peel off from the rest of the herd.*

Child rapists know which kid on the playground is vulnerable. Serial killers spot the woman desperate enough to take a chance on a ride with a stranger.

Truly gifted predators—those born to it—just *know*.

Marnie collected women who didn't mind simply basking in her glow; women who could accept that the reflection of greatness was in itself a worthy purpose.

Marnie Spellman and her products made promises that could not be measured by the FDA.

She promised women that clear and vibrant skin was the "outside-in" way to feel better about themselves.

And she wrapped that up in a stream-of-consciousness, buzzword-steeped theology that riled feminists but appealed to those with broken pieces that never quite fit the way they'd thought they should.

Lindsay slotted a CD into a player, and Marnie's voice filled the air.

How is the impossible achieved? Through perseverance and need. That's how I've lived my life from the moment I understood the power of the world under our feet and in the skies overhead. Ants lift leaves far beyond their body weight and carry them homeward without a bit of struggle. They do that because they need to in order to survive. I've never witnessed a mother lift up a car to save her child trapped underneath, but I know that has been done. It is the impossible, made possible.

That brings me to my beloved bees. The way God designed these creatures nearly makes the very idea of their flight a cruel joke. Especially the bumblebee. And yet they persevere, with brute force and determination, their innate inefficient aerodynamics work just fine. One undeniable component of the impossible in the case of bees

is the nectar that fuels every beat of their wings. Nectar is
honey transformed. Honey is life.

The next evening, Lindsay heard a thud at the door and found a yellow-and-black package waiting on her doorstep. Her Spellman Farms order had arrived. She put it on the coffee table and got herself a beer from the kitchen before settling in.

She'd ordered the starter pack, which included Royal Jelly Elixir, Honeycomb Scrub, and Bee Yourself.

The packaging was elegant, with the product name in the kind of calligraphy usually reserved for wedding announcements. A yellow-and-black ribbon encircled the top of each jar or tube.

Lindsay set them on the table in front of her while she read a letterpress card from the box:

Bee all that you dream. Bee beautiful. Bee strong enough
in your knowingness to face any day.
  This is all for you.
  Bee powerful,
  Marnie Spellman
  Spellman Farms
  Lummi Island, Washington

The words were over the top. Unapologetically so. Lindsay wondered who could buy into such New Agey bullshit.

The desperate. The lonely. Searchers.

That's who.

She opened the Royal Jelly Elixir and breathed in. The face lotion smelled wonderful, as if she could pour it on ice cream and eat it. Sweet, not cloying. Not fake. Just the slight hint of the lavender grown on Spellman Farms.

She rubbed a touch onto her palm and breathed it in again.

So good.

The texture was different from anything she'd ever used. It felt silky and soft. It made her skin feel that way, too. She opened the other two containers, and they, too, smelled wonderful. Almost intoxicating. The tube for the Royal Jelly Elixir noted that it "contains real royal jelly."

From her reading, Lindsay knew that royal jelly was the substance drones fed a bee to turn her into a queen. It was a mysterious biological substance that was impossible to duplicate. Marnie Spellman had been the first to include it in her product line.

Lindsay set down her empty beer and carried her Spellman Farms products to the bathroom. She'd try them in the morning.

Research, she told herself.

Chapter 45

When Marnie was thirteen, her parents took her out of public school. Notes from her teacher's file published by the *Bellingham Herald* years later gave this reason: "The Spellmans consider their daughter a prodigy, which is fine. Many parents do. They intend to provide her with a more intensive curriculum."

Lindsay read what Marnie wrote about that period in *The Insatiable Heart*:

> *Mother and Father wanted me home. They needed me to work on the farm. My brother was younger, smaller than me. So I got the brunt of their ire when things didn't go right.*
>
> *I remember one time when Mother told me she needed help with the apricots she was canning. I was excited because I loved all the smells and the stickiness of the process. Mother had me clean the jars by sterilizing them in a vat of hot water she kept going on the stove. A timer told me when to pull jars from the water to cool. While I worked, the radio played my favorite classical*

music from a station in Canada. It was Bach, who was never my favorite composer—in fact, the only composer after which I didn't name any of my precious pets. Too many spikes of sound. Bach always seemed to unsettle me.

Lindsay set down the book. If she'd been a casual reader of the memoir, she'd have thought that the woman writing it had an ego that stretched from here to wherever. What child listens to Bach? It was possible, of course, or was it a fabrication that matched her grandiose view of herself?

Mother had stepped out of the room when my brother, Casey—enlisted to wash the fruit—tugged at my apron as I was removing the jars from the boiling water. I would later wonder if it was Bach's fault—later still, I would know better—but the tongs slipped, and a hot jar that held about an inch of water fell to the floor. In doing so, the water poured over his leg.

Casey's scream is still imprinted on my brain today. It was the scream of a dying animal, so strong and so loud that it not only brought Mother running back to me, it literally rattled the windows.

"God! Marnie, what did you do?" she screamed.

"I'm sorry. It was an accident."

She dropped to her knees and looked at my brother's scalded leg.

"There are no accidents. Only mistakes that people make when they don't pay attention."

She lifted Casey up, pulled the vegetable sprayer from the sink, and ran cold water over his leg.

Casey continued to wail.

*"We might need a doctor." She looked at the kitchen
clock, a black-and-white Bakelite clock that I still have in
my kitchen today. "Last ferry is about to leave."*

"I'll get some dressings," I said.

"You've done enough."

"I'm sorry, Mother."

*"'Sorry' is for those who knew better and didn't do
the right thing."*

During Lindsay's visit with Marnie's exiled mother, she'd come off
as a woman who'd accepted her banishment over time. She didn't seem
cold or indifferent to her daughter. Mother–daughter relationships were
difficult. Lindsay and her mother had gone through their own little
battles when she was a teenager. She ran around, got into a little trouble,
and then eventually settled down. After Lindsay joined the Ferndale
Police Department, her mother often reminded her of the irony of it all.

"Now you enforce the same rules you used to think were for everyone else."

Lindsay smiled at the memory and went on reading.

I got the gauze and some salve.

She looked at me with accusing eyes. "What's this?"

*"I made it," I said. "Medicine. It's beeswax and
herbs. Like your soaps, but for cuts and stuff."*

*Mother looked at the blue Noxzema jar that I had
used to store the salve. Her eyes went back to mine as she
sniffed it.*

"Calendula?"

I nodded. "And honey. Some other things, too."

*Mother put the amber-colored salve on my brother's
leg. He stopped crying almost at once.*

"That feels better," Mother said. "Doesn't it?"

By then, we'd literally missed the boat. My brother went to bed, and the next day, he was already in the kitchen when I woke up, eating breakfast with Mother and Father. The Noxzema jar sat in the center of the table.

"Morning," Father said.

"How's Brother?" I asked.

Mother was teary eyed, but that didn't compute at first. Father and Brother were smiling. In fact, Father got up and gave me the biggest hug I'd ever had in my life. Mother joined him. Then Brother. We were one being right then, bound together in a harmony that I hadn't ever expected. Mother had been a taskmaster. Father had been too busy with the farm. And Brother—he was just a pain in the neck half the time. Not that morning. Everyone was crying. I started to cry.

"What is it?" I asked. "Why are we crying?"

"Look at his leg," Father said.

"It's a miracle," Mother added.

I pulled away and lowered my tearful gaze to my brother's leg. It was normal. Clear. There wasn't a trace of the burn from the day before.

Her word choices for her family members was strange. Mother? Father? Brother? They were a part of her story, but she wrote about them in a way that distanced them from her. Making them generic made her stand out. They were, Lindsay was sure, only devices in her storyline—real or imagined.

I write this now, and I can't help but connect the day the swarm took me to the elixir that I created for my brother's wound in that little blue jar. I know now as I knew then that none of it was a miracle. I knew that the bees led me to mix the ingredients that saved my brother from skin grafts. They had talked to me—not in words, but inwardly. They had let their will be known. If you've ever sat on a driftwood log facing the Pacific and heard the music and rhythm of the waves as they pound and caress the shore, then you just might know what I mean. If you listen carefully, there is a message.

The message is directed not to your brain, only to your heart.

CHAPTER 46

YouTube had scores, if not hundreds, of clips of Marnie Spellman before and after her rise and fall. Lindsay continued to find herself mesmerized by the outrageousness of Spellman's stories—and none were more fascinating than her origin story. The story of the swarm.

She clicked on a video headlined Spellman's Childhood BFF Talks the Swarm.

The TV camera focused on the woman's face at first, holding it a long time. Astra Ullman had black hair and blue eyes behind the cat's-eye frames of her glasses. Her top was a plain white blouse, accented by a large gold chain with a swallow pendant.

"She was your best friend, wasn't she?" the interviewer asked.

Astra smiled and gave a knowing, self-deprecating look. "More like only friend," she said. "Being raised on an island makes for slim pickings when it comes to things like kids your own age."

"You two were close."

"I thought we were."

"What do you mean?"

"I don't know. Marnie had a wall around her. Don't get me wrong: we had mostly good times on Lummi. We were back-and-forth friends. We hung out in the woods, picked mushrooms for the inn, that kind of thing. We spent a lot of time together, and if you told me back then that we'd be friends forever, I would have agreed. It just didn't turn out like that."

"I see. Let's talk more about Marnie as a girl. Did you see anything that told you she'd be so well known, that she'd be as famous as some of her celebrity clients?"

"You mean Dina Marlow?"

"Yes, and others. Did you imagine how far she'd take her dreams?"

Astra looked away from the camera, then back at the interviewer. "No. I didn't. Honestly, I thought a bunch of what she was saying was just a game."

"Like what? What did she say to you?"

She looked to someone off camera. "I don't feel comfortable talking about this." Then back to the interviewer. "I'm sorry. This wasn't a good idea."

"No, Astra. I'm sorry. Let's start over. Tell me what happened to your chickens."

"I'm still mad that people don't know the truth about her. I shouldn't have done this interview. I need to just leave it alone. I'm sorry you wasted your time."

"Your chickens were killed, Astra. Isn't that right?"

The video came to an abrupt end.

It took Lindsay all of two minutes to locate Astra Ullman's telephone number. Thank God for folks who still clung to their landlines. The oddness of her name didn't hurt. She hadn't gone far; she'd ended up in Anacortes, Washington.

Lindsay pushed back her chair and dialed Astra's number. A woman answered, and they exchanged introductions.

"I don't mean to be rude, Detective, but you can forget calling me again."

"I'm sorry, I'm in the middle of something, and I need to know more about Marnie Spellman."

"Middle of what?"

"A homicide case."

"Doesn't really surprise me. Marnie's a menace. Has been forever."

"How so?"

"Look," Astra said, "I'll be blunt. You don't know what you're getting into with that woman. I had to move from the island because I was stupid enough to speak out against her."

"What do you mean?"

"I'm not saying it was Marnie or one of her followers. Probably one of them. I really don't know. I won't ever know."

"What happened, Astra?"

An uneasy stillness filled the line.

"What happened to your chickens?" Lindsay persisted.

"You saw my misguided attempt at my fifteen minutes. So dumb to do that."

"I saw the video. This is just you and me. I need to know the story."

"All right. I was raising French Marans. Chickens. Every single one died. More than two hundred twenty birds. All dead."

"You think Marnie killed them?"

"Not exactly. The vet said the feed was bad. When I took a sample to Seattle for a lab analysis, they said the feed had been laced with arsenic."

"Why do you think Marnie was behind that?"

"When we were kids, her dad used arsenic to kill rats on the farm. Marnie told me that one time the chickens got into it and died. She was really mad about it. Said that they died after only a peck or two of feed. And now this call is over."

"You really think that she'd poison your chickens?"

No answer.

"Hello? Astra?"

The line was dead. As Astra had indicated, the call was over.

CHAPTER 47

April 1992
Lantana, Florida

Marnie knew the underlying power of anguish and heartache better than a Kennedy.

She stood on masking tape Xs on the shopping channel's floor two weeks after her brother's last visit to the farm. Marnie was on a mission. Her makeup was flawless; she had her regular girl apply a foundation a shade two tones lighter than what she customarily wore on air.

The makeup artist was skeptical. "Are you absolutely sure? You might look a little washed out. The lights are so bright, so cruel."

Marnie and the makeup artist both studied her face in the mirror. "Completely. Last time you had me on—and not your fault—I looked like I'd spent a week in West Palm Beach. Not the best look for my market."

When filming began, the host, a blandly handsome man who normally sold copper-clad cookware, stood next to her.

"Before we move on with your segment, Marnie, I can't help but acknowledge what you've been going through."

Marnie's eyes glistened. "Thank you, Ricky," she said, taking a deep breath before turning from the host and directly facing the camera's lens.

"It has been extremely difficult," she went on. "As many of you know, my beloved brother passed from an overdose of prescription drugs. Casey had struggled for years, fighting the fight. Winning. Losing. Of course, he's still with me, just as he always has been, by my side from the very beginning. He was a witness to everything that happened. I don't want to dwell on his ending, because none of us truly end. We go on to another life and continue to be all that we can be. Casey's there. As is our father."

Ricky gave Marnie a clumsy hug and then, just as awkwardly, redirected the conversation.

"Marnie, thank you for sharing," he said. "Truly heartbreaking. We are all full of grief for you. We in the studio and your countless fans share your pain."

The camera panned over her product line, the yellow-and-black jars that defined her brand, and Ricky pivoted.

"Let's talk more about being all we can be and how Spellman Farms continues to lead the way in making women—and, I admit, some men like me—be our best possible selves."

Marnie let out a protracted sigh.

"It's always been about the bees, Ricky," she said, energy returning to her pallid face. "They are nature's engineers, nature's lovemakers, as they pollinate all of the crops we need. Within their DNA, they have the knowingness that the center of the universe is female, not male. That's right, Ricky. Don't be offended: God is a female."

"My wife tells me that all the time," he said.

*A week after the swarm lifted me, I woke up in a hos-
pital in Bellingham. My parents nearly lunged at me
as I lay supine, dry mouthed. My eyes were slits, but I
could see them. I saw my mother's tears and that she
was caressing me, yet I didn't feel her touch. My father
was crying, too. So was my brother. I knew they were
tears of joy.*

    Something was wrong.

    Worse than being in the hospital.

    *I watched a man come to my mother. He was in a
white coat. A doctor? A nurse? He was patting her on
the shoulder in that gentle but firm manner that was
meant to comfort. I saw her recoil slightly and reach
for my father. Her fingers reminded me of a red rock
crab's spring-loaded pincers. She scooped my father up,
then pinned his shoulders tightly to hers and wailed at
the ceiling. Her screams reverberated, and my father
held her.*

    Neither of my parents came to me.

    Neither reached for my exposed, swollen hand.

Then my brother came to me and said everything would be all right.

We were always close like that. Even when he had his problems. And even at the end.

The Insatiable Heart
Marnie Spellman

CHAPTER 48

Marnie's brother was sixteen when his parents first sent him to rehab on the other side of the Cascades, just north of Spokane. Marnie, then nineteen, went with the family to drive him to the facility. Her mother and father sat in the front and brother and sister were in back.

Casey's rapid trajectory from smoker to pot smoker to heroin user wasn't surprising. In the late 1970s, Lummi Island was very much a rock with very little to do. Casey scored his first cocaine from a customer at the Wildwood Inn, where he was working as a busboy—at his parents' insistence.

Marnie was older and, frankly, more useful on the farm than Casey, who was prone to get lost in the music of his tape player when he was supposed to be working. At the restaurant, their parents reasoned, he'd build some character out of much-needed discipline.

Instead, Casey learned to size up restaurant patrons and their teenagers as potential sources of drugs. He was as resourceful as his sister.

Just not in the ways his parents had hoped.

Casey had curly black hair that he wore like a used-up shipyard mop. His eyes were always lazy and hooded, even before the drugs. He knew his place in the family. It was always Marnie first, then Casey.

Even when he was an infant, there'd been few pictures of only him in the family album. It was always his older sister who was the focus of every shot. Kate Spellman once told him that there were times when she'd forgotten he'd been *her* baby, not Marnie's.

"Marnie treated you like you belonged to her. She was the little mother. You were the precious baby doll that needed her attention."

Over that long stretch of empty highway from Ellensburg to the bridge over the Columbia, Casey kept his head against his sister's shoulder. She was asleep. He looked up and could see, beneath her slightly raised eyelids, that her eyes were moving furiously. A dream. A nightmare. He looked past her at the car door and could see that the lock knob hadn't been pressed down. If he'd wanted to push her out, he would only have to reach across her, undo her shoulder harness, open the door, and shove.

Marnie opened her eyes just then, and the fantasy that had passed through his mind stopped. He stopped it. It was like he needed to back up right then and think of something else. Fast.

Marnie could read him whether he was high or sober. She had a canny and unnerving ability to be inside his own head.

"What are you thinking now, Casey?" she asked.

"Nothing. Just about what this place will be like."

"You're lying," she said.

How did she know?

"Don't start with him, Marnie," their mother said.

"I'm not starting anything. He's a liar. We all know that."

Casey pulled away, retreating as far as he could to the other side of the seat. Maybe he should just open the door and jump out. Maybe that would be better for everyone.

"How much longer, Dad?" he asked.

"Couple hours, buddy."

"Okay." He looked over at his sister. The best thing about rehab would be the month away from her.

Drug addicts like Casey Spellman don't dream of ending up as they do. It isn't a destiny they chart out of a sense of purpose. After rehab in Spokane and another stint in outpatient at a clinic in Edmonds, Washington, he knew that he'd never make it out of the quicksand in which he'd found himself.

Everywhere he went, his sister's rise to fame and fortune was thrust at him. He'd seen her on TV. Her products in the window of a store. One time when he was wandering around the Western Washington University campus, waiting for his score, he even saw her picture in a magazine lying in the gutter. He picked it up and started to read.

When his dealer, a student from Kirkland, arrived, she remarked on Marnie's photograph.

"My mom thinks she's God's gift to womankind," she said.

"Oh," Casey replied as he let the magazine fall back into the gutter.

Where he felt she belonged.

Where he knew he'd end up.

"Yeah. Has her tapes and stuff. Always telling me how life changing her message is. Got the money?"

He handed over the cash he'd stolen from tips on tables where he tried to hold down a job.

"I said twenty."

"I only have seventeen."

"That's really sad. You're too old to be doing this, anyway."

She started to walk away.

He grabbed her by the shoulder. "I need this," he said.

She pulled away. "Maybe you should listen to those stupid recordings and you wouldn't be such a loser."

It took everything he had—which wasn't much—to stop himself from punching her in the face. She was like his sister. Full of advice.

Full of contempt.

And rich.

The pilot on the *Whatcom Chief* recognized Casey right away.

It was early March 1992—Casey was twenty-four—and the winds blew needles of cold air into his bearded face.

"Hey," he said, "aren't you the Spellman kid?"

Casey gave the man a nod. "Yeah. The one that got away."

"Haven't seen you in a long time around here."

"I moved out of state," Casey said, a lie that he'd preplanned in case anyone recognized him. It was better than saying he'd been off doing drugs for the past few years.

The pilot kept his eyes fixed on Casey's, perhaps wondering if he was like his sister, able to read people. Casey hoped not. Even though he'd truly hated his parents for their constant praise for his sister and their ceaseless nagging on his shortcomings, he didn't want anyone to know his true feelings. Being full of hate only made him feel more like a bitter loser, which was how his sister had already managed to make him feel with the note that summoned him home.

"Give your sister a hug for me. She's beloved here, as you know. The community center she built—just amazing."

The pilot went back inside the tollbooth-sized wheelhouse to maneuver the vessel alongside the island's dock.

"Yeah. Will do."

Casey, who no longer carried a valid driver's license, managed to hitch a ride with a woman and her two kids coming for the weekend.

She was about the same age as his sister, maybe a year or two younger. She drove an old VW Rabbit with a screwdriver stuck into the ignition where the key would normally go. He sat in front, while the kids sat in their car seats in the back.

"I'm here for a job interview," she said.

"At the Wildwood Inn?"

"Yeah, how did you know?"

"It was either that or Spellman Farms. Not a lot of other options. You'll like the inn. I used to work there."

She was a brunette with short fingernails that she'd gamely painted a light pink. She wore a pink sweater and black jeans.

"Nina," she said.

"Casey."

As she pulled off the dock and took the road around the island to the inn, she talked about the job—as a maid, full time.

"They have a fifth-wheel trailer in back that I can live in, or I can commute. The commute seems rough."

"I'd commute, though," he said. "I'm from here. Being stuck on this rock at ten o'clock at night and nowhere to go can drive you crazy."

"Their father is on a fishing boat in Alaska. I could leave the kids with his mom."

"I'd do the commute. Trust me."

She gave him a smile. It was a kind and friendly one. It made him wish that his life weren't stuck like that screwdriver hanging out of her dash—that he'd be able to make a life for himself.

Maybe he could do it.

It was the reason why he came back to Lummi.

"The inn's right here," he said, pointing out an old farmhouse that had been converted into a restaurant and hotel with ten rooms and a stunning view of the water. Trumpet vines lived up to their name as they amplified the split-rail fence and signage with bright-orange blossoms and crisp, green foliage.

"My interview isn't for an hour," she said. "Can I drive you the rest of the way?"

Casey liked her. He liked her because there had been no glint of recognition in her eyes when he mentioned Spellman Farms. In another time and place, she might have liked him for him and not as a means to get close to his sister, as others had.

"No, thanks, Nina," he said. "The walk will do me good."

Nina parked and twisted the screwdriver to shut off the Rabbit's engine. Casey got out and waved goodbye.

Marnie watched from the window as her brother ambled up the sweeping driveway. She'd taken off her expensive casualwear and jewelry—the trappings of her success—and put on a pair of jeans and a T-shirt. Later, she'd tell people that she did it because she didn't want him to feel that he'd been relegated to a level—or two—below her. She'd become a fixture on the home shopping channel when her father died. And in an unusual move, Johnny Spellman left full control of the multi-million-dollar one-hundred-acre estate to his daughter, not his wife. His son seemed to be a bit of an add-on, too. If Casey maintained sobriety for a period of two years, he'd be able to claim a share of the estate. In an arrangement she easily could have fought in court, Kate was given some cash and a promise that she'd be able to stay there until the end of her days. She didn't fight it, because her daughter was special, a gift for the world.

Marnie flung open the door and embraced Casey.

"I had faith in you," she said.

"I'm here for my share," he said, brushing her aside as he walked in. "I know you better than Mom and Dad ever did." He looked around. "Lots of upgrades, Sis. Hope you didn't spend it all."

She shut the door. "I have plenty of my own."

"I've watched you."

"I made Mom's lasagna," she said.

"Pass," he said. "I'm going to catch the next boat back. I just want what's mine."

He reached into his pocket and pulled out a letter from his doctor documenting twenty-four monthly tests confirming he'd been clean for the stated requirement.

"It's notarized. Witnessed. Whatever."

Marnie took the paper and read it through. "So I see."

"How much do I get?"

Casey was always the impatient kind, she thought. Always in a hurry. Always leeching on to whoever had drugs, until they didn't anymore.

"I have all the paperwork," she told him. She indicated a pitcher on the table. "I made honey lemonade."

He gave her an indifferent smile. "Like old times, right, Sis?"

She poured him a glass.

"Just like old times," she said, watching him take the glass, put it to his lips, and take a long, thirsty drink. "Mmm." He gulped down another. "Hits the spot. Surprised you haven't found a way to market this. Aren't you going to have—"

Suddenly, his eyes rounded and the glass shattered on the floor, sending a spray of liquid over the polished wood floors.

"You," he said. "Marnie. You . . . bitch."

Chapter 49

As she became more and more immersed in Marnie's story, Lindsay found herself picking up the phone to hear firsthand why others had thrown themselves in with her, had so passionately subscribed to beliefs and products—and why they had turned on her. Somewhere in their stories, she hoped, might be the answer to what had happened to both Calista and Sarah.

They were connected by Spellman Farms.

By Marnie's undeniable power.

Among the materials she'd collected was an article about a woman from Wyoming named Gina Krause. The source was her sister, Alexandra.

Lindsay found Alexandra's number and called her, explaining that she was a homicide investigator working a case with potential ties to Spellman Farms.

"Just one case?" Alexandra asked.

"Sounds like you have something to say."

"I do. And I have. And I will as long as people ask me."

Alexandra didn't know anything about Calista Sullivan beyond what she'd read in the news and on various message boards. She'd never heard of Sarah Baker.

While Alexandra talked, Lindsay took notes.

"Let me tell you about my sister."

Gina Krause could scarcely contain herself when she learned that she'd been selected to attend Marnie Spellman's weekend retreats on Lummi Island. Until then, most attendees of the Art of Beeing were members of the celebrity class: political, high society, Hollywood. According to the invitation, this particular weekend was a bit of an experiment, and as such, the six attendees were handpicked by Marnie to represent "women who have achieved their true potential quietly, unassumingly. These are the women who are already changing the world."

The cost for the retreat was only ten thousand dollars.

Gina withdrew all her savings and pawned her grandmother's art deco diamond brooch to pay the fee. She had no money for plane fare, so she drove her Ford Bronco to Washington State. She left her sister a voice message from a pay phone in Baker City, Oregon.

"I haven't even seen her yet, but I feel Marnie's love already. It's hard to explain the difference she's made in my life. I'm a broken record about that. Sorry. I can't wait to get there and learn more. Love you."

Alexandra said once her sister came home from that retreat, she was never the same.

"Gina was like a drug addict or something," she said, her story tumbling into Lindsay's ear and onto the pages of her notebook. "She didn't care about anything. She didn't go out. She didn't even get dressed. She just sat in front of her computer all day long, looking at that stupid message board. She was consumed by finding ways to add to what she called 'Marnie's army' by recruiting new members. I couldn't even budge her. I told her I was worried and thought that maybe she was being used."

"How did she react when you confronted her?" Lindsay asked.

"She didn't like that at all. Boy, did she tell me in no uncertain terms that I was wrong. Stupid to boot. I didn't know if it was a pyramid scheme or what at the time. I assumed she was getting paid. I didn't have the slightest idea she'd found a way to take out two mortgages on our parents' house and give the money to Marnie. So I guess Gina was right: I guess I was stupid after all."

"You weren't stupid, Alexandra," Lindsay said.

"You're just being nice. I was. And I'm still angry. Nothing good was happening on Spellman Farms. I hope you find out just what it was. There's a long line of us cheering you on."

CHAPTER 50

Thursday, August 22, 2019
Fairhaven, Washington

A couple weeks before Sarah Baker's body was discovered at Maple Falls, Greta Swensen buried herself in the stacks at Village Books and Paper Dreams in Fairhaven Village, an enclave of bars and boutiques just south of Bellingham. An avid reader, she eschewed online book browsing for the smell and feel of the real thing. It was a routine she'd started twenty-some years prior, a way to spend a Saturday, looking for a volume that would teach her something new or just help pass the time living alone. Greta had never married—not that she didn't have opportunities or suitors; she just preferred managing her life on her own. She was in the gardening section, looking over an old Ann Lovejoy book on the perennials of the Pacific Northwest, when she turned toward a familiar voice.

"How long has it been, Greta?"

It was Marnie, looking no different than the last time they'd seen each other—again by chance—downtown by the old Hotel Leopold, long after it had been converted into a residence for the aging. Today she wore a loose yellow sweater, cream slacks, and sling-back heels. Her signature bumblebee brooch—a Cartier—was pinned to her sweater near the neckline.

Greta must have looked surprised, because Marnie said, "Didn't mean to startle you, dear."

"Oh no. Just so happy to run into you. I didn't know you came here."

Marnie smiled. "I knew *you* do."

So this wasn't by chance.

"Do you have time for a little chat?"

To be fair, it was a question, but Marnie's intonation was so persuasive that Greta could see no way out of it.

"Of course," she said. "Love to."

"How's the house?"

"Oh, a work in progress. Like all things in life."

Marnie crooked her neck and looked deep into Greta's eyes. "I love making others' dreams come true."

They went across the street to a wine bar and ordered.

"I see you still love your reds," Marnie said as Greta sipped her merlot.

"Yes, I guess I do."

She wondered what Marnie wanted. It didn't take long. She was direct in asking for things that would specifically benefit her.

"I'm considering a reemerging," she said. That was, Greta knew, Marnie-speak for a comeback, a word that would never in a million years come from her lips.

"Oh really?"

"That's right. And well . . . what I'll be offering will be completely fantastic and sure to revolutionize the world. You know, I've always been ahead of my time. I was the first American woman to see the potential in stem cells as the basis for human improvement."

You were, and we stole stem cells for you, Greta thought. *We lied to the police. We did things that no human would ever want to do. For you. We did all that bullshit stuff for you.*

"Right," she said, waiting for Marnie to tell her whatever it was that she was developing.

But she didn't.

"I need some help. I've managed to replicate bee venom as a replacement for Botox. Its basis is natural. It lasts twice as long and will cost the user half as much. It will be huge. It will make us rich."

Again.

Marnie was breathless in excitement over her discovery.

"Us?" Greta repeated.

"Yes. You will be one of my investors."

Marnie always had a penchant for the assumptive close.

Greta looked away. Looking at Marnie directly was sometimes like looking into the sun.

"It sounds exciting, Marnie. However, I'm retired from the hospital. I'm living on a pension. I'm comfortable, but only barely."

"You, my Greta, are a liar," Marnie snapped back. "You're living in a house built with my money. A *lot* of my money. You took it from me at a time when I had enough of it and thought I always would. Getting you out of my hair and happy seemed worth it. And it probably was. But now . . ."

Marnie sipped her wine and wiped the condensation off the globe of her glass. Her fingernails were out of style: French manicure.

"Now you can mortgage this house."

"I can't do that, Marnie. I won't."

"Look," Marnie said, suddenly switching to a more sympathetic approach, "I changed the lives of millions. I can do it again. You owe me."

It was hard to argue with Marnie. She never missed the opportunity to seize the last word.

"You did amazing things," Greta said, picking her words carefully. "You did. I know that. And I know you have more to offer. This is something you have to do without me. And not because I don't respect and love you; it's because I simply don't have the means, Marnie. And to be honest, I just don't have the heart for it."

Marnie's expression flatlined. She sat quietly across from her former acolyte, a woman who had helped realize Marnie's vision.

"What about Marnie's army?" Greta asked. "You surely still have so many devoted followers. Maybe you could crowdfund your project?"

Marnie's eyes sparked. "I could never do that again."

"What about Heather? Dina? They have money."

"Heather has all but turned her back on me. Won't return calls. Letters. She's already forgotten how she got where she is. I'll remind her in person at a conference in Seattle. I won't be ignored. And Dina, she's probably in worse shape than I am. She's a washed-up actress with a drinking problem."

"Well, I'm sorry, Marnie. I can only repeat that—"

"Mortgage the house, Greta." Marnie cut her off.

"I can't do that. There's no way—"

"Do it. And soon. Time is running out."

"What exactly does that mean?"

"Let me put it this way: you and I both know what you did the night Calista's baby came."

"Are you making a threat, Marnie?"

"Don't consider it a threat. Consider it a gift. A chance for you to do the right thing. I need two hundred fifty thousand dollars, and I need it soon."

With that, Marnie got up, glancing at the bill for the wine.

"Pay the bill, Greta. It's due."

Chapter 51

Heather Jarred was the third of three girls.

There was the pretty one.

The smart one.

And finally, Heather, the tall one.

She grew up on a ranch near Goldendale, Washington, to parents who raised beef cattle for income and, for a while, sheep as a hobby. She spent her summers riding along the barbed and electric fences on her beloved horse, Mia. She endured the jokes her sisters made about her breaking Mia's back and the taunts of the local boys who, like her sisters, continually found new ways to pick her apart. When Heather was eighteen, she left for college in Spokane. She slimmed down, grounded herself in a future of helping people with a nursing degree, and never looked back.

When her sister Amanda—the pretty one—was diagnosed with breast cancer, Heather sent a note: "You made me strong, Mandy. I hope that you will find some strength of your own now that you are facing this. I won't be coming home to see you. You know why."

When she first met Marnie Spellman, in the late 1990s, she was trans-fixed by her beauty and her commanding presence. More beautiful than anyone she'd ever seen. More than that, she radiated love. Heather's eyes brimmed with tears when they embraced for the first time. It was as if Heather had come home. A safe home. A safe harbor.

"Greta told me about you," Marnie said, still holding her in her arms.

"She did?"

Marnie laughed. "Of course she did. She brought you to me, didn't she?"

Heat flushed through Heather from her scalp to her toes. "Oh. Right." So stupid. Greta was in her nursing pod at Whatcom Memorial. She wouldn't shut up about Marnie, but then Heather's annoyance became curiosity. Who *was* this woman? She'd allowed herself to be talked into visiting the island, and now here she was in Marnie's arms. Home. Making a fool of herself.

Again Marnie laughed. She held Heather at arm's length. "It's all right, seeker. You will never feel alone again. Do you hear that? You are a part of a sisterhood that transcends anything you could have imagined. I need you. I want you here on the farm. I desire for you to be and do all of the wonderful things that are waiting inside you."

Heather was weeping by then, tears hot on her cheeks. How could Marnie see her so clearly? How was it that she was able to go beyond the surface of her skin, to see her? The true her—the grown woman who'd never dared to dream until she left that ranch in Southwestern Washington.

Marnie took Heather's face in her hands.

"You," she said, "are divine."

CHAPTER 52

Friday, August 23, 2019
Seattle, Washington

That same voice, nearly two decades later.

Melodic. And terrifying.

It came from behind Congresswoman and US Senate candidate Heather Jarred as she nodded and smiled her way through the lobby of the Four Seasons in downtown Seattle.

"Heather!" said the voice. "I can't believe it's you!"

It was, of course, Marnie Spellman, dressed in royal-blue trousers with a silk blouse in her trademark yellow.

"Marnie," Heather said. "I'm stunned. How long has it been?"

"Too long," Marnie said, circling her long-lost friend like a hungry great white. "You look wonderful. Not sure about the suit. The hair is perfect, though."

The dig about the suit was typical Marnie. She could be the most giving person in the world, but when she saw the chance to work in some insecurity, it was heaven for her. It was as if, after making someone feel vulnerable, she'd be an even greater hero when she offered a life preserver.

"You don't like the suit?"

"Oh no, Heather, I adore it. I was just being silly. A little silliness keeps you from getting old."

"You look exactly the same, Marnie."

Marnie smiled. "Thank you. You look like you could use a little sun or something. Are you feeling all right?"

I was until I ran into you, Heather thought.

"What are you doing here?"

"I'm here for the homelessness summit," Marnie said. "Same as you. We have a break at noon. Are you free?"

Heather gamely tried to lie. "Oh no. I wish. I've got something at that hour."

"Come on, Heather, we haven't talked for the longest time."

Heather looked around. Her communications officer, Stephanie, and a group of associates were marching her way.

"I'll meet you in the hotel bar at ten o'clock tonight, Marnie. And I'll give you ten minutes."

Heather dissolved into the group as they trekked across the lobby, her heels leaving tiny indentations in the luxurious carpet.

"Was that who I think it was?" Stephanie asked.

"Uh . . . who?"

"You were just talking to her."

"Oh. Yes. Marnie Spellman. That was her."

"Wow. She's a big fish. Maybe a donor? How do you know her?"

"Look, Stephanie, it was a long time ago. Not a donor."

Marnie was coming.

Heather could feel it over the rest of the afternoon and evening like a cold sore coming on.

The idea of a reunion made Heather nervous and sick to her stomach. That part of her life was under lock and key—in her mind. It only seeped out into her dreams.

In the nearly two decades since Heather cut ties with Marnie, she had thanked God every day that the sum of their relationship had been pre–social media. There were absolutely no digital tracks leading back to the time in her life when she felt impelled to spend time at Spellman Farms with Marnie. She worked at the hospital in Bellingham during the week and spent her weekends on Lummi Island. She couldn't pretend she hadn't wanted to do it. She'd *needed* to. There was a kind of camaraderie at Spellman Farms and a sense of purpose that was like a drug to her. And getting close to Marnie—to feel *chosen* by her—that had been like mainlining that drug. It was the combination of her brilliance, her manner—kind, gentle—and her undying belief in an outward-inward beauty as the pathway to a purpose in life. It wasn't a cult. There were no bizarre rituals. It was simply a powerful message that resonated within the hearts of Marnie's many followers.

The mantra was simple: *You are lovely. You are loved. You can bee.*

As a nurse, the science behind what Marnie was doing with honeybee products not only intrigued Heather but moved her. Excited her. There was something so deeply affecting about Marnie's methods that Heather clung to her every word, every move. Later she'd almost feel embarrassed about her devotion. She'd watched as her mentor worked silently in the lab she had built in the new barn. Marnie kept a notebook and was constantly and ferociously writing in it, but she never let anyone see just what she was putting to paper. Heather saw the notebook left open one time but, out of respect, resisted the urge to look.

Whatever Marnie was doing was private until she deemed otherwise. She was measuring, distilling, and extracting the contents of nature—all for the purpose of finding "the gift Mother Nature has hidden in plain sight." She procured moss from the north end of the island, berries from her farm, barnacles from the shore. Everything was pulverized into a slurry into which bee pollen, royal jelly, and honey were added.

Sometimes Marnie would loll in the lavender field for hours, her eyes closed, her mouth open, moving ever so slightly as she recited an unintelligible prayer. No one dared disturb her as she communed with a higher power that spoke only to her. It was God's voice, she said. A woman's voice.

"She wants you to be everything you have ever dreamed of being, Heather," Marnie told her. "You are one of her most important people. You have a path to follow that is going to bring you great power one day. You will rise, and the people will follow your lead."

Later, Heather would have conflicting thoughts about what Marnie had said. In the beginning, she saw it as a prophecy, a message from far beyond meant for her ears and, in time, her heart. Not long before she decided to leave Spellman Farms, it appeared to Heather that Marnie was only saying what anyone would want to hear.

"You're awfully quiet," her husband said, snapping her back to the present. They were taking a few minutes in their hotel room, after the interminable opening banquet for the homelessness summit.

"Just thinking about her," she said.

She never said her name. Never had to.

"Sometimes . . . ," Richard started to say, then stopped.

"What?" she asked. "Sometimes what?"

"Never mind, Heather."

Heather was never one to be denied an answer. Not in Congress. Not from her staff. Not even from her constituents. And most assuredly, not from Richard.

"You don't get to start something and just leave it unsaid. Spit it out."

"I wish I'd never brought it up."

"What? You still haven't told me."

"All right," he said. "Fine. Sometimes you talk about her with such a wistfulness that I think your feelings for her were, you know, more than just friends or mentor and mentee."

She almost laughed, considering the sense of foreboding she'd been feeling about the idea of Marnie creeping back into her life. Wistfulness? But then she really heard what he'd said.

"Seriously?" she asked. "You think there was something between me and Marnie?"

Richard didn't blink. "Yeah," he answered. "I do. I'm not saying it was sexual, but I'd be lying to you right now if I said that the thought hadn't crossed my mind more than a time or two. And if you were, I don't care."

"We weren't. And, Richard, I do care."

"Sorry. It's just that . . . well, I've always felt she had her hooks in you one way or another."

"Ridiculous. I haven't seen her in years."

"Well, that's about to change. You said she wants something."

She waved that away. "She just wants what everyone wants. A little something for nothing."

Whenever he asked for more about Marnie and the farm and what the group was involved with that was so hush-hush, she shut him down.

CHAPTER 53

Winter 1997
Lummi Island, Washington

In the beginning, the trio of nurses—Heather, Trish, and Greta—didn't feel that what they were doing was of any real harm: a kind of victimless scenario—certainly not criminal—that would only seem wrong through the eyes of those who did not fully understand the mission.

Placentas and stem cells from umbilical cords following childbirths were considered hospital waste, after all.

Whenever Marnie needed more "material," as she called it, Greta, who had moved up to charge nurse on her way to an administrative position, fixed the schedule so that she and Trish would serve as labor-and-delivery nurses. The laboring mother would be wheeled in, and the obstetrician and anesthesiologist would go about the business of bringing a new life into the world, while Greta and Trish would do what they needed to do. Helping the doctor, helping the mother-to-be, was a responsibility that they both took seriously. It would be wrong to do otherwise. First the baby. The cry. The joy on the new mom's face. The father's, too, when he was present. When the placenta was delivered, the two nurses would huddle together to weigh it. The umbilical cords, however, were the great prize. All eyes were on the new baby and the mother, and it took only a moment to move the cord to its own plastic bag.

The most desirable deliveries were those aligning with the Lummi Island ferry's limited operating schedule. Freshness mattered to Marnie. The cords collected in the evening when ferry service was halted were kept on ice in an Igloo cooler Trish stored in the trunk of her car.

Greta knew she couldn't tell anyone about what they were doing or the reasons behind it. There would be no point to it. Anyone who'd ask would only seek to judge something beyond his or her understanding. Was it even wrong at all? Later, Heather would marvel that none of it seemed wrong or even strange, although she knew deep down that it was, and her heart always raced whenever she served as courier and got onto the ferry for the island.

Trish Appleton knew the stem-cell samples were being incorporated into the formula for Beautiful Six, a product that Marnie was convinced would revolutionize the holistic and natural beauty industry. Sheep stem cells were already a mainstay of a Swiss company, and the copacker who was handling the entire Spellman product line said she'd heard that Koreans were developing products that included human stem cells—nature's ultimate elixir for youth and renewal.

The Spellman Farms lab was barely functional, more for show than for scientific study. That's not to say Marnie didn't know her way around a lab, having seduced the professor that ran her university research facility. She was a quick study, only taking in what she needed to know to grow her empire. To be the authority. When investors came through— new followers with a sufficient income or influence—Marnie would put on a bright-yellow lab coat and provide a truncated tour of the facility in the back of the barn: a spectrometer, a centrifuge, microscopes, and various beakers, mostly for show. She'd whirl around and dazzle them with her theory that everything women needed to be their best was already there.

"In the world, in ourselves. We only need to learn how to unlock the secrets that are right before our eyes."

When a visitor would ask, as they almost certainly did, where the next breakthrough would come from, Marnie would give the same reply.

"I don't know. Here, I hope. I do know that it will come from a woman, because the earth is female. The earth and its women are life givers. Not takers."

"Are men the takers?"

Marnie would smile. "You've seen a man hold a baby, right? But have you ever seen a man *have* a baby?"

Everyone smiled or laughed at that one.

The line worked every time.

Trish once asked Marnie why she didn't tell people about stem cells and how they could revolutionize the cosmetics industry.

"People aren't ready for that, dear. Think about it. While the cells we withdraw from the cord blood are destined for waste disposal, people would freak out at the idea of using them. They're all twisted up about it, as though it's some kind of betrayal of the mother or the baby—as though either has the slightest connection to or need for those cells! Our whole misguided Western medical establishment would be up in arms."

"Someday, though," Trish pressed, "you know, if—*when* this works, you'll have to tell them. The FDA will need to know what's in Beautiful Six. Right?"

"Maybe so. Maybe not."

Later, Trish would wonder about that encounter. For all the secrecy about Beautiful Six and its formula, there seemed to be little effort being made to seriously embark on the process to get it to market.

Marnie wasn't a woman who didn't go after what she wanted with gusto. She had a knack for shifting gears when necessary and for staying sharply focused when nothing was in her way.

Not with Beautiful Six. It seemed that although Trish, Heather, and Greta were frequently bringing the red-and-white cooler packed with syringes of blood taken from the birthing and operating rooms, nothing seemed to be happening. Marnie took the cooler to her lab and unpacked it into the refrigerator. She seemed eager. Even grateful. But with no result. No formula. No next steps. It was like the revolution was on pause.

Though Marnie was full of confidence, no action followed her proclamations.

When Marnie was off with Dina—as she so often was, in those days—the other members of the Hive talked about the delay. They sat outside, looking down past row upon row of hives. By then there were more than forty.

Trish said what they all were thinking.

"Dina is the reason nothing is happening."

"I agree," Greta said. "It seems Marnie has no time for Beautiful Six. No time for *us*. She's focused on making money, building power."

Heather didn't say it, but she admired Marnie's knack for turning a for-profit enterprise into a cause. She thought Marnie's true brilliance lay in knowing how to market and manipulate. She saw a role for herself as a kind of CFO for Spellman Farms. She helped with the books.

"*Fame*, money, and power," Heather finally said.

They'd all found themselves on the same page—and it scared Trish a little.

"Dina is lovely," she said, backtracking. "I really like her. So down to earth."

"And down on her luck," Heather added.

The three women exchanged looks. No one had said an unkind word about Dina Marlow until that moment. Much less any about Marnie.

Trish hurried to fill the gap in the conversation. "Marnie has a way of finding people like Dina, and . . . well . . ."

They all nodded. *And us* is what she hadn't quite said aloud.

They, too, had been searching for meaning, a spot to land, when they first arrived on Lummi Island.

Heather had struggled as a premed student and switched her major to nursing. She thought it would be easier helping with the delivery of babies than being the one supervising the entire process. This went against her grain, and her family's. She came from forceful people, parents who knew that everything depended on a take-no-prisoners approach. They bred cattle to be the best in the market.

"I was analyzed from day one, like a 4-H project," she once told Trish. "My parents studied me like I was a science project, always watching and questioning my motives. The reality of it all was that I had no motives of my own. Everything I did was in anticipation of what I thought they'd expected of me."

CHAPTER 54

Friday, August 23, 2019
Seattle, Washington

Marnie Spellman had planted herself in the bar of Seattle's Four Seasons Hotel fifteen minutes before Heather was due to arrive and set about nursing a glass of sauvignon blanc. She was a die-hard red wine drinker, but as she ordered, she knew this was not a day to have red teeth.

How the tables had turned.

After she left the Hive, Heather retreated to the Seattle area, served in the PTA, then leapfrogged into state politics, then a US congressional seat. And now, a promising contender for the US Senate. Indeed, the tables had spun in circles. At 10:00 p.m. sharp, Marnie spotted Heather lingering by the door and waved her over. Heather, after looking around to see who might be watching, crossed quickly to Marnie and tucked herself into the deep leather booth.

"I saw what you did back there, Heather."

Heather cast her eyes downward before facing Marnie. "I don't know what you mean. Where?"

"Before. In the lobby, when we first ran into each other."

Heather picked up a glass Marnie had waiting for her and swirled her wine in the candlelight.

Garnets and rubies, Marnie thought. *So lovely.*

"Marnie, I don't want to get into anything with you."

"You treated me badly. You know you did. I know you did. She knows, too."

"She?" Heather said, then caught herself. "Oh! Yes."

She, of course, was God. Not that Heather had given her any more thought than she'd given Marnie for years now.

"I'm sorry about the lobby," Heather said. "I was distracted."

Marnie stared her down. "You were mortified."

"No, Marnie, I wasn't."

"I see it on you now. It's like the skin shed by a snake, hanging on you, unable to peel away. Shame is the opposite of love."

"I didn't come here for an assessment, Marnie. In fact, I don't know why I came."

An assessment. She'd retained Marnie's words, though. Her philosophy, or some watered-down version of it.

"Maybe it's the food," she said, nudging a menu toward her protégée. "Maybe that's why you're here."

"I'm here, Marnie, because we have a history. And to be very frank, it is a history that cannot help me do what I need to do in this life."

The waiter came, and they both ordered the spinach salad, dressing on the side. No croutons.

"See?" Marnie said when he'd left. "We're still alike."

Heather glared at her. "We are not."

Marnie rolled her eyes. "Take a joke, dear. You were always so serious." She swirled the wine in her glass and nodded at Heather's. "Come on, enjoy your wine. You've always loved your vino."

Heather rose up to protest, but Marnie just laughed, raised her palm to her. "Would you *drink*? You're positively about to detonate." She raised her glass. "Douse the fire!"

After sinking back into the booth, Heather shook her head and joined her in a drink.

And then another. They continued drinking in almost companionable silence until the waiter returned with their salads.

Marnie stabbed at hers. "Our history scares you."

Heather set her fork aside. "No. Actually, *you* scare me. You always have. I think that I mistook your power over me as something benevolent. Now I see otherwise."

"Because you have your own power? Is that it?"

"Possibly. But that's not what I'm telling you right now. I'm running for the Senate. I can't have one whiff of you associated with me. No one knows that I worked with you."

"Beneath me."

"Whatever you think, Marnie. I just need to know that you will stay away. You will leave me alone. You will never speak of us, our relationship, or things that we did that I can never forget, as hard as I try to."

"We didn't do anything wrong," Marnie said. "You know that."

"This was a mistake. Meeting you here like this. I need to go. I'm begging you, if you have any feelings for me whatsoever, stay away. I have a chance to make up for all of what I did, and I can't have it destroyed by you, or anyone."

"Look, sister," Marnie said. "You owe me. And I'm here to collect." And then she put it to her as clearly as she could. Heather's jaw dropped; Marnie almost laughed in her face, but she needed to be sure she was understood. "Hear me, Heather. I'm onto a breakthrough, and it's your duty as a member of the Hive to help me. You made a vow."

Heather had mostly regrouped—but only mostly.

"That boat sailed decades ago, Marnie," she said. "The Hive was not about female empowerment. The whole time, it was about you, you goddamn freak. Stay away from me."

With that, Heather got up, fidgeted in her purse, pulled out a ten and a twenty, and put the bills on the table. Her lips were pressed together, and Marnie could see the perspiration under her makeup. She was going to melt into a big mess right there.

"Don't ever bother or threaten me again, Marnie. I'm a congresswoman, and I'm about to be a senator. Don't think I couldn't or wouldn't crush you like a bug."

Marnie sat alone, ensconced in the leather booth. Everywhere around her, people were talking—no, boasting—about their lives and all that they had accomplished. At every table was a contest of sorts. Who had the better life? Who had the smarter kids? Who among their group had the fullest breasts?

She looked down at her plate. Her salad had wilted. Her wineglass was dry. The waiter saw her surveying the sorry scene and rushed over. When she waved him away, she caught her image on the back of a silver spoon. Not ordinarily given to much self-reflection, Marnie found herself wondering what Heather saw in her that she couldn't see. If there had been any truth to what she'd said. She had made terrible mistakes in her life, things she regretted, but she knew there were no do-overs. Life didn't stop and start. It was circular, always moving, revolving, changing. Heather was cruel, unforgiving. She was building her own empire, her own Hive in politics.

Marnie refused to be cast aside, ignored.

She couldn't understand why the women she'd been closest to had abandoned her. She'd only wanted the best for each of them. They'd been to battle together. They'd fought to enlighten the world. And now, they'd turned their backs on her.

Marnie started to fume.

She knew their secrets.

She'd tell if she had to.

That night, under eight-hundred-thread-count sateen sheets in their hotel room, Richard Jarred had sex with his wife. It was halfhearted, the kind that barely got the job done. It had been that way for them for quite some time. Too long. While they lay there watching the lights of the city flicker in a cloudless Seattle night, both of their minds were churning on the same subject.

Marnie Spellman.

Despite what he'd said to his wife, Richard had believed for a very long time that she and Marnie had been lovers. It was a long time ago, and it didn't make him love her any less, yet it troubled him now and then. He'd wondered more than once if their marriage was merely a means to an end. If Heather had ever felt a burning desire for him; if she was able to let go of the past. He despised how Marnie had assumed a kind of mythical presence in their lives. He hated himself for thinking that the absence of passion between himself and Heather was because she was a lesbian. Or bisexual. Maybe she felt no attraction for him because politics had completely seduced her. He could live with that, though not with the idea that his wife still held a torch for Marnie Spellman. That was humiliating. Crazymaking, too.

He watched Heather scroll through her phone to review her schedule, or perhaps check how many more likes she'd collected on her campaign's Facebook page. She glanced over in his direction and then tenderly pulled up the comforter to cover his shoulders.

And while Richard was thinking of Heather, she was thinking of Marnie.

CHAPTER 55

The second day of the homelessness summit was over. Heather's jaw hurt from smiling, and her right palm ached from shaking hands. One more morning of the same ahead of her. Why did the organizers of things like this so often insist on scheduling Sunday breakfast programming when all anyone wants to do is crawl home?

The Jarreds sat in the hotel bar, off in a dimly lit corner.

"You're drinking too much, Heather."

"Richard, you're being, as our daughter says, a little judgy."

Before he could respond, she changed the subject.

"I've been thinking," she announced.

He gestured to the bartender. "That's kind of what you do," he said before ordering a club soda with lemon, not lime.

"No, let me finish," Heather continued, raising the glass of whiskey to her lips. "All right. Maybe I'm worried. Concerned."

He read the hotel bar. Tasteful and boring. At this time of evening, quiet. Hookups from Match.com and Grindr had come and gone. Hell, they pretty much had the place to themselves. He wouldn't try to stop her from bingeing. Maybe she really did need to completely unwind, crash to the floor, wake up with an AK-47 blasting between her ears.

He'd been sober for more than a decade. He would do anything for Heather, yet he had to admit he didn't relish being posted as permanent designated driver. The very definition of a thankless role.

"My Achilles' heel will always be Marnie," Heather admitted, looking up from her drink.

You don't say. That's what Richard thought; what he said was "No one knows anything about her or that time in your life. Not like now when every utterance, every move, is captured and shared. God, be glad we didn't have to live in those days like we do today, fearing every post, every bystander with a camera and an insatiable need for attention."

"That's just about everyone." Heather returned to her drink, ice cubes rolling toward her mouth, then falling back into the bottom of the crystal tumbler.

"Seriously, babe, what are you worried about?"

"I don't think I could tell even you."

He sat quiet for a minute, then reached over to her. "I'm your husband. If you don't trust me, it must be really bad."

"It is," Heather said, "but it's not because I don't trust you. It's because if I tell you, then it will mean that it's out there. That I've told someone. I'd have to answer truthfully about what happened. You know I couldn't lie. I've never lied."

"Except by omission. Is that what this is?"

"In some ways, yes. I guess so. If it ever gets out, it can't be from my lips. I'd lose everything."

"Are you going to tell me?" he asked.

"Isn't my silence enough? If I say it aloud to you, then it's the same thing as making it public."

"If it's really that terrible, maybe you need a lawyer."

"I have two right now. That doesn't matter. It isn't necessarily a legal matter. It would be a question about my character and the road I took when I should have known better."

315

"You were young," Richard said. "Whatever it was, it couldn't have been solely your fault."

She knew that he loved her beyond measure and that he'd forgive whatever it was, no matter how dark. But even though she knew all that deep in her marrow, she still couldn't tell him.

"I love you," she said.

"I know."

That night they went up to their suite. Heather undressed and took a long shower. She was woozy from the liquor, and she planted her feet apart and braced her hands against the tile, holding herself up. The water ran over her back; it was the hottest she could endure. She was grateful for Richard, the support of the party, the idea that she still could do great things in the world. Make it better. Make it safer. Create opportunities for those who hadn't been given the ones that she had enjoyed.

Steam rose into a cloud, fogging the glass, creating a veil of privacy. She was as sorry as she'd been all those years ago when she complied with the will of the group, of its leader, at a time when she knew there were other options.

Options that would save a life.

After toweling off and changing into a nightgown, she caught a glimpse of herself in the mirror. Everyone marveled about her beautiful skin, crystalline blue eyes, commanding yet nonthreatening presence. Said she easily could have run for Miss America instead of the US Congress. She was approaching sixty and worked hard to keep herself looking the way she did. It was peculiar how her looks still mattered, how her campaign aides thought she was the most stylish and put-together woman on the floor.

In that fleeting instance, all Heather Jarred saw was the ugliness in the barn at Spellman Farms.

Heather left Lummi Island when Dina cemented her role as Marnie's favorite. Until then, she had seen herself as second-in-command, never second fiddle. Dina usurped her position without even trying. Heather was a fool for not seeing it right away. Marnie was akin to a vampire: she managed to suck the life force from her strongest advocates. She used them, coddled them, abused them, loved them. With Marnie in the room, there was no way of knowing what might happen next. The followers who stayed longest were not only true believers but adrenaline junkies. Marnie was the fix they needed to thrive.

It was, most ended up thinking later, a one-sided trade.

Richard dropped right off, but, Heather, still unable to sleep at midnight, dressed and returned to the bar with her laptop tucked under her arm. Seeing Marnie had brought back the worst thing she'd ever done. It was exactly as Marnie had intended. She wanted to remind Heather of what she held over her and how she could return the favor of her silence.

"You want money?" Heather had asked.

"No, I said I *need* money. Two hundred fifty thousand."

"A quarter million? Are you insane?"

"You can get it. I know you can. In a week. Less. And I also need access." Her voice lowered to a hiss. "I need you to hear me."

"What do you mean *access?*"

"I need a senator who will help me do what I was meant to do."

"I don't understand."

"You do. You will get on the committee that regulates consumer products." Marnie had leaned in even closer. Her gaze remained threatening. "I can make things difficult for you. I can send a YouTube link to the media that will show you were at the wrong place at the right time."

"You wouldn't," Heather said.

"Try me. I'm only looking for quid pro quo here, Heather. Not a complete annihilation of your career."

"I see."

Heather knew that favors were traded like baseball cards in the Senate, that senators often had oblique reasons for favoring one committee over another. What Marnie was asking—no, demanding—was within Heather's reach, so long as she reciprocated when the time came. Still, considering it now as she returned to the bar, she felt shaky and thought a healthy pour of Scotch would calm her nerves.

She'd done what she had believed was necessary all those years ago, and there was no way of minimizing it in a world that fed off of others' misfortunes. She had a target on her back.

Once Heather had her place at the end of the bar and her nightcap before her, she turned on her laptop. She'd fought the urge to look at the basis of Marnie's threat. It was foolish, she knew. By not looking at it, however, it seemed less real. Stupid reasoning, she knew. So, no more playing games with herself, as she logged on to YouTube. She'd always suspected it was there. Everything old and new found its way onto the site.

Sometimes there was a convergence of the two.

If people found out about what she'd done, everything they thought about her would vanish. Not only would she be forced to resign, she'd be an instant pariah. She'd lose her husband's unyielding loyalty. Her children would no longer boast who their mother was.

She'd be lucky to get a seat on a second-tier city council.

Heather watched the video and drank her Scotch in gulps. The image was of poor quality, a VHS tape that might have languished in someone's garage, just waiting to be uploaded.

Yellow crime-scene tape stretched across the beach where Calista had been found by the tourists on their Y2K tour of national parks. Heather kept the sound low, and she watched the lieutenant and tribal police as they worked the area in search of evidence. A fly landed on the lens, and Heather watched it until it moved to the left of the frame.

And there she was, where the fly had been, mixed in with young people who'd gotten off their shifts at the inn to check out what was happening. Everyone was straining to get an eyeful. Heather was twenty years younger, although either good DNA or the Spellman Farms products she'd used had kept her in remarkable shape since then.

That was a problem. There was no real change in her appearance. She looked youthful. Same hairstyle. Same figure. Some would say it's a nice problem to have, but not Heather. She'd done everything she could to wipe the past from her life. Yet none of it mattered now.

She was, as Marnie threatened, on that recording.

And she was readily identifiable as she drank in the lurid commotion attending the discovery of this tragic young woman's corpse on what should've been a desolate stretch of nowhere beach.

She could hear viewers—friends, constituents, and most annoyingly, the rail-thin right-wing pundit who sucked in controversy like others breathe.

"Wait—rewind. Isn't that Heather Jarred, the congresswoman? I mean, she's younger, but . . . that's her. God, look at the look on her face. That is *intense*! Is she crying? What in the hell is she doing there with those slacker kids? She's teed up to be senator, isn't she?"

Her heart hammering, Heather drew the curtain on that horrific scene. She thought to call Greta and remind her of their promise. She was drunk by then and didn't have her old friend's number, anyway. She found her way back upstairs and stretched out next to her snoring husband. She folded herself into the bedding and lay still, eyes open, scared that everything she'd ever wanted was caught in a mix of limbo and jeopardy, both tugging at her. She waited for the light to dim on her phone and closed her eyes.

Heather knew she had to do something. Everything was within her grasp. She was the heir apparent to a Senate seat that would not likely shift again in her lifetime. Senators were lifers. They clung to their positions because they craved being at the seat of power. They never let go.

This was her time.

Yet it was another time, now two decades gone, that her mind returned to, as it so often did during her darkest nights, when even the possibility of sleep was too fantastic to imagine.

Heather kept her eyes on the television in the break room at Whatcom Memorial. The local TV station, KVOS, was reporting on the arrest of Reed Sullivan for the murder of his wife.

"Sullivan had made several trips to Lummi Island in the weeks running up to the murder of his estranged wife. Calista Sullivan was employed on the island at Spellman Farms."

B-roll images of the body recovery were next.

"The victim was found on the west side of the island by beach-combers a month ago."

More background video, this time of the farm.

"Charging papers say that Marnie Spellman reported that she feared that Calista Sullivan was being stalked by her former husband. She told investigators that Calista had said her husband was very controlling and had visited the farm on at least two occasions and made threats."

Heather looked up when Greta joined her.

"Wow," Greta said. "This is seriously messed up."

Heather nodded. "We can't say anything, Greta."

Greta looked at her. "What do you mean? A man's been arrested for something he didn't do. He never stalked her at the farm. Marnie made that up."

"We don't know that."

Greta looked at Heather like she was crazy. "We do. We know he's innocent. We were there."

Heather fidgeted with a Styrofoam cup, pulling at its edges until pieces fell onto the table. "We didn't see anything," she said. "We don't know what really happened."

Greta whispered as another nurse came into the break room. "We do know that he didn't do it. And we know what we did."

After her shift, Heather went home to her apartment on Donovan Avenue in the Fairhaven historic district south of Bellingham. She stayed planted in her car for an extra few minutes as another news broadcast reported Reed Sullivan was already at the Whatcom County Jail, pending arraignment the next day.

She felt as though she was going to throw up.

Calista's ex-husband was an innocent man, raising two little boys.

This was so wrong. Everything was spinning out of control, and in her mind, there was nothing she could do about it.

Marnie had admonished the members of the Hive to toe the party line.

"Reed was a stalker. Calista was fearful. She told us. We don't know where she went. We can only guess."

Heather turned off the ignition and went inside, hurrying to the toilet.

CHAPTER 56

Monday, August 26, 2019
Seattle, Washington

Heather Jarred made a face when her communications officer informed her that there was a local reporter who'd been asking for an interview.

"You know the locals," Stephanie said with an exaggerated eye roll.

Heather considered local media the worst. She could handle CNN or even Fox. They only skimmed the surface to fill gaps in programming with anything that resembled news. The locals were another thing altogether. Puff pieces were no longer their mainstay; they'd figured out that more persuasive journalism promoting a point of view was what earned viewers. Clicks. Likes. Comments. It was, Heather thought, harder and harder to just fudge your way through the questions. Being smart and noncommittal had gone by the wayside.

This one was even worse.

A college student who was too green to embrace the rules of conventional media.

"She's called seven times. Texted. Posted on Instagram a picture of a broken clock, tagging you."

"Okay, fine," Heather said. "Young people are the future."

Stephanie gave her a look, and for good reason. She'd just delivered a hackneyed sound bite to someone who knew better.

"Inspiring," Stephanie said. "Would a sit-down tomorrow at three work for you?" She already knew it would. She was the kind of assistant who knew when her boss needed a bowel movement.

"Fine. Tomorrow. Fifteen minutes only."

Sarah Baker wore a black blazer and dark-dyed jeans. She put her long, dark hair up with a chunky wooden clip. Around her neck, she wore a pendant with a heart-shaped stone, amethyst.

Heather remarked on it when she greeted the college reporter in her downtown campaign office.

"My birthstone," Sarah said. "My aunt gave it to me when I went off to Western." She held it out to let the admirer have a closer look.

"It's beautiful," Heather said, fully aware that taking up this much time during the start of an interview with a hard stop in fifteen minutes was a proven method to ensure staying on message. She offered juice, coffee, water, and made some small talk.

Again, to fill the time.

"I'm doing a profile," Sarah said.

"Wonderful. What would you like to know? My position on climate change has rankled my Republican opponent."

"I know," Sarah said as she took a seat across from Heather's immaculate mahogany desk. "Just about everything rankles him."

Heather laughed. "I guess it does."

"I want to talk to you about your time up in Whatcom County."

"That was a while ago, Sarah. What would you like to know?" she repeated.

Heather looked at the clock on her desk. Seven minutes to go.

"Specifically," Sarah said, "I'm curious about your work at Spellman Farms."

Heather always knew this would come up sometime. She and Stephanie had planned for it. Role-played how to answer. She knew that denial was a trap. Never deny. Always deflect.

She gave her canned response.

"Oh, that was such a small part of my time up there. My work as a nurse at the hospital was really more formative in terms of what I'm doing now. Health care has always been my passion."

Sarah, however, was no pushover. "Spellman Farms ties into that, doesn't it? Marnie Spellman's whole empire was built on helping women to have happier, fuller lives."

"It was a cosmetics company, Sarah," Heather said, her tone a little cooler. "It wasn't founded on helping anyone be healthier. I don't know much about what Marnie Spellman believed."

"You were close."

"That's overstating things. I knew her, yes. Not well."

Sarah looked surprised. "Really? I must have been given some bad intel."

"That happens."

"I don't know why Ms. Spellman would lie to me," Sarah said.

The clock said two more minutes.

A career, Heather knew, could be ended in ten seconds.

"I don't, either."

"Are you two still in touch? I mean, casually, like at the homeless-ness summit?"

"We chatted briefly, yes."

One minute.

"Did you talk about Calista Sullivan?"

"Not at all," Heather said, feigning puzzlement.

Ten seconds.

Stephanie breezed in.

Thank God.

"Your next appointment is here, Congresswoman."

Heather shot up and extended her hand. "I wish we had more time, Sarah."

Sarah tightened her lips. Her eyes flashed a blend of anger and annoyance.

"Me, too," she said. "I'll keep knocking on doors. Just like you, I'm a determined woman."

Stephanie escorted the reporter out, and Heather slumped into her chair.

Marnie was an invisible vapor, always present, undetected until it was too late. Heather hadn't lied to the student reporter—well, not in any substantive way—although she'd wanted to. She took a deep breath, so deep that she nearly coughed. She let the air out. It was possible that Sarah really didn't know anything at all—that she was just fishing. The election was weeks away. She wondered if Marnie could be so stupid as to send a mere girl to do her bidding.

Heather pulled herself together and hoped it all would blow over before it destroyed what she knew was rightfully hers.

Hope was, she knew, for voters and the foolish.

Stephanie Haight fit her name; at least, many in the Seattle office of Heather Jarred for US Senate thought so. Stephanie ran the campaign like a navy ship, a trait that might have been owing to the fact that she'd been brought up near the Puget Sound Naval Shipyard.

As she wove her way past volunteers working the late-evening phones to her windowless warren of an office, her phone rang. She looked down, picked up the pace, and answered as she shut the door behind her.

It was her husband.

"Why are you calling, Albert? Did you not understand what I said?"

"Hey. I care about you."

"Are you really going back to that? That was a mistake. And by any measure, you're becoming a bigger problem with each call."

"I could give it to the press."

"You wouldn't do that."

"Why is that?"

"Because there'd be nothing in it for you."

"Revenge."

"For what? *You* dumped *me*, remember?"

"You'd like to think that, Stephanie, but you're wrong. I left you because you were going to dump me the next morning. I saw your list of things to do."

"That's silly."

"I will tell."

"Why?"

"Money."

"That can't happen. We're in the middle of a campaign. You'll have to back off and leave it be until after the election."

"I don't know. What if your girl loses?"

"She won't. She's born for this. America needs her."

"So grandiose, Stephanie. Your tongue must be Kool-Aid green by now."

Stephanie thought about what she might say or do to make her point. Nothing. At least, there was nothing she *could* say. Words didn't have any impact on Albert Haight. He saw them as obstacles to dodge or bounce from his head like a soccer ball. To the gut. To where it hurts.

"Don't do this," she said finally. "You will ruin everything."

"I love you."

Albert Haight had loved Stephanie at one point, yet as he saw his wife pulled ever deeper into the Heather Jarred universe, it became plain that he had little hope of seeing that affection reciprocated from her side of the galaxy.

Too cold there to support life.

He went outside into the warm night and sat down, the phone, now silent, still in his hand. The stars were out. Rare in Seattle, but there they were, dimly winking. Stephanie had receded from his life like a drifting satellite. He could pinpoint moments, although he could not perceive the velocity of their separation. Just how it happened and what he'd be able to do about it.

One pinpointed moment had been his discovery of the photograph.

It was late when she'd come home and thrown her purse, a black Kate Spade, on the table by the front door. She was exhausted and looked like hell.

"Glass of wine?" he asked.

She shuffled past him and threw herself on the couch. "Thanks, honey," she mumbled.

That's how they were before Heather. He was *sweetheart* or *honey*. Now he was just another aide to the aide, a nobody married to the communications officer for the next US senator from Washington State. *Deal with it*, he told himself. *Revel in it*. Other husbands surely did. They must. Then he wondered how many of the key female staffers in the Senate had husbands. Pretty all-consuming job, if the campaign was any indication. Being a senator's top aide probably made being a congresswoman's right hand seem like being VP of the PTA. Hell, did the women senators even have husbands? They must. He couldn't picture Elizabeth's husband, or Amy's or Kirsten's. Were they shunted off to the side to play golf? Or maybe just boarded in stables out in the Virginia countryside?

"Can you get my purse, babe?" she asked as he handed her a wine-glass full of a nearly black Syrah.

Albert returned to the foyer, picked up the purse by a single strap, and opened it on one side, sending the contents to the floor.

Crap!

As quickly as he could, Albert started to scoop the contents back inside. There was an envelope among the makeup, keys, and confetti of business cards. Later, when Albert thought of it, he couldn't come up with any legitimate reason why he did what he did. Mindless curiosity. Suspicion seemed dark and wasn't a feeling he'd have until much, much later.

He opened the envelope addressed to Heather with a return address belonging to Sarah Baker, a name he didn't know. Inside was an old photograph, black and white, and clear as could be.

It was taken at night, and it showed two women lifting a heavy, unwieldy object into the back of a pickup truck with SPELLMAN FARMS painted on a side panel. Strange. He put on his reading glasses to get a better view. He recognized one of the women as Heather Jarred. The other was unfamiliar.

The object was a body. It appeared to be a woman's body. A thin arm dangled.

He returned to the sofa and held out the photo.

"What is it?" he asked.

Stephanie had on her media face, a combination of a poker player and a person hard of hearing. "I don't know, Albert," she said.

"That's Heather, and what is she doing?"

Stephanie tucked the image into the envelope, then back into her purse.

"Photoshop prank by some hater," she said. "We get fakes all the time."

Liar.

Later that night, Albert heard his wife talking in the bathroom. Odd, he thought, because the line of light that would show under the closed door was absent.

Stephanie was taking her call in the dark.

For the most part, he couldn't hear what she was saying, except for the repetition of his name, which came from his wife's lips with disdain and frustration.

The next morning, while his wife was in the shower, Albert retrieved the photo from her purse. He carried it to the kitchen, where the light was better, and made a duplicate of it with his cell phone camera.

Again, just as when he'd first opened the envelope, he was uncertain exactly why he made the copy. But this time, it definitely wasn't just curiosity. It was something else. An insurance policy? A chip to be played in the war that was soon to become their marriage, maybe?

CHAPTER 57

It was Wednesday night, a day after the interview with Sarah Baker. Heather looked at her calendar for the following day and liked what she saw.

She had Stephanie fill each day down to the minute, except for Thursdays and Sundays. Thursdays were mostly open for personal things—it was so much easier to get things done in weekday, midday traffic—although there was often an evening obligation. Night events in the middle of the week were almost always local things in her district. She'd dress slightly down for such gatherings—attire that would signal she was one of them, whoever they were. Elks, Rotary, some skin disorder charity. She'd be asked to say a few words, but the emphasis was not on her campaign or how she wanted their vote. It was about them and how she was there to support them.

Nothing is more important to me than [FILL IN THE BLANK]. *I'm thrilled to stand with you as we* [FILL IN THE BLANK].

Heather had become jaded, and she knew it. She hoped that once she got to the Senate, she'd be able to reconnect with the person she used to be—that she'd no longer be the game player vying for a vote, but the woman with a passion for helping others. That sense of being a steward of people and their lives had brought her to nursing, and to Spellman Farms.

Almost impossibly, this Thursday was open. Truly wide open. She told Stephanie that she was going to use the free time to rethink her position on the Seattle homeless crisis. The previous weekend's summit had fired her up.

"Something has to be done, Steph," she said. "I'm not sure we're facing the root of the problem."

"You're sounding like a Republican," Stephanie said.

"No," she insisted, with some heat. "Not at all. I just want to make sure that my position is one that drives a genuine solution, one that will move the needle, not put more of them on Seattle streets."

"Good line," Stephanie said. "Use it."

Heather made a note of it. "I'll have my ringer off, so don't expect me to take a call. I'll answer by text if I have to. Understand?"

The morning's drive to Whatcom County would take two hours; the return, given a later time in the day, probably three. That meant Heather would have only an hour or two to get done what she needed to do. In Congress, she was known as a representative who didn't dally and always found a way to cut to the meat of a problem.

Her husband was asleep when she got up at 4:30 a.m. and hit the road. Her car was full of fuel, and she planned on making only one stop to get something that she considered a necessity.

She ordered a tall black coffee from a Starbucks just off I-5.

With classical music playing and caffeine pulsing through her tense body, she was ready.

Any calls she'd make would be on a burner phone, standard issue in modern campaigns. No trace. No records. No pings from cell towers that would put someone in the wrong place at the wrong time. A burner phone was the best-kept secret in modern politics. It fit nicely in her clutch bag, too.

Heather used the drive to weigh the evidence that might come back to haunt her. She let it spin through her mind while the music played and the speed of the traffic picked up north of Marysville.

She hadn't committed a crime. Not exactly. Calista had died in childbirth. It was a tragedy, but it wasn't anyone's fault. She'd gone along with the disposal of the body because it made sense in all the chaos. She had regrets about it, but she could chalk all of that up to fear and emotion, things that she knew were the flip side of most good intentions.

She could not, however, find any reason other than cowardice for having let Reed Sullivan stand trial. It was a snowball that had rolled into a mammoth avalanche, and she'd seen no way of stopping it. When Reed's DNA profile was recovered from under Calista's fingernails, she let herself believe that he was indeed, somehow, the killer. Had somehow sneaked into the barn and killed her, then spirited himself away. She hadn't thought to ask anyone—because to ask was to call attention to what Marnie (ahead of her time, as always) had posited as "an alternate truth"—how it was even possible to recover DNA from a body after it was in salt water for so long. It had taken too long for Reed's defense to push that issue and, finally, free him. No thanks to her.

Now, all these years later, her poll numbers surging, she knew that she was on the path to victory. She was going to do great things for the people whose faces she saw in every crowd—the women and men who, like herself, came from humble circumstances and needed a boost to get to where they rightfully belonged.

If anything came out about the time when she had been young and reckless, she'd be stripping her constituents of hope.

It started to drizzle in Mount Vernon just before the freeway snaked over fallow tulip fields and crossed the sluggish Skagit River. She turned on the intermittent wipers. Each time the rubber blades scraped across the windshield of her Mercedes, she heard the words *Watch it. Watch it. Watch it.*

It wasn't magical thinking. She heard the words. It was a warning.

She abruptly changed lanes and exited toward Chuckanut Drive, taking a slower but extremely scenic route to Greta's house.

For a woman who hated surprises and told her assistant to never, ever spring one on her, Heather Jarred was about to deliver one of her own.

An unexpected visit. Probably a very unwelcome one, too.

CHAPTER 58

The sun reflected splinters of light into the trees around Greta's glass cube. Heather hadn't been there before, but she'd heard that it wasn't far from Teddy Bear Cove. Greta, Trish, and Heather had decided to play free spirit one afternoon and make the trek down to the secluded cove's nude beach, a venue they had decided almost immediately was more for the younger college crowd and the obligatory dirty old men who also congregated there on sunny days.

Greta had stayed with Marnie the longest of the original members of the Hive; maybe that explained her compulsion to stay within sight of the island. Trish was the first to leave after Calista went missing, then Heather. For some reason—out of loyalty or some misguided feeling of being part of something important—Greta had remained for a few years. Heather couldn't have imagined doing so, but then, Greta was always a bit of a mystery to her. The two of them were never as close as Heather had been with Trish and Calista. Greta was smart, with a logic-above-emotion approach to things. Some saw it as a facade that kept people from getting to really know her. It was true. She was adept at reflecting whatever another person wanted or needed.

She was, Heather always thought, just like Marnie in that way.

Heather turned from the bay and regarded the house, which was wildly beyond the means of a hospital administrator, the job Greta took after leaving nursing and the Hive. No doubt feeling the need to address the issue—the hospital was a public institution, after all—Greta told the writer of a *Seattle Times* Sunday magazine piece on her place that an aunt had left her a sizable inheritance, which she'd poured into the house in tribute to her ("Aunt Dora had a wonderful collection of glass figurines; I knew she'd have loved it."). They never spoke about it, but Heather expected Trish and Dina shared her suspicions about the windfall that built the pricey home. It just made too much sense that the money had come from a collaboration with Marnie.

Payoff, she thought as she knocked on the door, was a better description than *collaboration.*

Heather watched through the twelve-foot-high glass front doors as Greta came into view. She was dressed for the day, looking as she always did: cinnamon-red hair cut in an angled bob, lightly freckled skin, and green eyes that always telegraphed alertness no matter the time of day or how much wine she drank. She wore a light-pink top, casual tan slacks, and ballet flats. As she did when they were young, she wore only mascara.

Greta returned Heather's wary smile as she opened the door.

"Senator," she said, "what a surprise."

"Actually, for both of us," Heather said. "And I'm not a senator, yet."

Greta's smile dissolved. "You're here because of the girl?"

Heather gave her old friend a long, hard stare. "Aren't you going to invite me in? And yes, I am."

The house was immaculate, a chilly shell of a human's abode, devoid of any personal touches that might indicate a life lived. It was beautiful, nonetheless, Heather thought as she looked it over. The furnishings were mostly cream, as were the walls and the floor. A splash of color had been placed here and there in the form of artwork and throw pillows so one could navigate the space without bumping into things.

"Your home is stunning," Heather said as Greta led her to the seating area in front of the windows that brought the outside into the space. "You're living like a queen."

"Bee—a queen bee," Greta said with a sardonic smile.

"Don't let Marnie hear you say that."

This earned an eye roll. "Not much chance, these days."

Greta went to get coffee while Heather looked out over the water. She returned with a tray bearing two white mugs, some honey, and a creamer.

"The girl is a college student, Heather. She can't do any harm. You must get a zillion requests for interviews."

"I do. And most of the media plays by my rules. I'm in politics, in the bluest of blue states. I'm on their team."

"So they know about you and Marnie, right?"

"That I knew her a long time ago, yes. And they know better than to ask about it. They know that Marnie Spellman's name carries with it a modicum of toxicity. I can't have that right now."

Greta pressed her. "You managed to skirt the issue in previous elections. Why worry now?"

"The US Senate election isn't just any election. It's a high-stakes game, and I have worked very hard to do everything I can to win a seat."

"You're beginning to sound like her."

Heather gave her a knowing look. "Funny," she said, "I've always thought that about *you*." Her eyes swept the room. "How is it that you managed to get a place like this? You were a hospital administrator at a third-tier medical center."

"Let's not get nasty, Heather. You could always flash from nice to mean in two seconds. I thought things would be different now—you know, so you can win people over to your position on various issues."

"We're getting off track here."

"You started it."

"Please, Greta. We need to talk."

Greta drank some coffee. "Fine," she said before starting to chuckle a little.

"What's so funny?"

"Us. We haven't seen each other in . . . what, two decades or so, and we're right back to where we always were: finding ways to fight over something."

Heather wore a grim smile. "Usually Marnie's approval, back on the farm."

Greta nodded. "Approval, acknowledgment . . . Hell, we just wanted her to see that we were more than hangers-on."

"More than worker bees."

This time they both laughed.

The clouds that had hung low in the distance, obscuring Orcas Island, had moved almost to shore, a foreboding, misty curtain drawn across the bay.

They sat still for a moment. Heather finally broke the silence.

"In my world, the cover-up is always worse than the crime."

"There *was* no crime, Heather. Calista died of natural causes, remember?"

"Of course I do. But she shouldn't have been there in the first place. She should have gone to the hospital to have that baby."

"She didn't, though."

"Right. Because we told her that the ferry was out of service. You and I both know it wasn't."

"I didn't know it at the time."

"Come on, Greta."

"Well, honestly, I didn't."

"You know that Marnie lied, and we just went along with it. She wanted the stem cells from Calista's afterbirth because they would be fresh. 'Still warm,' she said."

"I don't remember it that way," Greta said.

"Look, we both have a lot to lose. My future. Your house and early retirement."

"I didn't do anything. I have no exposure here, Heather."

"I was there. I know what we did. If it gets out, I'll lose my Senate seat, and you'll probably be up to your neck in legal fees. I know you only have this place because you put the screws to Marnie. No hospital administrator lives like this."

"Now wait." Greta clearly didn't like what she was hearing. "Why don't you just chill for a minute?"

"Have I ever struck you as someone who might 'chill' on request?"

"No," Greta said. "I remember that." She smiled a tight smile and tapped her own temple. "And I also remember that little pulsing vein you have going there just now. The way it rises and falls, ticking like a clock, when you get cranked up."

It was all Heather could do not to test her claim, press a fingertip to this supposed vein.

Greta's smile widened. "Take a breath, Heather. You need to stop and consider what I'm about to tell you."

Heather had always hated listening to Greta's ideas. They always seemed flat. Unimaginative. When they were part of the Hive, she'd sensed that Greta was only playing at enlightenment. That she didn't really have an authentic bone in her body. A fake, and a wannabe.

"Fine," she said. "I'll listen."

Greta poured more coffee and spoke while taking in the view.

"A smart woman would take her time, think things through. Don't go barking like a rabid dog and threaten the girl. That won't work. That would only encourage Sarah Baker to do whatever she is threatening to do."

"I never said her name, Greta."

"I know her name. I've never talked to her—and I wouldn't. I understand that you have different concerns. That it would be bad PR for you to deny a college student an interview. Just before the election,

338

you know. Anyway, my security camera caught her car, a beat-up Fiesta, on video. I asked a friend in the police department to run the plate."

"That's going to a lot of trouble—the kind of trouble that invites more problems. Why did you do that?"

"It was the sticker on her windshield."

"What kind of sticker?"

"A pass for the Lummi ferry."

Heather set down her cup. She imagined her little vein was now a bigger one, throbbing.

"Interesting."

"That's what I thought, but ultimately harmless."

"You wouldn't say that if you had seen this." Heather got out the photo and showed it to Greta.

She nearly fell backward. "Where in the hell did that come from?"

"The girl left it behind. Like a cat leaving a dead rat."

Greta took her eyes from the image. "Where did she get it?"

"I'm guessing from Marnie."

"That manipulative bitch. She sent us out to do her dirty work that night, and she took a photo of us."

"That's right, Greta. Now what are we going to do about it?"

CHAPTER 59

Wednesday, September 25, 2019
Mount Vernon, Washington

As Lindsay dug more into Marnie's world, a name that emerged from time to time was CiCi Whitman. Lindsay followed digital breadcrumbs left by CiCi in Marnie's online forums in the spring and early summer of 1997.

The way Marnie's proponents viewed her, CiCi was a bitter and dangerous Internet troll at a time when the web was served by search engines Alta Vista and HotBot.

Marnie was reviled by CiCi; then CiCi was gone.

With Spotify playing Hipster Pool Party, Lindsay sat at her desk in the police department and clicked on a long-since-abandoned bulletin board called the "Stinger," which she resurrected from Archive.org.

"If you're looking for salvation," CiCi posted, "you might as well look for it on the shelves at Rite Aid."

The post, short and to the point, brought a torrent of hateful messages from those who thought CiCi was mocking Marnie. She clearly didn't know that the anti-Marnie forum was a magnet for the true believers.

Someone named Honeygirl wrote, "This ugly bitch should drown herself in the Skagit River."

Honeygirl, Lindsay thought, was ahead of her time. She'd be perfect for Twitter. Election year or otherwise.

She followed the nasty rhythm of the trail of posts to the bottom of the page. CiCi pushing back. Honeygirl and a dozen others piling on. Then a link to an article that appeared in the *Skagit Valley Herald*.

Lindsay clicked on it and read on. CiCi Whitman had been living a quiet life in Mount Vernon, Washington, with her husband, Mark, a tulip grower specializing in heirloom varieties originating in Turkey, not the Netherlands. The article pointed out how CiCi had posted a few times on a forum for those who saw Marnie Spellman's outside-inside message as a way of thinking that made some feel they were less than, not more, because of the way they looked. Spellman Farms products were no better and no worse than anything that could be found on the shelves of a local drugstore.

CiCi said she was frightened by some of the zealots who posted threats, then placed phone calls, and finally performed honking drive-bys. When someone shattered their front window, Mark called the Mount Vernon Police, and a patrol officer took down the information.

A day later, a *Skagit Valley Herald* reporter named Justine Shaw did a brief story in its Crime Watch column.

Lindsay found Justine, now living in Bow, Washington, and called her.

"I'm investigating a murder case with potential ties to Marnie Spellman."

"It's about time," Justine said right away. "Can't talk on the phone."

Justine Shaw, now in her forties, wore her hair in a mass of Medusa curls and oversized RBG glasses that somehow stayed on her tiny knob of a nose. There was a tremulous quality to her words when she called Lindsay over to a booth in the back of the Plum Tree restaurant off I-5 in Mount Vernon.

Lindsay thanked her for agreeing to meet.

"Sure can't talk about Marnie Spellman over the phone."

Lindsay regarded her skeptically. "Seriously, Justine? It's been years."

"I don't want to end up like CiCi Whitman and her husband."

"I don't follow."

"Your murder case," she said. "You're working the Whitman case, right?"

"No. Sarah Baker, a young college-newspaper reporter."

Justine looked down at her coffee, then put her hands on the table.

"Oh God," she said softly, looking up. "Are you sure?"

Before Lindsay could reply, Justine added, "Don't tell me. I don't want to know."

"All right, then, Justine. Tell me about CiCi."

"This conversation never happened, all right?"

Lindsay agreed.

In a quiet voice punctuated by quick glances around the restaurant, Justine Shaw told Lindsay that the "Stinger" bulletin board and the smashed window had been the impetus for the feature article she'd planned to write for the Mount Vernon newspaper. She'd decided to put the focus on the personal connection CiCi had with Marnie when growing up together on Lummi Island. She conducted the interview in CiCi's kitchen.

Thursday, July 3, 1997
Mount Vernon, Washington

"Look, we were on an island, for goodness' sake," CiCi said with a half smile and a shrug. "There was very little to do. In the summers, we hung out at the beach. We picked fruit in the abandoned orchard near our place. Mostly we just talked."

"What did you talk about?" Justine asked.

"Nothing much. We talked about whether we'd ever get off the island, that's for sure. Funny how it turned out that I was the one who left for the mainland and, despite all of her money and fame, she stayed put."

"Did you have any idea that she'd become this phenomenon?"

CiCi selected her words carefully. "I did see her as someone who could spin a tale, sell something to people who might not even need it. I'd seen her convince people that she'd single-handedly developed a cultivar of an apple that was just a rogue tree in the old orchard."

"She was a very good storyteller," Justine said.

"Right, but there was always something behind her stories. There was always a little grain of truth to whatever she said. Like the story of the swarm."

"All right. Let's talk about that."

CiCi nodded. "I remember when she came up with that. I was with her, not her brother. We scored some marijuana from someone and watched a swarm of bees in a tree above us. It didn't lift her up. It didn't do much of anything. Next thing I knew, she was telling everyone that she'd had this transformative experience and that her brother could verify it. I knew she was making it up."

"So you're sure she made it up?"

CiCi poured some kibble into a bowl for her cat and looked back over at the visitor.

"Well, like I say, I saw what I saw—and didn't see what I didn't," she said. "Then I wondered if maybe there'd been another time, when it was just her brother there, like she said. Because listen, we were close. Very. I didn't want to cause trouble with that."

"So you don't really know for sure, do you?" the reporter said. "Although I admit it is fantastical, this idea of a moment in which she was imparted some kind of wisdom from God by way of an enormous swarm of bees . . ."

"I know Marnie," CiCi said firmly. "She can be an extremely convincing storyteller. At the time, I saw only good in her ability to get people to believe her. I never saw it as coming from somewhere else."

"I don't follow."

"I think you probably do," she said. "You just don't want to see it. If I were Marnie Spellman, you'd nod your head like a buoy in a bay."

"Would you mind spelling it out? I can't play a guessing game here."

"Fair enough. Here's what I think: she either made it up or it came from some source other than God. By the way, I prefer the male pronouns for God. Just in case you were wondering."

"Understood," Justine said. "But if it didn't come from God, then from whom?"

"That's not for me to say."

The next day she filed her story under the headline Childhood Friend Calls Spellman "Dangerous Fraud."

Two days later, before the article was even published, someone set fire to the Whitman residence using a crude firebomb that consisted of a mason jar, accelerant, and wadded rags. Thankfully, the Whitmans were away.

The only casualty was the family's cat, Felix.

The paper ran a story the following day.

Arson Suspected in House Fire

Wednesday, September 25, 2019

"They were pretty upset about the arson article," Justine said. "Concerned that the coverage would spark more violence against them, no pun intended. After that, they moved away. Lock, stock, and barrel. Didn't even tell the next-door neighbors, close friends of theirs."

"To be safe?"

Justine hesitated. "Yeah, I think so."

"But your story never ran."

"No. It didn't."

"What happened?"

Justine finished her coffee. "I don't know for sure, Detective. I have my suspicions, though. I asked my editor why my story never ran, and he hemmed and hawed before firing me for misusing the copy machine a week later. Someone told me eventually that the editor's wife was the one who killed the story. She was one of those Marnie followers."

They sat in silence for a minute while the waitress filled their cups with more coffee.

"The Whitmans," Lindsay said. "Did you ever get a bead on where they went?"

"That's just it," Justine said, her eyes glistening a little. "I felt kind of responsible for everything that happened next."

Lindsay let more silence fill the space between them. Justine was struggling. She took off her glasses and wiped away a tear.

"This is really hard," she said, finally finding her voice and telling Lindsay that two years after leaving Mount Vernon in the middle of the night, the family's van crashed into a deep ravine near Clarkston, Washington, where they'd moved to start a new life. The vehicle landed amid sagebrush and tumbleweeds and was only spotted by chance when a hitchhiker noticed sunlight sparkling off the front bumper. The bodies of the Whitmans were found inside.

"It was an accident," Lindsay said. "It wasn't your fault."

"You think?"

"Of course."

Justine looked nervously around the restaurant. "Then you don't know those Spellman people," she said, dropping her voice. "I called the lieutenant in charge of the case, saying I was a reporter. Which I wasn't anymore. Anyway, he told me that his techs said the brake line had been leaking. The vehicle was in rough shape, and it was impossible to tell if it had been tampered with."

Justine got up, plunked down a couple of dollars, picked up her jacket, and started for the door. She turned with a word of advice.

"Be careful, Detective," she said. "Those bee freaks are dangerous."

And with that, she was gone.

Lindsay sat there quietly before dialing the Asotin County sheriff. She identified herself and asked for information on the Whitman crash. A woman took the message and promised she'd get a call back.

Lindsay's phone rang on her drive back to Ferndale. The caller was a deputy with Asotin County.

"I worked that crash in '99," Gene North said. "Sent parts to the state crime lab. Nothing conclusive on the brakes. Seemed suspect to us, given what the reporter said. But nothing here. Found that book of Marnie Spellman's in the van."

"*The Insatiable Heart*?"

"Yeah, that book. What a load of crap. Inscribed, too."

"Really?"

"Yeah, I have it right here. Kept it as a souvenir or reminder. Hang on a sec."

Lindsay heard the rustle of paper and the sliding of the same kind of bric-a-brac that cluttered areas around her own desk when she was knee deep in a case. A minute later, the deputy picked up the phone and read,

> CiCi, it all started with you.
> Don't you ever forget it.
> Marnie

CHAPTER 60

Thursday, August 29, 2019
Chuckanut Drive, Washington

The two old friends, at odds over their shared past and frightened about what would happen if the world finally caught up with them, sat quietly for a minute after Greta finished her story about her encounter with Marnie just days before. She scooped up her cat and started the animal's motor as it purred in her lap.

"Marnie was angry, Heather. At you. At me. At the world."

"Anger was always a motivator for her."

Greta nodded. "She wants money."

"She came to me for money, too. Said she made a big discovery," Heather said.

Heather took a step back, once more looking over the home she knew had been built with Marnie's money. Greta was shrewd. Likely a blackmailer. Heather didn't ask Greta whether she had blackmailed Marnie, because she wasn't sure she wanted to know the answer—it would only need to be denied later.

If any of this Marnie stuff resurfaced. Which it had better not. Ever.

"Same old, same old," Heather said. "She's desperate for a comeback. Probably enlisted Sarah Baker in doing a story, a story meant to hurt us."

"You, especially," Greta said.

"All of us will go down," Heather corrected.

"Right," Greta said. "She's running out of funds. Followers are tired of waiting and giving. She played a winning hand like a loser. And now she's shaking the trees in the orchard to see what she can get to fall."

"You never hold back, do you?"

"Why should I? When you're right, you're right. You know that bumblebee brooch of hers?"

Heather nodded. "It was exquisite. What about it, Greta?"

"Remember how she said that it had five diamonds, one for each one of us, the members of the Hive?"

"Yes," Heather said. "I remember."

Greta held Heather's gaze. "While she was ranting at me, I just stared at it. Something was off. After she left, I realized that there were only three gemstones. I'm pretty sure it was a fake, a half-assed replica."

Heather shook her head. "She would never have parted with that. She said it was a gift from Princess Diana, a thank-you."

"Right," Greta said. "A story, like the swarm, that I no longer believe."

"I'm not sure I know what to do with that."

"Tell me, do you still believe it?"

"Some things, I guess, though I should know better."

"She's a fraud, Heather. Maybe you've been around politics so long now that you think when someone says something with conviction it must be true. You should, more than anyone, see that conviction now means a lie."

Heather stood to leave, but stopped and said, "I expect you are in touch with some of our old friends."

Greta didn't answer.

"Make sure everyone gets the message."

"I gave to your campaign, Heather."

"I know. That's another reason why I'm here. Don't do anything more for me. Let's bury the past and hope that Marnie doesn't force us into damage control. If she does, I'll drag you to hell with me. I know Marnie paid you off. No hospital administrator could afford this place."

Greta didn't take the bait.

Heather was right.

There were no goodbyes to end the visit, just a soft closing of the front door.

Chapter 61

It wasn't a social call. It was the same as any of the times Marnie had appeared at Dina's door over the years. Her eyes were bloodshot, and there was an unsteadiness to her gait that indicated she'd been drinking or was on drugs of some kind.

"I need money, Dina."

"I don't have any more to give you."

"I doubt that very much," Marnie said. "You know people. You can get cash with a phone call."

"I don't know anyone like that."

"You're a liar," Marnie said. "You're an ungrateful liar."

"I think you should leave now. Get some sleep. See a doctor. You're a mess."

"That's funny," Marnie said. "Giving me advice. Telling me what's best for me."

Dina wished she'd never answered the door. "How is that even remotely funny? You know I care about you."

Marnie's jaw tightened. "Bullshit! You are as facile a liar as the day I met you. Pretending, acting . . . in every situation, it's all you do. You aren't even a real person, Dina."

Dina started to shut the door.

"You can call another has-been right now and get me what I need to continue my work, to make the world a better place. Don't stand in my way."

Finally, and gently, Dina Marlow closed the door.

From the other side, she heard Marnie.

"You want me to tell what I know? You really want to push me there? Get me the money."

"What about you?" Dina asked through the door. "Anything I have to say will take you down, too."

"I know you better than you know yourself, Dina. As long as you think you have people out there that love you, you'll keep your mouth shut."

CHAPTER 62

Wednesday, September 11, 2019
Olympia, Washington

Richard Jarred felt the vacant space next to him and got up from bed to find his wife in her office on the main floor of their "remodeled, not reimagined" house in Olympia overlooking Black Lake.

She looked up from his phone. Her eyes flashed. She'd found the picture.

"Heather," he asked, "you okay?"

"Don't even start, Richard. Just stop your game playing."

"You're the one playing with my phone."

"Stephanie told me Albert got drunk and sent it to you. Neither one of you can stand being bit players in a woman's life. You're wondering what the photo means, right? You're thinking to yourself that this violation of trust that you suspect me of will destroy me."

"I wasn't sure," he said. "I didn't want it to."

She shook her head in disbelief. "You don't want me to win, do you?"

"Don't be insane, Heather. It's *all* I want."

"Then why are you sneaking around, spying on me, digging into things that are none of your business when the very act of doing so casts doubt on my candidacy?"

"I wasn't digging around. Albert sent it to me, unsolicited. He's pissed off at Stephanie. You know that. He'd sink you to sink her. I love you." He put his arm around her shoulders, and she didn't recoil. She turned and met his eyes.

"Two fucking months to go, Richard. *Poof.* If this gets out, I'm done."

"Sarah Baker was going to put it out there. Albert doesn't have the balls to do something like that. And I wouldn't. Stephanie told him about Sarah and the Marnie Spellman bullshit. But don't you see, now that the girl is dead, it can't get out."

"I don't know. Things this late in the game upend everything."

"It didn't for the president," he said.

She pushed the phone toward him. "Please don't offer that as some form of encouragement."

"I went up there the night Sarah Baker was killed," he said. "I was going to take care of it."

"Oh, Richard, you are such an idiot. How could you?"

She didn't tell him that she'd been in Whatcom County, too.

"I was going to tell the girl to kill the story," he said. "She had to be stopped. I knew what she was going to write."

"How could you?"

"She told me everything."

"What are you talking about?"

"Sarah sought me out the same day she came to interview you," he said. "Said she had something she needed help with. She told me about the woman in the photograph who was murdered on Marnie's farm . . . how it was covered up by members of the group you were in. The Hive."

Heather could scarcely believe her ears. "You're telling me this now?"

"You had already seen her. I didn't tell you because you have so much on your mind. And really, until Albert sent me the photo, I thought she was full of crap."

Heather got up and put her hands on his shoulders, drawing him in. His eyes had flooded by then, and she could feel the tremor of fear coming through his body.

"Richard! What did you do?"

"I would have done anything to protect you. I would have. But she was gone. I was ready. I cut the power to the security cameras in the parking area. God help me. I knocked on the door, no answer. I waited awhile in the car, feeling angry and stupid. I don't know exactly what I was going to do to her. Maybe just beg her. Pay her off. I don't know. I watched as her car pulled into her parking spot. She wasn't driving. Some guy was. In fact, she wasn't even in the car. The guy went inside and came out with a laptop. Then he left on foot."

"Stop," she said. "I can't know any more."

"I didn't do anything."

"Richard, take a Xanax and don't mention this to me again."

He nodded. "I didn't touch her. I never even saw her."

She pressed her lips against his and told him she'd be upstairs shortly.

After he disappeared, she texted Stephanie Haight on yet another burner phone.

Heather: We might have a problem.

Stephanie responded right away: What?

Heather: We need to get Richard out of town. Just until voting. Albert, too. They're too stupid to keep their mouths shut.

Stephanie: God, why did we marry these guys?

Heather: For votes, I guess.

Heather went into the garage and took a hammer to her husband's phone. She wondered why he hadn't asked about the meaning of the photograph. He just accepted the narrative that came to him as an observer. He didn't ask how she could have done what she was doing.

Maybe he wasn't so stupid after all.

Or maybe he actually loved her.

The next morning, Richard Jarred and Albert Haight were chauffeured to SeaTac for the long flight to Alaska.

"Are you sure it's okay?" Richard asked Heather as she handed him a new phone. "Leaving like this? Right now?"

"Once you get back to Washington, you'll start complaining again that there's no decent fishing for miles—and you'll be right."

"I don't have my gear."

"They have everything there. Send pictures."

Inside her Olympia home, Heather Jarred knew she had to take immediate action. Even the slightest whiff of impropriety would ruin her run for the Senate. The political landscape had been a Gettysburg of fallen candidates since the primary, and there was no way she would allow herself to be counted among the media casualties.

She weighed her predicament. There were three choices: pray that it would pass, get out in front of it, or make sure no one said another word.

Although she and her husband attended church, it was merely for show. Marnie had corrupted all of that. Heather didn't know if she believed in any god whatsoever.

So praying was out.

Chapter 63

Wednesday, September 18, 2019
Chuckanut Drive, Washington

Greta considered phoning Marnie after Detective Jackman's visit. She could clear the air. She could remind her of all the things that bound them together and how she'd lived up to every single promise she'd made. Every goddamned one of them. She went into her office and sat in the big leather Knoll chair that had been her first purchase when she knew she could buy really nice things. She gazed through the Douglas fir boughs that partially obscured the view of the slate-colored water from the window. A sailboat that had been caught in the rain and wind now enjoyed the choppy waters and a much gentler breeze.

Beside her was the bookcase she had had custom built of reclaimed wood from a bowling alley in Ferndale. She didn't keep any books there, choosing rather to decorate the shelves with items from her past, her travels, even her career at the hospital. A silver-and-black frame with a photo of her and a group of nurses held a prominent spot. Seeing their faces was a reminder not of happier times—although there had been those, too—but of things that were essential to remember so that they'd never be repeated.

The night before Calista went into labor, Greta had worked the morning shift at the hospital. She had grown to resent the job and preferred working at Spellman Farms, enjoying the company of Marnie and the other women who made up the Hive. She felt that she'd been cast as a bit of an outsider: always working, commuting to Lummi Island, and pulling extra shifts.

She was closest to Trish, who also worked at the hospital. The two of them had lunch together when their shifts aligned. They talked about how a newcomer like Calista could worm her way into the inner circle with such astounding speed.

Greta had picked at her salad, wishing she'd added more black olives and fewer sprouts.

"She shows up like all the others, and all of a sudden, she's the golden girl, Trish."

"Tell me about it," Trish had said. "Here we are, doing all this, and Dina, Heather, Calista, and Marnie are whooping it up."

Trish exaggerated. She always did. Greta doubted anyone was whooping it up.

"I do agree that Dina and Marnie are especially chummy," Greta finally said, exhaling.

"Chummy?" asked Trish. "How do you mean?"

Greta deflected Trish's curiosity. She was an expert at that sort of thing. It was more of a volley, innocent words charged with innuendo. "Never mind. Just me and my big mouth and overactive imagination at work. Like always."

Casually yet deliberately, Greta had lobbed a bomb. It was a stealth attack, one to keep her closer to Marnie, and keep Trish in ignorance—in a hole that Trish herself had helped dig.

Later, after Calista's death, turning her back on Marnie when she had been the single most important person in her life wasn't easy for

Greta. To be sure, however, the bond between the women had never been fully severed. Every day, when she woke up and looked at the fabulous house that was her home, she knew that it was payment for things she had done with Marnie Spellman. Greta was good with numbers, details. Both were weak points for Marnie. Marnie was a visionary, and that was her role. It fell to Greta to manage the business side, first as a quasi helper, later as Spellman Farms' business manager.

Sometimes the bonds of a relationship have nothing to do with friendship at all. Greta's glass house was a kind of metaphor for her life after Spellman Farms. It was always on the verge of being shattered by secrets from the past.

Chapter 64

Friday, September 20, 2019
Bellingham, Washington

Whatcom Memorial sat at the base of a hill northeast of Bellingham. At one time, it was the largest hospital north of Seattle and drew patients from all over the county up to the border with Canada. The gray granite facade of the oldest section of connected buildings jutted upward just four stories, a stub compared to the "new" hospital built in the early 1980s.

Greta Swensen roamed the parking lot, looking for an empty space. She hadn't been back in five years, when she'd returned for a ceremony honoring another staff member. The place hadn't changed. How she felt about it hadn't, either. She could feel her pulse quicken a little as she found a place for her most conspicuous status symbol, a midnight-blue Tesla.

A dermatologist she knew parked his Mercedes convertible next to her, and she kept her head down while he checked his teeth in the rearview mirror. Finally, after two minutes of fussing, he got out and went through the double doors of the lobby.

When Greta was satisfied no one would see her, she followed him, though at a deliberately slow pace. Returning to the place she'd worked after leaving Spellman Farms made her feel anxious. Very uncomfortable. A kind of ticking feeling reverberated inside her chest, and she tried to will it away. She'd been known as a strong, nearly unflappable administrator when she worked there. She'd go toe to toe with anyone—staff, insurance companies, even patients. In some ways, it was a game. And she was very good at it.

Carrying her laptop like it was a shield, she breezed past the front desk and waited by the drinking fountain while an employee swiped his badge to enter the staff corridor. She gave him a nod while his eyes scanned her for her badge.

She was beautiful. She smiled. The combination of that and a smart wardrobe choice—a stylish suit and blouse—made her look as though she belonged there.

"Do I know you?" he asked.

"Consulting. Used to work here."

"You look familiar."

She knew there was a risk in that. Someone whom she'd worked with, a visiting staffer—even someone who might have seen her photograph— might come across her when she needed to be alone.

While the man's admiring eyes lingered on her, Greta shifted her gaze toward the hall and walked right in.

"Have a nice day," she said over her shoulder.

Greta had chosen Friday for her return to Whatcom Memorial because the vault downstairs was closed on Fridays. In fact, it was seldom used. The documents stored in the basement had been deemed important enough to retain, but not important enough to digitize when the hospital moved to a paperless system for records and billing.

There was one hitch: the door had been equipped with a cipher lock.

While it was possible, Greta highly doubted anyone had changed the number since it had been installed more than a decade ago.

Down the back stairs, to the door, where she stood quietly, listening.

Not a single sound other than the ticking she was sure was her heart.

She pressed numbers for the lock securing the door—the factory-issued numbers that were supposed to have been temporary: one, two, three, four.

She turned the handle, flipped on the lights, and studied the cavernous space. She released a sigh of relief. Nothing had changed. She'd worried that records would have all been scanned by then—that what she needed had been committed to a data file somewhere and would be retrievable only by someone with a computer science degree. Maybe a hacker. But not her. She'd never learned those skills.

Greta worked her way toward the back, skipping past racks and stacks of records marked with the year. One after another. It was as if she were going back in time, getting younger as she went and heading toward the girl she'd been back then. Young. Impressionable. A follower.

The spark of memories made her shake her head. She'd come so far since then.

Greta Swensen had grown up on a farm in rural Nebraska, the second of three girls. She'd later tell people it was her "middleness" that made her chart an unexpected course in life. She hated the idea of marriage and children, both of which contributed to women being in that safe space between boringly quiet and colorfully obnoxious. She'd proudly worn her ERA button around a town that still saw women in the roles that defined them. When she told her parents that she was interested in a medical career, they pushed her into nursing.

"I don't want to be a nurse," she insisted. "I intend to be a doctor."

Intentions were always appreciated in the Swensen household; reality, however, was what drove each decision.

Greta graduated from the nursing school in Lincoln in 1978 and took a job in a hospital in Omaha. She was bitter toward her parents, estranged from her sisters, and simply marinated in negativity. It was as if she felt some deep hatred of her fate and was too weak to fight against the middleness that was consuming her.

That changed when she saw a beautiful blond woman on the shopping channel one Saturday afternoon. It was true that she was selling lotion and honeybee balm, but ingrained in every word of her pitch was a mantra that truly resonated: "You are special. You are worthy. You own your destiny. Be beautiful and brave."

Greta was transfixed by the saleswoman and her message. To say her message appealed to her was an understatement. It set her vibrating like a tuning fork. Greta felt her words pulse. She wrote down the woman's name and company on the back of an electric bill. She was fairly certain that the message she had heard on TV was directed specifically at her. Suddenly, she felt upbeat.

She looked down at her note and smiled. "Marnie Spellman, Spellman Farms."

A week later, all the pieces were in place. Instead of calling them to let her parents know she was moving to Washington, she wrote them a letter.

Mom, Dad,

Share this note with my sisters. Let them know that they were only bookends that held me in place when we were growing up. Ellie was the baby. Amy was the oldest. I was the girl in the middle. Remember her, the one who didn't smile as broadly as she should have whenever family photographs were shot in front of the fake tree you all loved so much.

Greta found what she was looking for on the label of a gray Bankers Box. It was at eye level, in her face. Written in clear cursive. It was handwriting that she immediately recognized as her own: "A. Arthur, patient records, 1967–1995."

She set the box on the floor and opened it carefully, as though she were dismantling some kind of bomb. In a way, she was. What had been carefully hidden inside the box of file folders and old, musty charts from a world in which every single word was noted by hand on a chart was waiting inside.

She found the file: Sullivan, Calista W.

Greta let out a breath she hadn't realized she was holding. She no longer heard the ticking of her heart, the noise that followed her across the parking lot to the front desk, then down to the basement.

She pulled Calista's file, put it in her laptop case, and returned the box to its place. She even adjusted it carefully so that the smear of dust that came off when she retrieved it was obscured.

Good. This is right. I'm doing what needs to be done because I am capable of doing anything. Anything! I am the power. I am me.

She heard the door open and a voice call out.

"Anyone in here?"

It was a woman's voice. Young. Slightly tremulous.

Greta was a deer. She was frozen. And while she allowed herself to breathe, it was shallow, soft.

"Hey!" the voice called out.

Greta crouched low.

She stayed as still as she could, all the while wondering what she would say if the woman calling out made her way that far back into the stacks. Should she call out now? That might be better. It might indicate that she wasn't doing anything wrong. She could say she was hard of hearing or something to explain the delay.

If that didn't work? What would she do to hide the reason for her intrusion into a space that she should never have entered?

The voice mumbled, even cursed.

"Damn! Why don't people turn off the lights?"

Next, the cavernous space went dark. Black. Not a single speck of light, save for the red blinking of the fire sensors affixed to the ceiling that looked like runways to no place in particular. The door closed, and the cipher lock secured it.

Greta waited a beat, turned on her cell phone, and cast a beam over the floor as she found her way to the door.

In a strange way, the close encounter had lifted her spirits. It made her feel as she had felt all those years ago when she arrived on Lummi Island. *Invincible* was the word that Marnie Spellman had used in a reading at the bookstore when Greta first arrived from Nebraska and met her.

Invincible was a good word.

No one would see her.

No one would stop her.

She'd gotten what she came for.

CHAPTER 65

The file folder with Calista's name on it sat on the Tesla's passenger seat and seemed to speak to Greta as she drove. She could almost hear Calista's voice telling her about leaving her husband and her children and making her way north to Lummi Island and a new beginning.

"Do you think what I'm doing is the right thing?" she'd asked once while they were working together in the barn.

"You mean your personal sacrifice?" Greta had asked.

"I guess that's what I mean."

"You are the only one who gets to decide what you do with your life, Calista. That includes the good and the bad. The sacrifices we all make are the price we pay for living this life as it is meant to be lived."

Calista bobbed her head as though she understood.

Greta knew her friend's sacrifice was deeper than just leaving a farm, parents, and sisters. She'd left her husband, her children. She'd abandoned them because she could no longer be just a mother and a wife. That, Greta was sure, was the greatest sacrifice. The other women in the Hive had only given up things and relationships that would fade with the life cycle, anyway.

"I miss my boys," Calista said finally.

"I'm thinking that's probably normal," Greta said, looking up from a computer screen on the big pine table brought in to create a workspace in the barn. The sound of a printer filled the space as labels were created for product shipments that afternoon. "Remember, they are bound to your husband. That can't be ignored by the law and the processes that govern the lives of women."

Calista put her hand on her abdomen. "Marnie says this one will be mine," she said. "Not Reed's. He doesn't even know."

They exchanged smiles and returned their attention to filling boxes for shipping.

Back in her glass house, Greta slammed the folder down on the kitchen table and dialed Trish Appleton.

"Someone knows," Greta said.

Trish kept her voice low. "I told you to stay clear of me."

"We all go down if one of us does."

"I'm already dead, remember?"

Greta let out an exaggerated sigh. "I guess I forgot."

"Leave me alone, Greta," Trish said. "We didn't do anything wrong."

Greta kept pushing. "Not technically. People won't see it that way."

"All right, fine," Trish said. "I'll listen."

"I got Calista's file from Whatcom."

"Why would you do something stupid like that, Greta? God, that would be a crime!"

"The detective—Lindsay Jackman—has been asking about her."

"She doesn't know anything. Trust me."

"Maybe. I'm not sure. *Someone* does. In any case, aren't you curious about what I found in the file? Or, rather, what I didn't find?"

"Okay. Okay. Tell me."

Greta opened the folder and spread out its contents.

"All that's here are the charts and copies of statements related to a rash she got from messing with some poison oak while hiking on Mount Baker."

Silence on the other end of the line.

"You need to do something. I can't do all of this on my own."

"Are you threatening me?"

"Don't think I won't."

"What's behind all of this? You? Marnie? Give me a break, Greta. I'm not getting pulled into one of your games."

With that, Trish hung up.

CHAPTER 66

Saturday, November 14, 1997
Bellingham, Washington

Trish Appleton was the fourth person to join the Hive.

She'd met Heather and Greta at Whatcom Memorial, where all three worked as nurses. Trish came to the profession by way of family tragedy. Her younger brother and sister had died of sudden infant death syndrome before they were six months old. In both instances, her mother had been the one to find the babies, who had turned blue, motionless in their beds. Trish was seven when Kit, her sister, died, nine when her brother, Will, passed.

Their losses had been devastating, however it was when she was twelve—when her mother gave birth to her fourth baby, Jasmine—that Trish's life changed forever.

It was the worst kind of dividing line.

Trish had early dismissal from school that particular day, a date that her mom had forgotten to mark on the kitchen calendar. When she got home, the TV was on, but the house appeared to be empty. This was strange. She went to Jasmine's room, where she saw her mother holding a pillow to her sister's face.

The scene was still, like a photograph, and then her mother's head swiveled to her in the doorway. Their eyes met.

Trish flew across the room, thrust herself between them, and grabbed the baby from her. *"What are you doing?"*

Her mom just stood there, blinking. "I don't know. She was crying."

Trish held her breath, processing it all.

"I know what you did, Mom."

Her mother had the scared eyes of an animal in a leg trap.

"Please," she muttered. "Don't tell."

Trish told her father what she'd seen, expecting him to do something to protect Jasmine. He listened to every word, holding her by the shoulders and insisting that he'd make sure it never happened again. Instead, the next day, Trish was sent to stay with her grandparents in Issaquah. When she returned home, her mother said she was under a doctor's care. What happened would never, ever happen again.

And it didn't.

Trish never told anyone else what she'd seen in her baby sister's room. Secrets were best kept locked tight. No key. In nursing school, she learned there was a name for what her mother had done to Kit and Will and tried to do to Jasmine, who'd survived with brain damage from being deprived of oxygen.

A few weeks after starting work at Whatcom, Heather and Greta invited Trish to come meet Marnie. They talked about her all the time, and Trish saw no way of wriggling out of the trip to Lummi Island.

When they arrived one Saturday morning, Marnie was on the phone and gestured to them to sit in the living room while she finished her call. She was absolutely bursting with joy when she hung up.

It was the home shopping channel.

"I'm going to be a regular now!" she said. "The world is going to know my name. Ladies, we are about to change the order of things. Women deserve to be on top."

Greta giggled at the accidental double entendre.

"You must be Trish," Marnie said, greeting the newcomer. She put her hand out, but lowered it as Trish extended hers.

"Oh my," Marnie said quietly, like a prayer. "You are such a petite marvel. I wish I had eyes like yours, beautiful and full of intelligence." She faced Heather and Greta, who sat rapt, ensconced on the big velvet sofa. "You two get some wine from the cellar. I'm going to show Trish my world."

Trish looked at her friends, and nervousness washed over her. It wasn't that Marnie didn't strike a chord somewhere inside, because she did. No doubt about that. It was the chord itself. She felt the woman before her was somehow able to see into her soul. She wondered why she would make her living from beauty products when she could so easily see through to the soul of another human being. What did the mere covering of the soul, the flesh, matter?

After a tour of the barn and the orchard, Marnie took Trish to the hillside that had changed her life.

"This is where it happened," she said.

"The swarm?"

"You've read my book."

"Twice. I didn't want to show up and seem like an idiot."

Marnie smiled and took Trish's hand. "You have a hurt deep inside, don't you?"

Trish only nodded.

"Everyone does."

"I guess so."

"Tell me, Trish. Tell me everything."

Chapter 67

Thursday, September 2, 1999
Lummi Island, Washington

Greta was looking for the shipping manifest for custom orders Marnie had promised to important clients. It was September, and the marine air carried a chill off the water and into the barn. She covered the barn nearly inch by inch, searching for the familiar yellow clipboard. When she couldn't find it, she returned to the house. Marnie was napping after a long day on the phone. Calista was on the porch with her feet up.

Where was it?

Marnie had to be right. All the time. Greta knew her place, but even so, it rankled her to think that the stupid clipboard would give Marnie a chance to say something about her competence. She did it whenever she could. It passed through her mind as she went upstairs that Marnie herself had been the one to put the clipboard somewhere just so she could lord it over her.

Marnie's door was open a crack, and Greta could hear Heather talking. It was odd that Heather was in there. Greta leaned a little closer, and through the narrow slit, she saw Heather lower a syringe and insert the needle into Marnie's upper thigh.

Royal jelly and saline, Marnie's latest concoction.

"When you do that," Marnie said, her eyes shut tight, "I can feel it happening."

Greta, mouth agape, took a step backward and quietly went downstairs.

Something was going on with Heather and Marnie. She'd wondered about that. They'd shared little private conversations that Heather always indicated were merely Marnie's way of "working" her.

"You know Marnie. She has a need to be close to all of us in her own way. It probably has to do with her childhood."

"Everything has to do with people's childhoods around the farm."

"Maybe so."

The conversation would switch, a change in topic always instigated by Heather.

The afternoon she saw Heather and Marnie with the syringe, Greta went outside to sit with Calista. She brought two black teas with honey.

"Blackberry honey. Your favorite."

Calista smiled and took the cup.

They didn't say anything for the longest time.

"Are you all right, Greta?"

"I'm fine. Just thinking."

"Can I help?"

Calista was like that. Of the Hive, she was the kindest. She had also given up the most to be there. Some of the others who came were there for reasons that Marnie thought were frivolous: a breakup with a boyfriend, a chance to be close to someone famous, a passing fancy. Not Calista.

"I'm fine. Just a lot going on."

"Me, too."

"I noticed you didn't drink wine last night," Greta said.

Calista nodded. "You don't miss much. It's early. I don't want others to know just yet."

"Are you happy about it?"

Calista kept her eyes on her tea. "I am, but I'm scared, too. I don't have much of a support system here in Washington."

"That's silly. You have all of us."

Calista nodded and drank her tea.

"I know that's true," she said, patting her belly. "Sometimes I think that I should just go back to Reed. This is his baby, too."

The two women sat on the porch, watching and thinking. One about what she'd seen. The other about what she planned to do. The silence between them carried with it a kind of comfort, the kind one feels when there is no need to talk. Just being there is sometimes enough.

"Listen," Calista finally said. "Do you hear them?"

Greta followed Calista's gaze. She was looking across the pasture at the hives. "The bees?"

"Yes, they're coming home."

CHAPTER 68

Wednesday, September 22, 1999
Lummi Island, Washington

Marnie put her hands on Calista's abdomen while they sat outside with the rest of the Hive on the expansive front porch, enjoying the vista of water and islands.

Greta didn't keep the secret.

Marnie had never had a baby of her own, but she reveled in the idea of giving life, of being a mother. The earth was her mother, she'd told people. Yet she frequently spoke of a yearning she'd had for a child of her own.

"Calista, wouldn't it be something if you had the baby here—a child of Spellman Farms, if you will? A baby that would know total love from the first moment she or he took in a single breath of air?"

Calista seemed to like the idea, although she had a reservation.

"It would be wonderful, but we don't have any doctors on the island."

"Who needs a doctor when we have Greta, Heather, and Trish here?"

"It's not the same," Calista said. "Being a nurse—no offense, ladies—is not the same as being a doctor."

Trish shrugged and gazed at Marnie and Heather, then back to Calista. "I guess you think a title—a title usually reserved for men—is more important than nature's way."

"I didn't mean that at all. Now you're getting defensive. Just like you, Trish. Always the one who knows the best way to do something—" She cut herself off.

"And sometimes behind Marnie's back, too," Heather said, suddenly interested in the conversation.

Calista replied, "Heather, you can be such a bitch sometimes. Whenever I suggest something that varies from Marnie's plan, you think I'm disloyal. *I* think I'm *empowered.*"

Marnie stood up. "Enough of this. I just thought it was a nice idea. In the matriarchies of the past, women gathered without men to welcome a baby into the world, surrounded by nature."

Calista shook her head. "I'm not having my baby in the orchard or apiary, Marnie."

Marnie waved this off. "In the barn, we can make a birthing room. It will be safe, beautiful. It will tell the child that the world is a lovely place, not cold, not antiseptic. It's all up to you, of course."

"I'm practically a midwife," said Greta, who'd stayed out of the conversation until she could gauge the shifting sands.

Calista looked up at Marnie, then the others.

"I don't know. I guess. All right. Maybe just as a backup plan."

Immediately, the rest of the group jumped up to join Marnie as they took turns hugging her.

"I know I've found my home," Calista said, tears brimming in her eyes, but not falling. "I don't think I've ever been this happy in my life."

This was all true. Not the whole truth, however. She was saying all the right words, telling them what they needed to hear. But as the day approached, Calista knew she would keep her mind fixated on the ferry schedule. Just in case.

The birthing room was painted pale yellow, as was the steel hospital bed that had been ferried over from the mainland. Marnie had the hired man paint the frame three times to get it just right.

"I want to see the color of the sun, but not on a bright day. A soft, clear morning. Early. Just after it rises."

"I don't know, Marnie." Greta thought Marnie could be completely ridiculous, and was the only one who seemed able to tell her so. "Looks more like the color of a Meyer lemon at two in the afternoon."

Marnie gave her a look. "Don't mock me, Greta."

"Just calling it as I see it. Definitely Meyer lemon. And maybe closer to two thirty."

"Two fifteen," Marnie countered, this time with a smile.

Both women chuckled, and the handyman was called in for another pass at achieving Marnie Spellman's very specific vision.

One afternoon not long before the big day, Dina came to help with the herb garden, and found herself working alongside Calista. They'd been harvesting calendula flowers for the restaurant that had called that morning for the frilly orange blossoms, an ingredient for a sorrel and calendula soup they'd be serving at that night's dinner service.

Dina asked Calista how she felt about having a baby.

"As you know, I've done it before."

"Right," Dina said. "That's kind of what I'm getting at. This time is different. You're on your own."

Dina had a way of posing difficult questions with a sweetness that proved she was a better actress than she was given credit for.

"My boys are with their father. They love him. He's a good man . . . just not what I needed in this life."

Dina picked at her fingertips, stained orange from calendula petals.

"Right," she said. "But isn't this baby his, too?"

"Right. I mean, no. Marnie tells me to see this as mine. *All* mine. I don't have to share parenting with a man in order to raise a child right. That's absurd. Plenty of single women have elected to have children. Most of nature is set up that way."

Dina had no children of her own, although one of her ex-husbands had a daughter that she had raised for two years. They were never close, Dina told everyone, except for when the girl wanted money or a free weekend at her stepmother's place in Palm Springs. Dina sold the house with its ridiculous statuary of Greek gods to a lovely couple from San Francisco just to spite the girl. She bought another place, albeit one that was a lot less grand, in Palm Desert.

She never told her ex or her stepdaughter about the replacement hideaway.

"It's not that you couldn't function on your own. I practically raised my stepdaughter, Trena, with zero help from that bastard father of hers, so I know," Dina said. "What I'm getting at is your baby has a father who'd probably want to be involved."

Calista nodded. "If he knew."

That surprised Dina. "He doesn't?"

"No. If he did, I know he'd do whatever he could to stop me from leaving him."

"He is violent?" Dina asked.

"The opposite. He was always decent. Hated Marnie's influence over me, but I told him over and over that she wasn't influencing me at all; her teachings were. It was a deeper connection to a place in this world that he just couldn't fathom."

Dina put her hand on Calista's belly and squinted into the sun. "What are you going to do when he finds out?"

"Finds out? He won't."

Just then, Marnie joined the conversation.

"Dina, I know that your Hollywood runs on gossip and innuendo; however, it doesn't rule the day here. Leave Calista alone. Let her have her own life. We are all connected here, and yes, we are individuals. We have our own private stories."

Your Hollywood.

Dina acted like she'd been slapped in the face.

In a way, she had been.

Calista looked over at Marnie and mouthed the words *Thank you.*

Inside, she felt like a fraud. Playing both sides. Unsure whom to trust.

Spellman Farms was a beautiful place, with beautiful people.

Beautiful liars with ulterior motives.

Calista realized she was one of them. It was at this instant that she decided she had no intention of having her baby on that farm.

Chapter 69

Sunday, March 5, 2000
Lummi Island, Washington

It was late in the afternoon when Calista's water broke. She'd been extracting royal jelly and mixing it with honey, a technique that Marnie had developed to preserve and extend the supply of the precious and miraculous food of a new queen. She was outside when it happened, standing in the garden. She'd had two children already, and she'd come to know her body better than ever before. The farm had done that. Marnie's counsel, too. The CDs that she'd listened to invited her—no, challenged her—to think about the purpose behind each word, each movement.

"Are you all right? Need anything?" asked Heather, who'd been there for a few days and was staying with Marnie.

"No, I'm fine. It's just that I think I should go to the hospital. I don't feel right about having the baby here. I'll catch the last boat."

Calista changed her wet clothes and returned to work, checking her watch between contractions.

Marnie and Greta found her in the barn. Trish showed up a few minutes later.

"Heather says you've changed your mind?" Marnie asked.

Calista indicated she had. "I'm sorry. I know you have gone to so much trouble here. A mother's instinct, I guess. I feel like the hospital is where I need to be. I better get going."

Greta spoke. "It's about that. The ferry's out for the rest of the day. Mechanical issues again."

Calista looked around, her eyes meeting Greta's.

"We can do this, Calista. You know we can," Greta said. "Trish and Heather are here. I think we know a thing or two about helping a mom have a baby."

"I was born in this barn myself," Marnie said. "Missed the ferry then, too."

It was the only option.

Later, Greta and Trish made final preparations in the barn while Marnie and Heather gave Calista a royal jelly milkshake. The minutes peeled away, and Calista was in the bed, inhaling and exhaling as the contractions began to force the baby down the birth canal. As the baby came, so did a pool of blood.

"Amniotic fluid mixes with blood," Greta said, catching Dina's concerned gaze. "It looks terrible, but not to worry. Here it comes, Calista! Push!"

Calista let out a loud cry.

"Here's your son!" Greta said.

"A boy?" Marnie asked, stunned by what she'd just heard. "A girl! I wanted a girl!"

Calista screamed. The sound erupted from a different, deeper, more panicked place. They all stood stock-still, staring at her.

"Something doesn't feel right," she said.

Dina's eyes were wide. Scared. The blood was still coming, too.

Greta handed the baby to Trish, who took him over to a table they'd covered with a white sheet.

"I want to hold my baby," Calista said, woozily straining to see past her swollen abdomen.

"Push again. Let's count. One, two, three!"

The placenta was delivered. So was more blood.

Marnie, visibly angry that it was a boy, took the placenta over to where Trish was working on the baby.

"This isn't good," Trish said, her eyes shiny with tears. "Mom's hemorrhaging." She kept her voice low—loud enough for Marnie to hear, but no one else.

"Greta knows what to do."

"I doubt that. She's not a surgeon."

"Calista will be fine. Did you get everything you need?"

Trish nodded as she studied the afterbirth and the bloody cord.

"You take the baby over to Calista. I'll put the samples in the refrigerator."

A moment later, Calista held her son. Her skin had gone pale, but the look in her eyes was the unmistakable gaze of a mother falling in love with her baby.

"He's mine," Calista said, looking up at Marnie, Heather, Greta, Dina, and Trish. "I don't have to share him with Reed or with anyone, do I?"

"No," Marnie said. "Not ever. He's part of you. You alone."

"I'm tired," she said, still unaware that the white sheet under her had turned red from the waist down and that blood was seeping onto the floor. "Need to rest a little."

"Good idea. Trish will take your baby. Oh, I'm sorry. I didn't even ask what you'll call him. Have you decided?"

"Scout," Calista said, her voice growing weak. "The most important role for a male in the hive."

She only said what she knew they'd want to hear.

All she wanted was to get her baby and leave.

CHAPTER 70

A scream came from the barn.

It was Trish. She stood frozen next to the bloody hospital bed that held Calista. Despite the hour, almost instantly others in the Hive arrived: Marnie, Heather, and Greta.

Marnie pushed past Trish, who was bunched up near the bed. She was inconsolable. Frantic.

"I thought she was doing better," Trish said. "I only left her for ten minutes."

"What happened?" Marnie asked.

Greta felt Calista's wrist, which hung limply from the side of the hospital bed.

"No pulse," she said.

"I tried chest compressions," Trish said.

"You're a nurse, Trish," Heather said. "For all that's holy, why didn't you get us?"

"I really thought she was getting better. I just acted. I went into lifesaving mode."

The women looked at each other, then at the lifeless body of one of the members of their tightknit group.

Heather spoke up. "We need to call the police," she said.

"Police? No," Marnie said, putting her hand up as though she were a traffic cop. "We can't bring them into this, Heather."

Trish knelt down next to the bed, still crying, though softly now. "What are you talking about, Marnie?" Greta asked.

"How are we going to explain why she was here? Why she had her baby here and not back on the mainland?"

Greta, as always, followed Marnie's lead. "We'll tell them that the ferry was out and we couldn't."

Marnie started pacing. Her fists were clenched as she walked from the bed to the TV set and then back again. "This will ruin me. It will. This is on me."

Just then, Dina appeared in the doorway. "This is insanity, Marnie. I can't be dragged into something like this. I have a public who adores me and all I stand for."

Marnie gave her an icy glare. "You're weak, Dina," she said. "Wear that word like a tattoo on your face."

By then Trish had gathered herself enough to say, "What are you two doing? It was an accident. We did the best we could. We all did. Except you, Marnie. This is your doing."

"I don't know what you mean, Trish," she said.

"You do," Trish said, pushing back. "You know perfectly well. You wanted her to have her baby here, didn't you?"

"What are you implying?" asked Heather.

Marnie and Heather.

Those two.

They were always wired together in a way none of the others in the Hive could quite articulate. When Heather was there, and later Dina, Marnie turned her attention away from the rest of them. When Trish and Heather left work at the hospital on Fridays and caught the ferry, they'd laugh and talk until they arrived at the farm. But then, when Marnie appeared on the front steps of the big house to welcome them, it was as if Trish vanished. Heather flashed from the car to Marnie like a bolt of lightning drawn to the tallest, most magnificent tree.

"The ferry didn't break down," Trish said. "Did it?"

Neither Marnie nor Heather answered.

Trish didn't need them to. She knew exactly what they'd done and why.

"I'll tell the authorities what you did."

"You wouldn't." Marnie was utterly unconcerned. "You'd be nothing if not for me."

Trish was reeling again. "What have we done?" she asked, her voice rising with panic.

Marnie put her hand out to her. "It will be all right. I promise." She drew Trish in close, stroking her hair, telling her that all of this had a purpose. That God wanted her to be everything she wanted to be. Trish folded herself into Marnie's arms, into her care. Her panic subsided.

"Trish," Marnie said, "you and Heather will do something for me tonight. It will be an act of love and respect. For me. For God. For Calista."

It was two in the morning when Heather and Trish wedged Calista's body into the back of the farm truck. Heather covered the body with a brown tarp and fastened it with a bungee cord to the truck bed.

"This is wrong," Trish said. "All of this."

"*Wrong* is a funny word," Heather said. "Circumstances can make wrong right in a split second. This is one of those times, Trish."

"Don't you see that Marnie made all this happen?"

Heather shook her head, sweating from the heavy lifting and the worry that she couldn't completely hide. "Honestly, I don't know."

Trish's mother had been a liar. Trish knew the cool look of a skilled fabricator.

"She lied about the ferry," she said. "She wanted Calista to be stuck here. She gave her that drink with God knows what in it. I've never said so before, but she's been poking her with needles like a pincushion in some grandma's sewing basket."

Heather got in the driver's side of the truck. "Really? So? Maybe she did. What has that got to do with what we need to do right now? We have to take care of this situation, or it will ruin our lives."

"It wouldn't have ruined our lives if we'd gone to the police, Heather."

"We didn't. So now we're dealing with it. Get in."

With Trish in the passenger seat, Heather backed the truck into the turnaround by the barn and then started down the driveway. She barely put her foot on the gas and kept the headlights off. The moon was out, sending a beam of illumination between the high clouds, filling the roadway with light.

"Marnie should be doing this, Heather. Not us."

"She's watching the baby. Do you think I'm happy about this? God, Trish, your constant doubts and questions aren't helping."

"I would have watched the baby," Trish said. "I didn't sign up for this. Stealing from the hospital was a mistake, too."

Heather kept her eyes on the blackened road as it unfurled along the shoreline. "It isn't stealing if it is going to go into the trash."

"That's what you tell yourself. Always have it figured out, don't you? If it wasn't wrong, why did we go to such lengths to hide what we were doing?"

"Changing the world from the outside in is worth a few transgressions, Trish."

"Boy, you are a true believer, aren't you?"

"Can we not do this? We have to get rid of the body."

"Calista Sullivan, Heather. The body has a name."

"Jesus, Trish," Heather said, "get it together. Stop this. We have a job that needs to get done, and in doing so, we are protecting the things that are the most valuable to us."

"My freedom is valuable."

"No one is going to find out."

"Right. People always think that."

Later, neither of the women wanted to remember what they'd done. How heavy Calista's body felt as they carried her to the outgoing tide. How they crouched on the barnacle-encrusted rocks and set her down, wrapped in the tarp, a giant cocoon.

Heather observed her friend.

Her sister.

Her accomplice.

She considered Trish among the weakest members of the Hive. Weakness always worried her.

"We need to get this off of her," Heather said, indicating the tarp. "Otherwise, she won't sink."

Trish was crying silently as they struggled to get the body out of the tarp and moving toward the current. With luck, it would drift north to Canada.

They waded out a few yards and gave Calista one final push.

"We should say something, Heather."

"This isn't a memorial service."

"She was our friend."

"Push," Heather said.

The word alone would have been enough; however, the intonation, the sense of urgency, induced Trish to shove as hard as she could. Calista's body floated on the surface of the inky water, the golden trail of moonlight heading back to shore.

"She's sinking, Heather."

"Good. She just needs to drift away from here. Let's get going. Marnie will wonder what took so long."

"She should have been the one to do this, not us."

"We need to get out of here without being seen by anyone."

"Who would be out and about at this ungodly hour?"

"*We're* out here, Trish. People like us. That's who."

When they got back to the farm, all the lights were off. Heather went up to the house, and Trish went into the barn. Every single trace of Calista's horrific delivery and death had been removed. Not a speck of blood anywhere. Even the bed was gone.

She went to the refrigerator in the lab part of the barn.

The cord blood was gone, too.

Everything except the baby—just gone.

CHAPTER 71

An agonizing five days after Trish and Heather dumped the body, Calista Sullivan's remains were found by the tourists who were exploring "the most beautiful place in the world" to find that sometimes things get ugly in paradise.

Heather watched the officers bring the body bag up from the beach to a waiting ambulance, the only one on the island. Trish was there, too. So was a KVOS news crew from Bellingham. No one said anything at first, but most of the onlookers assumed it was the woman in the photocopied handbill that had been posted around the island and at the ferry landing. It had a picture of Calista, cropped from one in which she stood next to Marnie and another woman who'd long since left the island. The "missing" poster included the phone numbers of both the tribal police and the sheriff's department.

"I heard that the police questioned her husband," one bystander remarked.

"Wow. Didn't know she even had one."

"Yeah, like some of those others from off island, she came here to be with that Spellman nutjob."

"She's not a nutjob. She's onto something with her bees, pollen, and such. We're lucky that she's here. She's helping people."

"Didn't help this one, if you ask me."

"I didn't."

"Whatever. The husband's going to have some explaining to do."

"I hope he fries."

Chapter 72

There was only one first bite of an apple, poisonous or otherwise.

It felt out of the blue when Marnie Spellman finally returned Lindsay's messages and agreed to an interview. As the *Whatcom Chief* pushed through the choppy waters from the mainland to Lummi Island, the detective sat in her car and planned the interview she was about to conduct with Marnie Spellman.

It would be a tricky one.

While Marnie was surely no Miss Havisham or Norma Desmond, she had existed off the radar for a few years. As far as a quick search of the Internet could tell, the media had evinced no interest in her for going on a decade. Given Marnie's previous propensity for reaching out to reporters for a sympathetic ear, it seemed this disinterest was likely mutual. Islanders saw her, of course, and generally waved hello, though they kept a careful distance. She was a complicated figure on the island. It was indisputable that Marnie Spellman's enterprises had brought much-needed jobs, but with time, this was overshadowed in the minds of most residents by the unwanted attention that came with celebrity, then infamy.

Unsolved murders can do that sort of thing.

Lindsay decided to play to Marnie's vanity, seeing if she could put her at ease before digging into the real reason for her visit—the murders of Calista Sullivan and Sarah Baker. It was an Alan Sharpe approach. He'd always found a way to catch witnesses and perps off guard with a corny joke or a nonthreatening compliment.

"My mother had a necklace just like that. Takes me back."

It was late in the afternoon when Lindsay turned into the driveway, marked by a wagon wheel at its entrance, and pulled up to the big white house and the even more imposing white barn. Once she turned off her engine, there was nothing to hear, not a single farm sound. The weather had turned, and the breeze off the water moved the paper birch leaves of the trees next to the driveway like silvery fishing lures waiting to be cast.

There was Marnie Spellman, standing on the wraparound front porch. Even from a distance, her beauty was undeniable—as was her resemblance to Dina Marlow. Though smaller than Dina; a good deal smaller than Lindsay had imagined she'd be. She'd always seemed such a formidable force on YouTube and in print media. She was likely only about five two or three. Backlit by the sun, her hair was a golden halo held with a tortoiseshell clip on the back of her head. Her eyes, forget-me-not blue, were penetrating, but not uncomfortably so. Not probing, just more open to capture the sight before her.

Lindsay introduced herself, and Marnie invited her inside, leading her to the living room that was a third as large as Dina's great room. Everything was tasteful and expensive. If Marnie and Dina were in competition, it would be difficult to declare a winner—until Lindsay noticed the Warhol silkscreen above the fireplace.

Marnie was the winner.

Lindsay, however, couldn't tell if it was Dina or Marnie that Warhol had immortalized.

They looked so alike.

"That was one of the last things Andy did," Marnie said. "People say he was a genius. His assistant took the Polaroid and someone else screened it. I'd say he was a genius at selling himself. Not so much his art."

She motioned for Lindsay to sit in an oyster-gray suede slipper chair across from a cream-colored velvet sectional. She offered some lavender tea cakes, but Lindsay declined.

Alan would have taken them and then pronounced them the best he'd ever eaten.

"Sure? I made them this morning."

Lindsay gave in. "Okay. Just one."

Marnie smiled. "That's what you say now. You'll want another. Guaranteed."

"I found your book fascinating," Lindsay said, dropping crumbs onto her lap. "Couldn't put it down."

"That's nice," Marnie said. "People liked it. Should have been a *New York Times* bestseller. They didn't know where to put it—memoir or fiction. I've battled that kind of thing all my life."

"You were a trailblazer," Lindsay said.

"I *am* a trailblazer."

"Right. Of course." Lindsay ate the tea cake and brushed away the crumbs from her lap. "Delicious."

"I didn't steer you wrong, did I?"

Actually, Lindsay hated the tea cake. It was dry and tasted like her grandmother's lingerie drawer.

"Not so far," she said.

It was time to shift the conversation. Gently. Respectfully.

"Let's talk about Sarah Baker," she said.

"I'm heartsick over that, Detective. She worked here as an intern."

Lindsay said, "I'd heard that. Why didn't you call and let us know?"

"I didn't have anything to add."

"I see. Were you two close?"

"Not especially. If I remember correctly, she was a hard worker. Happy to be here. Wanting to learn how to become her greatest self through the love of nature."

"She was a student of your teachings?"

Marnie smiled as though the question had never been asked of her. "Most that come here are. They've listened to the old CDs and read my book. Those who come here to work are already more enlightened than their counterparts on the outside could ever be."

"That's quite an endorsement," Lindsay said. *And quite a load of horse manure.*

Marnie's expression hardened as though Lindsay had spoken that last thought aloud. "I don't mean to boast, Detective. I don't mean to overstate, either. I'm just wary of people like you coming with preconceived notions about me, my ideas, the people that I care about."

Lindsay was sure her face was carnation pink by then. "I'm sorry if I seemed flippant. I didn't mean it like that."

Marnie looked her over, reading her posture. Her face. Even how she held her hands. Evidently she passed muster.

"I feel you're sincere," she said. "So I accept your apology." Her blue eyes continued scanning Lindsay's face, her body. Even the air around her. It was like she was copying the image before her and measuring it against whatever she'd use to make a determination. "Truth and trust are everything to me."

"Me, too."

"Now back to Sarah," Marnie said in a way that suggested she blamed Lindsay for wasting her time and getting off track.

"Right," Lindsay said. "Her aunt Mary Jo told me that it was her impression that Sarah and you were quite close."

Marnie deflected the idea with a shrug. "People make assumptions. We weren't close in the least. Now tell me, what exactly are you looking for?"

"Answers . . . information . . . the truth."

"Fine. In case others have polluted your brain with a pack of lies, then I will be brutally blunt about Sarah and Calista."

"I never mentioned I was investigating Calista's murder."

"This is an island," Marnie said. "We're powered by gossip."

Lindsay gave her an uneasy smile. "There's a connection, isn't there?"

Marnie adjusted the tray of tea cakes. "How so? What connection, please?"

"Well, Spellman Farms, for one."

"As I said, I barely knew Sarah. She wasn't here that long. A summer intern."

"But you found out something about her, didn't you?"

Lindsay was using a technique favored by some investigators, including Alan Sharpe. She moved around the story in circles, not loose ones. More like a spiral that encircled the information, tighter and tighter.

Marnie looked surprised. "What? That she was writing an article? What did I care about that? She was just one of many who came here with ulterior motives. I'm used to that. Some people arrive with an open heart. Some come to take."

"Were you worried Sarah would write something negative about you? Your philosophy?"

"I was certain she wouldn't."

"You said you weren't close."

The already taut, smooth skin of Marnie's face had tightened even more. Her face was now a drum, hard and impenetrable. "You've obviously never run a company. Everyone there resents you and envies you at the same time. It's how most things in business work. People are cold. Detached. I knew she was getting something out of it. That's fine."

"Right. Ms. Spellman, what about the other members of the Hive?"

Marnie shook her head. "I never liked the term. Hated it. The girls came up with it one night with too many bottles of blackberry wine."

This aversion was odd, Lindsay thought, considering how often Marnie herself had employed the term in her writings and interviews. She decided to let it pass. "Tell me the names of the members of the Hive."

"They weren't 'members.' You make it sound like some group or a sorority with a secret handshake. It wasn't that at all. Just six women."

"That's right. Six of you. You at the center, surrounded by the other five: Calista, Dina, Heather, Greta . . . who was the fifth . . . Trish?"

Marnie looked upward, as though she had to retrieve the name from a dormant memory.

"She left early on," she said slowly, putting the fragmented thoughts together.

Or pretending to.

"Earlier than the others, I mean," she went on. "Trish Appleton left and married a local around the time Calista vanished. I never saw her again. I don't believe any of the girls did." She shrugged. "Any of the girls were free to go at any time. That was apparently Trish's time."

"Uh-huh." Lindsay checked her notes—or, not averse to a little theater herself, feigned doing so—then looked up at Marnie. "And where might I find Trish Appleton? You say she married a local?"

"A tribal cop, as I recall. I think they moved to Idaho or Iowa. One of those. Died in an accident I heard."

"Where?"

"I don't really know. Just something someone told me."

They talked for another half hour, Marnie saying she had a hard break on the hour.

"A call from Hong Kong. Very important. Life changing."

Marnie said she was on good terms with the Hive, though they'd all gone their separate ways. She saw Dina and Greta only very occasionally. She ran into Heather at a conference not long ago.

"People grow, change, then they move on. Our sisterhood was strong when it needed to be."

"What do you mean by that?" Lindsay asked.

"Not what you are probably thinking, Detective. I know you're a cop and that your personality is one to constantly look for something ugly no matter where you are. You can't help it. It's who you are. I'm sorry. I really need to take that call."

"Life changing?" Lindsay asked, stifling an inner eye roll.

"Not for me," Marnie said with unabashed conviction. "For the rest of the world."

CHAPTER 73

Thursday, September 26, 2019
Ferndale, Washington

What had she missed?

The office around her had emptied out, but Lindsay couldn't stop shuffling through her files. As she often did, she returned to the photo she'd borrowed from Sarah's aunt Mary Jo. She now recognized everyone pictured:

Dina Marlow.

Heather Jarred.

Greta Swensen.

Marnie Spellman.

Calista Sullivan.

Those were the five smiling at the photographer. Another woman appeared in the background, off to the far right. She was bent over some boxes, apparently affixing labels or addressing packages.

Trish Appleton?

She'd vanished. A phantom. No trace. No credit history. No social security. No records of any kind. To disappear like that would take connections and access to databases and documents. Even dead, as Marnie had suggested, a person would leave a trace.

Mary Jo answered on the first ring, said yes, sure, she'd look for an email from her. Lindsay scanned the photo, sent it her way, and redialed her number.

"That's that same photo you borrowed," Mary Jo said in lieu of hello.

"That's right." Lindsay directed her to the woman in the background. "Do you know who that is?"

A little gutshot sound came over the line.

"Mary Jo?"

She cleared her throat. "Yes. I know who that is. It's my sister Annette. The rest of them are those kooks that ruined her life with that crap Spellman was peddling. I blame her—I blame all of them—for Annette's death. They twisted her up and tied her into knots with their so-called manifested reality."

Lindsay let Mary Jo spit out all that she'd kept inside.

Finally, she asked, "I don't mean to pry, just how did your sister die?"

"Suicide, supposedly," Mary Jo said, letting out a soft sigh. "Almost twenty years ago. Ran a hose into the exhaust pipe on her VW and let the engine run in a closed garage."

Ran a hose into the exhaust pipe. Closed garage.

"Supposedly suicide?"

"My sister was a lot of things, but she wasn't depressed. Upset? Yes. Angry? Often, and often enough with plenty good reason. Not depressed. That just wasn't her. She was on edge a little the last time we talked. More resolved about something than depressed."

"Tell me about the last time you spoke. What did she tell you?"

Mary Jo was quiet a long moment. "She said that something happened at Spellman Farms. Real upset. She told me that she was going to do something about it. That she felt like she had to, since no one else was going to."

"No specifics?"

"Nope. I asked her, too, but she kept it to herself."

"What exactly did she do out at Spellman Farms?"

"They gave her all the shit jobs," she said. "All the female empowerment stuff was only for a select few, handpicked by Marnie. If you didn't have something that woman coveted or could exploit, you were stuck, she said. You know, just being on the edge, never in the center."

"I see."

Something happened at Spellman Farms.

What would Mary Jo's sister have been able to tell her? She'd never get the chance to ask her. But maybe she could double back to the Hive members and rattle their trees, see what fell free. "What was Annette's last name?"

"Ripken."

Lindsay wrote it down, then cocked her head. The name struck a chord, but she couldn't place it right away.

"You still there?"

Lindsay started. "Oh sorry, Mary Jo. Thinking." The name Annette Ripken didn't ring a clear bell, but the name Karen Ripken certainly did. It went off like an alarm clock at 4:00 a.m. That was the name of the woman Reed had befriended down in California when he joined her support group for those whose family members were being sucked into the Marnie vortex.

When Lindsay asked Mary Jo if she happened to know a Karen Ripken, she shot back with "I certainly do."

"Annette was Karen and Sarah's mother," Lindsay said.

Mary Jo took a deep breath. "Yeah. We went to court, and I adopted Sarah. Changed her last name to Baker."

Lindsay sat at her desk, processing what Mary Jo had said. The connection between Sarah Baker and the members of the Hive had never really been about some story she was writing; that was only her way in to finding out more about her mother, Annette Ripken. Sarah had been rattling the cages of every member of the Hive in the weeks before she was murdered.

Now that Annette had been identified, Lindsay returned her eyes to the photo.

A seventh person was in the room. Five members of the Hive, outsider/worker bee Annette Ripken.

And of course, the photographer.

Lindsay looked closer. Her heart rate quickened. *The photographer.* She ran her fingers over the photograph and looked past the obvious, past the intended image. Squinting her eyes, her face nearly pressed to the paper, she could just barely make out the image of a figure holding the camera reflected in the mirrored surface of one of Marnie's in-store wall displays.

Who is that?

That had to be Trish Appleton.

Lindsay punched in Tedd McGraw's number and told him she was heading his way.

"Sorry, Detective. I'm locking this place up in half an hour."

"Look, Tedd, I need your help. It's important."

"I have a cookout to go to."

"You're going to be late, Tedd."

CHAPTER 74

Thursday, September 26, 2019
Bellingham, Washington

Tedd McGraw was waiting in the museum lobby with his shirttail hanging out and a deeply irritated look on his face. He unlocked the door to let Lindsay inside.

"I'll be stuck with a garden burger at the cookout."

Thank you for your service, Tedd.

"I'm sorry about that" was what she said aloud. "I'm going to need to use your scanner and your printer."

He sighed. "Hold on." He appeared a moment later with his obligatory courtesy coffee.

"You're a good man."

"I'm a prince."

Lindsay gave him the black-and-white print.

"How big do you want to be able to print it?"

"As big as you can without losing too much of the resolution."

Five minutes later, he returned.

"Hope this helps."

She'd barely finished her coffee. Tedd had the four-by-six photograph, along with the probably eleven-by-seventeen reproduction he'd made from it. He slid both across the table.

"Holy crap, Tedd."

"Like I said," he replied. "A prince."

It was remarkable. It didn't pay to get too close to the enlargement—the pixels muddied things up—but held about a foot away, it snapped to incredibly detailed life.

Only five of the women were there—Marnie and four of her Hive: Dina, Heather, Greta, and Calista. Why only five? Why not six? Where was Trish Appleton?

Six was kind of a magical numeral, according to Marnie's book. The cells of a honeycomb were six sided. Six was the number Marnie used in her product line, too. Elixir Six was a top seller, as was Beautiful Six.

From her reading of *The Insatiable Heart*, Lindsay recalled Marnie's adoration of the number six and how it applied to her world. "A hive," she'd written, "is made up of thousands of hexagons, six sides representing the power and strength of nature."

She even aligned six categories for each side of the hexagon to amplify her message.

Mind, Body, Spirit, Earth, Water, Sky.

Six was the number of members in the Hive.

In a group photo, one person is almost always absent. Lindsay thought back to her own childhood. Her mother, the family photographer, was missing from most shots. She was there, of course, present to capture the moment.

Someone had to be.

Lindsay moved the photo closer to examine the image. The reflection of the woman on the plexiglass display by the women was unmistakable. So was the camera. A Hasselblad.

Here was the elusive Trish Appleton, the missing member of the Hive.

Lindsay's heart raced, and her eyes became wet with tears. Her body knew it before her mind caught up. It couldn't be. The woman in the reflection had been there all along.

Lindsay had found Trish Appleton . . . and she was Patty Sharpe.

CHAPTER 75

Sunday, April 3, 2000
Lummi Island, Washington

It wasn't long after Calista's death and the announcement of Reed Sullivan's pending trial that Trish stopped going to Lummi Island every weekend. She made up excuses that her job was taking more and more of her time and she just couldn't fit it all in. Marnie sensed she was slipping away, but she didn't fight to keep her as she had tried to hold on to others she'd felt were especially useful. On what would prove to be Trish's last visit there, Marnie found her in the lab, looking over the latest formulas.

Trish looked up at her and just came out with it, as though she were helpless to hold it in. "You still believe in this, Marnie?"

Marnie took a step closer. "I believe in being all that we can be, yes, if that's what you mean."

"I'm getting married," Trish said.

"I heard. When?"

"Oh," Trish said, "we haven't set a firm date. But it's not going to be anything fancy. Just the justice of the peace. My parents and his."

"I see."

Marnie stared at her friend. "I'll never have to worry about you, Trish."

"No. Never."

"Good. That's what I need to know."

Trish watched Marnie as her eyes swept the length of the barn.

"Sometimes the hardest thing you ever did wasn't all that hard after all," Marnie said. "Not when there was so much at stake, right?"

Marnie had a way of making a threat seem oblique, but not this time. Trish knew exactly what she meant.

Then she hugged Marnie. In fact, she hugged her almost a little too tightly; a little tighter and she would have cut off her air supply. That, Trish thought at the time, would have been fine with her.

CHAPTER 76

Friday, September 20, 2019
Ferndale, Washington

Patty forced herself to finish the sad task of organizing Alan's things. She carried the boxes of her husband's old clothes that she'd already sorted to the garage and placed each atop the stack of things to be donated.

His car was where he'd left it. She found herself behind the wheel, wondering, as she often did, what Alan's last thoughts had been as the exhaust filled the space around him. She'd loved him more than anything, and yet at the same time, she now often found herself angry at him. His weakness. He'd acted strong at work, but inside and in their private times, Alan had been a very weak man.

The steering wheel felt cool to the touch.

Had it felt like that for him, too?

Had he looked around the garage and, surveying the things stored there, considered how each item told a story? The cooler from the beach. The dirt bike they bought for Paul when he was twelve. The barbecue supplies and croquet set that heralded the return of summer. Her craft supplies that nested in four boxes above the freezer.

A garage is not always a way station for things destined for the dump, but a living and breathing memory album of moments shared. And promises of more moments to come.

Though not this garage. Here, there were no more promises. It was all over.

She got out of the car and stared for some time at Alan's workbench, sprinkled with cedar shavings from a project he'd never completed.

Then, peeking out from beneath the far end of the workbench, there was *that* box. The box that held the clothes Sarah Baker had been wearing the night she was murdered, along with her laptop and phone.

It had been there quietly waiting for her to do what needed to be done during the days after Alan's suicide and the memorial service. She pulled it out, set it on the bench, lifted the lid, and peered inside at the cache of women's clothes—blue jeans, an Old Navy top, a bra, panties, socks, and shoes—and electronics. After stepping into the kitchen for a box of matches, she carried everything out to the burn barrel behind the house.

She tossed the clothing and electronics inside the open mouth of the barrel. She doused it all with briquette starter liquid, struck a match, and sent it into the barrel after the clothes.

Whoosh!

Patty stood back and watched, her eyes reflecting the flames as they began to lick the rim of the barrel, the bra, with its elastic construction, sending up a thin black column before quickly flaming out. The laptop and phone melted like a Dalí. She wedged in some brittle deadfall from a fir tree, and the smoke resumed, this time the color of yard waste, white and yellow.

Only yard waste was permitted by the county.

The shoes were another matter. Rubber sends up a black plume. She considered burying them in the yard but thought about the dog next door and his propensity for coming over and digging in the garden. That wouldn't do at all.

Patty decided to go to the store but took a circuitous route. Traffic was light to nonexistent. She hurled one shoe into a ditch, the other a mile later into the forest that met the roadway. She took a deep breath and hoped that she'd learned a thing or two from her husband's years of being a homicide investigator.

"The ones that get caught are the ones that talk about it," he'd told her at the dinner table on more than one occasion.

Holding her tongue was no problem for her, especially when the stakes were high. This wouldn't test her resolve in the least. Keeping quiet was something Patty Sharpe excelled at.

In fact, she had a positive genius for it.

CHAPTER 77

Thursday, September 26, 2019
Ferndale, Washington

Lindsay's eyes dripped tears as she drove home from the Whatcom Museum with Tedd's amazing, horrible enlargement. She'd started the investigation after her partner's suicide, bereft and lonely. She'd been a shoulder of comfort for Patty. She'd texted her. Checked on her and Paul. She'd sat next to Alan for years, never having any inkling that his wife had been part of something so bizarre as Marnie Spellman's world of bees and promises.

When she turned on her street, she saw a familiar Minnie Winnie parked in front of her house.

Kate Spellman was sitting on the front steps.

"Found your hide-a-key," Marnie's mother said as Lindsay approached, "but I resisted. Those fake rocks look, well, fake."

"How did you know I live here, Kate?"

"I might be old, but I know my way around the Internet. Probably surprises you that I was the one that helped set up Marnie's first website."

It did, but Lindsay didn't remark on it.

"What are you doing here?"

"You seem agitated, Detective."

"I am. But that doesn't answer my question."

Kate held an envelope in her hand, and she studied it now as if it had just appeared there. Then she lifted her eyes to Lindsay's. "I have something to show you."

Lindsay asked her inside. She'd never let anyone from a case come into her home, but it was late and the woman was elderly. One shove and her bones might splinter.

Once they were situated at Lindsay's kitchen table, Kate said, "I came back to Lummi from visiting my sister in Poulsbo a couple of days after Calista died."

"You mean after she was murdered."

"Call it what you like."

Kate sat still. Fixing her eyes on Lindsay in the way people do when they are about to drop a bomb.

"And Calista's baby," she said. "Her baby, too."

Lindsay didn't say anything. But inside, she was screaming at the top of her lungs.

What baby?

Annette Ripken had been out in the honey orchard for most of the day. She was hunched over a new hive that was being readied for a swarm that had been collected by amateur beekeepers on the mainland. Bringing swarms to Spellman Farms was considered a high honor among those circles.

Annette was crying.

At first, Kate didn't think much of the emotional display. Over time, she'd seen several women break down over some kind of revelation they'd had about their lives before coming to Lummi to be with Marnie.

Marnie encouraged women to dig deep into their pasts to determine why it was that they'd faltered in their careers, as moms, in relationships. As human beings.

"If you don't believe in you," Marnie said repeatedly, "I can't believe in you."

After this woman's tears didn't subside, Kate went to her.

"Are you all right?" she asked.

Annette looked up and shook her head. Her eyes were red, and the breeze coming up from the water dried some of her tears; pale streaks overlaid her tanned skin.

"I'm fine," she said.

"I know you're not, Annette."

"Right. I'm not. It's just that I don't understand things around here."

Kate took that as a reference to Marnie's obvious favoritism. Kate had seen plentiful evidence of that and the emotional toll it took on some of the women who were excluded. She was no stranger to this herself, but she'd learned long ago not to dwell on it.

This woman hadn't learned that yet. Maybe Kate could help her along that road.

"I've seen how the others treat you," she said.

"It isn't just that, Kate. I don't think I can be here any longer. Too much going on. Too much hurt, you know?"

"You're worried about Calista."

"Uh-huh."

"We all are. She'll be found. She's probably having her baby right now."

Annette didn't say anything for the longest time. Kate put her arms around her, and they watched the swallows dive-bomb the gnats that formed a wispy patch of air above them.

"You don't know what's going on here, do you?" Annette finally asked.

"I'm not a member of my daughter's inner circle. That's pretty obvious, isn't it?"

Annette looked up and stayed very still. When Kate turned to see what she was seeing, she found Dina coming toward them.

"You two mind if I join you?" she asked, her big Hollywood smile out in force. "Beautiful afternoon, girls."

"Just finishing up," Annette said. "Is the new queen here?"

Dina shook her head. "Next boat. Are we ready?"

"I think so," Annette said, giving Kate's hand a quick squeeze before starting back toward the barn.

"What was that all about?" Dina asked Kate. "She okay?"

"Emotional. Same as always. I'm heading back inside. Coming?"

"I'm going to enjoy the air for a while. We can talk later."

Lindsay offered Kate something to drink, and Kate surprised her with a request for a whiskey.

"No ice. No water."

Lindsay poured her a glass and one for herself.

"I never liked Dina," Kate went on. "My daughter was enamored with her. Thought that she was going to transform her business. She wanted to *be* Dina, if you ask me. Cut her hair the same way. Started buying clothes in Dina's signature color. Honestly, I thought it was embarrassing. I think Marnie had something special, a gift. Really, I do. Especially in the beginning. She was also a narcissistic attention seeker. Frankly, probably a sociopath, like Dina. That's just what I think."

Tell me how you really feel about your daughter, Lindsay thought.

Kate used the envelope she brought as a coaster on the kitchen table. Each time she sipped her whiskey, she darted her eyes to the envelope then back to Lindsay.

"What's in the envelope?" Lindsay asked.

"I'm getting to it, Detective."

Lindsay noticed Kate's nearly empty glass. "Another drink?"

"Maybe one more," Kate said. "Can't fly on one wing. Maybe a little water this time, though. Hard enough to drive that damned motor home as it is."

The next morning, Kate sought out Annette, who was on the front porch, drinking coffee alone. Marnie and Dina had taken the ferry to the mainland to do some shopping. Heather and Greta were at their jobs at the hospital. Trish was cleaning the floors of the barn with bleach diluted in a Home Depot bucket.

Kate asked Annette if she wanted to walk on the beach.

"Yes. I want to talk. You are the only one who's been really nice to me, Kate."

They made their way to the trail entrance marked by twin cedars and walked down to the pebble beach toward an enormous driftwood log, etched with initials and promises of undying love. They sat on the far end, where the log's roots fanned out like a sea anemone.

"They killed Calista and her baby," Annette said.

"That's not possible."

"I saw them. I know they did it. They don't know I saw."

Kate pushed back. "Calista's not dead. She's off having her baby. I think the girls are going to see her today."

"They wrapped up her body and took it somewhere. Baby, too."

"Are you sure, Annette?"

"I am. I know what I saw."

"What are you going to do?"

"I'm going to tell. I'm scared, though. I don't know if I can."

"Maybe you should just take a deep breath. We can figure this out."

They sat there for about an hour, long enough to feel the incoming tide lap at their feet.

"Don't do anything," Kate said.

"What did you do with this information, Kate? What were you thinking?" Lindsay asked.

"Honestly?"

"I hope that's why you're here."

"I am. And yes . . . what did I think? I thought that it was possible. I wasn't sure. When we got back, I asked Trish about it. She said Calista didn't have her baby there. That they wanted her to, of course. It just didn't work out. She thought that she might have gone back to her husband, who'd been around the island the previous week or so."

"What happened with Annette?"

"She was scared. The last time I saw her, a few days later, she told me she was leaving Lummi. And, Detective, she seemed scared. I told her that I was sure that Calista would turn up."

"And she did," Lindsay said.

"Right. After they found her body and Reed Sullivan was arrested, Annette called me. She asked for an alternate mailing address. I gave her my sister's."

"What did she want that for?"

"She told me she had something to give me but couldn't send it to a place where any members of the Hive could get to it."

"Why was that? What did she say?"

"She said they were watching her and she was scared that they'd kill her. Honestly, I didn't take this seriously; I just couldn't. When she committed suicide . . . I just let myself off the hook. Told myself that my narcissistic, megalomaniac daughter wasn't any of the things I knew her to be. When she fired me from that shop in Blaine, I was relieved. Really, I was."

Kate reached for the letter.

"Read it," she said, handing it to Lindsay. "It's all here."

Lindsay's adrenaline pumped with each word.

> *To whom it may concern:*
>
> *My name is Annette Ripken. I have information about the Reed Sullivan case. I know for an absolute fact he is innocent of killing his wife. I'm too afraid to come forward in person, but it is my duty to tell the truth when a man's future is at stake.*
>
> *I was working at Spellman Farms on Lummi Island the night Calista Sullivan was murdered. Yes, she was murdered. I wasn't in the inner circle, and I can't say that I know everything that happened in the so-called Hive, but I also have no reason to lie.*
>
> *Calista was nine months pregnant and went into labor early in the day. She was keeping track of the timing between contractions and indicated that she'd be able to stay until midday and then head over to the mainland with one of the Hive. (Those were the women—five of them—who were closest to our queen bee, Marnie. I was excluded from the circle. I wasn't much more than a drone. They treated me like a servant.)*
>
> *Later, I heard Marnie tell one of the girls that the ferry from the island to the mainland had some kind of mechanical failure and was out of service. I worried about Calista and her baby, but none of the Hive was concerned. I mean, all of them but Dina Marlow, the actress, were nurses—all of them, including Marnie. So*

I didn't think anything more about it, figuring they knew what they were doing.

That's what I figured, anyway, until I saw the neighbor next door come home to the farm that evening. I knew he worked in Ferndale and that he couldn't have arrived any other way but by ferry. I called the ferry office, and they told me that Marnie had been mistaken.

I went to her and told her what I'd learned. I thought she would be glad to know. The contractions were closer together now, and I offered to take Calista to the hospital. She told me to mind my own business. She said that Calista preferred to have her baby there on the farm.

I felt that I'd overstepped already, so I backed off. Marnie was like some kind of supreme authority to me and all the girls. She had great dreams for how she was going to bring out the inner light of all women in the world by her teachings and her creams and potions. Now it all seems so silly. At the time, it wasn't.

I went about the rest of my evening, processing honey for Beautiful Six and cleaning the beekeeper suits. Around ten, one of the girls told me that Calista had her baby and all was well. It was such a relief.

I had to finish what I was doing before I had any free time to go see her. It was around half past eleven, I think. It could have been later.

I went into the barn—and when I say it was a barn, that's really understating what the building was like. It really was part research facility, part recording studio, and part graphic arts studio where Marnie designed her own packaging. And now there was this birthing suite that Marnie had installed during Calista's pregnancy, even though Calista was pretty clear, I thought, that she intended to have the baby at the hospital in Bellingham. I heard some muffled cries in there, and God forgive me, but all of a sudden, I was frozen by fear. Calista was crying. She was asking about her baby. She said that what Marnie was doing was wrong and that she wanted to leave. Right then! Marnie was angry. Saying it over and over that it was supposed to be a girl, that Calista was a faithless liar.

Calista called Marnie a fraud and said she was going to tell everyone what had been going on.

I inched my way a little closer, and I saw Marnie tell her to shut up and then—this is the part that makes me so incredibly ashamed—Dina took a pillow and pushed it against Calista's face. I took a step, my feet were just going to take me in there so I could stop her—but then Marnie jumped on top of her to help, and I . . . I stopped where I was. I swear to God that I just couldn't believe my eyes. The baby was crying, and the whole barn was spinning.

The next day, Marnie came to me in my room in the big house. She asked me how I was doing and said she was sorry about the mix-up about the ferry. She said mother and baby were fine, and in fact, she insisted that Calista had gone home to Bellingham to be with her husband. I pretended to accept that as a good thing—when I knew I was being fed lies.

For the next few days, I acted as if nothing were wrong, all while the other members of the in crowd looked at me suspiciously: Dina, Heather, Trish, Greta, and Marnie.

I told them my youngest daughter was being abused by her father and I needed to go back to California and put a stop to it. I doubt they believed me. I didn't care.

I left the following week and never went back. Calista was a good person. In fact, we shared a bond. We'd both forsaken our previous lives, families, friends, to follow someone that I now think is the opposite of enlightenment and hope. Marnie Spellman is the devil.

All of this is true.

Sincerely,

Annette Ripken

Calista had been murdered by members of the Hive. They'd all played a part in covering up a terrible crime. They'd gone so far as to try to frame an innocent man to take the attention away from Marnie Spellman. They were a group of women bound together in silence.

Lindsay thought back to the report on Annette's suicide.

It was exactly the same as Alan's suicide: carbon monoxide in a car parked in a closed garage.

CHAPTER 78

Sunday, September 8, 2019
Whatcom County, Washington

Sarah Baker drove Paul Sharpe out to Maple Falls, a place they'd hiked for their first date. It would be quiet there, and Sarah wanted to explain everything without anyone hearing. The trailhead had been closed since Labor Day since a hiker had been mauled by a cougar.

Paul was fine with the silence between them on the ride. Just so long as he was with her, heading out into the dark. It hadn't occurred to him that he had anything to look forward to beyond time alone with her in her car, doing what they were accustomed to doing.

She didn't stay in the car, though, when she parked in the otherwise empty lot. She got out, and so he did, too.

Right away, over the roof of the old Ford Fiesta, Sarah dropped the bomb she'd been carrying for weeks. And after she did, she no longer looked beautiful to him.

She looked like a hateful monster. A messenger of a big, cruel lie.

"Your mom and dad aren't your mom and dad," she said.

Although she spoke with utter conviction, Paul questioned her as though he hadn't heard a single word she said.

"What are you talking about?"

His mind was a whirl of confusion. Sarah could see that. Paul was thoughtful. He was kind. The look on his face now was neither. It was angry. Bordering on unhinged. Frightening.

She took a step back, glad to have the car between them. He'd need some help taking this in, obviously. "I'm not saying they don't love you. I talked to your father, and I know for a fact they do. Very much. Even so, you aren't theirs, and you deserve to know it. We all need to know the truth."

"That's bullshit, Sarah. They would have told me if I was adopted."

"That's right. They would have. If you had been adopted." He already seemed a little less disturbed, she thought. She'd push on, get him clear on it all so he could absorb it, get past it. "But you weren't adopted."

"What are you talking about?"

"Look," she said, "I'm sorry. I've really gotten to like you. I hate being the one to tell you."

"Gotten to like me? What is that supposed to mean? I thought you were into me."

Sarah gave a little shrug and looked downward. It was easier to talk not making eye contact.

"Maybe I was, maybe I am. And the fact of the matter is, boys come and go—but the story of a lifetime, and that's what this is . . . well, it happens only once in a lifetime. I'd like to say I'm sorry, but you know what? I'm not. What happened is what happened—it's all on Marnie Spellman, that crazy bee lady on Lummi Island. You've heard of her? I've been working out there, working for her, but really for myself, undercover. It's all on her, and you're not the only one affected by her and everything she's made happen. Not by a long shot. She ruined my life. She ruined yours. I intend to fix things. To fix *her*. The truth will do that."

"You're lying about my parents. I don't give a fuck what you think you know."

"I saw the emails with my own eyes. Her and that actress Dina Marlow. They know what happened to your real mother."

She looked up at him again then and felt a jolt of disorientation, even alarm, when she couldn't find him right away. Then she did: he was at the back of the car. He'd begun pacing, apparently, because now he spun around and began retracing his steps. She could see how that might help, pacing. It was a thing people did. But then, seeing her watching him, he froze at the back corner of the car. There was something wrong with his face. It was his eyes—they were wide, and blank. And his mouth—it was opening and closing a little bit, on its own, like the mouth of a fish in a fishbowl. But then he was talking.

"Real mother? Is this some kind of a game?" he asked. "If it is, if you're lying, you are a fucking piece of trash, Sarah."

It was like he'd slapped her. He'd not only never raised his voice at her, she'd never even heard him curse, period.

"Hey," she said. "I'm just doing my job."

Paul's face was puffed up and red, even in the dark. *"Job?"* he repeated, the word dripping with sarcasm. "It's a tiny campus newspaper we're talking about, not the fucking *New York Times!*"

Now he was pissing her off. Royally.

"That's how people start out, Paul. One step at a time," she said. "One more. Then another. Then you're there." He was grinning at her, a really ugly, hateful grin. He looked like he was going to laugh at her, and she did not want to hear that. She'd spin them back on track. "Your parents probably knew that they'd eventually be found out."

The grin was gone. Paul stood mute, trying to process what Sarah was saying. "What? You make it sound like they, what, *stole* me? Like gypsies or something? Are you insane, or just stupid?"

"Neither," she said. "Just a reporter at a campus newspaper, who went around and asked questions to people like your dad the cop—by the way, he was very helpful—and dug into things until she got to the truth. And the truth is yes, your parents aren't your parents. Your real mom *died*, Paul."

This was so horrible to say that it stopped her. But it was true, it was part of the truth he needed to hear, and frankly, she was still really angry at him, so she went on.

"Your real mom died. She was killed, Paul. I'm sorry, but she was. By Marnie freaking Spellman and this other woman. And your parents, your . . . parents who aren't your parents, they didn't steal you, but they did *take* you. Your mom did; she was there, just like my mom. But again, neither of them killed your real mom—"

"You're crazy," he said. "Listen to yourself." He'd said it quietly, as if more to himself than to her. She could tell he was believing her, even though it did, undeniably, sound crazy. The truth was working on him, she was sure. He could hear it, feel it.

"You need to listen to me, Paul. This is the truth. Your mom didn't kill your real mom, and neither did my mom. But both of them knew about it. My mom *saw* it. It was this other woman, and Marnie Spellman. The two of them. And your mom took you away. She might even have saved you! And your dad knew about it, too. The two of them took you and passed you off as their own. Maybe partially to help cover up your real mom's murder, but also because they really wanted you. Obviously. You know how much they love—"

"You keep talking about the truth, Sarah." He was talking so quietly she could barely hear him. So it was okay that he'd come around to her side of the car. They were going to talk about this in regular tones. Reasonably. Kindly. Maybe they didn't really love each other, but they did care about each other. They were *something* to each other, whatever that was. "You keep talking about the truth as if it's a religion or something. Like you're born again."

"Well, no," she said. "But it's the truth."

"Okay. And to get it, you had to talk to my dad about it."

"I did. Yeah."

"And so to get to him, to get your once-in-a-lifetime story that's going to get you out of your little paper, you had to use me."

"No," she said, stepping back a little. He'd come up close to her, was almost whispering now. "It wasn't that. I like you, Paul. I do. I like you beyond this story and whatever it might do for me."

"Well, I'll tell you what it'll do for me. For my family, real or not. It will *ruin* us. You used me to get to my dad. You fucking set me up so that you could do whatever it was you wanted to do."

"That's not true."

"You are such a deluded liar."

Anger shot up in her. There was nowhere else for it to go but into his face. "Yeah, well you are not even Paul. You don't even *have* a name."

That's when he grabbed her by the neck. Tightly. Way, way too tightly. Then he released her. He must've realized what he'd been doing. He was going to plead with her to forgive him.

But no, he pushed her away toward the car, spun her around, and seized her neck again, even more tightly than before. He pressed her facedown onto the hood, still warm from their drive. Both of them were aware of that, surprised by it in some dim, dumbly recording part of their brains—how little time had passed since Sarah had turned off the ignition.

Then Paul's brain turned to more practical matters. He released his hold on her throat again—but only long enough to clamp his forearms on the front and back of her neck and pin her down again on the hood with all his weight.

He didn't want to leave any marks on his body.

He was the son of a detective.

He'd leave nothing to chance.

Tears came to his eyes. He wondered how many more seconds he'd have to endure while he waited for her to go limp. To die. To be murdered. It took too long, but she finally went still.

Paul needed to get her out from under the open sky over the parking lot. She was small enough to be carried slung over his shoulder. The trail was dark—so dark that the dim light of his cell phone would do very little to help him avoid the occasional tangle of roots and blackberry vines that crept into his way. He kept walking. His heartbeat was so loud that he was sure it could be heard by the nocturnal animals whose yellow eyes had observed what he'd done.

Maybe the cougar.

Paul knew it could be explained away to manslaughter, yet what about her? Sarah would get to be a murdered journalist, possibly a martyr. She'd be a media star. He would serve eight years, minimum. Maybe more if the judge wanted to make an example out of a cop's son.

It was, he was certain, a very real possibility.

Ten years. Maybe fifteen.

He knew he could manage doing the time, but his parents? What about them? Despite what they'd done, they didn't deserve this. His mom would wither away waiting for him. His dad would start drinking again, letting himself fall deeper into the abyss.

The right thing according to the law was to stop, turn around, and tell the police what had happened.

Instead, as he reached the Maple Falls overlook, he peered down into the blackness below, then gingerly set Sarah's body on a bed of ferns and peeled off his sweaty shirt. He spread his shirt on the ground beside the ferns and set about removing every article of clothing from her body and placing each carefully on his opened shirt. He found her cell phone and quickly turned it off. Cell tower ping. Shit! He was crying by the time he finished and lifted Sarah's still-warm, naked body from the ferns and held it before him. He couldn't, and probably shouldn't, hold her to him. He was grateful in a way for the tears, as they had formed a veil that kept him from clearly making out her features before he turned her around and held her over the edge.

"I'm sorry," he said.

Then he launched her into the dark with all of his strength, and her shining, pale form plummeted out of sight. After a terrible blank moment, he could hear the awful, dull sounds of body striking rock and then, finally, a splash.

There was no point in trying to see how she landed. Below him was a huge, dark hole with a silver strand of rushing water coming from above and showering the exposed rocks.

And Sarah Baker.

He gathered up her clothes and phone and went back to the car. It had been much easier to kill than he'd imagined when his father talked shop and police procedures. He also knew how hard it was not to get caught. He'd been careful to ensure that she didn't scratch him and collect DNA under her nails. But even if she had done so, he'd be able to explain that they'd had sex that morning.

He stood still, catching his breath. Thinking of a way out of what he'd done.

What he'd never meant to do.

"Things just got out of hand," he'd say later, if he had to. "At least, for my tastes. Sarah was more adventurous that way."

No. Keep himself out of it entirely. He'd say she was a party girl. He'd say that she got high a lot. That she'd been with several of the guys in the journalism program. That she probably went off with a Tinder pickup.

"She was up for anything. Anyone," he'd say.

CHAPTER 79

Monday, September 9, 2019
1:30 a.m.
Ferndale, Washington

Alan Sharpe was a big man, but just then, he managed to make himself look very small as he and Paul stood in the garage by the workbench. He had been working on a cedar carving of a sculpin, a hobby that occupied his "thinking" time when on a case, but now he had his arms around his son, who was crying as he told him about what he'd done to Sarah.

"Finish up, Son. I need to know everything."

Paul gulped some air.

"I drove back to Sarah's place, wiped the steering wheel, the door handles—anything I touched that night. Then I realized I didn't need to worry about my prints all that much, because I had been in that car a lot. I'd driven it before. I was her boyfriend, and she generally did the driving. Her car was more dependable—you know my damn fuel pump. And hers got better mileage. And she just . . . she liked to drive."

"Okay," Alan said. Though he seemed calm, his brow glistened. "Then what? Did you walk home?"

"Yes. She had picked me up, so I went inside her apartment, grabbed her laptop, and then I came home."

"Had you and Sarah been intimate that night?"

"No . . . I mean yes, earlier that day. But we both showered."

"Where are her clothes? You said you took all of her clothes."

"Yes. I did. I didn't want to leave anything behind, hair or fibers. Plus, I was thinking that it would look more like a sex crime if she were to be found naked. The clothes are in a box in my trunk."

"Her phone?"

"Turned it off. It's in the trunk, too, with her laptop."

"All right, Paul. All right. You know what's next, right?"

"I guess so."

"You cannot guess anymore. You have to own what I'm about to tell you, Son."

Paul stood motionless and let his eyes and ears consume everything his father said.

"Never, never talk to anyone about this. Not a single word. Not to your mother or another friend or girlfriend you might have later in life. Not five years from now. Not thirty years from now. Do you understand? Never. Can you promise me that?"

"I can. I promise."

"I'll need one more promise."

"Anything."

"No matter what happens, no matter what you see around you, close to you, you just need to know that you are loved. You have always been our son from the moment we both laid eyes on you."

Alan gave his son another hug, this time locking his arms as though he couldn't let go.

"It's my fault," he finally said. "She came to me, Paul. She told me that she was working on something that would expose things that I . . . that I couldn't let the world know."

Paul was a mess, beside himself. "Dad, she said . . . she said some crazy things. Is it all true?"

"I won't talk about it now," Alan said. "I couldn't talk to her about it, and now I see that I'm unable to tell you what I know. I figured the day would come. And now, all of this. Now the world has opened up to swallow all of us. Me. Your mom. You."

Paul pulled back and looked at his father. His eyes were red. "What are you talking about?"

"I won't let any more of this craziness happen, Paul."

"You need to tell me."

"You're in shock, Paul."

It was an understatement, and both father and son knew it.

"I killed my girlfriend, Dad. I killed her to make her shut the fuck up about whatever she was doing. Don't you think that I deserve to know all of the truth?"

"You do," Alan said, "but sometimes not knowing is a gift, Paul. Not knowing doesn't cause you to wake up in the middle of the night, wishing you had done things differently. Not knowing would have kept me off the meds."

"Dad, talk to me."

Awkward silence floated between them for what seemed like a very long time.

"Please."

"I need to fix things," Alan said. "We both do. You're going back to your place, and you're going to get some sleep. I'll fill you in on everything tomorrow. Just go about your day, Son. Be yourself."

Paul stayed silent.

"Remember, never, ever speak of what happened with the girl."

The line was familiar, though never before a command.

"Right," Paul said. "It's what trips up a killer every time."

It was one of Alan's dinnertime talking points.

Now his son was going to put it to good use.

Patty was already in bed, and the house was so quiet Alan could hear the hum of the mini refrigerator in his office from the hallway. He'd never heard it before. He entered the office and looked around the room, at the photos of his life in law enforcement. Awards. A plaster of paris hand-print made by Paul when he was five hung on the wall by a jute cord.

Sweat streaked his forehead, and he took a Pabst Blue Ribbon from the fridge and rubbed the cold can against his face. He slowly popped the top and drank.

A handwritten note was always best, he knew. There would be less quibbling over who had written it. He once had a case, a presumed suicide, that was upended by the fact that the laser-printed confession was indistinguishable from seven other printers associated with the case.

Always write a note by hand.

And always be somewhat vague in your missive to the world after death. Specifics invited more questions. Details were scrutinized and questioned.

He used the silver pen that had belonged to his grandfather to write on the sheet of Ferndale Police Department letterhead.

Brevity was important, too.

I'm very sorry for what I did. Please forgive me.
Alan

He wrote out a second note.

Your biological parents are Reed and Calista Sullivan.
Calista died in childbirth at Spellman Farms, and your
mom and I brought you home. We thought it was the
best thing for you. Mom and I love you like our own,

and now that we're gone, we hope you will forgive us.
Mr. Sullivan still lives in town. He did not know his
wife was pregnant.
    Dad

There was more to say, of course, but none of it would change Sarah's fate or undo what he'd done to Reed. He thought about the night it all happened and how none of it was planned. He could still feel Patty's anguish when she told him that Calista had died and that her baby needed a home.

A home with them as parents.

"This was meant to be, Alan," she'd said.

"This is wrong," he'd protested. "The boy should be with his father."

"He doesn't know. There isn't any wrong here."

Those words reverberated in his head just as he finished the second note. She might have been right in that moment. There was no wrong. Only need and desire. The wrong came over him like a thundering avalanche in the days that followed. Lies. A cover-up. Tampering with evidence.

Though none of it was his idea, he knew it was all on him.

He folded both letters, slid them into envelopes, and sealed them. He wrote Patty's name on the first one, Paul's on the second. He looked around his office one more time before dimming the light.

His son's note was delivered first. He put it in the bottom of the tackle box that Paul kept at the ready for when he came by for a visit from college. It would likely sit there until springtime, but that was fine. A little distance from Sarah's murder and Alan's own death would likely serve him better.

Next, he made his way into the bedroom, setting Patty's letter on his nightstand, where she'd be sure to see it. It would not surprise her. She'd often maintained that he was the weaker of the two of them and that his resolve could be penetrated with the right question.

Alan had lied, but he was not a liar.

"What happened?" she asked, her face turned to the wall. "I thought I heard Paul."

Alan told her what happened at Maple Falls. She took in everything, crying softly as she flashed back to scenes from Spellman Farms, moments in time she'd built a high wall around.

It was tumbling down now.

Alan tried to soothe her. "It's all right, Patty. It will be all right."

"I don't know that anymore, Alan. Really, I don't."

She remained facing the wall. She didn't want to look at him right then.

"It's all unraveling," she said.

Alan let out a soft breath. "Yeah, I think so. This girl was going to ruin us. If her story got out about what we did."

"We didn't do anything wrong," she said.

"*You* didn't," he said, "not morally, anyway."

"How could Paul have killed her, Alan?"

"He snapped. It happens."

"It will all lead back to Calista, won't it?"

"No," he said. "There is no reason any of Marnie's so-called Hive would talk. They are up to their necks in the cover-up, Patty. Though God knows why. Calista's death was an accident."

Patty thought carefully before speaking. "It wasn't, Alan. She was murdered."

"You never said that before."

"Because I didn't want to imagine that I had a role in it, but I did. I could have stopped her. Marnie gave Calista a drink that morning, a concoction of herbs and honey that she said would settle her stomach and ease the contractions she'd been feeling over the past few days. It was black cohosh. I remember her telling me about it. Native women used it for all kinds of medical reasons, including the inducement of labor. She'd dug up a plant from the garden by the back door to the kitchen and pulverized its roots in a blender with some other things. Pollen. Honey, I know for sure."

Alan stayed still while he processed what Patty had said. She'd lied to him for twenty years. Calista had been doomed from the start. Marnie, the Hive, all of them knew it. Somewhere in their twisted beliefs about empowerment, they'd played God.

His life was falling apart.

His future, gone.

He needed to be gone, too.

He could visualize the house now, empty. A **FOR SALE** sign stuck in the lawn he'd so methodically, so lovingly maintained. Neighbors would gossip and rewrite every encounter into some kind of referendum on his character.

Lindsay would be questioned about what she knew and, in time, possibly even in short order, would grow to resent his mentorship. She'd become embarrassed by their association.

And Marnie would be unscathed.

The queen of the hive.

Untouched.

"I love you, Patty," he told his wife.

"I love you, too."

He leaned closer and kissed her on the back of her neck.

"I don't regret our life together."

It was a goodbye, she knew, but she didn't say so.

"Everything will be better in the morning," he said.

Chapter 80

Patty Sharpe was alone in the part of the house that lived and breathed her husband. She paused and read the citations and certificates he'd hung on his office walls, a room that had been the nursery when Paul was little. When he moved his things in there one rainy Saturday afternoon, Patty told Alan that they should paint it first.

"Baby blue suits me," he'd said. "Matches my eyes. Also, makes me think of happier times."

She regarded him with skepticism. "Happier?"

It was exaggerated and playful, and yet there was an undercurrent of truth working its way through his words.

He shook it off and pulled her close.

"It has all been happy."

Patty's eyes landed on his police academy photograph. She could scarcely keep her fingers from taking down that picture. Alan's eyes followed her, and it unnerved her. She'd fully expected that they'd be together until the end of time, and through an afterlife that was far greater than what the minister said at the stone chapel. But now she wondered. She wondered if the man she had loved more than any other would want to have anything to do with her in the afterlife.

He knew everything. He knew what she'd done to him the day he took his life. How she'd made a choice to save herself from the disaster she was sure would come.

Patty left the office, went to the medicine cabinet, and examined the array of pills she'd collected over the years, bottles from her patients, some stolen from the hospital in the days when no one seemed to account for what was held in the storeroom. Samples from sales reps who insisted that what they had to offer was the latest and greatest.

He'd told her he would take them. He'd told her that he would do what he needed to do.

She knew, looking at the cache of pills, why he hadn't done it that way.

He'd saved the pills for *her*.

It was a love that could not be explained, an adoration that truly forgave. It was a love that allowed him to die on the battlefield for her.

When her phone buzzed, Patty reached down to answer, closing the medicine cabinet. It was Lindsay.

"Patty, I thought I'd stop by. Just feeling a little out of sorts. I'm thinking you are, too, and with far more reason."

"We're all broken over Alan's death," Patty said. "All in shock. Still. If you want to stop by, I'm home."

"I'm in your driveway now."

"On my way to open the door."

After hanging up with Patty, Lindsay had called for backup but told the responding officers to come quietly and park on the side road.

"I'll alert you if I need assistance," she said.

She sat in the car and took deep breaths, checking her face in the rearview mirror. Did she look calm? *Was* she calm? The entire way from her house to the Sharpe residence had brought a flood of memories. Alan had been moody as of late. His conscience was eating at him. He'd been married to a woman who had participated in a murder—its cover-up at the very least. Lindsay knew that Alan loved his family more than anything in life. He'd have done anything to keep the secret. She would never have thought that he'd been capable of murder. He'd never allow emotions to get the best of him.

Except he did.

He'd silenced Sarah. He'd tried to make sure his wife's involvement in the cover-up of the murder would never be known.

And then he'd silenced himself.

He'd told Lindsay one time that he'd take a bullet for those he loved.

"That's you, too, Linds. Don't ever doubt that I have your back. I know you'll always have mine."

She had parked behind Alan's car. Patty had put it up for sale.

"Too many sad memories," she'd said.

A kid from Canada had bought it and said he'd be down to pick it up at the end of the month.

Lindsay folded the enlarged photo in half and went to the door.

Lindsay followed Patty to the kitchen and sat down at the blond oak table.

Patty turned to pour the coffee. "Black, right?"

"Yes, Trish," Lindsay said.

Patty's body went limp, then rigid after she turned around to face Lindsay. The warmth had drained from her face, and the cups she was holding nearly slipped from her fingers. She looked down at the photograph that Lindsay had opened on the table.

"Do you want to call your lawyer?"

Patty sat down, her eyes riveted on the photo.

"No. No," she said. "Where did you get this?"

"Sarah Baker had it."

"Oh. She did. I didn't know a thing about it."

"She showed it to you?"

"Yes. She came by here, thinking that she could get some big story through all of us."

"'Us'?"

"The girls in the photograph. And Alan. I don't have any idea what she was up to. Not really. I told her that I didn't know anything. I wasn't even in the photograph."

Lindsay tapped her finger on the image reflected on the shiny display for Elixir Six.

"But you are. You and your Hasselblad. I recognize the camera now because it was on the shelf as a decorator piece in Alan's office. He said you used to be quite the photographer. Even had a darkroom at your other place."

Patty remained quiet. She took a sip of her coffee.

"Annette Ripken wrote a letter to Kate Spellman about what happened to Calista Sullivan that night at Spellman Farms."

"I had nothing to do with that."

"Really? How old is Paul?"

"Please don't go there, Lindsay. You're my friend. You were Alan's partner. We didn't do anything wrong. We did what we thought was the right thing."

Lindsay pushed. "Does Paul know who his birth parents are?"

Patty refused to answer. "Please. Just leave it." She reached for the cream, her hands shaking.

"Patty, what happened the night Sarah died?"

Silence took over. Patty didn't answer for what seemed like the longest time. Instead, she continued to stir cream into her coffee, the color now a light beige.

"Alan told me he killed her. He told me that she was going to tell Paul. She was even going out with him, using him to worm her way into finding out what happened. Alan tried to reason with her. Offered her money, but she just laughed."

"Then what happened?"

Patty looked up. Her face suddenly seemed haggard, and her eyes conveyed genuine remorse that Lindsay was sure couldn't be faked. "He said that he strangled her, stripped her of her clothes, and dumped her at Maple Falls. I swear to God that she must have made the ugliest threats to make Alan do something like that. He just lost it. He told me he wanted to scare her and then he couldn't stop. It was like he was possessed."

Patty said he concocted a plan to cover his tracks.

"The suicide was supposed to be a ruse. Just an attempt. A way to win sympathy. He said he'd start the car and I should wait a minute or two, then come out there and save him. He wasn't supposed to die. You were going to help him."

"Help him? How?"

"Get him out of it."

"How? I wouldn't mess with evidence, and I don't lie, Patty. I loved Alan, but I'd never do anything like that."

"Well, then," Patty said. "I got rid of the girl's clothes. Burned them in the yard. I admit I covered up the crime. And as far as that photograph goes, I admit that I was part of Marnie's inner circle, but I've stayed away from her and the others for a very long time. I felt like I was lucky to get out when I did."

"Annette Ripken wasn't lucky, was she, Trish?"

Patty's expression sank once more with Lindsay's second use of the nickname she'd long since abandoned. *Trish for Patricia.* Patty looked away, toward the window, then at the knife block with its set of Henckels blades gleaming—an anniversary present from her husband. Her eyes scraped over the entire contents of the kitchen before returning to her visitor.

"Lindsay, I really don't know what you're talking about."

This was difficult but necessary. Lindsay pushed a little harder.

"But you do, Trish. You know all of it, don't you?"

"Stop calling me by that name."

"I'm not trying to hurt you," Lindsay said. And she wasn't. "I'm trying to understand why Alan is dead and how it all relates to Calista Sullivan and Sarah Baker."

"He killed himself. Alan was a longtime depressive."

"I don't think so," Lindsay said. "He would have had to disclose meds on his fit-for-duty form."

Patty gave her a hard stare. "You didn't look at his private information, did you? That's way out of line."

"I didn't," Lindsay said. "Honestly, what's out of line is why you are covering for him."

"What do you mean, covering?"

"Alan talked to Sarah. Didn't he? He was worried about something—something awful. Something that spun out of control."

Patty took off her apron, folded it, and set it on the counter. "I don't know that. You don't, either. I thought you were his friend. *Our* friend."

Her protestations were feeble, and Lindsay knew it.

Outside, a car door slammed shut.

"Paul's here," Patty said. "You need to leave."

"We're not done."

"Please, Lindsay, just go. Leave all of this alone. There's nothing to be gained by digging into my husband's suicide, his old cases, the pain that forced him to take his life. Haven't Paul and I suffered enough?"

Lindsay looked at Patty.

"What happened the night Calista Sullivan died?"

"I think you already know."

"I know some, Patty."

"It was a long time ago."

"Tell me."

"I'm not sure I can. So much of it has been put away for such a long time."

"Go on, Patty. I'll bet you can get it out before Paul makes it inside, if you just start. Calista was having contractions?"

"Yes. Marnie had given her some herbs to induce labor. This is very difficult to talk about."

"I know," Lindsay said. "We have to, Patty. We have to put all of this to bed. We have two dead girls, and their connection is Spellman Farms and, well, frankly, the women of the Hive."

"I had nothing to do with what happened to Calista. Really."

"You were there. Do you know what happened, Patty?"

Patty's eyes grew wide and she pumped her fists to her legs. "She was dead when I went back into the barn. I swear it."

"And what about the baby?"

Patty was a mess, coughing and crying. "The baby died," she finally said.

Lindsay pushed the last button.

"No, *Trish*, the baby didn't die, did he?" she asked, using the name like a lash.

Patty had braced herself for the time when she'd hear her old name spoken by someone with ill intent. There could be no other reason. It would come, she knew, when the world found out what had been going on with Marnie and the others. The stem cells. How Marnie kept demanding she wanted to make sure they were fresh. "Off-the-OR-table fresh." It was crazymaking. Then the whole Reed situation happened. The criminal charges. The plan to ensure his conviction. All of it was a hall of mirrors, with no exit in sight.

"No, the baby didn't die," Patty admitted. "After the baby was born, I called Alan. He was about to get off shift."

"Tribal police in those days?"

"Right."

Just then the front door opened.

"Hey, Mom. Hi, Lindsay. Saw your car." He stopped and looked at the women. "Is everything all right?"

"Are you going to arrest me?" Patty asked Lindsay.

"You know I am." Lindsay stood up. "Trish Appleton, a.k.a. Patty Sharpe, you're under arrest for concealing a crime and destroying evidence."

Paul went to his mother and put his arms around her. "Mom? What's happening?"

She pushed him back to see into his eyes. "It's going to be all right. Don't talk to anyone, Son. Not a single word."

Chapter 81

Friday, September 27, 2019
Ferndale, Washington

Ferndale police officers were apprised of what was going on and rounded up Marnie and the other members of the Hive in a coordinated fashion so they'd have no opportunity to reach out to one another. Each was told that Trish had confessed to killing both Sarah and Calista and that they were needed for interviews that evening.

"No leaks to the press," Lindsay warned the other officers.

Dina was the first to arrive. She wore a beautiful pair of slacks and a long white sweater. Everything about her was perfect, as always. She almost floated like a drifting cloud into the department's conference room.

Greta was next. She came in black jeans and a forest-green twinset. Her hair had been cut shorter since Lindsay had seen her. She looked nervous and made small talk with Dina while they waited.

"How long has it been?" she asked, her voice echoing around the large, too-brightly-lit room.

Dina wasn't sure. "A long time. Ten years? You look wonderful."

"Thanks. You, too."

"I wonder if they can dim the lights in here," Dina said.

Then they fell silent, a relief for everybody. The banality of the exchange was tough enough to take, but their voices were incredibly hard on the ears in that room. Three walls were entirely covered in whiteboard material, and the other held only the door and a broad mirrored window. All members of the Hive had no doubt watched TV and suspected that the glass was one-way, but there were no signs of microphones anywhere—and as this was indeed a conference room, not an interview room, there were none. Which was just as well: factor in the linoleum floor and tile ceiling, and there was nothing but flat surfaces. It was as if the space had been designed to weaponize sounds.

When Heather showed up, she wasn't alone. Her assistant, introduced as Stephanie, was in tow.

"How long is this going to take?" Stephanie asked Lindsay. "Heather is in the middle of a campaign, and we can't spare much time."

"This is a murder investigation," Lindsay said. "You can spare the time now, or I can go on the news and wonder aloud why Heather Jarred isn't cooperating."

"We're cooperating, Detective. Just be quick about it, all right?"

Finally, as always, Marnie was the last to arrive.

By then, Lindsay knew Marnie was the kind of woman who never wasted an opportunity to be seen by everyone. That meant never arrive at anything first. Why would anyone? Arrivals are more important in the world of attention seekers than departures. She was dressed from head to toe in winter-white Chanel, a suit with matching shoes and only one adornment, her cherished honeybee brooch.

"Lovely pin, Ms. Spellman," Lindsay said.

Greta looked over at Heather and smiled.

Marnie hadn't responded to Lindsay's compliment with anything other than a narrow glare, which she kept drilled into the detective.

"Where's Trish?" Heather asked.

"She goes by Patty now," Greta said.

"Oh. Well, where is she?"

"She's in a holding cell at the moment," Lindsay said. "She'll be arraigned for two counts of murder tomorrow morning. More charges likely."

"Like what?" Heather, always the one for details, asked.

"Kidnapping Calista Sullivan's baby is also on the table. That's up to the prosecutor's office."

Marnie looked stunned.

Or at least pretended to be.

"I thought you said the baby died, Greta?"

Greta didn't say a word.

Neither did Heather or Dina.

Patty Sharpe was dressed in a Whatcom County Jail orange jumpsuit when an officer led her into the room. Her feet and arms were shackled with a too-long length of belly chains. It was clear that the jail didn't often serve child-sized residents. This was good news, Lindsay thought, tucking it away. She was making it a point to collect good news wherever she could find it these days.

None of the women spoke as Patty clanged and rattled into a seat at the head of the table. Marnie and Dina sat across from Heather and Greta.

"Taking sides," Patty said. "Just like old times."

"Hardly," Marnie said. "Now, what did you get mixed up in?"

"Hold that thought," Lindsay said. She'd just taken a seat of her own at the other end of the table, but now stood up, as though something had just occurred to her. "I need to take a call."

She left the room to give the women a few minutes to marinate in the awkward company of each other—old rivalries, perceived slights, memories of a time when Marnie Spellman was on top of the world.

With Lindsay gone, Marnie did what Lindsay had known she would do. Before the door shut, she seized control of the room. It had been a while since she commanded an audience, but she hadn't lost her touch for a hot start.

"What in the hell is going on here, ladies? What did you all do?"

"What did *we* do?" Heather asked. "That's pretty funny, Marnie. Everything points to you, and you know it. Right, 'ladies'?"

Greta spoke next. "I'd concede we all got our hands a little dirty, but we didn't do anything as awful as murder. How could you, Trish?"

Patty didn't answer right away, and when she did, she played to the big, two-way mirror. "How could I not? Only Heather has kids. So maybe she can understand. The rest of you, I doubt it. My husband is dead. Sarah was going to ruin me. Destroy all of us."

"I don't understand why the rest of us are here," Heather said, positioning herself above the fray. "Jesus, I'm going to be a US senator. I can't get caught up in something like this."

"Oh goody," Dina said, "your first scandal. Getting routed by the press is something that stays with you. I know."

Greta leaned toward Heather. "You aren't going to slime your way out of this, Heather. We all played a part in what went on at the farm."

"Water under the bridge," Marnie said, once more staking her claim as the woman with the answers.

"This isn't right," Heather went on. "None of this is fair."

Marnie waved her off. "Nothing's fair. Never has been. Not as long as men rule the planet."

Greta let out an exaggerated groan. "Can you just put a lid on your talking points?"

Marnie gave her a cold stare. "Truth is never a talking point."

"Look," Patty said, "Greta is right. We all have dirty hands here."

Heather pushed back from the table. "I don't."

"You forged the birth certificate," Marnie said. "You were part of the cover-up. You uploaded false information to vital statistics. Who knew you were training for a career in politics at that time?"

The two of them locked eyes for a long, still moment. The sound of the HVAC system sputtered in the room.

"Really, Marnie?" Heather said. "You're going to do this? Turn on me, with all that I know? All that you paid me to keep my mouth shut about? You are such a bitch."

Marnie's eyes swept the room and she glared in Heather's direction. "I'm not running for office. It would be a colossal shame to have an October surprise ruin your prospects."

"You wouldn't, you cunt."

Marnie laughed. "Your vocabulary is ever expanding, isn't it? Just try me, Heather. If I go down, you go down. And at the moment, the fall for you would be farther down than for any of us."

Heather took it down a notch. Marnie was all the things she said, but she was also a woman who would torpedo anyone that got in her way.

"Patty, uh, Trish was a friend," Heather said. "I forged the certificate because Paul needed one. He had to exist. That's what friends do, Marnie. They help each other. They don't search and kill."

"Please, Heather. You were trying to save your own neck," Marnie said. "You wanted everything to just go away."

"Didn't we all? And so what if I forged it? No one could prove it."

Greta looked over at Heather. "I could. I have the document."

"Then you stole it from the hospital."

"You bet I did. I didn't want nosy Sarah to get her hands on it. It was the one thing that could prove that Calista's death had been covered up—"

"By all of us," Patty finished.

"Trish and Heather dumped the body. Both bodies, I mean. Calista and her baby," Marnie said. "I watched you two load everything up."

"I didn't want to," Patty said, turning to Marnie. "You made me."

Every woman in the room wore a rosy flush when Lindsay returned with a recorder and a notebook—belt and suspenders, as Alan would say. Alan was, in fact, top of mind for her now, as the next bit she wanted to know was about her mentor's role in what happened. He was a police officer. He was in love with Patty. Obviously, the son they raised was not his. It pained Lindsay to no end, but Alan was neck-deep in the cover-up.

"I want to talk to my lawyer," Heather said.

"Must have something to hide," Greta shot back.

"Well, Detective, am I free to go or should I call my lawyer?"

Lindsay replied, "All of you can go. Except Patty. At any time."

Dina swiveled her chair and started to mention she'd played a DA on a show, when Marnie cut her off.

"Let's stay. This is the most fun I've had in years."

Heather stayed in her seat. Just knowing she could leave seemed like enough just then.

"Okay. Fine. All settled. Let's talk about the single hair inexplicably found under Calista's fingernail," Lindsay said, "a hair belonging to her ex-husband, Reed. You know, the evidence planted to make Reed look guilty? Which one of you came up with that gem?"

Lindsay looked around the room, then settled on Heather, who was looking down at the table like she was avoiding a teacher's question during a pop quiz.

Lindsay called on her.

"Heather, Reed's deposition says that you were the only one he met with in person."

"I did what I was asked to do," she said. "I regret it. It was wrong, but after stupidly getting involved in a cover-up, you do things you never thought you'd ever do."

She made eye contact with Marnie, then started talking.

Saturday, March 11, 2000
Ferndale, Washington

Only a day on the job at the Ferndale Police Department when Calista's body was found, Alan Sharpe was an amiable presence in court or out in the community. That he and his wife had recently adopted a baby "from a family member" only added to the goodwill many had for him.

The day Calista's remains were transported from Lummi to the autopsy suite—at that time, in the basement of Whatcom Memorial—Alan requested the night shift. He knew that what he was about to do was an insurance policy that, he prayed, would never need to be paid in full.

The hospital was quiet, but as a man in uniform, he was in his own way invisible. No one would tell him that visiting hours were over. No one would say a single word. In places in which cops were often seen but seldom urgently needed, they went about their duties in unremarkable fashion. Just people dressed in a uniform that announced their willingness to serve the public.

The morgue wasn't advertised in the way that, say, the gift shop or the maternity ward was. Alan swiped Patty's key card in the elevator reader and pushed B.

He swiped it a second time to get into the morgue.

Alan knew that there would be a record of his wife's breach of a space for which she could offer no reasonable excuse.

But she had done it, nonetheless.

Patty had gone down to the morgue earlier that day and left her favorite sweater.

It was a lame excuse, but even so, one she was convinced could work in the event it had to.

Alan put on a pair of latex gloves, turned on the old fluorescent tubes hanging loosely overhead, and made a beeline to the chiller. There was only one body on the racks, making it easy to find her. The smell, too. It was faint, acrid. And unmistakable. As he unzipped the dark-blue bag that held Calista's remains, he imagined he saw the odor rise up like cigarette smoke.

He had seen dead bodies before, but not like this one. First of all, he knew her story. She'd been part of something that had spun out of control. She didn't have to die. Her baby compounded the tragedy. The Salish Sea had been exceedingly cruel to her memory. Marine animals and fish had nibbled where the flesh had been damaged by the unforgiving elements. And the rocks. Against all odds, her face was mostly intact except her nose. That was gone. Bile rose up in Alan's throat, and he struggled to tamp it down. He retrieved from an envelope the hair sample Heather had procured.

Rigor had come and gone. He found her fingers and carefully moved the hairs from the envelope. He'd brought a nail file—ironic but sensible—and set the hairs parallel to the nails. Next, he held her hand steady and carefully pressed the hairs under the fingernails. He went deep. Deeper than a live person could stand, but it didn't matter. Calista was dead. He was giving her something to say about how she had died.

Alan had made Calista a liar in death.

They all had.

Earlier that day, Heather waited in the lobby of Whatcom Memorial for Reed Sullivan to arrive to ID Calista's body. It was Heather who had given the investigator working the case Reed's name as her friend's next of kin.

He was easy to spot. He was the only person she'd ever seen that looked so fit, so tan, and yet so sad at the same time.

"Reed?" she called out.

He looked her way, nodded tentatively.

"I'm Heather. I worked with your wife up at Spellman Farms. She told me all about you and the boys. I'm so sorry."

She flung her arms around him and started to sob.

At the same time, Heather reached behind his lanky frame and plucked a couple of hairs from the back of his head. She did it so quickly, letting out a yelp of her own personal agony that she doubted he'd notice.

He didn't, although he gently pushed her away.

"I'm sorry. I'm sorry that she ran away," Heather told him. "And all of this happened."

"She's run away before," he said.

"Last time," she said, unable to veer from the talking points of Spellman Farms, "she ran to something. Not away. To."

"You and the rest of the beekeepers can think what you want. Calista has been unstable for some time."

"*Unstable* just means she's not conforming to society's norms. She said you were controlling but kind. I'm beginning to wonder."

"Why did you come all this way to meet me?" he asked.

"I did it for her. I did it because I loved her. We all did."

Still holding the hairs, Heather scurried into the women's room and carefully slid them inside a paper envelope. She sealed it and returned it to her purse. Two hairs. It was the lightest thing one could imagine, but it felt heavy to her just the same. Like ingots of lead. Cement shoes. A weight that breaks one's back.

Later, she left the envelope on the corner of Trish Appleton's nurse's station as promised.

It was Alan Sharpe's first stop on the rainy night he planted evidence to frame a man who wasn't even near the scene of the crime.

Friday, September 27, 2019

Dina had lied to herself for years. Her fibs were never meant to harm, only to please. She thought of Marnie as a person out of her reach—in intellect, beauty, faith. She'd been around actors all her life and felt that her mentor possessed not a single false bone in her body. When Marnie talked of the swarm and the meaning imparted by nature, Dina hung on every word.

As the conversation careened from one part of Calista's death to the cover-up, she found her voice.

"The swarm was a fraud. Wasn't it, Marnie?"

Marnie put her hand on Dina's.

Dina pulled away. "No," she said. "I don't believe in you anymore. I've wasted my life on all of this. I did things that I can never undo."

Patty leaned forward, her chains rattling against the surface of the table. "What are you talking about? You didn't do anything that night. You looked the other way."

Dina didn't respond for the longest time. She just stared down at the table while the others watched.

Dina's best skill on the set was a very good pregnant pause.

"It was me," she finally said. "Annette saw it. She saw everything."

Lindsay was loving every minute of it. "Go on, Dina," Lindsay said. "Tell me."

"It isn't easy. It's ugly. You won't like me anymore."

Marnie rolled her eyes and looked at Lindsay. "See what I have to put up with? Most people are just like her. Desperate to be loved."

"That's true, Marnie. I won't deny it. And just so you know, this is me, standing my ground." Dina carried on. "The day she went into labor, Calista was still unsteady from whatever Marnie had been injecting her with."

Sunday, March 5, 2000
Lummi Island, Washington

For weeks, Calista had been complaining to Dina about the shots Marnie had been giving her—saline with minute amounts of royal jelly from hive number six. Despite Marnie's soothing words, each prick into her skin hurt like hell. They also made her feel funny. Woozy. Weak. Her last dose was while she was in labor.

When Dina went to see Calista in the barn after her baby was born, she didn't look good. Not at all. Her eyelids were heavy, and she fought hard to keep them open.

"They took him, Dina. My baby."

"Who did?"

"Trish . . . the others."

"What are you talking about?"

"Marnie is angry that I had a boy. She was sure it would be a girl. She told me it was my fault. That I didn't manifest a girl, a future queen. She's out of her mind. She actually thought I'd give her my daughter if I'd had one. Not a chance. She's a nutcase with all this royal jelly and stem-cell bullshit." She gripped Dina's hand. "You need to help me. You need to get my baby right now. Do it, or I'll tell everyone what I know. This isn't right, Dina. Help me."

Dina called out for Marnie and Heather.

"I'll tell," Calista repeated. Her voice was weakening as the color drained from her face. Her skin was parchment white.

"What will you tell?" Dina asked.

Calista croaked, "I'll tell the police what we're doing here. That you have been experimenting with that royal jelly and stem-cell garbage. What *you* and Marnie did to that childhood friend who'd talked about her online. CiCi, and her family, on the other side of the mountains."

"You wouldn't."

Just then, Marnie returned, her white pants streaked with blood.

"You took my baby," Calista said, her words clawing at her dry throat. "I want him back. Dina, tell her."

Marnie and Dina exchanged looks.

"She's going to tell," Dina said. "She's going to tell."

"The hell she is," Marnie said. "Do it."

Dina didn't ask for clarification. Didn't even blink. She took a pillow from the cart next to the hospital bed and shoved it onto Calista's face. As Calista struggled, Marnie joined in the fight to kill her. Calista writhed under the pillow, and more blood oozed onto the floor. Within a minute, she was motionless. Dina grabbed her by the shoulders and shook as hard as she could. Only a gurgling sound came from her lips.

Dina ran back into the house and locked herself in the upstairs guest suite.

And that was that. Calista's story was over.

Except for her baby.

Friday, September 27, 2019

Lindsay, her heart racing but her emotions hidden, moved on with the interview. She wondered if she was going to need a scorecard to keep track as denial and blame worked its way through the room, weaving in and out of the women on either side of the table.

"Patty," Lindsay said, "what happened to Sarah and Annette?"

Patty sat immobile. She barely moved her eyes, tracing the rest of the Hive as they looked on.

"You know that Alan killed Sarah."

"Yes. Did he kill Annette, too?"

Patty stayed mute for the longest time. "Yes, I'm afraid he did."

CHAPTER 82

March 2000
Bellingham, Washington

After leaving Spellman Farms, Annette Ripken turned inward, seldom allowing herself to think of her daughters and the life she'd left behind in California for the Pacific Northwest, the place of her childhood. Annette bought a little house north of Bellingham and tried to get on with her life, her new life. She painted the house a creamy yellow with teal trim— a color selection that she'd told everyone she regretted with the first swipe of the paintbrush. But no paint, no remodeling—nothing could fix her. She was humiliated beyond words and frightened. Mostly frightened. She watched the news of Reed Sullivan's arrest and was convinced that her constant worry over what she knew would give her a stroke. Or cancer. Most nights, she worked in the bar at Black Angus, a Samish Way steakhouse with a stainless-steel dance floor that overflowed most Fridays and Saturdays. Coworkers considered her a kind of sad figure, lonely, unable to hoist herself out of whatever it was that was dragging her downward.

Annette returned home from work late one night, her garage door rising to let her inside.

As she parked her VW bug, she noticed a car on the street, a silver Camry she knew belonged to Trish. She saw the Camry's dome light go on and Trish and Alan get out of the car.

She sat in the shadows of her car, entombed within the deeper dark of her garage, and wished she could just stay there forever.

Away from the memories. Away from the people coming at her.

She pressed the button and the garage door dropped like a drawbridge. Immediately, Annette heard a steady knocking that evolved into a pounding when she tried to ignore it. She got out of the car, walked in through the house, and swung open the front door. She left the porch light off, not wanting to be illuminated any more than her visitors did.

The Sharpes were waiting on the murky stoop. Trish had the infant in her arms.

"We need to talk, Annette," Alan said, without so much as a hello. "We're worried about Marnie and Dina."

She never really liked Alan, who reminded her of an ex. She turned to Trish. "Like you, Trish, I don't go there anymore. I have nothing to do with anyone at Spellman Farms."

"Right," Trish said. "We know."

"So what would I be worried about?"

"You know, Annette. You were there that night. I saw you. You know what happened."

The baby was working away at his pacifier. The sound was loud in the quiet night.

"Do you mean I know that you're holding Calista's baby? That I know that Dina and Marnie killed Calista and that the rest of you monsters covered it up?"

"Alan and I didn't do anything wrong, Annette. We saved this boy."

"He has a father, Trish. You can't just take a kid and pretend it's your own. You took advantage of a situation. An ugly one at that. Please leave. I don't want anything to do with any of this."

Trish dropped a baby toy, and Annette bent down to retrieve it.

As she got up, Alan jabbed her solar plexus with the prongs of a county-issued stun gun. She collapsed without a sound. Using the device was a risk. There was a chance that the medical examiner might see the telltale marks it left behind.

Alan, however, had an insurance policy.

He'd be one of the officers working the case.

He'd be able to help move it along to its sad, but predetermined, conclusion.

"I knew her from Lummi," he'd tell his colleagues. "She was suicidal back then. Surprised that she lasted this long. Always threatening something, hurting herself for attention. Something always a little broken in those gals who came to be with Marnie Spellman. Even left her kids. A really sad case, that one."

Friday, September 27, 2019
Ferndale, Washington

"I had no idea that Alan was going to do that," Patty said, raising her eyes from the table and over to Lindsay. "I stood there in shock. We were only going to talk to her."

"Really, Patty?" Lindsay asked. "You expect me to believe that?"

"I call bullshit," Heather said, pointing an index finger at Patty. "You didn't know he was going to do it? What did you *think* you were there for?" She'd honed her skills of the sharp attack on the campaign trail. Everyone at the table was an opponent. There would be no party unity among members of the Hive.

"It's the truth," Patty said. "Really."

Lindsay gave Heather a dismissive look.

She didn't need any help.

"Finish your story, Patty."

March 2000

"Put Paul in the car seat," Alan said after dragging an unconscious Annette from the porch into the house. It felt odd, wrong, dangerous to Patty to be talking in front of Annette, even though she was clearly out cold and resting on the carpet at their feet. "Then come back and give me a hand."

A few minutes later, she returned.

"I'm going to glove up. I have a pair for you, too." He dug around in his jacket pockets. "You'll get the garden hose from the backyard. I'm going to give the place a quick once-over to see if she's left anything that points to what happened."

"Part of me wants Marnie and Dina to go down for what they did," Patty said. "Heather, too. Greta. The lot of them."

"Understood, but if that happens, we all go down. Our hands are dirty, too."

"Dirtier now, Alan."

Alan gave his wife a hard look. "You wanted this, Patty."

"Yes," she said. "I did. And I agree."

Alan turned away and shook his head. "Agree? It was your idea."

"Don't get righteous with me, babe," she snapped back. "You love Paul, too. You know that taking him as our own was the right thing to do."

"'Right'?" Alan said. "Setting up a man for a murder he didn't commit. Killing Annette. None of this is the right thing to do."

He was wearing latex gloves by then and gave her a pair to wear.

"Now go get the hose and meet me in the garage."

When Patty returned, Annette was in the VW, seat belt strapped over her. The smell of alcohol filled the air. Paul had doused her blouse with vodka from a mini bottle in his pocket.

Alan took the hose from Patty, fed one end into the exhaust pipe, and sealed it with duct tape he'd taken care to cover with Annette's prints by placing her fingertips on the roll. He pushed the other end into the back window through a narrow slit on the driver's side.

"Now your turn," he said. His eyes were bullets aimed right at Patty. They were telling her very plainly this was not a one-person operation. It had to be the both of them.

"I can't do this," she said.

"You wanted this, Patty. Goddamn it. Now turn the ignition, and let's get the hell out of here."

Patty acquiesced and reached over Annette and turned the key. The bug's burbling engine turned over, and white exhaust began to leak into the car.

Then it billowed inside, a toxic, self-contained, deadly storm.

Annette's eyes fluttered. She started to cough, and Patty stifled a scream. Behind her, Alan cursed.

"Damn it, Patty. Be quiet."

Annette opened her eyes, though she appeared dazed. Then terrified, but still disoriented from the blow to the head, or perhaps the effects of the carbon monoxide had already gotten to her. Her hand clenched the door handle to get out, yet she couldn't open it.

With all of her strength, Patty kept her hip pressed hard against the door. Alan saw what she was doing and reached around her to add his weight to hers. It was almost an embrace.

Annette rolled the driver's window down and gaped at Patty as she shoved against the door. Then she turned away to scratch frantically at the seat belt's latch. Her coordination no match for this, she sagged in her seat and rolled her eyes back up to Patty.

"Don't do this," she said, her words punctuated by a loud, hacking cough.

And then, all of a sudden, Annette stopped trying. Her hands slid limply to her sides, and her head fell to her chest.

The garage rolled then like a ship on a pitching sea, and Patty was limp, too, wheeling down to wherever Annette had gone. Alan hooked his hands under her arms and dragged her from the car, back into the house, and away from the deadly fog.

Friday, September 27, 2019

Played for a fool. Embarrassed. Hurt. While Lindsay was devastated, she refused to show it. She moved her hands from the conference table to her lap. She kept her eyes on Patty and did her best to shift her emotions to anger.

"Patty, I don't know you," she said. "I didn't know Alan, either. I hope you go to prison for everything you've done. Paul will have to live with this for the rest of his life. You make me sick."

She turned to the others.

"The lot of you sicken me."

The other women sat without saying a word. Only Marnie and Dina had really understood what had happened to Calista. The others knew only that blood had been spilled, panic had ensued, and they needed to make every trace of her go away and point the finger of blame far away from them.

Ironically, it had been their strict adherence to rule number one of Alan Sharpe's folksy, but spot-on, instructional handbook for criminals desiring to go undetected—never, ever talk about a crime once it has been committed—that had been their undoing. For too long, no one reached out as Sarah Baker started digging into their past. No one thought to warn the others.

Until it was too late.

Epilogue

Marnie Spellman was granted immunity in exchange for testifying against Dina Marlow. Despite Dina's acting experience, she'd been unable to convince prosecutors that Marnie had been the instigator. Marnie, it turned out, was the better actress. She returned to Lummi Island and was seldom seen again, save for a single comeback attempt. She appeared on CNN to talk about her newest product line, teas cured with Spellman honey and herbs. The reinvention didn't catch on. Marnie's army, which once numbered in the hundreds of thousands, had dwindled to only a handful of loyalists. She tried to auction her Warhol, but Sotheby's was unable to authenticate it.

Kate Spellman died in a freak accident the following year when the propane tank in her RV sprung a leak. The explosion killed her instantly. The Picasso was found burned among the debris. Police investigated and determined no foul play had been involved.

Dina Marlow was convicted of second-degree manslaughter in the death of Calista Sullivan and was sentenced to four years at the women's prison in Gig Harbor, Washington. She served two. Her novel about her ordeal, *Escaping the Hive*, was a bestselling roman à clef. Names were changed, but the story of a Hollywood actress taken in by a huckster of dreams and potions had readers flipping pages. She also starred in two Hallmark movies after her prison stint. She now lives in White Rock, British Columbia, where she can dream of a comeback—and drink in peace.

Greta Swensen sold her Chuckanut Drive residence for three million dollars to a Seattle Amazon millionaire who considered it perfect for a summer cottage. She bought land in Billings, Montana, and started a line of goat's milk products: soaps, creams, and even an eyelid serum. She now holds the record for having appeared on the home shopping channel more times than any cosmetics entrepreneur, including Marnie Spellman.

Patty "Trish" Sharpe pled guilty to second-degree manslaughter in the death of Annette Ripken. She is serving a fifteen-year sentence at the women's prison in Gig Harbor, Washington. Her son, Paul, visits her whenever he can. Patty tells other inmates that the worst thing one can do is buy into the desires of others. She teaches a workshop on achieving true potential after incarceration. There is a long waiting list.

Heather Jarred was elected to the US Senate and publicly commented on her connection to Marnie Spellman only once. It was during a town hall event in Spokane a few days before the election. "Back then, my generation looked for leaders to make the world better. I carry the mantle from those days on Spellman Farms when we were young, hopeful, and ready for change." There are no mentions of her in any Whatcom County judicial records—police or court. Period. Heather was good at pulling the right strings.

Reed Sullivan, fully vindicated of a crime that dogged him for two decades, still lives with his aging cat, now an astonishing twenty-seven-years old, in the same wisteria-draped house in Happy Valley near Bellingham. He's reached out to the son he never knew he had, and after a couple of meetings, he and Paul agreed that blood doesn't always make a family.

Lindsay Jackman remains a detective with the Ferndale Police Department, though now lives in a Bellingham craftsman with a peekaboo view of the bay. She stays in touch with Paul Sharpe and occasionally visits Reed and his bag-of-bones cat. Not long after the cases connected to Marnie Spellman were closed, she started dating a network engineer from Seattle. The pair are planning a summer wedding next year. She's hoping no one thinks it would be funny to send her a Spellman Farms gift pack.

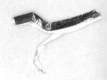

About the Author

Photo © Claudia Olsen

Gregg Olsen is the #1 *New York Times* and Amazon Charts bestselling author of more than thirty books, including *If You Tell, Lying Next to Me, The Last Thing She Ever Did,* and *The Sound of Rain* and *The Weight of Silence* in the Nicole Foster series. He's appeared on multiple television and radio shows and news networks, such as *Good Morning America, Dateline, Entertainment Tonight,* CNN, and MSNBC. In addition, Olsen has been featured in *Redbook, People,* and *Salon,* as well as in the *Seattle Times, Los Angeles Times,* and *New York Post.* Both his fiction and nonfiction works have received critical acclaim and numerous awards. Washington State officially selected his young adult novel *Envy* for the National Book Festival, and *The Deep Dark* was named Idaho Book of the Year. A Seattle native who lives with his wife in rural Washington State, Olsen's already at work on his next thriller. Visit him at www.greggolsen.com.